THE IRISH
Lite Fairy

ROBERT BOU

Ordering Information:

Prime Seven Media
518 Landmann St.
Tomah City, WI 54660

Printed in the United States of America

This book was translated from
Spanish to English by Maria Jose Cuartero

Table of Contents

Introduction

Imagine a world where every action we take, every fleeting thought, and every emotion not only affects our tangible environment but also reverberates through invisible dimensions intertwined with the very essence of our being. This book, crafted to be more than mere entertainment, is an invitation to explore the vast and hidden realities we weave with each everyday act.

In the course of our daily existence, we construct castles in these invisible dimensions through our choices, often unaware of whether we are nurturing the light or the darkness. Even a simple gesture can tip the scales. The arrogance of believing we know it all and closing our minds to new ideas blocks the entrance of possibilities capable of transforming our reality. This self-imposed blindness creates fissures in the social fabric, spreading malaise and collective depression. However, those who manage to connect with this esoteric truth understand the profound responsibility of this immaterial connection. Sages from all cultures have spoken of dimensions perceived only by them, offering fragments of wisdom to those willing to listen and learn.

This book not only narrates a universal truth but also immerses you in the intimacy of its characters through an original soundtrack. Each character has their own melody that reveals their essence, their story, and invites you to understand their deepest decisions. These songs, available at INL Sound, serve as portals to their hearts, offering a unique and immersive experience. You can choose to listen to them as you progress through the plot, allowing each note to add another layer to the tapestry of their lives.

Ultimately, this work poses a crucial question: To whom do you give your power, to good or to evil? As you close its pages, the choice is yours. The paths you trace afterward are in your hands, interconnected not only with humanity but perhaps with other planes of existence we have yet to discover.

I hope you find in this work an opportunity to reflect on your place in the universe and, above all, enjoy the journey that is about to begin.

My life changed radically after the adventure. Beyond seeing the magic in small details and appreciating each moment with a new perspective, one of the most important things the fairy, named Aisling, taught me was about the true nature of the universe and the forces operating in dimensions beyond our perception—or perhaps, they led me straight to God.

Aisling, the little Irish fairy, explained to me that night when I met her in the forest that the universe has an infinite number of dimensions and that our understanding is limited. She compared it to trying to explain life in a city, a bank account, or our complex concepts to a shark or another marine animal; they simply wouldn't comprehend any of it. In the same way, we are also unable to perceive these parallel dimensions, even though they exist right here on Earth. Sometimes we think life comes from other galaxies, but why couldn't it be from other dimensions right here on our planet?

Furthermore, Aisling revealed to me that good and evil also exist in these dimensions, and our proximity to either depends on our own perspective and actions. This explains why, sometimes, our lives seem to fall apart for no apparent reason. In that dimension, many beings of light constantly work to balance the scales of good and evil in our world. However, there are times when the balance tips more toward evil, as in our current era, affecting our lives in ways we cannot always understand or control.

From that revelation onward, I began receiving images in my mind and even dreams that seemed to be messages or visions from these other dimensions. Now, let me tell you one of these incredible stories that Aisling, the Irish Lite Fairy, helped me to comprehend.

Now, after this enlightening adventure, I wake up each day with a mind open to the infinite possibilities the universe offers us, knowing there is much more than we can see or understand. I also feel more aware of my actions and thoughts, understanding the impact they can have on that cosmic balance. Each dream and vision is a reminder of the magic and complexity that surround us.

With love,

Robert Bou

The Beginning

It all began when I was comfortably immersed in my daily routine. I lived a quiet life, devoid of much excitement, wrapped in the normalcy of my days. Nothing seemed to foreshadow that my life was about to take an unexpected turn.

One day, while delving into ancient Celtic tales, I stumbled upon a mysterious legend about the *Irish Fairys*—fairies said to bring light and clarity to those who encounter them. This discovery sparked an insatiable curiosity within me, igniting a desire to embark on a quest to uncover their secrets.

I had no idea where to start until I met an old and wise mentor, an expert in Irish folklore. He provided me with ancient maps and invaluable advice on how to recognize the signs of the fairies. He also gave me a protective amulet, something that would become a vital tool during my journey.

With a heart full of hope and uncertainty swirling in my mind, I left behind my mundane life and ventured into the unknown. I boarded a flight to Ireland, where my search would begin.

Ireland presented numerous challenges: cold nights in the wilderness, rugged terrain, and the constant doubt over the truth of the legend. Each obstacle seemed more daunting than the last, yet my resolve never wavered.

To get closer to my goal, I shifted my approach. I immersed myself in the local culture and traditions, speaking to village elders who shared stories and clues about the fairy sightings. I adapted, blending their wisdom with my own intuition.

The most harrowing moment came one stormy night. I found myself lost in a dense forest, with no clear signs and the amulet seemingly failing me. Fear and despair nearly drove me to abandon the search.

Then, when all seemed lost, a brilliant light appeared between the trees. It was the *Irish Lite Fairy*. I had found her. She not only guided me to safety but also granted me a profound understanding of life and my purpose.

But what left me stunned was her face. It was the same young girl I had seen on the plane.

The flight to Dublin had begun with the typical calm of a morning journey. Thick clouds blanketed the landscape below, and the gentle hum of the plane provided a constant backdrop to my wandering thoughts. As I settled into my window seat, a brief flash of golden light caught my attention—a girl, no older than eighteen, walking down the aisle behind her mother and grandmother.

What struck me most was her gaze, a mix of curiosity and wisdom that seemed to reach beyond her years. A strange familiarity tugged at me, as if I had seen her somewhere before. I tried to shake the feeling, chalking it up to those moments when we think we recognize strangers from our daily life.

Throughout the flight, I found myself stealing glances at the girl and her family. Her mother, a serene-looking woman, flipped through a magazine filled with images of Irish landscapes. Beside the girl, her red-haired sister—a typical Irish beauty—gazed out the window, captivated by the world from above. Their grandmother, with the air of someone who had lived many lives, smiled warmly at her granddaughters. There was something touching and timeless in their bond.

In an attempt to calm my restless mind, I struck up a conversation with the mother while we waited in line for the bathroom.

"It's a long journey, isn't it?" I said, offering a casual smile. "Seems I'm not the only one heading to Dublin in search of adventure."

The mother returned the smile, though her eyes held a knowingness that transcended words.

"Yes," she replied softly. "My daughters are eager to visit the place where our family once lived. There's something almost mystical about returning to your roots."

The conversation drifted into trivial topics, yet that unshakable feeling lingered—something indescribable, but potent.

Upon arriving at my destination, the memory of the girl stayed with me. Her face continued to surface in my thoughts, the spark of recognition never fading. But life moved on, as it always does, leading me down other paths—until that fateful night.

I was deep into the writing of a new book when, in a moment of introspection, a vision seized me. A story unfolded in my mind: magical beings fighting in a world of light and shadow, and that same girl, now a powerful fairy, leading the charge with her innate courage and light. It might sound irrational, but the connection was undeniable. She radiated with the same vitality I had sensed on the plane, and the realization filled me with renewed energy.

Later, I realized this family appeared repeatedly in my dreams and visions, reliving scenes from that flight. I had no explanations, only theories. Could they be echoes of themselves in other dimensions? Reflections of lives crossing over into parallel worlds?

As I completed my book, a dedication naturally formed in my mind:

"Dear reader, if you ever unravel the mystery of this connection between the family on the plane and the world depicted here, I would appreciate you sharing your thoughts with my publisher. Together, we might bridge the gap between the inexplicable and understanding."

Thus, my strange but inspiring encounter with that young girl became not only the catalyst for this fantasy tale but also an enigma that will accompany my thoughts at every step of my journey.

The experience with the fairy not only helped me complete my research but also gifted me a new vision of life, the importance of light in times of darkness, and the magic that resides in the everyday.

I returned home with newfound clarity and a heart full of gratitude. I shared my experience with friends and family, who also benefited from the lessons I had learned.

After the adventure, my life changed profoundly. I began to see the magic in small details and to appreciate each moment with a fresh perspective. My daily routine was now sprinkled with the light the fairies had shown me.

So, dear friends, always seek the light in your life, even in the darkest moments. Magic surrounds us, waiting to be discovered. Sometimes, we just need the courage to look for it.

CHAPTER 1

A Magical Journey

Aisling

A father walked along the dusty road of the English countryside, pulling a cart drawn by a massive ox. Sitting on the cart's bench was a six-year-old girl, her eyes wide with fascination as she took in the woods and meadows surrounding them. It was a time of war and betrayal, the era of the Wars of the Roses, where King Edward IV and Henry VI fought for the throne.

The girl, who was in fact the fairy Aisling in her childlike form, watched the world with a wonder only children could possess. Her large eyes sparkled as she discovered every nook and cranny along the road.

"Father," Aisling called up, looking at him with excitement, "do you hear those beautiful bells? What a lovely sound!"

The father, a robust man hardened by years of labor and the conflicts of the time, frowned in mild confusion. He paused, then smiled down at her with a touch of indulgence.

"My sweet girl, your imagination is boundless. There are no bells here, only the silence of the countryside and the plodding of the ox."

Yet Aisling knew what she heard wasn't just in her mind. The chime of those bells was a reminder of the magic that lingered, even in times of war and hardship. Though her father couldn't hear them, she was sure they came from somewhere special, a parallel dimension that only the eyes of innocence could glimpse.

A few moments passed before Aisling spoke again, her small finger pointing towards a distant tree. She looked up at her father, her voice filled with certainty.

"Look, Papa! Mama's there, under that tree. Can't you see her?"

The father's brow furrowed further, his heart tightening. He halted the cart, turning to his daughter with a sad, tender expression.

"Sweetheart, your mother passed eleven months ago," he said softly, kneeling beside her. "She's with God now, watching over us, especially over you, from heaven."

Aisling, her face set with determination and anger, stared at him, defiant.

"That's not true! She's right there! I see her!"

The father, his heart heavy with sorrow, glanced toward the tree but saw nothing. He knew his daughter had a vivid imagination, but there was something unsettling about her certainty. Children often spoke truths adults had long forgotten how to see.

Swallowing his doubts, the father urged the ox forward, moving closer to the mysterious tree where Aisling was so sure her mother stood. As they neared, the clatter of hooves grew louder, the sound of a troop galloping toward them.

The father, now alert, glanced back, steering the cart to the side of the road as the rumble of the approaching horses grew. Just as they passed the tree, the father took one last look but saw nothing. His face briefly clouded with disappointment.

Suddenly, a commanding voice rang out, sharp and authoritative.

"Make way for the king! Clear the road for King Henry!"

The father, filled with both urgency and unease, tried to move the cart further, but the ox, startled by the horses and the clang of armor, jerked wildly to the side. In that tragic moment, the cart hit a large stone, sending it lurching violently. Aisling was thrown from her seat, her small body colliding with a rock, the blow instantly fatal.

Panicked and heartbroken, the father leapt from the cart, rushing to his daughter. Tears filled his eyes as he cradled her limp form, blood trickling from her nose. He pulled her close, holding her tightly as he wept.

"No… please, no. Not you… please, not you," he sobbed, his voice breaking with the weight of his grief.

As the sound of horses grew closer, signaling the army of Edward IV, the future King of England, the father knelt, lost in his anguish. But in the very spot where Aisling had insisted her mother stood, a figure appeared—a beautiful woman with clear eyes and dark hair, dressed in green, her golden wings shimmering behind her. It was Aisling's mother, the fairy who had come to collect her daughter, knowing the tragedy that awaited.

In a voice filled with love, the mother approached her grieving husband, whispering words of comfort only the soul could hear.

"I know you cannot see me, my love, but I've come to take our daughter. I knew this would happen, but do not fear. My mother and I will care for her with love in the City of the Fairies in Cork, and she will grow to be extraordinary."

Though the father couldn't see her, he felt a brush of air against his face, a soft, cool touch that sent shivers through his body, as though his wife's spirit was near, offering him an unspoken comfort.

Through his tears, he looked down at his lifeless daughter and murmured, "Go with your mother, Aisling. She's waiting for you…"

Not far from the cart, the army stood still, watching the scene in respectful silence. King Edward himself dismounted his horse and approached the grieving father, his voice filled with sympathy.

"I am deeply sorry for your loss. That coward Henry is to blame. How is your daughter?"

The father, unable to speak through his tears, simply shook his head, too overwhelmed by the weight of his sorrow. King Edward, his voice solemn, placed a hand on the father's shoulder.

"I give you my word, Henry will end his days in the Tower of London. You have my promise."

With a nod of gratitude, the father accepted a pouch of coins from the king's officer, given so he could bury his daughter with dignity.

As the soldiers withdrew, the mother of Aisling reached out, gently lifting her daughter's spirit from her earthly form. In a soft, celestial glow, Aisling's soul rose into her mother's loving arms, cradled in a tender embrace. Together, mother and daughter ascended, their forms glowing as they faded into the air, leaving behind a lingering sense of peace, love, and hope.

CHAPTER 2

The City of the Fairies

Aisling's mother ventured into the dense woods of the fairy dimension, where the glowing light of blooming nasturtiums illuminated the path, and a celestial melody filled the air. Carrying Aisling tenderly in her arms, her mother walked with a sense of purpose, driven by an unknown force that pulled her beyond the boundaries of the familiar. As she moved through the tranquil forest, an Irish elf, small with a fiery red beard, suddenly appeared before her, catching her by surprise.

"What has happened?" the elf asked, his curious eyes fixed on Aisling lying peacefully in her mother's arms.

Without wasting time, Mirebelle spoke with urgency, "Quick, go to the city and tell them to prepare for an emergency. And inform my mother."

El Renacimiento en la Ciudad de las Hadas

The elf, with swift and nimble movements, darted toward the City of the Fairies, carrying the urgent message that Aisling's mother had sent. As he neared the breathtaking city, he was met by a sight of incomparable beauty: forests bathed in the luminous glow of magical flowers, with a perpetual shimmer filling the air, thick with magic and wonder. A soft, celestial melody wove through every corner, creating an atmosphere of peace and enchantment that resonated throughout the city.

The elf rushed to deliver the message to the Fairy Queen and summoned every available fairy to assist in Aisling's recovery. The city hummed with energy, an anticipation reverberating through every branch and leaf, as the fairies prepared for the task of restoring the child's life.

The Rescue in the Fairy Palace

Upon reaching the grand City of the Fairies, Aisling's mother was greeted by the majestic Queen Mother, Aisling's grandmother, along with a multitude of fairies who had gathered in response to the urgent call. The group swiftly organized and escorted Mirebelle and her daughter to the central castle, surrounded by magical houses seamlessly woven into the enchanted forest.

Inside the castle, Aisling was laid in a special room, where the air buzzed with the healing energies of the fairies and a magical light bathed every surface. The room was adorned with sparkling crystals and exotic flowers that emitted a soft, soothing glow, creating a space of serenity and restoration.

Aisling's mother stood by with hope in her heart as the fairies gathered around her daughter, enveloping her in a radiant aura of healing energy. The atmosphere was charged with magic and determination, each fairy focusing their powers to help revive the little girl.

"Dear one," the Queen Mother said softly, her voice filled with wisdom, "it is vital that we understand the role Aisling will play in our kingdom. She must be taught the ways of justice and wisdom, so that one day she can rule with fairness and love for all creatures."

"I understand, Your Majesty," Mirebelle replied, her voice steady with resolve. "I will do everything in my power to prepare Aisling for that great purpose."

At that moment, Aisling's Aunt Fairy, the delegate from the Mediterranean Seas, entered the conversation. She was the daughter of the Queen Mother and sister to Mirebelle. With her striking turquoise eyes and matching blue hair, her presence was like that of the ocean's waves—both calming and powerful.

"Sister," Aunt Fairy said, her voice melodious as the song of the sea, "I've brought a gift for Aisling, one that will help her understand the heart of the ocean, and with it, the heart of our kingdom."

She extended her hand to reveal a small, luminescent seashell, shimmering as though it held a piece of the moon within.

"This shell," Aunt Fairy continued, "is a gift of wisdom. Within it are the whispers of the sea, the stories of the creatures who live in its depths, and the secrets only the ocean knows."

Aisling, mesmerized by the glowing shell, moved closer to her aunt. With a warm smile, Aunt Fairy gently explained how to listen to the secrets of the shell and feel the strength of the sea within her.

Eyes wide with wonder, Aisling eagerly listened, her heart and mind diving into the mysterious world hidden within the seashell. In that moment, the Queen Mother, watching her granddaughter closely, recognized the potential within Aisling. The wisdom of the ocean, with its depth and mystery, would be a perfect complement to the knowledge she would need to rule.

Just then, the Queen Mother's expression shifted slightly as Aunt Fairy approached her and spoke in a low, serious voice, casting a shadow of gravity over the lighthearted scene.

"Grandmother," Aunt Fairy whispered, "it is time we speak of the shadows looming over the land. Dark forces are stirring, and in their wicked schemes, they aim to bring suffering and despair to the Third Dimension—our beloved Earth."

Her words carried the weight of urgency, as the seriousness of the situation filled the room. The Queen Mother, her eyes aglow with ancient wisdom, nodded solemnly, understanding the gravity of the challenge before them. United by love and purpose, they knew they must prepare to face the coming darkness and protect the light that guided their realm and the world beyond.

Suddenly, Aisling's innocent voice cut through the weighty conversation, her tone bright with curiosity.

"Auntie, Grandmother, why couldn't I see you before? And where's Daddy?" she asked, her eyes shining with the excitement of being surrounded by her family.

The Queen Mother smiled warmly, brushing a tender hand across Aisling's cheek. "Sweet Aisling, all will be explained in time. For now, just know that we're always with you. Now, give your grandmother a kiss, dear."

Aisling, not fully understanding but filled with affection, leaned in and gave her grandmother a soft kiss on the cheek. In that moment, the warmth of love passed between them, a bond that transcended time and space in their magical homeland.

After embracing Aisling one last time, Aunt Fairy turned to her sister and the Queen Mother with a look of determination. "I must leave now, sister, Queen Mother. The kingdom of Aragon is in turmoil. I must return to Barcelona. The almogavars—the soldiers of Aragon and Catalonia—are at war, and conflict is inevitable."

Hearing this, the Queen Mother's brow furrowed slightly, considering the weight of her sister's words. With calm but firm resolve, she replied, "Go with caution and courage, daughter. Let wisdom guide your actions and the light protect you. May the fairies' protection be with you at all times."

With a final nod, Aunt Fairy left the enchanted city, her heart full of determination as she prepared to face the storms gathering in the human world. Meanwhile, in the fairy realm, the bond of love, magic, and duty remained steadfast, as Aisling's future unfolded before her like a tapestry woven with both light and shadow.

The Revelation and the Warrior's Choice

In the vast ocean of existence, the waves of time often carry unexpected revelations. The battle between good and evil is not only a cosmic clash of forces but also an internal struggle within every human soul. In this delicate balance, a new day dawned in Barcelona, filled with both promise and peril.

As the first rays of sunlight bathed the port in golden light, Aislin's aunt, still shaken by the events of the previous night, returned home. Their conversation revolved around the signs and omens they had both witnessed, an air of strange anticipation and hope hanging between them. It was then that a wise old man, renowned for his vast knowledge of the metaphysical and the occult, approached them. His gaze, deep and serene, confirmed the gravity of the situation.

"Aislin," he said, his voice trembling yet firm, "her destiny is intertwined with forces beyond our understanding. An ancient prophecy speaks of a warrior who will balance the scales between good and evil. That warrior may be her."

The revelation struck Aislin's aunt like lightning. Could it be? Could her niece, an ordinary girl, be destined for such a monumental role in this cosmic war? With a steady hand on the old man's shoulder, she offered her strength and support.

The wise man presented a relic—an ancient amulet glowing softly with an inner light. "This," he explained, "is the symbol of her mission. Only the true warrior can activate its power."

With equal parts doubt and determination, Aislin's aunt accepted the amulet. Yet she knew they wouldn't face this journey alone. She, along with the sage, would guide and protect the young girl as she stepped onto this path that stretched out before them. The wise man promised that within a year, he would bring Aislin to Barcelona—or, if necessary, travel to the fae city in Ireland to meet with her mother and queen.

The sage spoke of a trial Aislin must undergo to claim her destiny: she must seek a celestial sword hidden within a secret cave beneath the monastery of Sant Pere. The journey would not be easy, but the stakes were far too high.

As preparations for the mission began, so too did an intensive training regimen. Aislin would learn combat tactics, the use of the amulet, and the power of faith and will. With each passing day, her physical abilities would grow, but more crucially, she would develop the inner strength needed to fulfill her destiny.

One night, as she practiced, a dark shadow slipped between the trees, whispering threats and promises. It was a minor demon, sent to gauge the strength of the emerging warrior. The encounter was brief but telling—the forces of darkness would not underestimate Aislin or her purpose.

Then, in the midst of a playful moment with Lumina, her new friend, a sudden attack caught them off guard. The sense of security they had felt vanished in an instant, replaced by an overwhelming awareness of the looming danger. The battle had only just begun, but already they faced trials that tested their unity and courage.

The chapter closed with Aislin staring down the menacing silhouette of her enemy, the intensity of the confrontation reflected in her eyes. The mission was clear, but the obstacles ahead were greater than they had ever imagined. The balance was tipping, and their ability to restore it would depend on every choice and action they took from that moment forward.

CHAPTER 3

The Watcher of Shadows

The Revelation and the Warrior's Choice

In the heart of the ancient, noble city of Barcelona—where centuries of history and secrets entwined in every stone—the night had drawn its cloak of stars over the majestic cathedral. At that hour, its stained-glass windows glittered like jewels, though the building was closed to mortal souls. Silence reigned, broken only by the soft murmur of the wind weaving through cobbled streets.

Before the great doors of the Gothic cathedral stood a tiny figure of light. His name, Alastar, was spoken with reverence in the fae tongue. A loyal spy of Liriel, the graceful goddess of the seas and protector of pure hearts, he was also known as the aunt of the brave Aislin.

Alastar, diminutive but radiant, kept a vigilant watch as the shadows stretched across the cool night. The bells had already chimed ten when a disturbance in the air caught his attention. In the parallel dimension, unseen by common eyes, a breathtaking spectacle unfolded. From deep within the cathedral's hidden passageways, creatures of darkness began to emerge. Demons and fallen angels, with twisted wings and faces filled with malice, formed a menacing army.

Legend spoke of the cathedral's endless corridors that led straight to the pits of Hell itself—a dominion from which few escaped with their sanity intact. The sounds accompanying the dark parade were inaudible to mortals, but if any could hear, their ears would be tormented by eerie melodies and soul-piercing wails.

As the dark music filled the air, one of the demons sensed Alastar's presence and lunged at him with a grotesquely open mouth, attempting to devour the small, pure light. Quick and nimble, Alastar hid within the very shadows, seeking refuge among the grand statues and pillars of the cathedral.

The threat had not passed. The dark army, swift and overwhelming, took flight into the night sky, tearing the serenity apart with their malevolent intent. Alastar, now safely concealed, knew he had to return to Liriel with utmost urgency. His heart of light flickered with the weight of the message he carried. The inevitable conflict was coming, and Barcelona, with its hidden wonders and secrets, would soon bear witness to a battle that transcended the human plane.

The Confrontation at San Pere

At the summit of the majestic Mount San Pere, which soared over a thousand meters high, stood an imposing convent—one of the oldest and most sacred in the region. At its feet, a breathtaking landscape of dizzying cliffs plunged into the restless waters of the Mediterranean. In the stillness of the night, Jesus, with his serene and contemplative gaze, was on the mount, uttering a prayer that resonated with the eternity of the cosmos.

A short distance away, in a dark tower from the ninth century, lay the stone graves of illustrious noble houses. Yet, among the guardians of the deceased, two empty tombs mysteriously stood intact, carved from the very rock itself. Suddenly, the entire scene was illuminated by a crimson light, and with a dull roar, two figures emerged from the vacant tombs.

Satan, appearing as a man of indescribable beauty, emerged, followed by his consort, a woman of celestial allure but crowned by an aura of darkness. After exchanging a knowing glance, they swiftly ascended towards San Pere, where Jesus awaited them. The night was thick with palpable tension, and the eyes of the night sky shimmered with the brilliance of immortal stars.

Upon reaching the summit, the confrontation began:

"Jesus," Satan declared, his voice dripping with seduction and defiance, "you are the son of man, not of God. I, a fallen angel, have wandered this world for millennia. I know better than anyone the dark corners of creation. The Father was wrong, for nature itself is a psychopath. From the beginning, it requires one being to thrive at the expense of another's misery. This planet is mine; it belongs to me. And what will you achieve with mere love? Nothing! You will never stop me!"

Just as Satan's last words hung in the air, Jesus vanished, swept away by a divine power that defied all earthly logic. The energies of the mountain vibrated with the tyrannical clash, a reminder of the eternal conflict raging beyond human perception. In the stillness of the night, the decisions made by these beings touched the lives of men, who remained oblivious to the cosmic drama unfolding above them.

In that moment, behind Satan rose an army of dark beings—infernal specters and mighty multi-headed dragons. It was a terrifying vision, a parade of nightmares made flesh.

From the heavens descended Archangel Michael, clad in resplendent armor and wielding the sword of justice. Beside him stood Mary Magdalene, her countenance radiating hope and purity. To the right, Saint Gabriel, an angel of formidable strength, with hair golden as the sun, took his stance before the adversaries.

"Satan, have you forgotten the day you fled from me and hid in the dark bowels of the earth?" Saint Gabriel thundered, his voice resonating like a storm. "Let that history not repeat itself. You will not claim victory."

Satan and his wife laughed, their cackles chilling the very air around them. With determination, Archangel Michael raised his sword and hurled it forcefully at Satan. However, with a swift and supernatural maneuver, the couple evaded the attack. The sword continued its relentless trajectory, embedding itself in an inaccessible cave of the nearby mountain, firmly lodged in the eternal rock.

The air throbbed with power as the gazes of the adversaries locked once more. The moments that followed would determine the fate of many, and the battle between light and darkness was just beginning in that sacred enclave.

The mantle of night cloaked the mountain, setting the stage for a tense confrontation. Both forces of good and evil braced themselves for the clash that would decide the fate of countless human souls. As these celestial and demonic entities prepared for battle, humanity continued its course, oblivious to the cosmic drama unfolding around them.

The celestial and demonic figures embodied the eternal struggle between good and evil. This battle transcended the physical realm, touching the deepest fibers of the spiritual. We, as humans, though often unaware of this war, are influenced by forces beyond our comprehension. This conflict is not merely metaphysical; it is profoundly spiritual and human.

Thus, we reflect on the duality that defines our existence. The actions and beliefs of human beings are intrinsically linked to these invisible forces. The struggle between good and evil shapes not only our present lives but also our eternal destinies. This battle serves as a poignant reminder of the importance of faith, courage, and our connection to the divine in our quest to understand and confront the challenges of life.

Dreams of Aisling

Lumina and Aisling

In an ancient, enchanted city where the sea breeze sang ancestral songs and magic lingered in the air, lived Aisling with her mother, grandmother, and childhood friend Lumina. Her mother, Mirabel, whose name resonated with the power of the waves and the wisdom of ages, possessed a wondrous gift. Whenever she sang with the passion of her heart, everything around her froze; even the fiercest foes fell into a deep slumber, ensnared by the enchanting melody that flowed from her lips.

In their grand family residence, adorned with shimmering tapestries and ancient books of arcane knowledge, Aisling's grandmother, the venerable Queen Mother Eithne, was a figure of respect and love. Her eyes held the wisdom of a thousand autumns and her voice carried the weight of divine authority. Aisling and Lumina spent their days amidst mischief and play, sheltered under the watchful care of their family and the whimsical sprite, Fergus. This little Irish creature, though mischievous and prankish, guarded the girls with devotion and unbridled joy.

Within the city stood the Lysandra School of Magic, a place where young talents learned to harness their gifts and understand the art of the arcane. Aisling and Lumina, along with other apprentices, attended this school where the walls whispered secrets of bygone eras. Under the tutelage of wise instructors, they practiced enchantments, potions, and the ancient science of divination.

One morning, as dew still adorned the garden flowers and the sun peeked timidly over the horizon, Eithne summoned Aisling to her chamber: "Aisling, dear," said Eithne, her voice as gentle and firm as a brook between stones. "Today is of great importance. You must accompany me, as the trial of two witches from the east of Ireland, accused of disturbing the sacred balance of our lands, will be held."

The young friends, Lumina and Aisling, set out under Fergus's attentive gaze. The sprite clambered up trees, whispering secrets to the wind, making every day an adventure. Through lush paths and hidden forests, Lumina and Aisling played, unraveling magical riddles and challenges that Fergus left in the shadows for pure amusement. Their laughter filled the air with life, painting every corner of their path with joy.

As Aisling neared the grand council hall, her heart thundered, knowing that the trial would require not only her grandmother's wisdom but also an act of divine justice. In the majestic courtroom, two hooded figures stood, their hands bound with shimmering chains glowing with a light of their own. The eastern witches, though formidable, were not immune to the power of justice resting beneath the august ceiling.

Eithne raised her voice, clear and powerful, resonating in every corner: "Today, in this blessed land, we must judge these two women accused of disrupting the order and peace we treasure. Let truth and justice prevail, and may magic never turn to misfortune for our land."

The trial commenced, and the fate of the eastern witches would be decided under the watchful eye of ancient traditions. Aisling watched intently, knowing that each lesson learned today would add a link to the chain of her knowledge and her future as a guardian of her home.

Thus, in the enchanted city, the lives of Aisling and her loved ones continued, weaving together magic, learning, and the adventures that only lie at the heart of legends.

In the venerable spell book, zealously guarded in the most sacred halls of the Lysandra School of Magic, there was a special chapter dedicated to young fairies and their innate powers. This chapter, penned in beautiful and ancient script, which Aisling took to the forest, read:

"Varbreatha," Aisling whispered, her melodious voice mingling with the wind. At her call, tiny green lights began flickering among the leaves, creating a natural spectacle that could only be described as a visual symphony.

"Look there," Aisling pointed out to her best friend, Lumina, who watched, wide-eyed. "The flowers... they're coming to life!" And right before their eyes, hyacinths and daffodils began to stretch, moving to the rhythm of a melody that was silent to all but them.

Lumina, fascinated and amazed, asked, "Can you always talk to creatures like this?"

"Yes, but only when I listen with my heart," Aisling replied as a family of squirrels approached trustingly. "They know when we have good intentions."

As they walked deeper into the woods, they reached a clearing where the sun shone with a loving intensity, caressing their skin with warm, gentle touches. There, a gleaming deer lay wounded.

"This is where we need Varbreatha most," Aisling said decisively. She extended her hands and murmured ancient words filled with power and kindness. Instantly, plants with healing properties sprouted at her feet, enveloping the deer with their colorful leaves, healing its visible and perhaps invisible wounds as well.

The deer, now fully recovered, rose and looked at Aisling with deep gratitude in its eyes. With a slight nod of its head, it paid homage to the young fairies before rejoining its herd.

"It's a magical place," Aisling said, twirling around with a radiant smile, "where we can make what's inside us come true."

Lumina nodded, "Aisling, I think the Luminous Forest is peaceful not just because of its magic, but because it's full of love and hope."

At dusk, Aisling and Lumina sat beneath the great oak at the heart of the forest, watching the sun set behind the hills. The forest creatures joined them, creating a picture of perfect tranquility.

"It's the home I always imagined," Aisling whispered, feeling the peace wrap around her like a comforting blanket.

Lumina smiled, "Yes, and you are its guardian."

So, they concluded their day in the Luminous Forest, a sanctuary of harmony where Aisling's magic shone not just through enchantments but in every small act of kindness.

In the heart of enchanted realms, where the echoes of the zeitgeist vibrated and the stars seemed to sigh secrets of old, Aisling prepared for a new challenge. Under the shelter of a bright moon, her connection with the Luminous Forest was about to prove its true power.

"Aisling, are you ready?" asked Lumina, her green eyes gleaming with curiosity and a hint of nervousness.

"More than ready," Aisling replied, feeling her heart beat in harmony with the forest.

The forest creatures gathered, forming a circle of presence and expectation. Aisling looked up to the sky and whispered, "Varbreatha!"

Instantly, the air began to vibrate, and green lights flashed, dancing among the trees.

"It's amazing!" exclaimed Lumina, astonished to see roots and branches expanding, responding to Aisling's call.

Aisling smiled, feeling the power flow through her like an untamed river. "This is more than magic; it's understanding and being understood."

From her hands, Aisling began to form whirlwinds spinning with luminous majesty. Spirals of light twirled, absorbing all lingering shadows in the air until the clearing shone with restored purity.

"Look at those whirlwinds!" cried Lumina, amazed by the wondrous destruction of darkness in spirals of brilliant splendor.

The clearing in the forest transformed into an extraordinary stage. The earth vibrated in unison with these bright whirlwinds, reflecting the energy that Aisling unleashed.

"Can you feel it too?" Aisling asked, her voice ringing with certainty.

"Yes, it's as if the forest is breathing with you!" Lumina responded, feeling the rhythms of the earth beat alongside their own.

Suddenly, a dark shadow attempted to breach the edge of the clearing, but it was swiftly absorbed by the luminous whirlwinds, deforming and disappearing in the radiant energy.

"You won't cross," declared Aisling with assurance, her words filled with renewed energy.

The shadow retreated, dissolving as if it feared the light emanating from her.

"See how even darkness yields to the light," murmured Lumina, impressed.

Aisling descended from her natural pedestal, the forest around her returning to its usual serenity.

"Power isn't always about strength but knowing where and how to apply it," said Aisling, as the forest creatures returned to their normal activities.

Lumina embraced her, "You've found your true path, Aisling."

As the sky began to darken, Aisling knew she would carry that moment in her heart—a symbol of the power of knowledge, camaraderie, and the light that never fades.

At the school, every third week, the young witches left the classrooms to practice what they had learned in the magical forests. This time, Aisling and Lumina were chosen to team up, merging their unique skills in preparation for their descent into the human dimension. Both shared a special destiny and knew this would be a crucial step in their training.

"Today will be interesting," commented Lumina as they walked toward the Luminous Forest, her golden hair reflecting the morning light.

"Certainly," Aisling smiled, her eyes shining with excitement. "I always learn something new when I spend time with you."

The leaves whispered at their passing, creating a unique melody that resonated in their hearts.

"Remember, we're here to practice the best of ourselves," Lumina said, as she gently slid her hand through the air, leaving a trail of silver light. "Solas na Gealaí."

"It's fascinating how you can heal and purify with just a gesture," said Aisling, admiring her friend's work.

"Thank you," Lumina replied, blushing slightly. "Your ability to communicate with nature is equally impressive."

As they ventured deeper into the forest, Aisling paused for a moment. "Do you feel it? The forest speaks to us."

Lumina closed her eyes for a moment, listening. "Yes, it welcomes us."

As they moved forward, Lumina began to sing softly. Invisible magical threads began weaving through the air, forming an intricate pattern that glowed faintly beneath the canopy of leaves.

"This is my Amsugach," Lumina explained, although she struggled with the pronunciation at times, her voice a melodic whisper that filled the air. "I weave it to protect us and guide our energies."

"It's incredible," murmured Aisling, feeling enveloped by a comforting warmth, a clear manifestation of Lumina's power.

Just then, a threatening shadow stretched from the forest's depths. Aisling reacted quickly, whispering "Varbreatha!" as she created whirlwinds of light that danced around them.

"Together we can do this," Aisling said, her voice firm and full of confidence.

"Always together," Lumina reaffirmed, focusing on strengthening her moonlight shield to protect them.

The shadows crashed against the luminous barrier, dissipating in a flash of light. The combination of their power was unbeatable, and the forest once again shone in peace.

Once the danger had passed, Aisling sighed in relief. "It's amazing how our magics complement each other."

"Yes, it's as if they were meant to be one," Lumina replied with a warm smile.

"I'm excited for what's to come," said Aisling, gazing at the horizon. "I feel like our mission in the human dimension will be unique."

Lumina nodded, her eyes reflecting determination. "Together, there's no challenge we can't overcome."

Conclusion: As their day of practice ended, the sky was painted in warm hues by the setting sun. Sitting in a clearing, surrounded by the songs of the forest creatures, Aisling silently gave thanks for the bond she shared with Lumina.

"This is the beginning of a powerful friendship," Lumina said, full of gratitude.

"Yes," Aisling responded, smiling, "and we're ready for anything that comes our way."

With newfound confidences and an even stronger friendship, both knew they would face any challenge together, even those beyond their dimension. They were convinced that, thanks to their skills and their bond, they were destined to shine beyond the barriers of time and space.

The Final Challenge: Star Fusion

The week of trials, affectionately dubbed "Practice Week," was drawing to a close at the Bright Magic School. It had been a series of intense challenges for Aisling and Lumina, testing their connection and abilities in a real-world setting. The instructors had reserved the most difficult challenge for the final day: facing a formidable enemy as a team, using their combined powers.

"Ready for the grand finale?" Lumina asked, a mischievous spark in her eyes. "If we do well, maybe they'll give us a trophy... made of chocolate."

Aisling chuckled softly. "I hope we can share it. I always crave something sweet."

As they walked to the designated clearing for the trial, the forest lights seemed to dim, creating a tense atmosphere filled with expectation.

Suddenly, a dark figure emerged from the shadows: the Guardian of Oblivion, an entity formed from fragments of lost memories, able to erase the memory of anyone it touched.

"Well, this is unexpected," Aisling admitted, a teasing tone in her voice. "Looks like the jokes are over."

"So, no chocolate trophies then," Lumina added with a slight pout. "It'll be a tie... until we win, of course."

The Guardian advanced, filling the air with an unsettling chill. The two friends quickly prepared themselves, knowing that facing this creature would require more than their individual magic.

"Star Fusion!" they shouted in unison, placing their hands one over the other. The energy around them swirled, sparking with vibrant colors and powerful radiance.

When their combined magic reached its peak, Aisling and Lumina unleashed a blast of divine light. The creature staggered as the brilliance enveloped it, dissipating the shadows that formed its body and transforming its dark core into hope and renewal.

"I bet it didn't expect that," Aisling declared with satisfaction, slowly lowering her hands.

"Definitely not," Lumina replied, her eyes sparkling with their recent triumph. "Do you think we practically lit it out of existence?"

They both laughed, the sound a balm after the tension of battle. They knew that no matter how dark the future seemed, their power together was an unstoppable force of light.

As they returned to the school, the twilight painted the sky with warm orange hues and the first stars began to twinkle. Along the way, Lumina couldn't help but smile and say, "Maybe we need to give a lecture on how to chase away shadows... with style."

"Absolutely," Aisling laughed, "though we must remember to include a demonstration with chocolate trophies."

With the week of trials behind them and their bond stronger than ever, Aisling and Lumina were ready to face any future challenge eager to cross their path. They already looked forward to the well-deserved respite of the weekend, confident that as long as they were together, no shadow could withstand them.

In the golden classroom of the Lysandra School of Magic, the fairy teacher Ceallach, known for her wise teachings and good humor, watched Lumina closely as she practiced an ancient enchantment.

"Lumina, dear," said Ceallach with a mischievous smile, "make sure to pronounce the ending of the Amsugach spell correctly. If not, you might find yourself tangled in a net over your wings."

Lumina grinned, knowing of her teacher's occasional pranks, and began to recite the enchantment carefully. However, at the last moment, she stumbled over a word, and a small spark of energy escaped her hands, playfully weaving a chaotic web that clung to her wings.

Ceallach let out a soft, motherly laugh: "Don't worry, young apprentice. Even the wisest fairies make mistakes. That's how we learn and grow."

Aisling, observing from her seat, couldn't help but smile and give her friend an encouraging nod, sure that next time Lumina would perform the spell perfectly.

Full of hope and perseverance, the young fairies knew that every lesson brought them closer to mastering the mysteries of the magical world and to becoming the guardians their ancestors dreamed of.

The weekend had flown by in the blink of an eye, those well-earned hours of rest filling the air with a nearly tangible calm. The queen mother, timeless in her elegance, decided to visit her beloved granddaughter Aisling before the new week began. With a firm yet leisurely pace, she headed toward Aisling's room in the towering palace, a place crafted for her granddaughter to find a sanctuary of peace and creativity.

Aisling's room was a corner of the palace that exuded magic and serenity. Large arched windows allowed light to stream in, filtered through delicate lace; soft colored rugs spread across the polished wooden floor like welcoming meadows. The walls were adorned with portraits of enchanted landscapes and shelves overflowing with spell books and tales waiting to be explored.

"My sweet Aisling," her grandmother announced in a voice both soft and radiant, warm as blankets on a cold night.

Aisling looked up from the book she was reading, her face lighting up with a smile. "Grandmother! I didn't know you were coming today."

"Well, I can't let too much time pass without seeing you," joked the queen mother, her eyes sparkling with affection as she drew closer for a hug.

Aisling quickly stood up, wrapping her grandmother in a tight embrace. "I've missed you," she murmured.

The queen mother pulled back to look into Aisling's young face, so full of hope and potential. "How was your practice week in the forest?" she asked, genuinely interested.

"Oh, Grandma, it was spectacular. Lumina and I faced a Guardian of Oblivion. Our Star Fusion spell worked perfectly," Aisling recounted with enthusiasm, her eyes shining like stars.

The queen mother nodded with approval. "You are so brave and brilliant, just like your mother at your age. Speaking of which, do you still enjoy weekends with her at the dream house?"

"Yes, it's our magical getaway," Aisling replied with a laugh. "The electric flower garden remains my favorite place to meditate."

"I remember planting those seeds with you, they seemed simple, but I always knew that with you they'd grow into something special," the queen mother smiled nostalgically.

"Grandma, is there more to your visit today?" Aisling asked, noticing a more serious expression on her grandmother's face.

The queen mother took a deep breath before answering. "Yes, I have to take you to an important event: the Witches' Judgment."

"The Witches' Judgment?" Aisling asked, a hint of concern in her voice.

"It's an ancient ritual where the skills and behavior of witches are evaluated," her grandmother explained. "It's not a condemnation, but an opportunity to demonstrate your abilities and learn."

Aisling pondered for a moment before smiling, feeling a mix of nervousness and excitement. "I understand, Grandma. Thank you for preparing me for this."

"I will be with you every step of the way," the queen mother promised, gently holding her hand. "You will face some challenges, but I'm sure you'll shine as always."

Time flew by as they prepared for the judgment. As they walked together through the palace's illuminated corridors, Aisling felt her grandmother's support like a warm, invisible hug.

"Visit me soon," Aisling requested, looking toward the future beyond the imminent judgment. "I want to learn much more from you, no matter the challenges."

"Promise, my star," the queen mother replied as they headed out to the event, a silhouette filled with grace and wisdom that inspired confidence.

With the judgment ahead and an unbreakable bond fortified, Aisling was ready to face whatever came her way, confident that with the love and guidance of her family, no challenge was too great nor shadow too dark for her to shine through.

CHAPTER 5

Judgment and Wisdom

The great doors of the courtroom opened with a deep creak, revealing a vast, luminous space. The hall was adorned with curtains of green and gold velvet, reflecting the light of enchanted crystals lining the walls. At the center, an imposing throne awaited the queen mother. Beside it, a smaller but equally dignified seat was reserved for Aisling.

The queen mother, her eyes sparkling with endless wisdom and her presence majestic, held Aisling's hand. Together, they headed to the main castle, where the trial of two witches was about to commence. The queen mother understood that this was a crucial moment for Aisling's growth, offering her a clear insight into the justice and fairness she would one day need to uphold.

The two witches bowed reverently as the queen mother and the young fairy entered. One of the witches, enveloped in a faint aura of confusion and regret, stepped forward first.

"Your Majesty," she began with a trembling voice, "my name is Grimhild. Your son fell in love with a young woman and sought to win her hand. My longtime friend, Morgana, asked to borrow my lake, promising to return it as soon as her son married. I agreed in hopes of helping, but now my lake has turned to mud, and my neighbors blame me."

The queen mother nodded slowly, turning her wise gaze to the other witch, who nervously wrung her hands.

"Your Majesty, my name is Morgana," she continued. "It is true, I borrowed the lake from Grimhild with the intention of helping my son. But what Grimhild didn't know is that when I made the vow, I crossed my fingers, nullifying its validity. My son never married, and now the lake is in a deplorable state. I felt it fair to keep it due to the efforts I invested."

The room fell silent as fairies, sprites, and other attendees watched the tension between the two witches. Aisling listened intently, her eyes shining with intelligence. The queen mother, with a half-smile, leaned toward her granddaughter and whispered softly:

"Aisling, my light, what would you do in my place?"

Having spent the past three years observing and learning in the Fairy City, Aisling answered with a clear, confident voice:

"Grandmother, I believe both are at fault in this matter. Grimhild erred by letting her area dry up, causing the death of fish and plants, which is harmful to the environment and those who depend on the lake. Conversely, Morgana cannot buy love; love cannot be purchased with money or materials. Neither acted with integrity."

The queen mother chuckled softly and nodded, pleased with her granddaughter's insight.

"I see that you have learned well, Aisling. Your wisdom and sense of justice are strong even at a young age. Now, let us see how we proceed with this matter."

Addressing the witches, the queen mother rose from her throne with regal grace.

"Grimhild and Morgana, you have been brought here to dispense justice. Grimhild, you have allowed your lake to become mud and mire, affecting the entire community. You are ordered to work with the nature fairies to restore your lake to its original splendor so that fish and plants may flourish once more."

Grimhild nodded solemnly, grasping the gravity of her negligence.

"Morgana, you sought to obtain something precious under false pretenses and deceit. Love is not a currency. No matter how much you wish something for your son, you have no right to take what is not yours and then break a vow. You are ordered to relinquish the lake and find a way to compensate Grimhild for the damages, working alongside her in the restoration."

Morgana lowered her gaze, feeling the weight of her actions.

"Remember, both of you, that integrity and honesty are the pillars of our realm," the queen mother concluded, regarding them both with severity and compassion.

The witches bowed their heads in acknowledgment and left the courtroom, ready to fulfill the decreed conditions. The queen mother returned to her seat, smiling softly and proudly at Aisling.

"You have shown great understanding, my dear. I know you will one day be a just and wise ruler. I am confident I will leave the kingdom in good hands."

Aisling smiled, feeling the warmth of her grandmother's love and trust, knowing there was much more to learn and experience, but feeling more prepared and assured with each step she took.

Lilith

The Demon's Dining Hall

In a vast, dark, and opulent hall, towering columns of onyx and obsidian soared towards a ceiling so distant it seemed to merge with the shadows. The light from the hanging chandeliers, each adorned with gems stolen from the very sky, merely provided a dim glow that cast long, sinister shadows across the walls. Between these walls, abysses of eternal fire roared, where condemned souls burned in perpetual flames, their screams silenced by the demon's power.

At the center of the hall stood a banquet table, a long slab of dark crystal supported by intricately carved stone claws. Upon it rested celestial delicacies and goblets carved from the same obsidian as the columns.

Seated on ebony thrones adorned with fiery rubies were Satan and his wife, the beautiful and dangerous Lilith.

Satan, with eyes burning with restrained fury and a presence that could chill the blood of any mortal, sliced a piece of meat with a knife that seemed to glow with darkness itself. Beside him, Lilith, with the grace of a queen and beauty that transcended the limits of this world, was dressed in attire far advanced for the era, a mix of black silk and light armor that gleamed like silver in the dim light.

Behind them, the servants—fallen angels with blackened wings—moved in the shadows, attuned to every subtle desire of their masters.

Lilith raised her goblet of blood, the liquid swirling gently. Watching her husband, she spoke with soft cunning:

"Men always seek brute strength, my lord," Lilith said with an enigmatic smile. "But we must use not only muscle but also mind."

Satan, his brow creased in disdain but with growing interest, lifted his gaze from his feast and fixed his burning eyes on her. His voice was deep, rough as the echo of a thousand storms.

"Speak, woman. What's on your mind?"

Lilith let the goblet drop, dark red splashing onto the crystal table like drops of poison as she leaned forward, her eyes alight with a ruthless intelligence.

"Time passes swiftly for humans. Their greed, their ego, blinds them. Let us create societies where leaders are increasingly thieves and avaricious, craving more power and endless wealth," she began, her voice both seductive and dangerous. "Let them believe they're preserving the planet while they actually destroy it. Encourage division among the people and, then, introduce a global government where you shall reign supreme."

Satan, intrigued and slightly less angry, took a sip from his own drink, listening intently. "How long will this plan of yours take?"

"Only five hundred years," replied Lilith, her smile widening to reveal glimpses of fangs. "By the year two thousand thirty, everything will fall under our dominion. Faith in God will wane, and men will believe in money and the illusory power they think they wield. They will abandon religions and worship abstract idols."

"Abstract idols?" Satan questioned, one eyebrow raised.

"Like science, technology, the universe," Lilith replied, "and their own overwhelming egos. They will cease to reproduce, for man's selfishness will be such that they will do nothing for anyone else."

Satan reclined in his throne, pondering deeply for a moment before nodding slowly. "You are clever, Lilith. Very clever."

Lilith smiled triumphantly, raising her goblet once more. "To our future reign," she said, and they toasted with the sinister echo of lamenting souls within the walls.

The plan was set in motion, woven with threads of greed and deceit, and the clock on humanity's destiny had begun to tick.

CHAPTER 6

The Lawyer and the Struggle

The Price of Triumph

Ashley's mansion stood grand and solitary atop a lush green hill, a modern palace constructed of white marble with expansive tinted windows that bordered its magnificent walls. At night, the city lights could be seen like a distant horizon, encapsulated by the serene silence that enveloped her fortress. Inside, the decor exuded elegance and accomplishment; every corner reflected decades of success.

Ashley, 44, a lawyer so renowned and impeccable in her craft that her face had become a symbol of justice on American television, sat in a sumptuous velvet chair, lost in thought. Her blond hair perfectly styled and her clear eyes, which had seen the depths of many human souls, pondered the cruel irony of life. In her lap rested her loyal pet, the dog Lassie, while the cat Moon lazily curled up on a nearby cushion. Despite her successful career and the great fortunes she had won against large companies that always had something to hide, Ashley once decided to help those most in need or citizens unjustly trampled by big corporations. In legal circles, she was called "America's Lawyer" for her television prominence, which led her to design her courtroom suits in the pattern of the stars and stripes.

From the television still playing in the background, she listened to the recounting of her achievements over and over. Cases won, criminals locked away, justice served. Yet, Ashley felt an overwhelming emptiness. An inner voice reproached her for mortgaging her personal happiness to reach professional heights. There were no children running through that vast living room, no partner with whom to share her triumphs and defeats. Only Lassie and Moon, and her assistant, Martha, who at this hour was at home with her own family. As the song "I Don't Have Love" played on the television, she reflected:

"What have I done with my life?" Ashley asked herself in a whisper. There were no answers in the ostentatious serenity of her home, only the echo of her solitude. Adorned with works of art and luxuries that few could even imagine, her mansion did not fill the void in her soul. "I could have had a family... children..." she murmured as she gently petted Lassie, reflecting on the decisions of her life.

Her thoughts were interrupted by the shrill ring of the phone. Martha had already retired for the night, leaving her alone with her thoughts. Always hopeful for a call at this hour, Ashley picked up the phone quickly: "Yes? Who is this?"

The voice on the other end of the line was Sandra, one of the mothers she assisted in the organization "Mothers on the Border." After years dedicated to her work, Ashley had found a new purpose in helping to rescue children from human trafficking.

"Sandra, what's happening?" she asked with seriousness and caution.

"We need you to come in tomorrow, Ashley. It's urgent. There's a new case, and I fear time is not on our side."

Though Ashley had closed numerous cases with the precision of a surgeon, this field was entirely different. These children, these families… their lives hinged on every move and action. Every second counted, and every mistake could be fatal.

The next day, Ashley met with the people she now considered her new family. There were four mothers, each with stories of bravery and tragedy: Maria, who had lost her daughter to a kidnapping and now dedicated her life to helping other mothers; Jessica, who had managed to escape a trafficking ring with her two children; Rebecca, with a past of abuse, who used her knowledge of the system to fight those trafficking children; and Priya, traumatized by the disappearance of her youngest son, who vowed not to rest until every child was safe.

Also among them were two fathers: Adolf, a cybercrime expert tracking child trafficking networks worldwide, and George, a private detective with an infallible instinct for uncovering secrets and dismantling criminal organizations.

The new case revolved around a group of children last seen on a route crossing the border of two states. Daniel had tracked the financial movements of a supposed charity, which was a front for a trafficking network, and George had confidential police reports indicating suspicious activity in certain abandoned warehouses.

Ashley spent endless hours, sleepless nights studying every detail, every clue. She knew she could not fail. Her training and experience were her weapons, but her passion and dedication to this new cause were her new motivation.

Together, they managed to dismantle a crucial part of the trafficking network. Children were rescued, and the perpetrators were put behind bars. Each success not only saved lives but filled Ashley with a satisfaction that no courtroom victory had ever provided.

For the first time in many years, Ashley felt she had a life mission far beyond the courtroom. She realized that her personal struggles and sacrifices had not been in vain, but a path to prepare her for something even greater: to give voice and justice to the most vulnerable.

That night, as she returned to her mansion and cuddled Lassie and Moon, Ashley understood that her life had taken on a new meaning. There was no traditional family, but she had a cause, a group of people to fight for, and, above all, a new reason to carry on.

At that exact moment, the phone rang again. Ashley picked it up, more ready than ever for action and the call to justice. They had marked a new trail and needed her cunning to once again save lives and bring hope to darkness.

The setting sun bathed the land in golden and reddish hues, while the cool breeze of County Meath, the most magical and legendary in all of Ireland, gently rustled through the leaves. Aisling's home, a charming cottage draped in moss and wildflowers, stood at the heart of the enchanted forest.

Aisling, a loving and wise mother, was setting the table with carefully gathered forest fruits and the exquisite flowers they themselves enjoyed as food. Lite Fairy and Lumina sat at the table, surrounded by vibrant nature.

Lite Fairy, a delicate fairy with golden hair and radiant eyes, approached her mother with a question she had long held in her heart.

"Mama," Lite Fairy said with a voice sweet yet filled with longing, "I haven't seen Papa in ages. I want to see him."

Aisling, with her radiant tranquility and eyes full of love, gave her a compassionate look as she placed a dish of delicious plant nectars and magical honey on the table.

Aisling sighed softly and sat next to Lite Fairy. She gently stroked her hair and said in a soothing voice, "My dear light, I understand your desire, but some things are difficult to explain."

Lite Fairy looked at her with eyes brimming with curiosity and hope, eagerly awaiting a response that would ease her heart.

Aisling continued, "Humans live such short lives compared to us. While they may reach up to 90 years, we live up to 1,800. Their existence in both time and space is very different and hard to reconcile."

Lite Fairy furrowed her brow and asked hesitantly, "So is Papa already gone? Did he die of sadness?"

Aisling nodded sadly, "Yes, my love. Your father loved this land and us so much that the sadness of our absence was too much for him. But my light, you must understand that he is not in this dimension with us."

Lite Fairy, with a tear running down her cheek, asked, "If he's dead, why isn't he here with us? Why can't he be in this dimension?"

Aisling, somewhat at a loss, replied delicately, "Your father took a wrong path in his sorrow. His spirit couldn't find its way here to this dimension. But this, my dear, is something better explained by Grandmother."

Lumina, who had been quietly listening, recognized her friend's growing sadness and decided to step in. "Don't worry, Lite Fairy," she said with a kind smile. "I lost my mother twice too, in the human dimension and our parallel one."

Lite Fairy looked up, surprised, as Lumina continued her tale. "I lived with my mother in the human world, but she had to go for work in our dimension. Unluckily, two men saw her and debated whether she was a fairy. One of them denied our existence, and every time someone denies fairies while we're in the human dimension, we die. She was unfortunate enough to be in the third dimension when it happened."

Lite Fairy felt a mix of sadness and understanding. Seeing Lumina's strength in the face of her pain inspired her and filled her with hope, knowing she wasn't alone in her sorrow.

Lumina smiled tenderly and concluded, "Since that day, I've lived with your mother, Aisling, who has treated me as her own daughter. Here, I've found a new family and much happiness."

Aisling took Lite Fairy and Lumina's hands, looking at them with deep love. "We are together, and in this magical forest, we will always find strength to move forward. We are not alone, and our souls are nourished by the love and nature that surround us."

Lite Fairy felt a comforting warmth in her chest, embracing the love of her mother and the friendship of Lumina with a serene smile. She had realized that magic resided not only in their powers but in the unbreakable strength of their love and the unity of their hearts.

CHAPTER 7

Dimensions and Insights

In the dim light of night, Lilith's figure materialized in an ethereal glow, surrounded by an aura that seemed to exude pure malevolence. Her steps echoed softly on the obsidian floor, moving with unparalleled grace as the light from the eternal flames of the crematorium reflected off her delicate features. Her finely sculpted face, perversely beautiful and seductive, radiated infinite satisfaction as she prepared to unveil the orchestrated plan for humanity. Her eyes, bottomless pits of darkness, gleamed with an inner fire at each word that flowed from her blood-red lips.

"In the times humans call 1530," Lilith began, her voice a seductive whisper snaking through the heavy air like a serpent, "the Spanish have discovered what they call America. A land rich, a New World destined to be forged under the swords and creeds of the conquistadors."

The demon, his grotesque face marred with scars, lit up with a malevolent grin, his eyes shining with dark enthusiasm. He nodded slowly, showing an expression of vicious delight. "They think to build universities and churches in their zeal for expansion," Lilith continued, "but we know that in those lands dwell savage tribes, our worshippers, who invoke our names with human sacrifices. Yet the invaders will seek to silence these practices."

Lilith began to walk towards a large glass wall. Behind the glass, the eternal fires of the crematorium roared in a macabre dance, with damned souls writhing in unending agony. Her steps were slow and calculated, filled with sinister grace. Her face twisted into a grimace of wild pleasure. "They aspire to free those tribes from our dominion, but not without cost. The greed and avarice of other nations, like those in the north, will lead to the massacre of the indians at the hands of the English, who will blame the Spanish. Once again, wars will ravage Europe."

The demon, whose claws intertwined with palpable anticipation, watched Lilith with growing malice. His eyes, beginning to glow a terrifying yellow, reflected a diabolical joy. Lilith's words unveiled plans beyond human comprehension. "Centuries will pass," she continued, "and another pandemic will ravage humankind. Then, world wars will stain the Earth with blood, and we will place in power the most sadistic and psychopathic leaders the world has ever known. Humans, drawn to corruption and despotism, will gleefully follow these rulers, causing millions of deaths."

Lilith smiled, her white teeth flashing in the firelight. "And then, economic power will concentrate in a few hands. Another pandemic will arise, and we will ensure that political and economic leaders centralize control. Then, the entire planet will be yours."

The demon, with a guttural laugh that rumbled like thunder in the darkness, asked, "How soon will this happen?"

"I doubt," Lilith replied mysteriously, "that it will go beyond the year 2040."

The demon's laughter grew louder, and his eyes, like a goat's, shone with unparalleled malevolence as darkness deepened around him. "Sometimes, dear Lilith, you surpass me in wickedness," he commented between laughs, his face reflecting twisted pleasure.

Lilith turned slowly, an enigmatic smile adorning her crimson lips. "Then together," she murmured, "we can forge a hell on earth that even humans cannot imagine."

The demon's eyes sparkled with manic enthusiasm as his laughter echoed in the shadows, mingling with the cries of tortured souls beyond the glass.

with a guttural laugh that echoed like thunder in the darkness, asked, "When will this happen?"

"I doubt," Lilith responded in a mysterious voice, "that it will be later than the year 2040."

The demon's laughter intensified, and his yellow eyes, like those of a goat, glimmered with unparalleled malevolence as the darkness deepened around him. "Sometimes, dear Lilith, you outdo me in wickedness," he chuckled, his face contorting with twisted pleasure.

Lilith slowly turned, an enigmatic smile gracing her crimson lips. "Then together," she murmured, "we may forge a hell on Earth that even the humans cannot imagine."

The demon's eyes sparkled with frenzied enthusiasm as his laughter filled the shadows, mingling with the shrieks of tortured souls beyond the glass.

The Gas Station in Texas

On a scorching summer afternoon, a lonely gas station in the arid lands of Texas appeared to be just a quick stop for a traveling mother and her seven-year-old daughter. The mother hurried into the store to buy some drinks and snacks to continue their journey. The old radio played the tune "Old Station in Texas." The sales clerk, a beautiful blonde woman in her late forties, covered in tattoos, glanced at her customer while the sweltering heat was stifled by a fan that whirred louder than the music.

Meanwhile, her car remained parked beside the pump, a sight that would soon awaken the greed of two men lounging in the shade, sipping beers.

Among them was Lilith, enchanting in her elegance, with fiery eyes watching the scene unfold from the shadows. With a seductive smile, she approached the two men and whispered in a melodious voice that slithered into their consciousness like a stealthy snake.

"Do you see that car?" Lilith said softly. "It's full of opportunities. Money, valuables... Everything you need is right there, just waiting for you to take it."

The men exchanged quick glances, greed mingling with anxiety. Lilith pushed them along, maneuvering her words like pieces on a sinister chessboard.

"Don't worry about the mother; she isn't going anywhere. No one will notice," she smiled, urging them with her persuasive power toward the vehicle.

Consumed by temptation, the thieves moved swiftly toward the car. As they rushed, Lilith gracefully distanced herself, taking her position by the gas pump, watching with dark satisfaction. The thieves spotted the purse and the keys left in the ignition, and without hesitation, they jumped inside and started the car.

The mother emerged from the store with bags of groceries in her hands. Upon seeing her car pulling away, she let out a desperate scream:

"My daughter! My daughter is in the car!" Her voice cracked as she ran after the vehicle in vain.

Inside the car, the thieves suddenly felt uneasy. The driver looked to his passenger with uncertainty.

"Hey, did you hear that?" he asked, his voice trembling. "I think the mother said her daughter is in the car."

"What?" The passenger turned and saw the little girl in the back seat, rubbing her sleepy eyes. "Shit, there's a kid in here!"

"I can't do this." The driver began to slow down, his face contorted in a mix of regret and fear. "I can't with a child in the car."

Meanwhile, the distant sounds of ZZ Top's music reverberated from a nearby festival. The iconic song "La Grange" filled the air with its energetic beat.

Lilith approached a well-dressed, sophisticated demon who stood patiently beside the patrolling police officers. The demon, immaculately tailored and smiling in a way that concealed his true intentions, spoke to the officers.

"Officers, I just witnessed what seemed like drug addicts stealing a car at the gas station. You should act quickly." His voice was convincing, seemingly filled with concern.

The police, without suspecting the true identity of their informant, dashed towards their vehicles to respond to the situation. As the officers departed, the demon's gaze met Lilith's, and they exchanged a malicious smile.

Seeing the police arrive, the mother clutched her hopes tightly. Breathing heavily, she pointed frantically in the direction her car had vanished.

"There! There! Please, get my daughter back!" she begged, tears streaming down her face.

The police accelerated after the escaped vehicle, their sirens piercing the sultry afternoon air. Moments later, a helicopter joined the chase, its blades slicing through the air, amplifying the tension of the scene. The thieves, feeling the pressure, decided to stop the car and run away, leaving the girl unharmed but scared in the back seat.

Seeing more police approaching, in a panic, they turned back to the car. Their jaws clenched from the impulses of the cocaine they had snorted, they revved the car before abandoning the little girl

In a magical corner of the parallel dimension, hidden among lush forests and enchanted mountains, lay the fairy city. On a clear day, Aisling, Lumina, and their mother soared through the sky like fighter jets, flying at incredible speeds. Their wings glimmered with iridescent sparkles as they deftly dodged objects, rocks, and tall fir trees, rising and falling with skill and grace.

"Mama, look at us!" Aisling shouted, her voice bursting with joy as she performed a daring aerial flip.

"We're going to beat you!" Lumina chimed in, laughing with a melody that danced softly among the trees.

Their mother laughed and puffed, trying to keep pace with them. Finally, they reached a high peak where they all came to a stop. Aisling and Lumina were giggling, their faces alight with the thrill of their flight.

"By all the flowers, how you girls fly!" said their mother, resting her hands on her knees as she caught her breath. "You're amazing at this. Truly, you are fairies through and through."

The three looked at each other affectionately. The mother, still recovering, observed her daughters with a mixture of pride and nostalgia.

"With all the teachings your grandmother and I have provided over the years," she continued softly, "and soon the school will be ready for you. You will venture to the human dimension."

Her face grew somber for a moment as she gently caressed their cheeks with tenderness.

"Soon, you will go with your aunt to learn about the oceans and seas. And then..." Her voice softened even more. "Then you will enter the human dimension."

Aisling moved closer to her mother, her voice trembling slightly. "Mom, I want to stay with you and Grandma. I love you so much. I don't want to go back."

Lumina nodded, her eyes welling up with tears. "Neither do I, Mama. Can't we stay here with you?"

Their mother embraced them tightly, trying to soothe their restless hearts. "My loves, I will always be with you, even if not physically," she whispered lovingly. "But you have an important duty. You have been chosen to carry our knowledge and teachings to other places. It is an honor and a responsibility."

Aisling looked at her mother, trying to understand. "Will we really be okay on our own? What if something goes wrong?"

"You will never be alone, my dear," the mother kissed both their foreheads. "The wisdom of your grandmother, my love, and the teachings you will receive from your aunt will always guide you. And remember, you can always come back here. This is and will always be your home."

Lumina sobbed, clutching her mother desperately. "I'm going to miss you so much, Mama. I don't want to leave…"

The mother took Lumina's face in her hands, looking deeply into her eyes. "Lumina, be strong. What you will learn and experience will help you grow, and you will be able to help others. This separation will be only temporary, and when you return, we will be stronger and wiser together."

An emotional silence enveloped the peak as the three fairies embraced, comforting one another. Their hearts literally beat as one, knowing that despite the distance soon to come, the bond of love between them would never break.

"I love you unconditionally," the mother whispered. "And I will always be by your side, in every thought and every dream. Fly high, my little ones, and do so with pride and courage."

They remained in silence for a moment, enjoying each other's company. Then, the mother took a deep breath and looked at her daughters with determination.

"My dears, the task you are going to undertake is crucial for our existence and the world's completion. In the human world, there is much beauty, but there are also many challenges," she explained, her voice filled with calm wisdom. "Mother Earth is suffering. Us fairies and all magical beings must aid in her restoration. You carry the lineage of the forest fairies, and with that, immense power. The trees need your help; they are subjugated by man."

Aisling and Lumina listened intently as their mother continued. "You will have the power to heal plants and animals, to purify water and cleanse the air," said the mother, gently touching the heart of each girl. "But you must also learn to guide good-hearted humans. There are many humans who wish to help the planet but do not know how. You will be their guides and their inspiration. Through your presence, they will connect with nature in ways they have never experienced."

"And our aunt? What will we learn from her?"

"Your aunt is the guardian of the oceans," their mother replied. "With her, you'll learn to care for and protect the marine creatures, to clean the waters, and to maintain the balance of aquatic ecosystems. The oceans are vital for life on Earth, and you will learn to defend them."

Aisling looked at her mother, a newfound spark of understanding lighting up her eyes. "So, our purpose is to help both humans and nature?"

The mother nodded, pride swelling in her chest. "Exactly. Your purpose is to be the bridge between the magical realm and the human world. In doing so, you will assist not only the good-hearted humans but also all of nature in recovering its balance and beauty. Always remember, my dears, that every action you take must be guided by the love and wisdom you have learned here."

Lumina and Aisling exchanged looks, still a bit nervous but also filled with determination.

"We can do this, Mama," Lumina declared.

"Yes," Aisling added, "we will do whatever it takes to protect our home and help the world."

The mother embraced them once more, knowing that the future of their lineage and the well-being of the world lay in good hands.

"I am so proud of you both," she said softly. "Follow your hearts and instincts. Always radiate the light you carry within you. With that, you can achieve anything."

The First Contact with Fairies from Other Communities

The sun filtered through the leaves of the forest, painting the clearing with golden flecks. Lumina was playing with tiny magical lights, laughing as they danced around her in the warm afternoon air. Her mother, Mirabelle, watched from the shade of the trees with a tender smile.

"Lumina, come here, dear," Mirabelle called.

Lumina stopped in her tracks; the lights faded gently as a new emotion washed over her. She ran to her mother and, upon reaching her side, noticed they were not alone. Three fairies Lumina had never seen before stood there, wearing vibrant emerald-toned outfits.

"Lumina, these are Aeloria, Brystal, and Nymia," Mirabelle said with a warm voice. "They come from the Dew Fairy community. They have come to make their first contact with our lands."

Lumina's eyes widened in awe. She had always heard stories about other fairy communities but never imagined she would meet any.

"It is an honor to meet you, Lumina!" Aeloria said, curtsying slightly in a respectful bow.

"The honor is mine," Lumina replied, awkwardly returning the gesture with charming innocence.

Learning Basic Healing Spells

A few weeks later, Lumina found herself in the clearing once again, this time surrounded by the visiting fairies and her mother. They felt different, as if the very air vibrated with magical energy.

"Today, we will teach you the first healing spell," Brystal announced with an encouraging smile. "It is fundamental for any fairy."

Lumina glanced at her mother and saw the pride shining in her eyes. Taking a deep breath, she began to follow Brystal's instructions, reciting the ancient words and channeling her inner energy.

"Luxiastra. Senera."

"It's like feeling a river of light inside you," Nymia explained, placing a hand over Lumina's heart.

With great focus, Lumina tried once more. A small spark of green light erupted from her hands, illuminating her face with a warm glow.

"I did it, Mama!" she shouted, jumping for joy.

Mirabelle approached, her eyes sparkling with tears of happiness. "I'm so proud of you, my little one," she said.

"It's an honor to meet you!" said Aeloria, bowing slightly in respectful reverence.

Lumina followed suit, her face aglow with excitement.

CHAPTER 8

Cycles of Light and Darkness

Adventure in the Enchanted River

The fresh air of the forest embraced Irish and Lumina as they walked towards the enchanted river, a magical place they often visited in search of new discoveries.

"I've heard that the river keeps secrets beneath its surface," Lumina said excitedly.

"Then we must explore it," Irish responded with a daring smile.

Upon reaching the riverbank, they both knelt, gazing into the crystalline waters. Suddenly, a radiant flash emerged from the depths, capturing their attention.

"Did you see that?" Lumina whispered, her eyes wide with wonder.

"Let's check it out," Irish said, reaching her hand toward the glimmer.

The water responded to her touch, spiraling open in a magical swirl that revealed a luminous underwater path. The two fairies exchanged determined glances, their excitement igniting their spirits.

Lessons on the Cycles of the Moon

Later that night, Irish and Lumina sat beside Mirabelle in the clearing, bathed in the soft glow of the full moon. Mirabelle held an ancient book, its pages filled with ancestral wisdom.

"Tonight, I will tell you about the cycles of the moon," began Mirabelle. "The moon affects not only our emotions and powers but also the energy of all nature."

Irish listened intently, captivated by every word. Learning about the cycles of the moon was not only important; it brought her closer to the roots of her magical existence.

Sharing a glance with Lumina, their hearts swelled with gratitude and love for their mother and mentor. In that moment, they understood that their journey was filled with adventures, but also with learning and growth.

The Dark Dining Hall of the Demon Castle

The air in the dark castle's dining hall was thick and oppressive, an overwhelming mix of spilled blood and eternal despair. The mighty demon, a being of immense power and infinite cruelty, presided over a table of suffering. Beside him, with an enigmatic smile, was Lilith, the first woman and mistress of the underworld.

Odran, now a reluctant servant of the demon, moved awkwardly and in fear. In his hands, he clutched a golden goblet brimming with the blood of infants, that precious and sacred liquid feeding the insatiable thirst of the infamous being.

"Be careful with that goblet, mortal," growled the demon, his red eyes blazing with malevolence.

The uncontrollable tremor in Odran's hands proved fatal. A momentary slip, a slight stumble, and the goblet spilled slightly, its contents staining the rich fabric of the black tablecloth. The demon erupted in fury, his voice resonating like thunder in the vast, shadowy chamber.

"Damn you, useless wretch!" he roared, rising from his infernal throne. "What have you done? You dared spill the sacred blood, miserable sinner! You deserve to be thrown into the eternal flames!"

Odran fell to his knees, terror filling his eyes. He knew he had no defense or hope against the wrath of the Demon King.

Before the demon could carry out his sentence, Lilith intervened, raising a delicate yet authoritative hand.

"My lord," she said, her voice soft but firm, "allow me a word before you condemn this poor wretch."

The demon, barely containing his rage, nodded slowly, his gaze fixed on Lilith, intrigued yet wary.

As Odran awkwardly made his way out of the hall, Lilith stepped closer to the demon, her dark eyes glinting with cunning.

"My lord, I urge you to remain calm," Lilith whispered. "This man is not a mere mortal. I have brought him here with a deeper intention."

"How dare you?" the demon roared. "What depth could a clumsy servant like him possess?"

Lilith smiled with a cleverness that only she commanded. "This man has fallen into our dimension for more than just an accident. I sense his fate is tied to ours in a way we do not yet comprehend. His misfortune and weakness could render him a valuable tool for our purposes. Let us not waste this opportunity."

The demon, intrigued yet skeptical, leaned in closer, his curiosity piqued by Lilith's words.

A Dark Dining Hall in the Castle of the Demon

As Odran lingered in the hall, Lilith approached the demon, her dark eyes radiating a cunning light.

"My lord, I urge you to remain calm," Lilith whispered. "This man is not an ordinary mortal. I have brought him here with a deeper purpose in mind."

"How dare you?" the demon roared. "What depth can a servant this clumsy possess?"

Lilith smiled with a cleverness that only she possessed. "This man has fallen into our dimension for more than mere accident. I sense that his fate is intertwined with ours in ways we do not yet comprehend. His misfortune and weakness make him a valuable tool for our schemes. Let us not squander this opportunity."

The demon's anger simmered, but intrigue flickered in his eyes. He leaned back in his throne, his fury subdued by curiosity.

"You are cunning, Lilith," he murmured, his gaze now reflecting interest. "What do you propose we do with this wretch?"

Lilith leaned closer, lowering her voice to a conspiratorial whisper. "Leave this matter to me. I will ensure that he serves our dark purposes. Allow me to manipulate his fragile mind, and you'll find that his servitude will be more beneficial than you could ever imagine."

The demon, contemplating for a moment, slowly nodded. "Do as you see fit, Lilith. But remember this: if your intuition fails, neither of us will escape the infernal wrath."

Lilith smiled, performing a respectful bow. "I won't fail, my lord," she promised, and with that pact sealed in the dark dining hall, she left to find Odran.

In the Shadows of the Castle

She found the trembling Odran wandering the dim hallways, his face resembling that of a lost soul. Lilith approached him, her gaze dripping with feigned compassion.

"Look up, Odran," she said, her tone imbued with a deceptive tenderness. "Not all is lost for you."

Odran raised his eyes, filled with despair and confusion. "What do you want from me, milady?" he whispered. "I am a broken man, without worth."

Lilith gently clasped his hand. "Your value lies in your very weakness. I know you have suffered, and I am aware of the dark chasm into which you have fallen. But I also know that you can still find redemption, even here, in the deepest shadows. Help me, and in return, I will guide you to discover yourself amidst this chaos."

Odran, clinging to the faint hope Lilith offered, nodded slowly. His days of misery and doom appeared to find new purpose. Little did he know that his redemption would come through twisted, dark service under the cunning Lilith.

The Years of Learning

In the enchanted corner of the world, hidden among lush forests and bewitched mountains, lay the fairy city. On a clear day, Aisling, Lumina, and their mother soared through the sky like fighter jets, flying at full speed. Their wings shone with iridescent sparkles as they deftly dodged objects, rocks, and tall fir trees, diving and ascending with impressive skill and grace.

"Mama, look at us!" Aisling shouted, her voice brimming with joy as she performed a daring twirl in the air.

"We're going to beat you!" Lumina added with a light-hearted laugh that rang sweetly among the trees.

Their mother, gasping with laughter as she struggled to keep pace, finally reached an elevated peak where they all came to a halt. Aisling and Lumina were beaming with excitement, their faces lit up by the thrill of their flight.

"By all the flowers, how you girls fly!" said their mother, placing her hands on her knees as she caught her breath. "You truly are nothing short of remarkable."

The three shared affectionate glances. With pride swelling in her heart, their mother watched them with nostalgia and love. It was in this tranquil moment that the seeds of their future adventures began to take root, revealing a destiny just beyond the horizon of their understanding.

"Oh my goodness, how you girls can run!" their mother exclaimed, resting her hands on her knees as she caught her breath. **"You're already outpacing me! You've truly become little fairies."**

The three exchanged affectionate glances. The mother, still recovering, observed them with a mix of pride and nostalgia.

"With all the teachings your grandmother and I have provided over the years," she continued softly, **"the school will soon be ready for you to attend."**

Her expression turned somber for a moment as she tenderly caressed the faces of her daughters.

"Soon you'll have to go with your aunt to learn about the oceans and seas. And then…" Her voice softened even further. **"Then you will enter the human dimension."**

Aisling stepped closer to her mother, her voice trembling slightly. **"Mama, I want to be with you and Grandma. I love you both so much. I don't want to leave."**

Lumina nodded, tears welling in her eyes. **"Neither do I, Mama. Can't we stay here with you?"**

Their mother embraced them tightly, trying to comfort their restless hearts. **"My darlings, I will always be with you, even if not physically,"** she whispered lovingly. **"But you have an important duty. You have been chosen to carry our knowledge and teachings to other places. It is both an honor and a responsibility."**

Aisling looked at her mother, striving to comprehend. **"Will we really be okay on our own? What if something goes wrong?"**

"You will never be alone, my little one," the mother kissed their foreheads. **"The wisdom of your grandmother, my love, and the teachings you will receive from your aunt will always guide you. And remember, you can always come back here. This is and always will be your home."**

Lumina sobbed, clinging to her mother in desperation. **"I will miss you so much, Mama. I don't want to leave…"**

The mother gently cupped Lumina's face in her hands, looking straight into her eyes. **"Daughter, be strong. What you are about to learn and experience will help you grow."**

A warm embrace surrounded them, a moment filled with love and understanding, promising that their bond would remain unbroken, no matter where their journey took them.

"Daughter, be strong," her mother said softly. "What you are going to learn and experience will help you grow and empower you to assist others. This separation will be only temporary, and when you return, we will be stronger and wiser together."

An emotional silence enveloped the mountaintop as the three fairies embraced, seeking comfort in each other. Their hearts beat in unison, knowing that no matter the distance soon to come, the bond of love between them would never break.

"I love you unconditionally," their mother whispered. "And I will always be by your side, in every thought and every dream. Fly high, my little ones, and do so with pride and courage."

They stood in silence for a moment, basking in each other's company. Then, taking a deep breath, their mother looked at her daughters with unwavering determination.

"My dears, the project you are about to undertake is crucial for our existence and that of the entire world. In the realm of humans, there is much beauty, but also many challenges," she explained, her voice rich with wisdom and calm. "Mother Earth is suffering. We fairies, along with all magical beings, must help in her restoration. You carry the lineage of the forest fairies, and with that comes immense power."

Aisling and Lumina listened closely as their mother continued.

"You will have the power to heal plants and animals, purify water, and cleanse the air," the mother said, gently touching the heart of each girl. "But you must also learn to guide kind-hearted humans. Many humans wish to help the planet but don't know how. You will be their guides and inspiration. With your presence, they will connect with nature in ways they have never imagined."

Lumina looked up, intrigued. "And what about our aunt? What will we learn from her?"

"Your aunt is the guardian of the oceans," their mother replied. "With her, you will learn how to care for and protect the sea creatures, clean the waters, and maintain the balance of aquatic ecosystems. The oceans are vital for life on Earth, and you will learn how to defend them."

Aisling gazed at her mother, a new spark of understanding igniting within her. "So, our purpose is to help both humans and nature?"

Their mother nodded, pride swelling in her heart. "Exactly. Your purpose is to be the bridge between the magical realm and the human world. In doing so, you will help not only kind-hearted humans but also all of nature in its quest to regain balance and beauty. Always remember, my dears, that every action you take must be guided by the love and wisdom you have learned here."

Lumina and Aisling exchanged determined looks, still a bit nervous, but filled with resolve.

"We can do this, Mama," Lumina stated confidently.

"Yes," Aisling added. "We will do whatever it takes to protect our home and help the world."

Their mother embraced them once more, knowing that the future of their lineage and the well-being of the world rested in capable hands.

"I am so proud of you both," she said softly. "Follow your hearts and instincts, and always radiate the light within you. With that, you can achieve anything."

Intensive Courses Until Age 18 for Fairies in the City and Kingdom of the Fairy Dimension and Magical Beings

1. First Flight of Aisling and Lumina
2. Encounter with the Wise Trees of the Forest
3. Discovery of Their Initial Powers
4. Celebration of the First Solstice in the City
5. Friendship with Talking Animals
6. First Teachings from Their Grandmother
7. Magical Hide and Seek Game
8. First Encounter with Mischievous Goblins
9. Visit to the Magical Library
10. Learning Enchanted Songs
11. Creation of Their First Magical Garden

Second Year (Ages 7)

1. First Contact with Fairies from Other Communities
2. Learning Basic Healing Spells
3. Adventure in the Enchanted River
4. Lessons on the Cycles of the Moon
5. Festival of Lights in the Forest
6. Discovery of a Magical Flower
7. Tales of the Fairy Kingdom Ancestors
8. First Meditation Sessions with Their Grandmother
9. Collecting Magical Ingredients Creating Simple Potions Flight Competition in the Community First Event Interacting with Humans

Third Year (Age 8)

1. Exploring Magical Caves
2. Learning about Crystals and Precious Stones
3. First Alchemical Experiments
4. Discovery of an Interdimensional Portal
5. Rescue of an Injured Small Animal
6. Festival of Golden Rain
7. Journey to the Summit of the Sacred Mountain
8. Guardians of the Secrets of the Forest
9. Restoring the Health of the Elder Tree
10. Celebration of the Starlit Night
11. Invoking and Understanding Wind Spirits
12. Magic Skill Competition

Fourth Year (Age 9)

1. First Classes with Aunt about the Oceans
2. Rescue of Marine Creatures
3. Maintaining an Aquatic Ecosystem
4. Finding the Pearl of Wisdom
5. Becoming Guardians of a Magical Island
6. Finding and Protecting a Coral Reef
7. Learning about Marine Flora
8. Conserving Nesting Areas for Magical Turtles
9. Quest for the Marine Crystal
10. Water and Fire Festival
11. Reconstructing a Sunken Ship
12. Creating Underwater Defenses

Fifth Year (Age 10)

1. Reunion with Human Friends
2. Mysteries and Secrets of the Ancient Forest
3. Advanced Alchemy Lessons
4. Uniqueness of Enchanted Objects
5. Magical Protections for Loved Ones
6. Bonding with and Caring for Baby Dragons
7. Journey to the Edges of the Fairy Kingdom
8. Magical Events and How to Control Them
9. Trip to the Kingdom of Friendly Giants
10. Festival of Tales and Legends
11. First Encounter with a Dark Enemy
12. Formation of a Protective Circle

Sixth Year (Age 11)

1. Lessons on Climate Change and Its Impact
2. Eruption of a Magical Volcano and Protection
3. Manipulating Elemental Energy
4. Creating a Sanctuary for Forest Creatures
5. First Steps toward Leadership in the Community
6. Challenges Related to Acid Rain
7. Learning about Magical Constellations
8. Journey to an Enchanted Forest at Night
9. First Counsel with Grandmother about Destiny and Mission
10. Strengthening Sisters' Bonds
11. Protection against an Evil Spell
12. First Meeting with the Council of Elder Fairies

Seventh Year (Age 12)

1. Forming Alliances with Other Magical Beings
2. First Attempts at Diplomacy
3. Exploring Unknown Territories
4. Researching Ancient Relics
5. Challenge of the Enchanted Mazes
6. Advanced Enchantments and Protections
7. Meeting Diverse Magical Cultures
8. Lunar Festival and Artistic Skills
9. Resolving Magical Conflicts
10. First Steps towards Managing Dimensions
11. Reinforcing Connections with Their Grandmother
12. Experiences with Celestial Creatures

Eighth Year (Age 13)

1. Advanced Lessons on Space and Time
2. Guardians of Portals and Their Secrets
3. First Approach to the Dimension of Darkness
4. Becoming and Rebirth: A Journey Through Cycles
5. Collaboration with Nature Realms
6. Magic and Technology: A Symbiosis
7. Tournaments of Magical Skills
8. Festival of Ancient Knowledge
9. Teachings of Stellar Wisdom
10. Councils about the Human Dimension
11. Expanding Their Protective Circle
12. Findings of Time Artifacts

Ninth Year (Age 14)

1. In-Depth Study of the Dimension of Light
2. Protecting a Mystic Sanctuary
3. First Work in Advanced Alchemy
4. Interdimensional Journey with Their Grandmother
5. Learning Ancient Runes
6. First Contact with Interdimensional Guardians
7. Balancing Energies of Light and Darkness
8. **Creating Objects with Mystical

Thirteenth Year (18 Years)

1. Arrival in the Human Dimension: First Impressions
2. Adapting to Human Life
3. Finding Their Place in the New World
4. Building Connections with Kind-Hearted Humans
5. First Meetings with Hidden Magical Beings
6. Discovering Challenges and Opportunities in the Human Realm
7. Responsible Use of Their Powers in Our Reality
8. Guardians of the Balance Between Both Dimensions
9. Learning the Complexities of Humanity
10. Initial Adventure in the Human World
11. Establishing a New Home and Community
12. Mission of Light: Beginning Their Legacy in Our World

First Contact with Fairies from Other Communities

The sun filtered through the leaves of the forest, casting golden glimmers across the clearing. Irish Lite Fairy, a young fairy with radiant eyes and translucent wings edged with silver light, observed the landscape from her perch on a branch. Below, Lumina played with tiny magical lights, laughing as they danced around her in the warm afternoon air.

The two fairies had blossomed into delightful adolescents. In human years, they were about 17; in their realm, they had existed only a few months, as time flowed differently there. In human terms, they would be over 500 years old.

Suddenly, delicate footsteps approached. Mirabelle, Lumina's mother, appeared, accompanied by three unfamiliar fairies: Aeloria, Brystal, and Nymia. Irish gracefully descended from the branch and landed beside her friend.

"Lumina, Irish, these are Aeloria, Brystal, and Nymia," Mirabelle said warmly. "They come from the Dew Fairy community. They have come to make their first contact with our lands."

Lumina's eyes widened in awe. She had always heard stories about other fairy communities, but meeting them in person was truly exhilarating.

"It is an honor to meet you!" Irish exclaimed, offering a slight bow of respect.

"The honor is mine," Lumina said, mirroring her friend's gesture with an enthusiastic smile.

Learning Basic Healing Spells

Weeks later, in the same clearing, the visiting fairies organized a special class for Irish and Lumina. They sat in a circle, the air vibrating with magical energy.

"Today, we will teach you your first healing spell," Brystal announced with an encouraging smile. "It's essential for any fairy."

Irish glanced at Lumina and then at the visiting fairies, feeling a mix of nerves and determination. Following Brystal's instructions, she began to recite the ancient words, channeling her inner energy.

"It's like feeling a river of light inside you," Nymia explained, placing a hand over Aisling's heart.

With great focus, Irish attempted the spell again. A small spark of green light erupted from her hands, illuminating her face with a warm glow.

"Look, Lumina, I did it!" Irish exclaimed, her eyes sparkling with excitement.

Lumina clapped enthusiastically, her joy infectious, spreading around the clearing.

Mirabelle observed proudly, filled with admiration for her daughters. Although her role was secondary in this journey, her unwavering support was crucial.

Adventure in the Enchanted River

The fresh air of the forest wrapped around Aisling and Lumina as they approached the enchanted river, a magical place they often visited in search of new discoveries.

"I've heard the river holds secrets beneath its surface," Lumina said excitedly.

"Then we must explore it," replied Aisling with a daring smile.

When they reached the riverbank, they knelt, gazing into the clear water. Suddenly, a luminous flash emerged from the depths, capturing their attention.

"Did you see that?" Lumina whispered, her eyes wide with wonder.

"Let's go see," Aisling said, stretching her hand toward the shining light.

The water responded to her touch, swirling open in a magical spiral that revealed a glowing underwater path. The two fairies exchanged excited glances, their hearts racing as they prepared to embark on their next grand adventure.

Lessons on the Cycles of the Moon

The air hung heavy in the clearing that night, the soft glow of the full moon illuminating Aisling and Lumina as they sat beside Mirabelle. The ancient book she held, filled with the wisdom of ages, seemed to shimmer in the moonlight.

"Tonight, I will share with you the secrets of the moon's cycles," Mirabelle began, her voice calm and soothing. "The moon not only influences our emotions and powers but also the very energy that flows through all of nature."

Irish listened intently, captivated by every word. Learning about the cycles of the moon was not merely important; it drew her closer to the roots of her magical existence.

"Each phase of the moon carries its own magic," Mirabelle continued. "Knowing how to harness these energies will make you stronger and wiser."

Lumina and Aisling exchanged a glance, their hearts brimming with gratitude and love for their mother and mentor. At that moment, they realized their journey was not just filled with adventures but also rich with learning and growth.

The Dark Dining Hall of the Demon Castle

Meanwhile, in a dark castle, the air in the dining hall was thick and oppressive, an overwhelming concoction of spilled blood and eternal despair. The great demon, a being of immense power and infinite cruelty, presided over a banquet table of suffering. Beside him, with an enigmatic smile, sat Lilith, the first woman and mistress of the underworld.

Odran, now a reluctant servant of the demon, moved about with clumsy fear. In his trembling hands, he held a golden goblet brimming with the blood of innocents—a precious, sacred liquid that fed the insatiable thirst of the infamous being.

"Be careful with that goblet, mortal," the demon growled, his red eyes flaming with malice.

Odran's uncontrollable shaking proved to be his downfall. A careless misstep, and the goblet tipped, spilling its precious contents onto the rich fabric of the black tablecloth. The demon exploded in fury, his voice echoing like thunder in the vast, shadowy chamber.

"Cursed fool!" he bellowed, rising from his infernal throne. "What have you done? You've spilled sacred blood, you miserable sinner! You deserve to be cast into the eternal flames!"

Odran fell to his knees, terror flooding his eyes. He knew he had no defense, no hope against the wrath of the Demon King.

Before the demon could carry out his sentence, Lilith intervened, raising a delicate yet authoritative hand.

"My lord," she said with a voice both soft and commanding, "allow me a word before you condemn this poor wretch."

The demon, his fury barely contained, slowly nodded, his gaze fixed on Lilith, curious yet wary.

As Odran scurried out of the hall, Lilith stepped closer to the demon, her dark eyes gleaming with shrewdness.

"My lord, I implore you to stay calm," she whispered. "This man is not just any mere mortal. I have brought him here with a purpose that runs deeper than you may realize."

"How dare you?" the demon snarled. "What depth could a clumsy servant such as he possibly have?"

Lilith smiled, a cunning twinkle in her eye. "This man has fallen into our dimension for reasons beyond mere accident. I sense that his fate is intertwined with ours in ways we have yet to understand. His suffering and weakness could make him a valuable asset for our plans. Let us not waste this opportunity."

The demon, still angry but intrigued by Lilith's words, leaned back in his throne, his fury tempered by curiosity.

"You are cunning, Lilith," he murmured, his eyes now reflecting interest. "So, what do you propose we do with this miserable wretch?"

Lilith leaned in closer, whispering softly. "Leave this matter to me. I will ensure that he serves our dark purposes. Allow me to shape his fragile mind, and you will find that his servitude will be more beneficial than you can imagine."

The demon contemplated this for a moment before nodding slowly. "Do as you see fit, Lilith. But remember this: if your intuition fails, neither of us will escape the infernal wrath."

Lilith smiled, bowing her head respectfully. "I will not fail, my lord," she promised. With that pact sealed in the dark dining hall, she departed to find Odran.

"Look up, Odran," she said, her tone imbued with a hint of tenderness. **"Not all is lost for you."**

Odran raised his eyes, filled with hopelessness and confusion. **"What do you want from me, milady?"** he whispered. **"I am a broken man, worthless."**

Lilith gently took his hand, her grip warm yet firm. **"Your worth lies within your very weakness. I know you have suffered, and I understand the dark abyss you have fallen into. But I also know that you can find redemption, even here in the deepest shadows. Help me, and in return, I will guide you to rediscover yourself amidst this chaos."**

Clinging to the faint glimmer of hope that Lilith offered, Odran nodded slowly. His days of misery and despair seemed to take on a newfound purpose. Little did he realize that his redemption would come through twisted and dark servitude under the cunning Lilith.

CHAPTER 9

Justice in New York

The air in the courtroom was charged with tension as the case of the Hernández family captured the attention of the media and public alike. The parents, devastated by the loss of their children—Emily and Jake, aged twelve and fifteen—were grappling with their grief after their lives had been shattered by a serial killer whose cruelty had sent shockwaves nationwide.

Ashley Mills, a defense attorney with an impeccable reputation, braced herself to face what seemed like the toughest challenge of her career. She was determined to seek justice for the Hernández family, aware that the stakes had never been higher.

In the courtroom, the atmosphere was thick with anticipation. Across the aisle from Ashley was Gareth Hart, the prosecutor—a relentless man known for his severity and precision in court. At the helm of this tense judicial arena sat Judge Samuel Whitaker, whose stern expression and piercing gaze commanded respect.

Courtroom Dialogue

Ashley rose to address the jury, her voice firm and emotional.

"Ladies and gentlemen of the jury, we cannot bring Emily and Jake back to their parents. But we can deliver justice. The Hernández family deserves to know that the man who shattered their lives will face the consequences of his heinous acts."

She paused, scanning the faces of the jurors, the prosecutor, and the judge. Her voice trembled slightly, yet her conviction remained unshakeable.

"The evidence is clear and indisputable: the defendant, Patrick DeLuca, not only murdered these innocent children, but he did so in the most brutal and inhumane manner imaginable. It is our responsibility to ensure that there are no more victims at the hands of this monster."

Gareth Hart stood, ready to counter. His voice was unwavering, each word calculated.

"The defense claims we must seek justice. And I agree wholeheartedly. But justice isn't merely about punishing Patrick DeLuca; it's about preventing more families from enduring the pain that the Hernández family has suffered. The evidence we have is irrefutable: DNA, fingerprints, and testimonies place the defendant at the scene of the crime. This is more than enough for a guilty verdict."

Judge Samuel Whitaker interjected with a grave tone.

"Ms. Mills, do you have anything to add before we proceed with the testimonies?"

A chill crept down Ashley's spine at that moment. Something dark, a negative presence, seemed to torment her. It felt as though a shadowy claw was digging into her mind, hindering her thoughts.

"Yes... yes, Your Honor," she managed to stammer, attempting to regain her composure. "I would like to continue..."

But the words tangled in her throat. Gathering her courage, she finally steadied herself.

She looked directly at Patrick DeLuca, who sat smugly next to his defense attorney. His expression was calm, even arrogant, as if he knew he wielded power over the proceedings.

"Mr. DeLuca," she said, her voice tense, "I have questions about the night of the crime. Can you tell us exactly where you were between 7 and 10 PM on May 14, 2024?"

A flicker of something passed through Patrick's eyes—a hint of mischief. A twisted smile crept onto his lips.

"I don't exactly recall," he replied coolly. "Maybe I was at home... or maybe not."

"How convenient," Judge Whitaker interjected. "However, we have witnesses who saw you near the Hernández residence."

Ashley took a step closer, determined. "Do you deny being in the vicinity of that residence that night?"

Patrick exhaled slowly, his smile unwavering. "I can deny many things, Ms. Mills. But sometimes, what one denies doesn't matter when the minds of others have already been made up."

Those words rang loudly in Ashley's mind. There was more at play here—something Patrick's intention evoked that sent chills down her spine. Ignoring the feeling of cold dread creeping into her bones, she redirected her focus to the evidence at hand.

"Tell us, Mr. DeLuca, how do you explain that your DNA was found under the nails of both children?"

Patrick paused, silence stretching as he considered his response. Then, his tone turned mocking. "Maybe you should ask the dead, not me."

Judge Whitaker banged his gavel, his voice thundering in the stillness of the courtroom. "Enough of this game, Mr. DeLuca!"

Ashley felt the dark presence intensify but took a deep breath, determined to maintain her focus and strive for justice.

"Proceed, Ms. Mills," the judge instructed, now calmer.

Ashley paused, allowing clarity to sweep over her, before addressing the jury with pleading, determined eyes.

"Members of the jury, our choices in this room will have lasting repercussions. Let's not allow the empty words of a murderer to distract us from our objective: justice for Emily and Jake. The evidence is clear…"

As she finished her speech, Ashley felt a slight easing of that dark presence, as if her determination and willpower were finally beginning to prevail. The fight for justice was not only against Patrick De Luca but also against the shadows that sought to twist the very essence of truth and decency within that modern

CHAPTER 10

Legacy and Power

In the Shadows of the Castle

In the dimly lit corridors of Satan's castle, Lilith stood before an imposing door carved from obsidian. To her left, a large crystal reflected the eternal fire and the tormented souls writhing within it. With a firm knock, the door swung open, revealing the father of shadows, whose face, illuminated by Lilith's presence, displayed a mix of respect and fear.

"You have promised me many favors, and it's time for you to start repaying them," Lilith said, her voice serene yet laden with authority.

The demon nodded solemnly, knowing he could not oppose the wishes of the Queen of Darkness. Lilith explained that she would grant him a crucial favor: to free him from his eternal damnation so that he could search for his daughter, Aisling—a name that resonated with beauty and mystery.

The father, gratitude lighting up his features, accepted the pact, but Lilith warned him solemnly, "You must swear by the eternal flames of Hell that you will find Aisling, or else the fire will be your final resting place, you man of flimsy faith."

With sincerity, he vowed to uphold his end of the bargain. Satisfied with his oath, Lilith gave him a threatening yet magnetic glance before disappearing into the shadows of the infernal castle.

The place, described in archaic terms, exuded a heavy and gloomy atmosphere. The walls were inscribed with ancient runes carved into black stone, and the air was tainted with the smell of sulfur and despair. The red glow of the fire reflected in the crystal dimly lit the hall, casting dancing shadows that faded into darkness.

Now a man on parole, the father ventured deeper into the castle's shadows with renewed purpose, guided by the promise made to Lilith and the hope of reuniting with his beloved daughter, Aisling, in some forgotten corner of the afterworld's dimensions.

The Enchanted River Adventure

In the land of magic and mystery, sisters Iris Lite Fairy (Aisling) and Lumina frolicked in an enchanted garden, discovering hidden wonders in every nook. Suddenly, they spotted a radiant flower emanating a magical aura.

"Look, Lumina! That flower seems to have special powers!" Iris exclaimed.

"It's incredible! I heard that if we eat from it, we'll be able to fly at the speed of sound!" Lumina replied, her eyes sparkling with excitement.

Without hesitation, the brave sisters took a bite of a petal, and in an instant, they soared into the air, leaving a trail of light and laughter behind them.

After their thrilling adventure, the sisters encountered their grandmother, the wise matriarch of the forest, Mother Belle, who welcomed them with open arms and a warm smile.

"Come here, my dear ones," Mother Belle said. "It's time for you to learn how to relax and find peace within yourselves."

"How do we do that, Grandma?" Iris asked.

Mother Belle taught them the magic of meditation and the art of connecting with their inner being, enveloping them in a sense of serenity and tranquility.

As Mother Belle shared her ancient teachings, the sisters listened attentively, captivated by their beloved grandmother's words of wisdom.

"Remember, love and understanding are the most powerful weapons in times of adversity. Always support one another, and you will find strength in familial unity."

With their hearts brimming with gratitude and shared knowledge, the sisters bid farewell to their grandmother, ready to face any challenges ahead, guided by the light of family and the eternal love that bound them.

As Iris Lite Fairy and Lumina made their way toward the bustling city, they were suddenly met by their mother, who waited for them with worry and affection etched on her face.

"My dear daughters, I've been so concerned for you. Don't stray too far, and make sure to keep me informed about where you are at all times. I sense dark energies in the air, and I wish to protect you with every fiber of my being."

The girls nodded in understanding, recognizing the sincerity and yearning for protection in their mother's words.

"We understand, Mama. We will always be careful and stay aware of our surroundings," Iris replied.

"Don't worry, we'll be fine. We promise to take precautions," Lumina added.

Back in their cozy, moss-covered home on the outskirts of the city, their mother prepared a delicious meal to share in their welcoming abode. As the enticing aroma filled the air, laughter and familial warmth intertwined, creating an unbreakable bond between mother and daughters.

With love in her heart, their mother watched her girls enjoy their meal, knowing that no matter the adversities they might face, the love and unity of their family would be their greatest strength.

In the Shadows of the Castle

"Look up, Odran," Lilith commanded, her voice tinged with false compassion. "Not everything is lost for you."

Odran raised his eyes, swimming in despair and confusion. "What do you want from me, my lady?" he whispered. "I am a broken man, devoid of worth."

Lilith gently took his hand, her grip as soft as a whisper. "Your worth lies within your weakness itself. I know you have suffered, and I understand the dark abyss you have fallen into. But I also know you can find redemption, even here, in the deepest shadows. Help me, and in return, I will guide you to rediscover yourself amidst this chaos."

Clinging to the flickering hope Lilith extended, Odran nodded slowly. His days of misery and condemnation seemed to gain a new purpose. Although he had yet to realize, his redemption would come through dark and twisted servitude under the astute Lilith.

CHAPTER 11

Meetings and Encounters

In the year 2024, María, a brave and compassionate woman, sought solace from the pain of losing her husband by organizing a group of mothers dedicated to finding and helping abandoned children at the border and in the desert. Alongside four close friends—three Americans and one Indian—along with the collaboration of two separated fathers, they embarked on a mission to rescue children left to fend for themselves in the harsh wilderness of crossing borders.

One of María's allies in this noble cause was "The Computer," a nickname given to the tech expert who once worked for an oil company. After a tragic accident forced him out of his regular work, he decided to invest his insurance money in purchasing the motel that now served as their operations base.

The other women in this diverse and committed team were essential. Vanessa, of Indian descent, contributed her ancestral wisdom to the rescue missions. Caroline, the indomitable American woman, handled logistics and communication for the group with her ingenuity and organizational skills. Meanwhile, Emily, the mother of three and a community volunteer, provided warmth and emotional support to the needy children they rescued.

As they gathered in the makeshift meeting room of the motel, María spoke with determination. "Ladies, we have received information about a potential urgent rescue. We know the situation is dire, but together we have the strength and determination to make a difference in the lives of these vulnerable children."

The other women nodded in conviction, ready to face the challenge ahead. With a spirit of solidarity and courage, the group prepared to venture into the dangerous terrain of the desert in search of the children desperately needing their help.

CHAPTER 12

Aisling's Birthday

In the enchanted realm, on the day when the young fairy Aisling turned eighteen and blew out the candles on her birthday cake, an event of far greater significance unfolded. Although in her world she was merely eighteen, she had the astonishing age of 500 years, due to the peculiarities of time in her dimension.

All the inhabitants of the kingdom—fairies and elves alike—cheered joyfully for the young princess as Queen Belle and Mother Mirabelle observed with pride. A dazzling spectacle of dance and magic unfolded around her, illuminating the streets with sparkling fairy lights and magical glows.

Now more mature and confident, Lite Fairy expressed her gratitude to everyone with grace and elegance, speaking with a poise that surprised even her shy sister Lumina, who was more recognized for her skill in flight and magic than for her words.

Radiating pride, Grandmother Belle approached Lite Fairy and whispered affectionately, "Dear one, soon you must journey to the sea to learn from your aunt and recover an amulet from the hands of an ancient wizard." Demonstrating her newfound maturity, Lite Fairy responded respectfully, "Yes, Your Majesty, I will leave when you say so. But may I at least finish the party first?" Laughter erupted around them as her mother interjected, "But you still have six months left before you go!" The young princess smiled, relishing the warmth and joy of her family and her people.

Thus, amidst laughter, joy, and the magic enveloping their world, Lite Fairy prepared to embark on a new and thrilling chapter in her life, ready to uncover the secrets of the sea and face the challenges that awaited her on the path ahead. What adventures lay in store for her journey into maturity and wisdom? Only time, magical and eternal, could unveil its mysteries.

In the luminous kingdom of fairies, as the celebration continued in honor of Lite Fairy, an unexpected event shattered the tranquility. Lite's father, Odran, guided by angels and dragons, entered through a dazzling multicolored tunnel filled with sparkles and lights that defied earthly description. Absorbed by a mysterious tube of energy that resonated with the intensity of a black hole, Aisling's father was transported in an instant, his face reflecting panic and confusion.

In the Shadows of the Castle

Believing he was embarking on this mission alone, Aisling's father could not contain his screams of terror as he was dragged away by an unknown force. Yet, in that crucial moment, Lilith, shrewd and determined, approached two shadowy angels who were watching in silence and ordered them in a firm tone, "Follow my father without being seen and make sure to bring me along."

The two angels, obeying Princess Lilith's command, vanished into the shadows, ready to follow Aisling's father and execute the intriguing mission of kidnapping the princess herself. Meanwhile, Lilith observed the scene with a fierce determination in her bright eyes, aware that fate was leading her down an unexpected path filled with revelations.

In the center of that whirlwind of lights and energy, Aisling's father vanished into the unknown, his voice silenced by the tumult of interdimensional travel. What mysteries and challenges awaited him on the other side of that energetic threshold where he had disappeared? More importantly, what revelations would await Lite Fairy when her loved ones returned from that journey beyond all comprehension? The destiny of the young princess and her family hung in the balance, wrapped in the mystery and magic of their extraordinary world.

Aisling turned to her grandmother and said, "Grandma, I had a vision. My father is coming this way." The grandmother brushed off the concern, replying lightly, "Then let him be welcomed." The young fairy walked toward the enchanted party, while the Queen Mother gestured for her lieutenant.

"Lieutenant, order the watchmen to guard the city's entrances and exits," she commanded.

"Yes, Your Majesty, right away," the lieutenant responded.

In the Dark Dining Hall of the Demon Castle

In the vast, sinister dining hall that always served as a backdrop for the machinations of evil, the demon, with his dark eyes fixed on the spectacle of souls burning beyond the glass, received a visit from Lilith. In a silence charged with complicity, the demon broke his reverie and directed a penetrating gaze toward Lilith, a mocking smile playing on his lips.

"These foolish, ignorant beings, struggling for all eternity only to end up burning," rumbled the demon's guttural voice, accompanied by laughter that echoed through the hall's walls. Lilith replied, her tone calculated and firm, "My lord, Odran has already departed in search of his daughter; everything is in motion."

The demon erupted in laughter, his eyes sparkling with a supernatural glow that revealed the true power he held. "Ha! I want everything to go perfectly; this strike will be definitive, and this planet will belong to me," he declared, his voice dripping with malice as his eyes turned a menacing yellow, taking on a reptilian appearance.

In that moment, the scene encapsulated the instant before a cunningly devised move, where the fate of entire worlds dangled by a thread. Lilith's figure, driven by ambition and a twisted loyalty to her new master, unveiled her true face hidden behind a mask of deception and manipulation.

Thus, the dark drama unfolded in the shadows, weaving a tale of treachery and unbridled power, where the forces of evil conspired to reclaim their supremacy over a vulnerable, unsuspecting world. The pieces were in motion, forging an uncertain future riddled with dangers for anyone daring enough to challenge the forces of darkness.

CHAPTER 13

Rescue and Freedom

In the dilapidated motel on the border of Mexico, just outside the town of Las Tres Cruces in Texas, the mothers, including María and Ursula, sat in a dimly lit and tense room, whispering about the perilous report they had received. The presence of the fathers, The Computer and Don Lázaro, added a layer of grave concern to the charged atmosphere.

Meanwhile, in the cantina of Ciudad Juárez, María and Ursula occupied a shadowy corner with the fearsome Roadrunner and his henchmen, listening cautiously to every threatening word of the conversation that resonated in the room.

"Cheers, friends!" proclaimed the Roadrunner, raising his glass arrogantly as the others nodded with feigned respect. The tension grew as their dialogue darkened and intensified, exposing the harsh realities of the dangers lurking in every corner of that shadowy world.

María and Ursula exchanged glances laden with unspoken meaning, both feeling the heavy weight of responsibility resting on their shoulders. They were the protectors of their families, guardians of hope in the midst of despair. As El Corre Caminos boasted of his wicked plans to his accomplices, the women listened with steely determination, knowing they had to act with both cunning and courage to safeguard their loved ones and challenge those who threatened their peace and security.

At Ursula's motel, the murmurs of anxious voices and the latent fear in the air created a thick atmosphere of worry. Mothers, fathers, and others in the small gathering braced themselves for the imminent danger, bound together by ties of solidarity and mutual protection as the darkness threatened to engulf them all.

In the cantina, María and Ursula stood unshaken, facing the evil before them with unwavering resolve. In their eyes burned the spark of resistance and hope, ready to defy anyone who dared to threaten the lives and freedoms of those they loved. Together, united by a shared purpose and an indomitable spirit, they prepared to face the challenges ahead, determined to battle the growing darkness that threatened to consume their dreams and their future.

THE CUSTOMER MOMS

In a quiet town on the Mexican border, a group of mothers had built a safe and peaceful routine despite their economic struggles. María, a dark-haired mother, worked at a small shop, while Ursula, with her calm demeanor, taught at the local school and managed her modest motel. Both women cared for their families with dedication, their friendship forming a strong bond of mutual support and loyalty.

One day, disturbing news reached the town: a shipment of fentanyl was on its way to cross the border from China. Word also spread that the ruthless coyote known as "El Corre Caminos" was involved, planning to traffic not only the drugs but also migrants. Upon hearing this, María and Ursula knew they had to act to protect their families and their community.

At first, María and Ursula hesitated. Fear gripped them—fear of the consequences and of putting their loved ones in danger. They discussed the situation at Ursula's motel, where other worried mothers and fathers from the town voiced their own concerns and uncertainties about how to confront this looming threat.

In the dimly lit motel, an elderly and wise man from the town, Don Lorenzo, approached María and Ursula. He shared stories of past resistance and assured them that together, they had the strength to face the perils ahead. He offered his knowledge of the desert and his connections along the border, giving the women hope that they were not alone in their fight.

Armed with newfound courage and Don Lorenzo's support, María and Ursula decided to infiltrate the dangerous world of El Corre Caminos. Disguised, they ventured into a cantina in Ciudad Juárez, a notorious gathering place for bandits and smugglers, to eavesdrop on conversations and gather critical information.

In the cantina, María and Ursula overheard El Corre Caminos boasting about his vicious plans. They faced the challenge of staying hidden while carefully gathering information. With the help of a sympathetic bartender, Ramón—who had his own tragic history with El Corre Caminos, having lost his 14-year-old niece to the criminal, never to be seen again—the women managed to escape undetected and brought the information back to the motel.

With their newfound intel, María and Ursula devised a plan to intercept the fentanyl shipment before it crossed the border. They rallied the town's residents, who, inspired by the bravery of these two mothers, decided to stand together and fight for their future.

Return with the Elixir

In the end, the mothers had transformed their community. No longer were they passive caretakers; they had become active defenders of their world. The bonds among the townspeople had been strengthened, and they had learned that true protection comes from unity and constant vigilance. Though the threat of El Corre Caminos remained, they had proven that with courage and collaboration, no adversity was insurmountable.

Thus, the heroic journey of the border mothers became an inspiring story of courage, unity, and resilience in the face of overwhelming challenges.

It was a scorching summer afternoon in El Paso, Texas. María, a strong woman with dark hair tied up in a scarf, sat on the porch of her modest home, reflecting on her late husband, a Marine who had died in service. Since his death, María had devoted her life to her two children and helping her community.

Suddenly, her phone buzzed. It was a message from Ursula, the owner of the Buenaventura Motel and María's closest friend. Ursula ran the motel for a living but also dedicated one of its rooms to the office of "Custom Moms," an organization she had started with María to support immigrant families.

Ursula's message was urgent: "María, come to the motel now. There's something you need to see."

A chill ran down María's spine as she got into her car and headed toward the motel. When she arrived, Ursula was waiting at the entrance, her face lined with worry.

"María, come inside. This can't wait."

They entered the office quickly. On the table lay a report, accompanied by photos and maps.

"What is this, Ursula?" María asked, her brow furrowed.

Ursula sat down across from her, sliding the documents toward her. "This just came in from a reliable source. There's a fentanyl shipment about to cross the border from China. And that's not all... El Corre Caminos is involved."

María's face went pale as she looked up from the report. El Corre Caminos was notorious for his cruelty, a coyote known for trafficking both people and drugs with ruthless efficiency.

"No... this can't be happening. How are we supposed to stop something like this?"

"I don't know," Ursula admitted, her voice steady, "but we can't just stand by. We have to protect our families, our community, María."

María thought of her children and all the families who depended on them for protection. Her mind wandered to the lessons her husband had taught her—a brave man who had always fought for what was right.

"You're right," she said, exhaling slowly. "We can't let this happen. What do you suggest we do?"

"First, we need to inform the other mothers on the border. They need to be on high alert. Then, we'll figure out how we can intercept that shipment without putting ourselves in too much danger."

María nodded, a mix of fear and determination rising within her.

"I'll take this home and study it, Ursula. We need to be smart and careful. We can't afford to fail."

"Yes, María," Ursula replied, her voice filled with quiet resolve. "But remember, you're not alone in this. We're in this together."

The two women embraced, sharing a moment of solidarity and strength. The road ahead was perilous, but they were ready to protect what they loved most.

Doubts and Fears

The sun was setting over El Paso, Texas, painting the sky in hues of orange and pink. María and Ursula sat together in the "Customers Moms" office, located at the Buenaventura Motel. They had called an emergency meeting with other mothers and fathers from the town. The small room was packed, but the air was thick with tension, almost palpable.

María stood and took a deep breath before addressing the room. Her voice trembled slightly, but she did her best to sound firm and convincing.

- **María:** "Dear friends, we're gathered here because we have a serious situation on our hands. We've received word that a fentanyl shipment is about to cross the border, and El Corre Caminos is involved."

A murmur rippled through the room. Some women hugged themselves tightly, while the men furrowed their brows in concern.

- **Ursula:** (interjecting) "We all know what this means for our community. But what can we do? We're not the police or federal agents. We're just mothers and fathers."
- **Ana:** (one of the attendees, voice cracking) "My son is in high school. If that drug gets here... I can't even think about it."
- **Robert:** (a father) "This is dangerous. El Corre Caminos isn't someone you mess with. They'll kill us if we try to interfere."

María felt the fear rising in the room. She was terrified herself, but she couldn't let fear paralyze them.

- **María:** "I know, Robert. We're all scared. I feel the same way. The last thing I want is to put my children in danger. But if we don't act, we're letting that danger walk right into our homes without any resistance."
- **Elena:** (another mother) "But what can we do? We don't have the resources or training to deal with something like this."

Ursula stood, her face a mix of determination and doubt.

- **Ursula:** "We're not suggesting that we take these people on directly. But we can't just sit by and do nothing. We know the families, the children; we know who's at risk. We can organize a watch, warn the families, and work with agencies that can take legal action."

A heavy silence fell over the room as everyone considered Ursula's words. Finally, María found the strength to speak again.

- **María:** "We came together to protect and support each other. This threat is big, yes. But together, we're strong too. We don't have to face this alone. We can be the eyes and ears for the authorities, helping them where we can."
- **Mikel:** (a father) "And what if we uncover something bigger? What if we get into real trouble?"
- **Anna:** "María's right. We can't sit idly by. The families crossing the border trust us, and we have to be worthy of that trust."

Anna's words resonated through the room. Slowly, the murmurs of uncertainty began to transform into voices of determination.

- **Ursula:** "So, are we agreed? We'll form watch groups to keep an eye on our homes and children. And we'll contact the authorities for help."

One by one, heads began to nod in support.

- **María:** "Thank you, everyone. I know this is scary, but it's our duty to protect those we love. Together, we'll get through this."

The meeting ended with a renewed sense of purpose. Though the fears hadn't entirely disappeared, the community was united, ready to face the threat as best they could.

Meeting Don Lorenzo

The twilight sky deepened as María and Ursula, fresh from the intense meeting at the Buenaventura Motel, stepped outside for air. Waiting for them was Don Lorenzo, a retired sheriff who had seen more than most could imagine. He had witnessed the best and the worst in Tres

Cruces. With his wide-brimmed hat and deliberate stride, his presence commanded respect.

- **Don Lorenzo:** (in a low, steady voice) "Good evening, ladies."
- **María:** (smiling weakly) "Good evening, Don Lorenzo."
- **Ursula:** "Thank you for coming, Don Lorenzo. We need your wisdom now more than ever."

Don Lorenzo tipped his hat slightly, a gesture of respect, before taking a seat on a nearby wooden bench. The two women followed, exchanging glances of worry and hope.

- **Don Lorenzo:** "I hear you've got trouble with El Corre Caminos. That man's a scourge. His grandfather, though in shady business himself, had some morals. I knew his grandfather, back when times were different."
- **María:** (anxious) "What can we do, Don Lorenzo? We know he's using children to smuggle drugs. And then… he sells them. He's a monster."

Don Lorenzo frowned, his deep-set wrinkles deepening as memories of darker days flashed in his mind.

- **Don Lorenzo:** (sighing) "He's worse than a monster. Using children… that's something I'll never forgive. His grandfather would never have stooped so low. But his grandson… he's got none of that twisted honor his granddad had."

Ursula shuddered. Don Lorenzo's words confirmed their worst fears.

- **Ursula:** "Can we stop him? We need to protect our children, our youth."

- **Don Lorenzo:** (nodding) "You can, but it won't be easy. El Corre Caminos has eyes and ears everywhere. But there's something he doesn't understand. The strength of a united, determined community. You've got something he'll never have—the love and protection of your families."
- **María:** (tears welling in her eyes) "We don't even know where to start."

Don Lorenzo stood slowly, surveying the area, choosing his words carefully.

- **Don Lorenzo:** "The first step is to organize. Set up a quiet watch, alert the authorities without drawing attention. I can help coordinate. And, above all, don't act rashly. I know the routes and tactics these men use. But we need to be smart, and we need to be cautious."
- **Ursula:** (resolute) "We'll do whatever it takes. We can't let them keep hurting our children."
- **Don Lorenzo:** (with a faint smile) "That's the spirit we need. This fight won't be easy, but always remember: you're fighting for what's sacred. For your families. And that gives you a strength that nothing can break."

The eyes of María and Ursula shone with renewed determination. Don Lorenzo, old and wise, still had the fire of justice in his heart, and the right words to ignite the courage in others.

As the last rays of the sun dipped behind the horizon, leaving a blanket of stars over the desert sky, Maria's heart pounded with determination. She stood firm, her gaze steely, the weight of the moment pressing down on her. Beside her, Don Lorenzo's face, worn by years of hardship, showed both worry and resolve. The battle had begun, and there was no turning back.

- *María:* (with a firm voice) Thank you, Don Lorenzo. With your guidance, we will face El Corre Caminos and protect our children.
- *Don Lorenzo:* (nodding gravely) You're not alone in this, never have been. And remember, justice may be slow, but it always comes.

The desert night seemed to hold its breath as his words sank in, giving the group the quiet strength they needed. They knew the road ahead was treacherous, but they also knew that together, they were unstoppable.

Planning the Interception

Back in Tres Cruces, Maria and Ursula wasted no time. They called a meeting in the town's small church, bringing together every able leader they could trust. The gravity of the situation hung heavy in the air. The threat wasn't just looming—it was here, and it had to be dealt with carefully.

- *Don Lorenzo:* (looking sternly around the room) We all understand the danger we face. But our children's lives are at stake. We must act, and we must act with precision and bravery.
- *Villagers:* (nodding in agreement) Yes, Don Lorenzo!

Maria and Ursula stood before the crowd, their faces etched with both fear and fierce determination.

- *María:* Ursula and I will return to Juárez. We need to learn the exact route they plan to take. By the time we return, you all need to be ready.

The Second Incursion into Juárez

Once again, dressed in the modest habits of nuns, Maria and Ursula slipped into the shadows of Ciudad Juárez, finding their way back to the dimly lit cantina. The place buzzed with activity, but the two women kept to the edges, scanning the room. Then, they heard it—the unmistakable voice of El Corre Caminos, his plans spilling out to his men.

- *El Corre Caminos:* (speaking confidently to his crew) The truck leaves at dawn, taking the old desert road. Two cars will escort it. No one will see us coming.

Maria and Ursula exchanged a glance. This was it—the information they needed.

- *Thug:* Wouldn't it be safer to take the highway?
- *El Corre Caminos:* (sharply) No. The police have checkpoints all over the main routes. Nobody bothers with the old road.

With hearts racing, the women slipped out unnoticed and hurried back to Tres Cruces. The entire village was on edge as they delivered the vital information. Don Lorenzo wasted no time, immediately setting the plan into motion.

- *Don Lorenzo:* We'll have to disable the escort cars first, then stop the truck without endangering the children.
- *Juan (a brave young man from the village):* We can use spike strips across the road. That'll take out their tires.

As the moonlit hours stretched on, the villagers prepared. They set traps along the desert road, hidden in the sand. Maria and Ursula, still disguised, positioned an old, broken-down car in the middle of the road as part of their ruse.

When dawn finally broke, the sound of engines pierced the desert stillness. The truck, flanked by two cars, barreled toward them. Maria stepped into the road, waving her arms frantically.

- *María:* (shouting) Please! Help! Our car is broken down—we can't move it!

The escort cars skidded to a halt, their drivers suspicious but uncertain. The truck driver rolled down his window, his eyes narrowing.

- *Driver:* Didn't I see you at the cantina?
- *Ursula:* (her voice trembling) We had an accident… We just need help. Please…

The hesitation lasted only a moment. But that was all Juan needed. From behind a sand dune, he signaled. A set of compressed air spikes shot out, puncturing the tires of the escort cars before the thugs knew what had happened.

Chaos erupted. The men from the village sprang from their hiding places, surrounding the vehicles.

- *María:* (shouting) Stop the truck! For the children!

The truck driver panicked, trying to reverse, but the broken-down car blocked his path. One of the traffickers, realizing they were cornered, fired his gun into the air, attempting to scare them off. The desert echoed with the gunshot, but far in the distance, the flashing blue lights of police cars signaled that help was on the way.

The Final Showdown

In the heat of the moment, Maria's instincts kicked in. She sprinted toward the armed thug, her years of self-defense training sharp in her mind. Before he could react, she disarmed him with a swift move, knocking him to the ground. A struggle ensued, but Maria, fueled by desperation and the knowledge that her children's lives were on the line, overpowered him.

With the traffickers subdued, the villagers opened the back of the truck. The sight was enough to break anyone's heart—children, terrified and huddled, stepped out into the arms of their protectors. The victory was theirs, but it was hard-won.

- *Don Lorenzo:* (his voice strong) Today, we proved that together, we are unbeatable.
- *María:* (tears in her eyes) And we will always protect our children, no matter the cost.

As the sun rose over the desert, a new day dawned for Tres Cruces. They had faced down a monstrous evil and emerged victorious. Yet they knew the fight wasn't over. They would have to remain vigilant, always ready to stand together against whatever darkness came next.

With the children safe and the traffickers in custody, Maria and Ursula stood side by side, their bond stronger than ever. They had faced fear and come out the other side. Though the battles ahead might still be fierce, they knew that, united, they could face anything.

The stillness of the desert night wrapped around the barren landscape like a heavy cloak. Beneath the cold brilliance of the stars, María stood on the precipice of the hardest decision of her life. Ursula was in the hands of a ruthless mobster, and the success of their mission hung by a fragile thread.

"Let her go," María demanded, her voice steady as she faced the mobster. "You won't find mercy if you don't."

The mobster's lips curled into a sneer, his grip on Ursula tightening. His eyes gleamed with cruel delight. As tension thickened the air, Don Lorenzo stepped forward with deliberate calm, his presence commanding the attention of everyone around.

"You've lost this fight," he said, his voice firm but measured. "Release the nun, and I'll see to it that you have a chance for redemption."

The mobster's laughter rang out, harsh and dismissive. He ignored Don Lorenzo's words, his henchmen closing in around María and Don Lorenzo, their postures threatening.

"You think you can stop me?" he snarled. "This is my empire. You're nothing but an inconvenience."

María's gaze never wavered. "I won't let you hurt any more innocents. Your reign of terror ends tonight."

She could feel the moment of reckoning drawing near. Her muscles tensed, her mind focused. The confrontation was inevitable.

The Final Showdown

In an instant, chaos erupted. The people of Tres Cruces surged forward, joining the fray with unwavering courage, outnumbered but undeterred. Fists flew, and the sharp crack of gunfire echoed through the night.

"For freedom and justice!" María shouted, her voice cutting through the bedlam. "We will not yield to the darkness you bring!"

Don Lorenzo fought with a quiet ferocity, protecting the vulnerable while leading the charge. The clash of weapons and the sounds of battle filled the air, punctuated by cries of defiance and hope.

"Finish them!" the mobster roared in fury, his empire crumbling around him. "I will not let you destroy everything I've built!"

But no amount of rage could overcome the bravery and solidarity of María, Ursula, Don Lorenzo, and the villagers. With strategy and sheer willpower, they disarmed the henchmen one by one, pushing forward toward the mobster for a final confrontation.

Don Lorenzo faced him squarely, his eyes cold. "Your tyranny ends here. Justice will triumph over the oppression you've brought."

In a final, desperate struggle, the mobster was subdued, his reign over the desert territory brought to a swift and just end. The night's violence faded into an eerie calm, the stars above silently bearing witness to the courage and determination of those who had fought for what was right, even in the face of overwhelming danger.

A New Dawn

As the dust settled, the familiar figure of El Corre Caminos, always cunning, slipped away into the shadows, evading capture for another day.

With the mobster in chains and the immediate threat neutralized, a tense silence settled over the desert once more. María, Ursula, and Don Lorenzo stood among the people of Tres Cruces, weary but victorious.

The first hints of dawn began to break over the horizon, bringing the promise of a new day and the beginning of a new chapter for the villagers.

"We've struck a significant blow against El Corre Caminos' operation," María said, her voice low with exhaustion. "But we know he'll be back. He'll want revenge."

Don Lorenzo nodded gravely. "The fight isn't over yet. But tonight, we've shown that courage and unity can defeat even the most powerful enemies."

Ursula approached María, her face soft with gratitude. "Thank you, María," she said quietly. "Your bravery saved us all."

María smiled humbly. "I couldn't have done it without all of you. We're stronger together."

As the first rays of sunlight stretched across the desert, painting the sky in soft hues of pink and gold, the people of Tres Cruces readied themselves for the battles that still lay ahead. But they knew that with determination and solidarity, they could face whatever threats the future might bring.

Far away, hidden in the shadow of a towering cactus, Lilith and Satan watched the unfolding events with grim fascination.

Lilith scowled. "The bad guys lost! Damn it! Now they'll free the children in the truck and find the drugs."

Satan chuckled, his eyes gleaming with amusement. "Don't worry, my dear Lilith. The bad guys are going to prison, and they're going to suffer. Right?"

Lilith nodded, her lips pressed into a thin line.

"Well then," Satan said, a malevolent smile spreading across his face. "As long as someone suffers, what does it matter who?"

Maria

Prelude and Warnings

The Awakening of Iris

Moonlight streamed through the window of Iris's room, bathing the space in a silvery glow. She slept soundly in her mother's cozy bed, immersed in dreams that were anything but ordinary. In her dream world, she found herself in a clearing deep within the forest, a gentle breeze caressing her hair.

Suddenly, a golden light illuminated the scene, revealing an ancient guardian with a presence both imposing and serene. His voice echoed in Iris's mind like a distant thunderclap.

"Listen, young Iris. The demon is strong, but there is a power within you that you have yet to discover. Seek within your heart and remember: light will always triumph over darkness. This dagger,"—the guardian extended his hand to reveal a glimmering blade—"is the key. Use it wisely."

With a start, Iris awoke, the guardian's message still reverberating through her thoughts. Drawing in a deep breath to calm her racing heart, she slipped out of bed and hurried to her mother's room.

"Mom, Lumina, wake up," she whispered urgently, shaking her sister gently. Their mother, always perceptive even in her sleep, was already stirring awake.

"What is it, darling?" her mother asked, propping herself up.

"Iris, why are you awake at this hour?" Lumina grumbled, still half-asleep.

"I had a dream... no, a vision," Iris explained, her voice a breathless mix of fear and excitement. "A guardian spoke to me about a power I possess. There's a dagger I must find and use against the demon."

Her mother nodded with calm assurance. "We need to speak with Grandma. She'll know what to do."

Without delay, the three of them rose and made their way to the kitchen, where the scent of fresh petals filled the air. Their breakfast consisted of their favorite feast: a delicate assortment of Edulis flowers. Iris struggled to focus on her meal, but she knew they needed energy for what lay ahead.

"Eat well," her mother encouraged with a warm smile. "The cockscomb and jasmine flowers will give you the strength you need."

After a hasty breakfast, Iris felt the excitement of the message still buzzing within her. She sprang to her feet. "Let's go to the castle before it's too late!"

Once they ensured everything was in order, they set off toward the queen mother's castle. Iris led the way, her determination evident in every stride.

The castle gleamed in the distance, a majestic silhouette against the clear sky. Iris's mind raced, replaying the vision, each step drawing her closer to a revelation that could change the world's fate.

Upon reaching the castle, they were greeted by the guardians, who, recognizing them, allowed them to pass without delay. The interior was as grand as ever, adorned with banners and tapestries that narrated tales of past glories.

The queen mother awaited them in the great hall, seated with a grace that only time and wisdom could bestow.

"Iris, what news do you bring?" the queen mother inquired, her smile warm yet knowing.

"Grandma, I've had a vision," Iris began, her voice resonating with newfound purpose as she prepared to recount every detail of what she had seen and learned.

The Force of Brotherhood

The first light of dawn began to timidly filter through the castle's windows. Aisling and Lumina had spent the remainder of the night training in the castle's secret garden, a place where flowers shone with their own light and magic flowed with every step. They knew their abilities had to be honed to face the realm of darkness.

As they practiced their spells, Lumina paused for a moment, observing her sister with pride. "You know, Aisling, I've always admired your courage," Lumina remarked, casting a sphere of light to disperse a lurking shadow.

Aisling, smiling warmly, replied, "And I've always envied your skill and grace. You always seem to know exactly what to do."

The shadows, aware of their presence, swirled around them menacingly. The sisters joined hands, creating a barrier of light that held the creatures of darkness at bay.

"Lumina, together we are unstoppable," exclaimed Aisling as they intensified their combined magic, their light blazing more brilliantly.

"We will always be together, no matter what," Lumina affirmed with unwavering determination.

With one final push, the barrier of light expanded abruptly, sweeping away the shadows. The sisters exchanged a knowing glance, aware that this was merely a small victory before the real confrontation.

"It's time," Aisling said with a deep sigh, heading toward the portal that would lead them to the realm of darkness. Together, they stepped forward, crossing the magical threshold that transported them to a world where light barely penetrated.

There, in the heart of darkness, even the air felt denser, laden with unseen threats. The shadows moved with a life of their own, whispering in forgotten tongues.

"Aisling, stay close," Lumina said calmly, squeezing her sister's hand, offering strength and protection.

Together they began to weave a spell of light, ancient and powerful words flowing from their lips, creating a beam that cut through the darkness. The shadows recoiled, unable to withstand the brilliance of their magic.

"We're doing it!" Aisling exclaimed, feeling the power surge through them.

Finally, they found what they'd been searching for: the core of evil, a pulsating orb that radiated tangible darkness. United, the sisters channeled their energy into it, disintegrating it and freeing the dimension from its shadowy grip. The atmosphere shifted, as if a heavy burden had been lifted.

"I think it's time to go back," Lumina suggested as the portal to their own dimension began to reopen.

They crossed back in an instant, feeling the fresh, vibrant air of the fairy realm. It was as if they had taken their first breath after being submerged in the depths.

"We did it, Aisling," Lumina said, releasing a deep breath of relief as they returned to the castle. "And we will do it again, whenever needed."

Aisling looked at her sister, filled with gratitude and love. "Together, we are unstoppable, Lumina."

With a bond stronger than ever, the sisters made their way back home, their hearts united both in battle and in the love that would always guide them.

The bond that held them together was unbreakable. The final battle still awaited them, but they knew that with their bond intact, they would always possess the power to confront the darkness.

The Unexpected Encounter

The sun began its descent beyond the horizon, casting a golden veil over the castle's garden. Aisling and Lumina sat beneath the ancient oak, practicing their spells, when the soft sound of footsteps disrupted their concentration. They looked up to see a mysterious-looking old man approaching. He was dressed as if he'd stepped out of a 16th-century book, wearing heavy velvet cloaks and a hat adorned with a long feather.

"Greetings, young fairies of the dimension of light," the old man said with a voice that seemed to hold centuries' worth of knowledge. "I am Don Alejandro, and I come from distant lands, from the city of Barcelona."

Lumina exchanged a glance with Aisling, a mixture of curiosity and caution in her eyes. Aisling, however, felt a chill of recognition. "Lumina, he... he is the sage I saw in my dream."

Don Alejandro smiled, his eyes sparkling with serene wisdom. "I've come because fate has willed it so. There is an object of great power I entrusted long ago to your aunt, the goddess of the seas. This object is crucial to your mission."

"What object?" Aisling asked, as Lumina nodded, intrigued.

"It is a special amulet, a mystical key that will allow you to enter the cave of Saint Pere," Don Alejandro explained while adjusting his hat. "Inside that cave lies the sword of Saint Michael the Archangel, a powerful weapon against evil. But a formidable guardian awaits you: a six-headed serpent, created by Satan to protect the cave."

"How are we supposed to face such a creature?" Lumina questioned with concern.

"First, by trusting in your bond and the inner strength each of you possesses," advised Don Alejandro. "Always remember what an ancient sage once said: 'True magic lies not in the spell, but in the heart of the one who casts it.'"

Aisling nodded, taking the old man's words as a mantra. "So, we must seek the amulet from our aunt in the sea?"

"Indeed," the old man replied. "Your aunt awaits you in the depths. You must hurry before time works against you. Only the chosen one can extract the sword from the stone. And once you succeed, the confrontation with Satan will await."

Lumina grasped Aisling's hand, trying to instill her with courage. "We will succeed. We are destined for this."

"Yes, Lumina," Aisling affirmed. "We must do it together."

The old man nodded one last time, his figure glowing under the twilight. "The wisdom of the ages accompanies you, young fairies. Use your knowledge and courage to face this challenge."

With these words, Don Alejandro bade farewell, leaving behind a gentle echo of magic in the air. Aisling and Lumina looked at each other, understanding that the road ahead would demand all their ingenuity, as well as an unwavering trust in themselves and the power of their bond.

Determined, they prepared to embark on their underwater adventure, knowing the fate of the world rested on their success.

The Zoology Class

The chatter of youthful voices filled the classroom, bathed in the warm light filtering through the tall windows. Aisling and Lumina sat together amid the bustle, surrounded by other students who shared their enthusiasm for the lessons of Miss Selene, known for her captivating and enlightening teachings.

"Today, dear students, we will explore a peculiar creature: the human," began Professor Selene, a smile playing on her lips as she hung a large map of the human world on the board. "Although this creature does not reside in our dimension, its influence stretches beyond its own world."

Lumina furrowed her brow slightly, a restless curiosity sparking in her eyes. "Professor Selene, we're often told about humans. What are their virtues?" she asked, leaning forward.

The teacher nodded, smoothing her long green dress that mirrored her affinity for nature. "Humans possess a remarkable capacity for love, invention, and perseverance. They create art and literature, and have the unique talent of imagining things that do not yet exist."

"And their dangers?" Aisling interjected, recalling warnings she had heard before.

"Ah, therein lies the great contrast," the professor continued, folding her arms across her chest. "The potential for evil also exists within them. They are often prone to consumed by the desire for power, and their fear of the unknown can lead them to violence. And when they are violent, their cruelty can be astonishing."

Lumina raised her hand, her gaze intense and serious. "Why, then, do so many fear humans?"

Professor Selene gave her a compassionate look. "It's natural to fear what we don't fully understand, Lumina. But I must say, not all humans are bad. Many are good and seek peace just as we do. Their kindness can surprise if given the chance."

A raised hand from the back interrupted the discussion. "But haven't they harmed other creatures and their environments?" a classmate asked with concern.

"It is true that some have," Selene admitted with a momentary look of sadness, "but there are also those who dedicate their lives to protecting the planet and all the creatures within it."

Aisling pondered the journey she and Lumina were about to undertake. "How can we connect with the good humans, then?" she asked with genuine curiosity.

"Understanding and dialogue are key, Aisling. The more we know about each other, the closer we can become," the professor replied, drawing a circle in the air that briefly shimmered. "Knowledge and empathy are the first bridges."

The class continued, each of Selene's words planting more seeds of thought in the young fairies' minds. As Aisling jotted down some notes, Lumina leaned toward her, whispering, "Perhaps there is more in common between us and humans than we think."

Aisling nodded with a slight smile. "It seems that our quest for the sword and the demon is not just about magic. Maybe it's also about better understanding those with whom we share this existence."

The class concluded with the soft ringing of the bell, and as the students gathered their belongings, Selene's voice left them with one last thought. "Remember, young fairies: every creature has the potential to illuminate the world or darken it. It's up to us to choose which path we take."

With those words echoing in their hearts, Aisling and Lumina headed outside, with much more to learn and even more to accomplish in their world full of wonders and challenges.

CHAPTER 15

Ashley's Decision

Under the starry skies of Texas, an unnamed restlessness began to weave itself into the soul of Ashley. She found herself gazing at the vastness before her through the grand window of her mansion when a melancholic melody echoed in her heart. This moment, fleeting as it was, ignited a spark within her, a spark that had lain dormant beneath layers of routine and responsibility.

Ashley had achieved much in the tangible world: a distinguished career, reputation, and success. Yet, she learned over time that conventional measures of achievement did not always translate to eternal satisfaction. Something beyond the visible was calling her, a gentle whisper from her intuition, that silent voice speaking from deep within the soul, connecting our thoughts to the vast web of existence.

Intuition, Ashley believed, was the manifestation of thoughts from beyond, sparks of universal knowledge filtering into human consciousness. It was as if her higher self, her true spiritual self, was trying to guide her to a path she could not yet fully comprehend. Listening to this call required courage and the willingness to embrace the unknown. But Ashley had always believed intuition was the bridge between the material and the ethereal, an unfailing compass for navigating the mystery of life.

It was this deep intuition that whispered she must go, though she knew not the why or the wherefore. She realized the journey was not just physical; it was a voyage into the heart of her own being. Determined to honor this call, she embarked on her departure to Ireland, a land rich in legends and ancient secrets.

In Ireland, Ashley felt enveloped by a vibrant yet serene energy, as if the ancient stones and gentle hills were alive, whispering forgotten stories to the wind. She found herself lost in landscapes seemingly imbued with a timeless era, where each fragment of nature resonated with ancestral wisdom. Her interactions, guided by this intuition, led her to Maeve, who helped her explore the metaphysical depths of her own essence.

"It is in silence that the soul whispers its secrets," Maeve had told her, her words infused with an understanding that transcended time and space.

deep her than a simple explanation ever could. "I suppose," she began thoughtfully, "it's the search for something I couldn't find back home. A deeper connection to myself, an understanding of life that goes beyond the surface."

Robert nodded, pondering her words. "Ireland has a way of calling to the soul," he said. "It's as though the land itself whispers secrets from ages past, challenging each person to see beyond the ordinary."

Their conversations, which unfolded beneath the flickering candlelight or surrounded by the rich scent of old books, became a source of inspiration for Ashley. Robert's insights and tales illuminated the path she was on, helping her navigate the complex labyrinth of her thoughts and feelings.

In this enchanted land, where history and myth intertwined seamlessly, Ashley began to realize that her journey was about more than just facing exterior challenges; it was about accepting the light and darkness within herself. Each step across this vibrant landscape reinforced her faith in her intuition—an anchor in the sea of the unknown as she embraced her spiritual journey. It was a bold move, unlike anything she had done before, spontaneous and recklessly brave.

As the days turned into weeks, Ashley found herself at home in the quaint Irish village, surrounded by reminders of a bygone era. The stone walls entwined with vines seemed to wrap her in a sense of timelessness, as if they whispered the stories of those who had once called this place home. Her newfound friendship with Robert enriched her experience, making the foreign feel familiar and the distant surprisingly close.

Ashley realized that this journey—marked by introspection and unexpected connections—was guiding her toward the discovery of her true self, a self that resonated with the harmony of the universe and found wisdom in its quiet symphony. b reasons. "I believe I'm seeking the kind of answers that aren't found in courtrooms or city streets," she confessed, her eyes fixed on the flickering fireplace. "I feel that the untold stories here might help me understand myself better."

Robert regarded her with a sympathetic smile. "The lands of Ireland have a curious way of unveiling hidden truths. This place tends to bring out the stories we carry within."

Ashley found solace in these conversations. Her exchanges with Robert became nightly rituals, a dance of words and thoughts that deepened her personal understanding. "The stories we live and the adventures we choose are like novels," Robert once remarked. "They shape and define us, often when we least expect it."

"I think learning to listen is one of the greatest challenges," Ashley replied, feeling the weight of truth in her own words. "In life, as in reading."

In the simplicity of these meetings, Ashley found unexpected guidance in the writer next door. Their evenings together in those old Irish homes became a beacon of personal transformation, steering her through her own internal landscapes and guiding her on a path illuminated by the understanding that sometimes the deepest answers emerge from honoring the journey itself.

Memories By The Hearth

The crackling fire filled the ancient Irish home with a comforting murmur, its flickers illuminating stone walls steeped in history and mystery. Ashley sat lost in thought before the warm hearth, watching the flames dance and whisk her memories far away to the heart of Texas.

The image of the grand mansion in Redwood Hills surfaced in her mind, surrounded by the rose garden she adored. Those fragrant blooms that perfumed the air were the perfect backdrop for the day Maria, Ursula, and Don Lorenzo emerged from their car, their mission evident in their determined gazes.

The day unfolded once more in her mind. She envisioned Maria and Ursula, dressed as nuns, moving with elegant determination along the cobblestone path, and Don Lorenzo, whose serene demeanor inspired trust for even the darkest of secrets.

In the Rose Garden - The Unexpected Meeting

A gentle breeze, heavy with the scent of roses, caressed her face as she stepped into the garden. The sight of Maria and Ursula in their disguises had brought a smile of disbelief to her lips.

Maria: [With genuine delight] "Ashley, we're so glad to find you here."

Ashley: [Curious and amused] "What's the purpose of this unexpected attire?"

Ursula laughed softly, her voice twinkling and candid. "Sometimes, you have to dress up to catch the devil, isn't that right, Don Lorenzo?"

Don Lorenzo's eyes, sparkling with stoic wisdom, locked onto Ashley's. "We've heard about the escape of the convict and the situation in Ciudad Juárez," he had said firmly, his deep voice resonating like a bell within her.

The memory of that moment rekindled a spark of determination in Ashley's chest, even now as she was enveloped by the gentle comfort of her Irish sitting room.

Maria: [Stepping forward with resolve] "We've unmasked the Roadrunner and captured part of the fentanyl ring. But your help remains crucial."

At that time, Ashley felt how her skills and sense of justice converged into a single intention. "I'm ready to help in any way necessary," she had responded, her words almost transforming into a mantra that continued to echo in the silence of the Irish night.

Back Within the Stone Walls

The present called her back, solidly anchored in the old Irish house that was now her temporary refuge. Remembering the mission at the abandoned convent where the children had been rescued filled her heart with a blend of hope and compassion. She thought of Don Lorenzo, his fleeting smile as he laid out plans to infiltrate the dark web.

She knew that was only a small part of the journey she needed to undertake. As the fire cast gentle orange hues across the room, Ashley stood up, driven by an unusual desire to see beyond. She approached the window, drawing the curtains open softly to peer outside, into the quiet street where that welcoming Irish home awaited her next act Would, the storyteller of present and past tales, come by to share yet another unexpected chapter of wisdom and companionship? There was something in him, in the way he turned each visit into a fruitful exchange of ideas and emotions, that invited introspection.

She didn't quite understand why this urge to speak with him was so pressing, but she allowed her intuition to guide her, free of judgment. In the serene Irish night, anticipation shimmered in her spirit. As she leaned out, she welcomed the fresh air, rich with history, grateful for the knowledge that every meeting, every conversation with the writer, added another piece to the mosaic that was the unfolding image of her own soul discovering itself.

Wthih a menacing grace, eyes glinting in the dim light. Each head hissed softly, a symphony of sinister whispers that echoed through the cavernous space.

Between Cliffside Legends

Carved by centuries of Mediterranean storms, the majestic and feared cave stood resolute amidst the turbulent cliffs. Its entrance, flanked by rock formations resembling stone guardians, gaped wide like a dark, voracious mouth. Inside, a perpetual twilight reigned, defying the daylight. The cave walls were covered in dark moss and arcane symbols, etched by ancient hands. Sharp stalactites hung from the ceiling like the fangs of a colossal beast, dripping with a disquieting moisture. The echo of each drop reverberated in the vast darkness, amplifying the omnipresent silence.

Supernatural Encounter

Lilith and Satan strode into the cave, moving confidently through the dense shadows. A few steps further, the flickering torchlight revealed the sword of Archangel Michael, embedded deep within a rock as a symbol of divine hope and power. The sword emitted a heavenly glow, starkly contrasting with the darkness that surrounded it.

Lilith: (strikingly elegant, laughing with a mix of mockery and intrigue) "Ha, ha, ha. It seems I am not the chosen one for this task."

Satan, by her side, smirked with condescension, his gaze fixated on the sword embedded in the stone. From deep within the cave, an overwhelming noise vibrated—a rattlesnake's echo.

Lilith: (with a mixture of curiosity and fear) "What is that sound, my lord?"

Satan: (with a wicked smile, recalling fondly) "Do you remember the hair you lent me that I transformed into a serpent?"

Lilith: (her eyes glistening with wonder) "Oh yes, my lord! I was amazed to witness that miracle, creating a serpent from a single strand. You are truly magical."

The serpent, enormous and majestic, slithered towards them, its six heads weaving with a menacing elegance. Eyes glinted as they met the flickering light, hissing softly—a sinister symphony echoing through the cavernous expanse. synchronized perfectly. As the serpent reached Satan, it lowered its heads in an act of submission and adoration.

Lilith: (wide-eyed with amazement) "My lord, how it has grown! And with six heads?"

Satan: (laughing with a malevolent tone) "Of course, no human can withstand her. Even if they manage to sever one head, she still has five more."

Satan stroked one of the serpent's heads, which exhibited behavior almost canine in its devotion. Another head vied for his touch, while a third snapped at the one being petted, desiring exclusive attention. Satan chuckled, pleased.

Satan: (laughing) "Do you see, Lilith, how they adore me?"

Lilith: (astonished and admiring) "My lord, you leave me speechless. You are the greatest thing I have ever seen. Creating such a creature with such devotion to you is a marvel."

The Feared Cave

Beyond the silhouette of the ancient, rust-covered sword and the multi-headed serpent, the cave extended into a tangle of labyrinthine tunnels.

The air was thick with the briny scent of the sea and stagnant moisture. As they turned every corner, shadows danced and took on grotesque forms, deceiving perception. In the depths, the eternal roar of water echoed as it crashed against the rocky walls. In some hidden corner, a dark altar stood, laden with items of occult worship, profane symbols, and candles blackened by fire. Within its eerie and iron-clad aura, the cave harbored secrets few dared to seek.

As Lilith and Satan lingered in the cave, a silent threat permeated the air. They knew Saint Michael's power was a formidable foe, yet they, steeped in their darkness and mysticism, prepared to face it with their magic and the formidable serpent, hoping that their dominion would prevail over the light.

Delving Deeper into the Darkness

Lilith watched the magnificent serpent and the dancing shadows within the cave as she moved closer to Satan, intrigued and captivated. After a pause, she spoke with reverence and curiosity.

Lilith: "My lord, five hundred human years have passed since we began our reign in the shadows. How is it that time loses its meaning for us, the eternal?"

Satan regarded her with an enigmatic smile, his eyes reflecting the knowledge of infinite eras.

Satan: "Lilith, time is a concept born of the human mind. A chain that binds mortals in an endless cycle of beginnings and endings. But to us, everlasting beings, time is merely a thin thread in the vast tapestry of eternity."

He calmed the serpent's heads with serene strokes as he continued.

Satan: "They measure their lives in days, years, and centuries, always. fearful of the end. But we are the weavers of history, moving through it untouched. Eternity for us is a vast and mysterious ocean, with no beginning or end, where each moment is merely a wave in its immensity." Lilith nodded, pondering the depth of his words.

Lilith: (thoughtful) "Yes, my lord. We witness the rise and fall of empires, the passing seasons, and the lives of men as mere blinks in our endless existence. Do we, being eternal, lose the sense of urgency that shapes their lives?"

Satan smiled, appreciating his companion's reflection.

Satan: "Precisely, Lilith. The urgency that mortals feel defines every decision they make, driving them with both passion and fear. But for us, outside their wheel, time's illusion becomes a tool, a device that we can manipulate at will. They cannot grasp the true power of eternity, with my six-headed serpent and our longevity."

His gaze shifted to the sword, embedded in the rock.

Satan: "However, in objects like this sword, the power of time manifests in ways that surpass even our perception. It's anchored not only in matter but in an essence that transcends the temporal. That is why only the worthy—or rather, the chosen—can unleash its power."

Lilith gazed at the sword, its reflection fractured in the rock.

Lilith: "My lord, that perception of time both fascinates and terrifies me. Perhaps it is that sense of temporality that imbues our lives with meaning, even in their transience."

Satan chuckled softly, his laughter echoing through the cave like a magnificent resonance.

Satan: "Lilith, we create our own meaning. Beyond the mortal constructs of time and morality, we forge our destiny with will and power. That is why, though time does not exist for us, within each moment lies an eternity of possibilities."

The serpent hissed with its six heads, as if affirming its master's words. Lilith smiled, deeply satisfied and devoted to Satan's arcane wisdom.

Lilith: "Yes, my lord. Let us continue weaving our fate on this eternal tapestry. While the mortal world consumes itself in its urgency, we shall remain the timeless masters of darkness."

Together, they stood contemplating the sword and the cave that housed it, their minds drifting through the unfathomable ocean of time, knowing that in their immortality, the true power and meaning of each moment were both a blessing and a formidable responsibility eternal curse.

The Cave of Darkness

Satan, eyes fixed on the coveted prize, extended a resolute hand toward its hilt. As his fingers brushed against the gleaming metal, a sudden surge of energy jolted through him. The lightning was so forceful that it hurled him violently against the stone wall. Slowly rising, he let out a laugh that echoed through the cave with an almost playful tone.

Satan: [Laughing, brushing off the dust] "Ah, it seems it doesn't like me. An electrifying touch, I must admit."

Lilith watched the scene with a mix of caution and curiosity. With a hint of reverence, she approached the sword and attempted to draw it as well. Her steady hands gripped the hilt, but no matter how hard she pulled, the sword remained immovable. Yet, she did not experience the shocking jolt that had affected Satan.

Lilith: [Looking at Satan] "No reaction with me, my lord. But it still won't budge."

Satan walked back toward her, a contemplative look in his eyes as he traced one of the symbols carved into the cave wall.

Satan: [Thoughtfully] "Hmm... how curious. It seems the chosen one will be female. I suppose we must await the arrival of someone worthy— or shall I say, someone more persuasive for the sword."

Lilith's eyes sparkled with a flash of forbidden knowledge as she gazed at her lord with assured confidence.

Lilith: [Confidently] "I know, my lord. It will be Aisling and Lumina who come to claim it, but they face an unexpected obstacle... their father. Soon he will be near them, and we will know exactly when they will arrive."

Satan chuckled, pleased by the revelation, his laughter echoing diabolically through the vast darkness of the cave.

Satan: [With a malicious smile] "Indeed, and when they succeed in extracting the sword, we shall be the ones to take it."

They laughed together, their mirth reverberating in the vast abyss of the cave, transforming the echo into an ominous promise of what's to come. The shadows seemed to dance around them, secretly sharing in that moment of complicity between the two, while the six-headed serpent kept watch, its eyes glittering in the dim light.

CHAPTER 16

Love and Farewells

Ashley stood against the window frame of her old Irish home, her gaze lost in the landscape speckled by the gentle drizzle falling over the eternal green of the rolling hills. As the fine mist enveloped the village, her thoughts drifted back to the courtroom in New York, where, just weeks ago, she had experienced one of the most intense moments of her career.

The courtroom had been suffused with fear and tension during the pivotal trial of the Hernández family. She remembered correcting Attorney Rinaldi just before the judge entered, and how the weight of the verdict descended upon everyone like an inescapable shadow. The murmur of the jury declaring the accused guilty still echoed in her ears, alongside the fleeting satisfaction on the defense attorney's face.

Yet beyond the victory, what struck her most was the unexpected escape of the convict, his threatening gaze and the chilling words that echoed in her mind: "You're next." Ashley recalled the ensuing chaos, the alarms blaring, the frantic attempt to stop the fugitive, and how everything spiraled into an almost surreal sequence. The adrenaline of that moment intertwined with the city lights she barely glimpsed during her hurried departure.

Back in Ireland, with the echo of that tumultuous episode still lingering in her thoughts, Ashley sought solace in the Irish landscape before her eyes. She realized that despite the distance, the shadows of that trial followed her, embedding themselves deeply in the emotional archives of her memory.

As she pensively watched the dusk descend, a figure caught her attention. There, half-shrouded by the rain and twilight, she glimpsed the unmistakable silhouette of her neighbor, the writer, making his way down the path to her door. The mere anticipation of his presence reminded her that even after the darkest days, there's always a new story to hear and share.

Adjusting her jacket with the intrinsic intuition that had guided her so many times before, Ashley rose, feeling an unexplainable need to speak with him. Knowing that perhaps, in that exchange... in words and dilemmas, she would find the remote solace her spirit so desperately needed after all she had experienced. Ashley moved to the door, propelled by a mix of curiosity and the need for companionship. Upon opening it, she found her neighbor Robert, the writer, standing there with a shy smile and his hands buried in his pockets against the cold. Robert: [Tilting his head slightly] "Hello, Ashley. I hope I'm not interrupting..."

Ashley: [Smiling, attempting to break the ice] "Not at all, Robert. I was just thinking of stepping out for some fresh air."

Robert swallowed nervously, the nervousness almost palpable, while his eyes reflected the soft light emanating from Ashley's home.

Robert: "Well, I was thinking... I wondered if... you'd like to go to the village pub for a pint. It's quite cozy, especially on nights like this."

A moment of expectant silence hung between them. Ashley realized that Robert's proposal had the hesitant charm of a teenager asking for a first date. She found this nervousness endearing, and warmth spread through her chest.

Ashley: [With a gentle smile] "That sounds great. I've been wanting to get to know the village better, and a pint seems the perfect way to start."

Robert exhaled, relieved, and nodded quickly, pleased with her positive response.

Robert: [Blushing slightly, laughing nervously] "Great, that's... great. The path is a bit slippery, so we can take it slow."

As she closed the door and they prepared to head to the pub, Ashley reflected on her past visions of an ideal partner. Once, she might have sought someone who fit the mold of a TV series protagonist—grand, successful, striking. But life's experiences had taught her the value of something deeper. What she truly desired now was someone who could connect with her soul, understand her silences, and offer the much-needed emotional solace.

Ashley: [As they walked side by side] "So, what brought you to this small corner of the world to write, Robert? There don't seem to be many distractions here, which I suppose is perfect for a writer."

As rolled, Robert's gaze lingered on the ground with a modest smile as he explained his search for a place where stories could flow uninhibited. In this village, he felt time seemed to pause, granting space for the imagination to take charge. He believed that certain places offered their tales to those willing to listen.

Ashley nodded, resonating with his perspective. She too had come seeking answers and tranquility, and this place seemed to provide both. As the brisk wind brushed against their cheeks, their steps began to align, perhaps signaling the beginning of a connection that transcended the words they had exchanged.

Upon reaching the pub, cloaked in ivy and warmly glowing from within, the laughter and conversation trickling through the cracks barely pierced the night's stillness. Together, they entered, ready to share new stories and embrace the familiar charm of a small town where life, though unhurried, was savored intensely one moment at a time.

In the dimly lit subterranean chamber, the flickering infernal torches cast long, dancing shadows across the gothic furniture, lending an aura of ominous authority to the setting. Behind a formidable obsidian desk, seated upon a throne carved with agonized figures of lost souls, sat the Supreme Demon, intently examining a ceremonial letter. The rhythmic sound of footsteps echoed through the darkness, and soon, General Balthazar emerged. Clad in a uniform eerily reminiscent of the dreaded SS, his presence was a chilling blend of military precision and raw malevolence. Without breaking his posture, he offered a militaristic salute and spoke with unwavering firmness.

Balthazar's report on humanity was delivered with the precision of a scientist dissecting a species. The Supreme Demon, curious and sinister, listened intently.

"Speak, Balthazar. What news do you bring of those insignificant creatures?" the Supreme Demon inquired, his eyes glinting with sinister curiosity.

General Balthazar, with the air of reciting a documentary narrative, began his meticulous exposition. "Humans, my lord, are a study in simplicity and complexity. They constantly oscillate between reason and instinct, forming societies and systems that, while advanced, are inherently fragile. They experience profound emotions like love and hate and are capable of creating wonders as well as committing horrific atrocities."

The Supreme Demon drummed his fingers on the obsidian desk, contemplating Balthazar's insights. "Go on, General. How might we leverage these observations to our advantage?"

Unfurling a map over the desk, Balthazar revealed highlighted marks on major human cities, with red dots indicating centers of power and influence. "Herein lies the crux of our strategy, my lord. The most influential humans—those at the helm of governments, economies, and societies—hold the key. We have identified these individuals, and if they refuse to comply with our demands, we propose a decisive strike to unleash chaos and subjugate their world to our dominion."

The Supreme Demon's eyes gleamed with malicious anticipation, savoring the prospect of bending humanity to his will. Together, they stared at the map, envisioning a new era of darkness orchestrated from their shadowy domain.

...well-coordinated coup. The Supreme Demon leaned forward, scrutinizing the map with keen interest.

"How do you intend to execute this coup, Balthazar?" he inquired, his voice a blend of curiosity and command.

Balthazar smiled coldly, his response a mix of military precision and pure Machiavellian strategy. "We have embedded agents within their ranks, beings capable of manipulating minds and corrupting wills. Should the human leaders resist our domination, we will unleash chaos and destabilization. We will turn their very own technology against them, undermining critical infrastructures and inciting civil unrest."

The Supreme Demon reclined in his throne, satisfied with his general's plan. "Excellent, Balthazar. Ensure our agents strike with precision. We must attack from the shadows, like venomous snakes, leaving humans oblivious to the true cause of their downfall until it's too late."

Balthazar bowed deeply and prepared to exit the chamber, but not before receiving one last directive.

"And remember, General," the Supreme Demon intoned, "our strength lies in patience and precision. Humans are like cattle, and we will steer them to the slaughterhouse at just the right moment. Execute this plan flawlessly, and their world will fall into our hands, with no mortal force able to stop us."

General Balthazar nodded solemnly and withdrew to coordinate the operation. Meanwhile, the Supreme Demon remained in his throne, contemplating the shadows and savoring the thought of impending conquest. Outside, the flames of hell burned brighter, heralding the approaching storm for the human race.

General Balthazar

A Journey to the Unknown

Mirabelle ventured into an unknown dimension, a dreamlike mosaic where colors defied imagination and dreams. The sky, draped in hues of the northern lights, shifted with every breeze, painting strokes of turquoise, violet, and gold across the landscape. Mountains floated like islands suspended in the air, their peaks adorned with crystalline structures that captured every ray of light. Rivers of pure, liquid luminescence meandered lazily, reflecting the whimsical shapes of the clouds like mirrors.

Everywhere, giant flowers swayed rhythmically, their petals radiating a rainbow of colors. Their fragrances blended in the air, creating a symphony of aromas that Mirabelle breathed in with fascination. Dragons, their scales shimmering as if made of polished glass, glided across the sky gracefully, leaving rainbows in their wake.

The Challenge of Melody

In a clearing surrounded by this surreal beauty, Mirabelle began to sing. She enjoyed challenging herself, seeking the precise harmony capable of soothing fiery hearts. Suddenly, an emerald dragon descended from the heights, rising before her like a living jade statue. As the notes vibrated from her lips, Mirabelle watched as the creature succumbed to the gentle enchantment of her melody, its movements slowing to stillness, contemplating her with eyes of gold, full of unknown wisdom.

The Encounter with the Dwarf

Just as Mirabelle perfected her melody, an unexpected twist interrupted her song. From the shadows cast by a great tree with shimmering leaves emerged a stout dwarf wearing a jacket of fossilized leather that glowed with its own light.

The mischievous-eyed dwarf grinned wickedly, saying, "Oh, what a delightful discovery in this steppe! What is a magnificent treasure like you doing in such a perilous place?"

Mirabelle paused, her song lingering in the air like a gentle breeze. She eyed the dwarf cautiously, aware that not all things in this wondrous dimension were benign. Despite the interruption, she held her composure, ready to learn whether this was friend or foe, knowing that every encounter in this realm was a step further into its mysteries.

Mirabelle tilted her head slightly, an air of mystique enveloping her. "I'm here for reasons that do not concern small mischief-makers who have strayed from their lairs," she replied, her voice carrying the weight of untold secrets.

The dwarf, a figure of comically disproportionate features, edged closer, his eyes glinting with curiosity and yearning. "Oh, but I love secrets as much as gleaming treasures and pretty faces," he chuckled, his laughter ringing like silver bells. "Allow me a kiss, and perhaps we can share a bit of both."

Mirabelle laughed softly, shaking her head. "I'm not so easily impressed, little dwarf. Besides, I know your nimble fingers hide intentions far less noble than a simple kiss."

Feigning mock offense, the dwarf exclaimed, "What poor judgment of my natural charm! I merely wish to... get to know you better."

With friendly banter and cunning glances exchanged, Mirabelle decided to take control of the situation, fully aware of the dangerous power hidden in the caress of that dwarf. With a graceful flourish, she sang a high note that flowed like an unbreakable current.

The sound lingered in the air, vibrating through the atmosphere and shaking even the tallest leaves of the monolithic trees. The dwarf, unable to resist, froze in a comical expression of surprise, his own powers temporarily banished by Mirabelle's innate ability.

The Triumphant Return

Having successfully disarmed the mischievous dwarf and unleashed the full potential of her song, Mirabelle knew she was ready to face the looming challenge, the inevitable confrontation to protect her daughter. In the realm of the fairies, predicting the future was not a matter of guesswork. Mirabelle, understanding that Lumina and Aisling were strong but unversed in the ways of cunning, felt more determined than ever.

With one last glance at the landscapes of indescribable beauty that seemed to defy all logic, she stepped into the portal, ready to return to her dimension.

Irish Night

The pub was bathed in warm amber light, the atmosphere humming with the friendly buzz of conversations and laughter. Ashley and Robert sat by the bar, surrounded by pints of beer and shots of Irish whiskey. The unexpected delight of a shot glass sunk into a pint had proven to be a surprising treat.

Amid animated chatter and laughter, Ashley gazed at Robert with a playful grin. "Well, you sort of know my life," she began, swaying slightly as she leaned toward him, "but you must tell me yours," she chuckled, her voice slightly louder and freer now. "Oh God, I sound tipsy, forgive me!"

Robert, laughing along with her, raised his glass. "There's nothing to forgive, Ashley. A day is a day, and spirits are the potion of truth, aren't they?"

Ashley, giggling as she brushed a strand of hair from her face, regarded him thoughtfully. "The truth, huh? So tell me, do you know how old you are?"

Robert pretended to ponder deeply, placing a hand on his chin. "How old do you think I am?"

Ashley looked up, engrossed in her appraisal. "Hmm, I'd say... 58?"

Robert burst out laughing, waving his hand in a grand gesture. "No! I'm 62."

Ashley erupted into laughter, her contagious mirth reverberating in the warm ambiance of the pub. "Hahaha! Forgive me."

Robert, bemused but amused, shrugged. "I'm not sure if that's a compliment or what."

Ashley, still catching her breath from laughing, looked at him sincerely. "You know, just ten years ago, I wouldn't have looked twice at you, because, well, I was looking for a fairytale guy." She paused, letting her words linger in the air before continuing, "And look at me now... I actually like you. (Smiles) You're 17 years older than me, but does that matter?"

Robert, touched by the honesty and levity in her words, simply smiled. "Not in the slightest. Sometimes things don't turn out as we expect, and that's what makes them perfect."

Their conversation melted into shared laughter, a spark that lingered in the air, illuminating the warmth of the moment, as they both savored the unpredictability of life and the surprising joy of unexpected connections.

marked the beginning of something unexpected and welcome. In the small Irish pub, beneath the glow of warm light, they both felt the barriers dissolve, revealing a new chapter in their lives. Surrounded by soft music and the constant hum of conversation, they discovered a connection amidst life's surprises, one that was nourished by the authenticity and charm of the moment.

As the night wore on, the laughter and shared stories flowed as freely as the drinks. Each anecdote unveiled layers of their personalities, drawing them closer together. Ashley found herself enchanted not just by Robert's humor, but by the way he listened, truly listened, as if each of her words held a significance he was eager to explore.

"You know," Robert said, leaning closer, his voice barely rising above the lively clamor, "it's rare to meet someone who makes you feel seen in a world that often overlooks the little things."

Ashley felt a warmth spreading within her, a tinge of recognition that this evening was no ordinary encounter. "I feel the same way," she replied, her eyes sparkling with newfound interest. "It's as if we were both searching for something, and we stumbled upon each other in this cozy corner of the world."

Their eyes met, and for a moment, the bustling pub faded into the background. It was just the two of them, enveloped in a cocoon of shared understanding and laughter, the possibilities of what lay ahead unfurling like the first light of dawn. It was a reminder that amidst chaos, there could be serenity, connection, and perhaps the start of something truly special.

As the clock chimed in the distance, signifying the late hour, the atmosphere shifted ever so slightly, and Ashley realized she didn't want the night to end. With a heart full of anticipation, she raised her glass to Robert. "To new beginnings," she toasted, her smile radiant against the backdrop of the pub's warmth.

"To new beginnings," Robert echoed, clinking his glass against hers, both aware that whatever came next, they would face it together, unafraid of the unknown.

** 17: LOVE AND GOODBYES**

Feeling the warmth of the pub and the curious glances of a few patrons, Robert smiled gently and leaned slightly closer to Ashley. "Perhaps we should be on our way. I wouldn't want to take advantage of the truth potion more than necessary. Let me walk you home."

Ashley paused for a moment, worried that she had revealed too much. "I'm sorry if I've offended you, Robert," she said, a hint of guilt in her voice.

He looked at her, his eyes shining with a blend of honesty and humor. "The truth doesn't offend, Ashley; it merely displeases at times. But there it is, and it must be accepted."

Just then, the melancholic yet vibrant notes of a violin began to fill the pub. A subtle drum accompanied the violin, establishing a rhythm that resonated against the walls and within their souls. The atmosphere shifted, enveloping them in a cloak of tradition and nostalgia. A young woman stepped onto the makeshift stage and began to sing with a clear, heartfelt voice, delivering a lamenting Irish folk melody that spun tales of times gone by and brave hearts.

Ashley smiled and turned to Robert, allowing the music to envelop them in a comfortable silence, the honesty of the moment forging an unexpected connection. "I've never heard anything so beautiful," she murmured, her gaze lingering on the impromptu performance.

Robert nodded. "It's the magic of this place. It reminds you that beyond words and time, there's always a song to bring us closer together."

They exchanged glances, and amid the music and the bustle of laughter and chatter around them, they discovered a silent understanding. While the journey home loomed inevitable, in that moment, all that mattered was what was being said and felt, regardless of what lay ahead.

Together, they let the music wash over them, savoring the shared moment until the last note faded into the air.

As the music came to an end and the pub was once again filled with voices and laughter, Robert and Ashley decided it was time to leave. Slowly, they rose from their seats, moving toward the exit, each step heavy with unspoken emotions and the bittersweet knowledge that their evening together was drawing to a close.

As they stepped outside, the cool night air enveloped them like a gentle embrace, and the stars twinkled overhead, mirroring the spark that had ignited between them. With each step they took down the quiet street, the warmth of the pub lingered in their hearts, promising that this was just the beginning of something extraordinary.

cool night air with the warmth of their conversation, took a moment to savor the evening that had unfolded.

As they stepped across the threshold, the cold air enveloped them, a stark contrast to the warmth they were leaving behind. The cobblestone street, worn and weathered, evoked a sense of time long past, as if they had traveled to the heart of another century.

"Here," Robert said, pulling on his jacket. "Take this, Ashley. I wouldn't want you to catch a chill."

"Thank you, Robert," she replied gratefully, wrapping the jacket around her shoulders. "I always thought I'd live in the tropics. I never quite got used to the cold."

As they strolled down the street, the shadows of the ancient buildings stretched beneath the soft glow of the streetlamps. The beauty of an Irish night enveloped them, making time feel as if it was standing still.

"Hey, Ashley," Robert said, a curious tone slipping into his voice. "Do you believe in fairies?"

Ashley laughed, responding playfully, "The ones from Walt Disney?"

CHAPTER 17

The Specter of Past and Future

Ashley climbed the wooden stairs carefully, each step emitting a familiar creak that resonated in the silence of the old house. The banister was gently worn by time and use, telling stories of those who had ascended these very steps before her. Upon reaching the top, she pushed open the heavy oak door to her room, revealing a cozy sanctuary that radiated warmth and a sense of timelessness.

The room was decorated in an antique yet elegant style: a floral-patterned quilt covered the four-poster bed, while sepia-toned photographs adorned the walls, capturing moments from a bygone era. A small table lamp cast a soft glow from the corner desk, shadows dancing gracefully across the walls.

Typically, Ashley was meticulous; everything had its place, every garment carefully folded or hung. However, this night felt different. After that magical evening with Robert, her spirit was light, almost effervescent. For the first time in a long while, she let that internal mess flow outward. With a contented sigh, she plopped down onto the bed, unconcerned about undressing.

As her eyes fluttered closed, the ease of sleep pulled her into a dream world that soon morphed into a vivid replay of the most intense trial of her career. Amid the ebb and flow of her slumber, she could clearly hear the voice of the jury foreman, a voice that echoed from only three days earlier.

Jury Foreman: "In the case of the State of New York versus John Doe, the jury has reached a verdict. We find the defendant... guilty of the charges of first-degree murder."

A murmur rippled through the dream courtroom. In her reverie, Ashley wore a satisfied professional smile, recognizing it as a mechanical reflection of her past victories. But as the dream progressed, an unsettling feeling began to stir within her.

The atmosphere shifted, and she sensed a heaviness in the air, the triumphant moment of the verdict overshadowed by an ominous weight. Images of the courtroom began to blur, replaced by flashes of the defendant's piercing gaze—taunting and defiant. The echoes of the crowd faded, replaced by whispers that twisted around her, questioning her choices, her path.

Ashley felt the heat of anxiety rising within her, a reminder that every victory was a double-edged sword. The need for reassurance grew strong as she threaded between the past successes and the uncertainties of the future.

Just as she grappled with this inner turmoil, the dream twisted again, and suddenly she found herself standing precariously on a ledge, overlooking an abyss of doubt. The colors of her reality merged and distorted, creating an unsettling landscape that reflected her fears— fear of failure, fear of loss, fear of what lay ahead.

Determined to conquer this haunting vision, she steadied her breath. "This is just a dream," she reminded herself, gripping the edges of her consciousness. "I control this narrative."

With that declaration, Ashley willed the dream to shift, to become a canvas for her own design. As clarity began to emerge, she envisioned the courtroom not as a battleground of anxiety, but as a stage for her expertise, a place where justice rang true.

In that moment of revelation, she could feel the weight of the past lifting, replaced by the lightness of possibility. The future could be shaped by the courage she was willing to embrace. And, with Robert's laughter still echoing in her heart, she knew she wasn't alone in this journey.

As she steadied herself on the brink between past and future, the dream began to dissolve into dawn's soft embrace, hinting at new beginnings waiting just beyond the horizon

The judge delivered his harsh verdict as Ashley watched the officer escort the defendant down to the basement. But things took a quick turn in this fleeting version of events when the defendant managed to escape, approaching her with a face twisted in malice.

Defendant: [With a sinister smile] "You're next. Ha, ha, ha!"

The dream spiraled into chaos, sounds jumbled together, and the defendant seemed to be everywhere, casting a threatening shadow. A whirlwind of confusion swirled around her, but just as she was about to plunge fully into the nightmare, Ashley jolted awake.

She found herself back in her tranquil room, the warm glow of the lamp caressing the space around her. Her heart raced, but with each deliberate breath, her anxiety gradually yielded to the tranquility of her surroundings. Somehow, the special evening she had shared with Robert had left a lasting impression, transforming that old room into her true home, providing the emotional refuge she desperately needed.

The judge adjusted his posture slightly, fixing his gaze directly on the defendant. "John Doe, you have been found guilty of two counts of first-degree murder. According to the laws of the State of New York, I sentence you to two consecutive life terms without the possibility of parole."

The court officer moved closer to the defendant and began to lead him down a small staircase that descended to the lower levels, where provisional cells awaited his transfer to prison. However, in a calculated move, the defendant suddenly lunged back, delivering a precise and brutal headbutt that knocked the officer to the ground. Seizing the moment, the defendant grabbed the officer by the neck, squeezing tightly until the man was either unconscious or possibly dead.

Quickly, the defendant bounded back up the stairs to the courtroom. With great cunning, he opened the door carefully and saw that the room was nearly empty. He snatched the keys from the incapacitated officer and freed himself from the handcuffs, stepping into the courtroom with determination.

Upon seeing him, the few people present began to scream.

Defendant: [Locking eyes with Ashley, a cruel smile stretching across his face] "You're next. Ha, ha, ha!"

Ashley tried to confront him, but the defendant reacted swiftly, throwing a punch that sent her stumbling backward. Leaping over the backs of the benches, he dashed down the hallway, leaving chaos in his wake.

Adrenaline surged through Ashley's veins as she realized the nightmare from her mind had now burst into reality. She couldn't stand by; she had to fight back and protect herself. The echoes of her dreams intertwined with the urgency of the moment, urging her to summon the strength she had always carried within. Refusing to be a victim, she steeled herself and pursued him through the corridor, ready to confront the specter of her fears head-on.

At that moment, a deafening alarm blared throughout the building, signaling the escape alert. The defendant sprinted down a corridor, desperately searching for an exit. Spotting a small door, he raced toward it. He opened the door and quickly climbed a narrow flight of stairs, only to find a solid iron door at the top—locked tight. Beside it, he noticed a tiny window that he managed to pry open with great effort, squeezing himself through.

Once on the terrace, he closed the window carefully, ensuring not to leave any traces behind. He surveyed his surroundings and saw a vast expanse of rooftop cluttered with large air conditioning units. He ducked behind one of them just as the sound of a helicopter grew louder.

Crouching low, he pressed himself against one of the machines, his heart racing as he contemplated his next move. Night was falling over New York City, and the lights below twinkled like stars in an increasingly darkening sky. The hunt had begun, and he knew that every second counted in his quest for freedom.

As he crouched there, resting his head against the cold metal of the helicopter's window, he reflected on the improbability of it all. It felt surreal—like a movie, with him cast as the protagonist. His thoughts raced, questioning the luck he was experiencing.

"Why is this happening?" he wondered, recalling how quickly everything had unraveled. Just then, he caught a glimpse of Lilith beside him, a sly smile gracing her lips.

Lilith: [smirking] "Nice show you put on there. You're quite the performer, aren't you?"

Her calm confidence contrasted sharply with the chaos of his thoughts. He blinked, still trying to process the scene unfolding before him. Shaking off the surreal sense of disbelief, he realized that somehow, she had become a part of his improbable escape.

Taking a deep breath, he tried to focus on the present, tuning out the surrounding noise and his jumbled thoughts. Every instinct within him screamed to keep moving. The night was thick with tension, but amidst it all, there was an unmistakable thread of anticipation coiling around him.

With Lilith at his side, he felt an unexpected surge of confidence. Perhaps, just perhaps, the night was in his favor. The city's cacophony faded away, leaving only the steady beat of his heart as he prepared to embrace whatever came next in this twisted narrative of his life.

Ha, ha, ha!

The defendant emerged from his hiding place, clearly bewildered.

Defendant: "Where did you come from?"

Lilith, with an air of natural elegance, fixed him with a steady gaze.

Lilith: "I'm everywhere. Just say the word, and I'm right there with your ego."

The defendant, skeptical, stepped closer to her, attempting to seize her. But Lilith was quicker. With a deft movement, she grabbed his arm and performed a flip in the air, throwing him to the ground with surprising strength. Before he could react, Lilith pressed the toe of her stylish stiletto against his neck, a lethal threat.

Lilith: [applying just enough pressure with her heel] "If you move, you'll lose your vein." [She raised an eyebrow, exuding both elegance and beauty as she added] "You call for me, and then you fear me. It's hard to understand you."

The defendant, realizing the gravity of his situation, froze. Lilith's commanding presence began to calm him. She eased off slightly, extending her arm toward him with grace.

Lilith: "Relax, kid. I'm here to save you."

He hesitated for a moment, but the clarity in Lilith's eyes and the confidence in her voice convinced him. Taking her arm, he rose slowly, feeling an odd blend of relief and respect.

Lilith dusted off her dress with care before speaking again.

Lilith: "Now, you need to follow my lead. We have to get out of here before reinforcements arrive. Do you understand who's in charge now?"

The defendant nodded, choosing to trust this enigmatic figure who had appeared at the most critical moment.

Defendant: "Sure. What do we do next?"

A faint smile played on Lilith's lips.

Lilith: "Follow my lead and don't ask unnecessary questions. Let's go."

With a blend of urgency and elegance, Lilith and the defendant moved swiftly across the terrace, strategizing their next move to evade imminent capture.

A police helicopter approached rapidly, its flashing lights casting an ominous glow against the night sky. The defendant shot a furious glance at Lilith, suspicion etched across his face.

Defendant: "You bitch, you sold me out!"

Lilith remained composed, a hint of amusement dancing in her expression.

Lilith: "Calm down, kid. How foolish you are. I'll let you go once you're safe, but for now, just let me handle this."

The helicopter landed precisely on the terrace. Without wasting a moment, Lilith and the defendant boarded. Lilith moved towards the pilot, her eyes blazing with determination.

Lilith: "Take us to New Jersey. Drop us off at the first clear spot you see."

The pilot nodded and lifted the aircraft into the sky, quickly disappearing among the city's towering skyscrapers. The journey was silent, tension thickening the air. Finally, the helicopter touched down in a clearing in New Jersey. Lilith and the defendant disembarked hurriedly.

Lilith: "Later, boys."

As Lilith and the defendant walked away, already over fifty meters from the landing site, the pilot turned to his co-pilot, confusion etched across his features.

Pilot: "What are we doing here?"

The co-pilot remained silent, his face reflecting the same bewilderment. As they glanced between the seats, they stumbled upon a bundle of hundred-dollar bills.

Co-pilot: "And what's this? Can you tell me what's going on?"

The pilot shook his head, baffled. Suddenly, the helicopter's radio crackled to life with an urgent voice from headquarters.

Voice from HQ: "Give your call sign and real names, New York Police. Where are you? Where are you? We saw you from a building across the street loading two passengers. Could it be the defendant? A woman and a man. Head to the station immediately."

The pilots exchanged bewildered glances, utterly confused. The situation was becoming increasingly surreal, and they knew they would eventually have to provide a detailed explanation for this unusual detour.

Meanwhile, Lilith and the defendant hurried across the clearing, the night wind rustling their clothes as they moved toward their next refuge.

Defendant: "What are we going to do now?"

Lilith met his gaze with a look full of purpose.

Lilith: "We will blend back into the shadows. I have contacts here who can help us disappear."

For the first time in a long while, a spark of hope ignited within the defendant. Maybe this mysterious woman was indeed his savior, beyond all suspicion.

The noise of the police helicopter faded into the distance as Lilith and the defendant found themselves in an open field after their bold escape from the terrace. They stood in a location surrounded by dense woods, tall trees whispering their secrets to the night breeze. The full moon illuminated the starry sky, casting enigmatic shadows over the ground blanketed with tall grass and wildflowers.

As they stood there, still catching their breath from the intense chase, they found themselves face-to-face in the middle of the field. The defendant, a rugged man with steel-gray eyes, regarded Lilith with a mixture of gratitude and wariness.

"So, what now?" he asked, a hint of uncertainty creeping into his voice.

Lilith smiled, unfazed by his hesitation. "Now, we move forward. Trust me when I say I have a plan. You need to follow my lead, and we can navigate through this together."

He searched her eyes, weighing his options. In that moonlit moment, he realized he was no longer alone in this fight—he had a partner willing to risk it all. The night was far from over, and as the shadows danced around them, the promise of escape ignited a sense of possibility that had once seemed lostLilith: [Taking the initiative] "You escaped this because of me, but don't be mistaken—just as I've saved your life, I can lock you away again, and much faster."

The defendant nodded, acutely aware of the truth in her words but keeping his guard up.

Defendant: [In a low voice] "What do you want from me?"

Lilith smiled, a grin that mixed danger with cunning.

Lilith: [Stepping closer] "There's a price for my help. When I need your services, you'll come without question. You will do what I ask, without protests or complaints. Understood?"

The defendant weighed his options, knowing he owed his freedom to her. Although cautious, he nodded slowly.

Defendant: [With determination] "Understood. But I want to know what kind of jobs you need me for."

Lilith raised an eyebrow, her expression a blend of amusement and threat.

Lilith: "You'll find out when the time comes. For now, enjoy your freedom, but remember… I'll always be watching."

The defendant tensed, reflecting on the whirlwind of recent events as he sat on a stone, absorbing everything that had happened. Just as he began to gather his thoughts, he was interrupted by the sound of his savior's voice, feeling the weight of her words. Before he could react, Lilith made a subtle gesture with her hand, pointing to a spot in the woods.

Lilith: [In a soft voice] "Now go. You'll hear from me soon."

The defendant nodded and started to walk away, but he couldn't resist casting a final glance back at Lilith. When he turned to look again, she had vanished. The spot where she stood was merely a shadow now, blending into the dimness of the forest.

Perplexed, he searched his surroundings, looking in every direction, but Lilith had disappeared without a trace, as if she had never been there. Only the whisper of the wind and the distant song of a nocturnal bird accompanied the night in the dense, mysterious woods.

With a final sigh, the defendant realized the magnitude of the pact he had made. He ventured deeper into the forest, fully aware that his life had irrevocably changed and that he was now a pawn in a much larger and more dangerous game than he had ever imagined.

On a warm summer afternoon in Ireland, Ashley sat in a quaint café within a local bookstore. Though physically present in her surroundings, her mind and heart were with her companions—Maria, Ursula, and Don Lorenzo—as they ventured into a mysterious convent on the other side of the world. Taking advantage of the patchy Wi-Fi connection, she connected with the group through a video call, anxiously observing the ancient structure that loomed large, filled with hidden secrets.

As the signal on her phone fluctuated, Ashley could see through the screen how her friends cautiously navigated the dust-laden hallways of the old convent. The air was thick with a solemn silence, broken only by the soft creak of wood beneath their feet. The rooms appeared frozen in time, with scattered toys and tattered blankets hinting at the recent presence of children.

Ashley: [With a slight tremor in her voice] "I can't believe what I'm seeing... those things, those toys. Were they keeping children here?"

Maria: [Holding up a worn doll to the camera] "Yes, Ashley. It seems this place has served as a refuge for them."

Then Don Lorenzo, his voice resolute and a spark of fervor in his eyes, shared his unsettling suspicion and bold plan.

Ursula

Don Lorenzo: [Determined] "We can't ignore this. I suggest we hack into the rogues' online systems to learn more about their operations and future moves."

His resolution and strategy ignited a spark of action within the group, aware that this could be the key to dismantling the Roadrunner's criminal network.

Ursula nodded, embracing the challenge with conviction. They understood that they were not only confronting a dangerous organization but also holding the lives of innocent children that needed their protection. As Ashley urged them to take every precaution possible from her corner of Ireland, the others geared up to simultaneously gather evidence and close down the dark enterprise.

United now more than ever, the group forged a path toward justice, with the hope of dismantling the Roadrunner legacy and paving the way for a safer future for the most vulnerable among them.

CHAPTER 18

The Family Reunion After 500 Years

The Reunion of Iris and Odran

Iris Lite Fairy, heart racing and hands trembling, moved through the thick forest, the leaves crunching softly beneath her feet. The golden hues of sunset filtered through the treetops, creating a magical and ethereal atmosphere. She knew that her father, Odran, awaited her on the other side, and after so many years of separation, her mind was a whirlwind of memories and emotions.

Finally, she spotted him. Odran stood near a clearing surrounded by wildflowers, his imposing figure radiating warmth. Iris ran toward him, relief and joy spilling from her eyes as tears streamed down her cheeks.

Iris: [sobbing] "Dad!"

Odran: "I've missed you so much, my daughter."

But their moment of peace was suddenly shattered by a gust of icy wind. The dark angels who had followed Odran were near, and their threatening presence hung heavy in the air.

1.   The Magical Storm

A clearing in the forest flickered under the relentless flashes of lightning. The wind began to twist with an almost supernatural fury, carrying a chill that cut to the bone. Leaves danced in chaotic spirals, foreshadowing the conflict about to unfold. Odran, his eyes sparkling with determination and love, embraced his daughter Iris Lite, communicating his strength and reassurance through the warmth of his embrace.

As their emotions intertwined, the surrounding atmosphere crackled with tension. Iris could feel the weight of the menace lurking just beyond the trees. Odran, ever the guardian, steeled himself for the battle that was undoubtedly coming, knowing that the dark angels wouldn't be far behind.

Odran: [Whispering fiercely] "Stay close to me, Iris. No matter what happens, we face this together."

Iris nodded, drawing strength from her father's presence. She had dreamed of this reunion for centuries, and though she had longed for a tranquil moment, she was ready to stand by him in the face of danger. Their bond, forged through years of separation and longing, shone brighter than any darkness that threatened to encroach upon them.

As the first crack of thunder erupted overhead, sending tremors through the ground, Iris and Odran prepared to fight for their reunion and their legacy. Together, they would defy the storm and confront the shadowy figures that sought to disrupt their hard-won moment. The battle ahead would test not only their strength but also the enduring power of a familial bond forged over centuries.

2.   Strength.

What should have been a moment of tenderness and welcome quickly morphed into a premonition of confrontation. The whispers of dark angels were no longer distant tales; the danger was palpable, tangible.

Odran: "I've missed you so much, my daughter…"

His words hung in the air, abruptly choked by the emergence of a threatening shadow. Before silence could reclaim its dominion, the dark angels unleashed a storm of terrifying proportions. Black bolts of energy shot from the sky, intent on annihilating everything in their path. Craters multiplied on the ground beneath the forceful impacts, leaving scars upon the earth.

Without hesitation, Odran and Iris intertwined their hands, channeling their combined energy into a powerful golden shield. The sphere of light rose up between them and the chaos, bracing against every dark blow.

Iris: "Father, I can feel the strain… we can't hold this forever."

Her voice trembled, reflecting the intensity of the battle. Sweat trickled down her forehead as she focused all her strength. The barrier flickered and wavered under the relentless assault. With each bolt that struck, the power of darkness seemed endless. The clash had only just begun, yet the determination in their hearts burned with renewed vigor.

Siege of Shadows

The forest morphed into a sea of twilight, where shadows appeared to have a life of their own. Initially mere distorted silhouettes that flowed across the ground and tree trunks, the shadows soon rose, materializing into sinister forms that approached with clear intent.

Iris Lite raised her hands, summoning a white glow that temporarily pushed back the shadows. Around her, the clearing filled with a pure, potent light, as if daylight had been torn from the grasp of night. The shadows halted, blinded by this extraordinary act of bravery.

Iris: "Father, they are surrounding us from all sides!"

Desperation tinged her voice, but determination never abandoned her. Odran, tapping into his own magic, crafted a protective sphere around them—a barrier that repelled the shadows with every pulse.

Odran: "Stay focused, Iris. Don't let the shadows play tricks on your mind."

Together, they stood firm against the encroaching darkness, ready to fight not just for their lives, but for the light they refused to let fade.

Her voice was a steadfast beacon amid the chaos, a guiding force that helped Iris maintain her focus. Yet the shadows, undeterred, resumed their assault with renewed ferocity. They hurled themselves relentlessly against the magical barrier. Each impact tested Iris's resilience, her brow gleaming with sweat as she channeled her magic to neutralize them. The effort felt endless—a battle against an enemy that showed no signs of exhaustion or surrender.

But with each shadow that fell, a spark of hope ignited in Iris's heart, for she knew that her light was her most powerful weapon. It was a bright flame in the darkness, a reminder that even in the face of overwhelming odds, she had the strength to push back against the night.

As the shadows pressed closer, fueled by a primal rage, Iris drew upon every ounce of her power. The intensity of her magic grew, illuminating the clearing with an ethereal glow that cut through the darkness, creating a stark contrast that momentarily held the shadows at bay.

She fought with a newfound determination, her mind racing with memories of the loved ones she was fighting for.

In a moment of clarity, Iris realized that she wasn't just battling for survival; she was fighting for the spirit of hope, a light that could not be extinguished. The connection with her father, the weight of their shared legacy, filled her with strength as she took a deep breath and prepared to unleash her greatest spell yet.

With a fierce cry, she focused her energy, intent on casting away the shadows once and for all. As the world around her began to flicker, she felt the tide starting to turn. Each beat of her heart resonated with the belief that even in darkness, the light would always prevail Amidst the chaos, a new enemy materialized from the shadows—one that toyed with the very edges of perception. A dark angel, bolder than the rest, began to conjure illusions with a disturbing mastery. The illusions warped the clearing, transforming reality into a landscape of nightmares and shattered memories. Odran was struck by an echo from the past: visions of happier times, now distorted and corrupted.

Odran: "Don't be fooled, Iris. What you see is not real."

His words served as an anchor in the turbulent sea of confusion, a constant reminder of the truth. Iris, shaken by emotions that surged like a torrent, struggled to maintain her clarity.

The forest clearing, now a battleground between light and shadow, twisted under the influence of the dark angel. Iris Lite's perception contorted, and the world around her began to fracture into shards of dreams and nightmares. Before her, reality morphed into a chaotic canvas where images from the past emerged in false hues. A chilling whisper filled her mind as familiar scenes played out before her eyes.

The first vision was of Iris's childhood. She saw herself in the meadow of her youth, running alongside her father, Odran, who laughed and lifted her into the air. It was a memory so vivid that she could almost smell the wildflowers. But Odran's smile began to fade, and the meadow darkened, transforming into a barren, desolate wasteland. The flowers withered into a sigh of dust.

Iris: "Father! Why is everything wilting? This can't be... this isn't real!"

In that moment, Odran, right beside her, sensing the internal struggle of his daughter, spoke with a voice that sliced through the illusory daze.

Odran: "Iris, remember who you are. Don't let these images control you. Find the truth."

A second scenario unfolded before her. She was now in a library, surrounded by books whose pages tore themselves free and soared like birds in the wind. The images and words within them seemed to come alive momentarily before fading into nothingness. It was a reminder of her moments of learning, of nights spent under the tutelage of Mirabelle, her mother, who taught her the secrets of magic.

As the chaotic scenes swirled around her, the lessons learned in that sanctuary of knowledge coalesced into something powerful within Iris. She drew upon the strength of those memories—each one a piece of her identity, a spark lighting the way through the darkness. The dark angel's threats echoed, but so did the wisdom of her past, urging her to reclaim her power.

With renewed strength and clarity, Iris stood tall against the encroaching shadows, ready to confront not just the illusions, but the deeper truths that lay beneath.

"I Know father"

Aisling responded, her tone resolute, though her eyes betrayed a flicker of fear. "But we can't let them destroy this forest."

The air suddenly turned frigid, signaling the approach of the ice angel. Almost immediately, a spark of heat surged from the fire angel, igniting the tension in the atmosphere. Aisling and Odran braced themselves, aware that they would need every resource and ounce of ingenuity to emerge victorious.

Dark angels descended from the sky, a disturbing fusion of flames and frost pushing their powers to the limit. They attacked in perfect synchrony: one unleashing a wave of sharp ice while the other sent forth furious tongues of fire.

"Watch out, Aisling!" Odran shouted, deflecting a barrage of icy shards with a barrier of wind.

Aisling's heart raced as she harnessed her water magic to counter the flames, summoning a thick mist that dampened the searing heat. "We need to separate their attacks!" she yelled, beads of sweat forming on her brow. "It's clear they're much stronger together."

Odran nodded, his gaze fixed on the enemies. "I'll handle the ice. You neutralize the fire."

As the battle raged around them, Aisling began to channel her inner energy, drawing upon the calming essence of the forest to empower her spells. A gentle storm materialized from her hands; the water danced through the air, dazzling with fierce grace as it absorbed the encroaching flames.

Embers crackled and sputtered, extinguished by Aisling's magical water, reducing the threat of unrestrained fire to little more than wisps of smoke. However, the danger escalated with every passing second, shards of ice slicing through the air like invisible blades.

Odran fought with equal intensity, summoning winds that wrapped around the icy shards, redirecting them away from their deadly path.

"Now!" Odran shouted, signaling Aisling to escalate her attack.

Aisling closed her eyes for a brief moment, focusing not just on her powers, but on the harmony of the forest surrounding her. She let that energy flow through her, amplifying the current of water as she unleashed an unstoppable wave that crashed against the fire angel, extinguishing its fury.

In the midst of battle, the bond between father and daughter fortified their resolve, as they fought not only for their home but for every living creature that called the forest its sanctuary. Together, they had become a formidable force, united by their love and the unyielding spirit of the nature they were determined to protect

Finding herself quickly surrounded, the figure of the ice angel faltered, retreating for the first time.

"Father, this is our chance!" Aisling exclaimed.

Without hesitation, Odran gathered his remaining strength, entwining wind currents to send the ice debris far away from them, disarming any remnants of threat that the ice angel could still pose. As the angels fled, defeated and diminished, Aisling and Odran stood firm, their breaths heavy with adrenaline and the triumph they had just achieved.

Once everything settled, Aisling sank to her knees among the damp leaves, shaken by both relief and the terror she had experienced. Odran embraced her, his expression a mixture of pride and deep paternal love.

"You did amazing, my daughter," he whispered, his voice calm now after the storm of battle. "I knew you could do it, even if it was difficult."

Aisling offered a tired smile.

The air still carried the scent of smoke and steam as Aisling slowly recovered from the intense battle. The wounds of the recent confrontation were fresh, and her body ached from expending so much magic. Beside her, Odran remained vigilant, his watchful gaze scanning the sky for any signs of danger.

However, their brief moment of reprieve was abruptly interrupted by a chilling shift in the atmosphere. From the horizon, soaring with dark majesty, a new malevolent angel approached, its intentions written in the gleam of its eyes.

"Aisling, back on your feet!" Odran urged, sensing the escalating power of the new adversary.

Aisling staggered to her feet, her energy not yet fully restored. "I didn't think another one would show up so soon," she gasped, struggling to gather her strength.

The new enemy leader, radiating an ominous presence, raised his hands. With a simple gesture, he began to manipulate the terrain. Massive rocks and shattered fragments of trees lifted from the ground, floating threateningly in the air.

"Father, watch out!" Aisling warned as the debris began to rain down upon them, guided by an invisible but lethal telekinetic force.

Attempting to protect her, Odran conjured a swirling shield of wind, deflecting some of the rocks but not all. The dark leader smiled with dangerous delight, intensifying his assault.

"We need another strategy," Aisling murmured, her mind racing to find a new angle of attack as she skillfully dodged the projectiles.

Every second under the relentless assault drained their reserves further. The weight of each attack pressed not only on their bodies but also on their spirits.

The Battle in the Clearing

Iris clutched her father, feeling his warmth and strength. However, their moment of tenderness was abruptly shattered by a chilling wind and the looming shadow of a malignant presence. The dark angels had found them.

Odran: [In a low, firm voice] "Iris, prepare yourself. I won't allow them to touch you."

The first shadows began to materialize around them, unsettling in their twisted forms, eyes gleaming with malice. Without a moment's hesitation, they lunged at the pair.

Iris raised her hands, conjuring a bright glow that illuminated the clearing. The shadows halted momentarily, blinded by the light. But this was merely a fleeting reprieve. The dark angels adjusted their strategy, merging with the environment and attempting to attack from all angles.

As they prepared for the inevitable confrontation, the bond between father and daughter crystallized in that moment, a shared determination to confront the darkness together. Together, they embodied the hope that could push back against the encroaching shadows

: [Desperate yet determined] "Dad, they're coming from every direction!"

Odran conjured a protective shield around them, a glowing sphere of energy that repelled the encroaching shadows.

Odran: "Stay focused, Aisling, let the shadows deceive you."

The shadows relentlessly launched themselves against the barrier, and Iris, sweat beading on her brow, summoned her magic to dissolve them. But the attacks showed no signs of stopping; it felt like an endless struggle.

The Rescue of Mirabella

Just as Iris's strength began to falter, a brilliant burst of light pierced the clearing, momentarily scattering the dark angels. Mirabella, Aisling's mother, appeared at the edge of the glade, flanked by a group of soldiers clad in pure white, exuding radiant energy.

"Now it's my turn," declared Mirabella, her voice steady, her gaze firm yet **compassionate as she assessed the threat.**

Mirabella: [With a powerful and serene voice] "Stay away from my family!"

Iris and Odran watched with relief and astonishment as Mirabella advanced with unwavering determination. The white-clad soldiers, with precise and coordinated movements, began to engage the dark angels, unleashing bursts of luminous energy that forced them to retreat and fade away.

White Soldier 1: "Protect the family!"

With each strike, the dark energies weakened, pushed back by the radiant offensive. The benevolent presence of the white soldiers rekindled hope in Iris's heart.

Aisling: Mom!!

Mirabella reached Aisling in an instant, enveloping her in a tight embrace.

Mirabella: "I'm here, my girl. I won't let anyone harm you."

The warmth of her mother's reassurance enveloped Iris, igniting a newfound strength within her. Together, they stood united, ready to face the shadows looming over them. With Mirabella by her side, the fight didn't feel so daunting anymore; it felt like a chance to reclaim their strength and love against the encroaching darkness.

Odran stepped closer, and the family embraced in a strong hug, each member drawing strength from the other. The remaining shadows, helpless against the arrival of the white soldiers and the united power of the family, began to disperse, whispering promises of vengeance before vanishing into the night.

The clearing fell silent, the twilight slowly washing the sky in warm hues, while Mirabella, Odran, and Aisling stood surrounded by the soldiers, allowing themselves a moment to breathe.

Odran: [Looking at Mirabella with gratitude] "You arrived just in time."

Mirabella: "I always will. Always."

With the family reunited, they understood that this victory was just a step on a long and perilous journey, but for this moment, they were together and at peace.

Reunion of the Soul

As the dark angels scattered and the white soldiers kept vigilant watch, Odran and Mirabella found themselves face to face, the weight of past memories reflected in their gazes. In this dimension, they had been husband and wife, bound by a love that had begun among the stars and had given birth to their wonderful daughter, Aisling.

Mirabella stepped forward, and Odran followed, silent tears spilling down his cheeks. Finally, they embraced, merging in a gesture that conveyed everything words could not express.

Odran: [His voice trembling] "Forgive me, Mirabella. I was consumed by pain and darkness when I lost you… when we lost Aisling. I let despair take hold and destroyed everything I loved."

Mirabella looked at him with tenderness, her hand gently caressing his face, weathered with scars from time and internal battles.

Mirabella: [Her voice soft and filled with love] "Odran, you don't have to make mistakes to be loved. I understand your pain; I felt your loss from the other side. We both suffered, but I always knew our love would bring you back."

Odran bowed his head, his sobs shaking his body.

Odran: [Barely above a whisper] "The day the soldiers of Henry VI attacked us... the day I thought I'd lost you forever... I also lost Aisling. I left her alone, **I abandoned her in her despair.**"

Mirabella: [With firm resolve] "Don't blame yourself, Odran. Those were dark times, and each of us fought the best we could. What matters now is that we are together again. We will learn to heal our wounds together."

Hope filled Odran's eyes, reflected in the unconditional love of Mirabella.

In that moment, Aisling, who had been observing the emotional reunion, couldn't help but chime in with evident emotion mixed with a hint of playful mischief.

Aisling: [With a teasing tone] "Hey, we're still here! Come on, you two, we have a world to save!"

Mirabella and Odran smiled and turned toward their daughter. Mirabella placed a hand on Aisling's shoulder, while Odran took the other.

Mirabella: [Smiling] "You're right, my brave daughter. But before we move forward, we need to rebuild what we've lost."

Odran: [With renewed determination] "Together, we can face anything."

Their reunion not only strengthened familial bonds but also reignited the hope within their hearts. United, they knew they could tackle any challenge that lay ahead. The white soldiers regrouped around the family, offering their protection and support.

And so, with renewed love and unbreakable strength, Aisling, Mirabella, and Odran prepared to confront the challenges awaiting them, ready to restore peace to their world and protect one another against any adversity.

The Feast of the Queen Mother

The family made their way toward the city, escorted by the white soldiers who had rescued them from the shadows. As they approached the grand city gates, they noticed not only security but also an atmosphere of celebration. Flags fluttered high overhead, and citizens cheered for the return of the royal family, their faces glowing with joy.

Upon reaching the palace entrance, the Queen Mother stood at the top of the staircase, radiant and sporting a smile that lit up her entire face. The relief and happiness in her demeanor were palpable as she gazed down at her daughter and grandchildren, safely returned.

Queen Mother: [Opening her arms wide] "Welcome home! We worried so much about you."

Mirabella and Odran greeted her with warm smiles and heartfelt embraces.

dashed into her grandmother's arms, laughter spilling forth as she reveled in the joy of being home.

The Celebration

That night, the Queen Mother organized a grand feast in honor of the reunited family. Tables overflowed with exquisite delicacies, and the air was filled with music, creating a jubilant atmosphere.

In the grand hall, as courtiers danced and celebrated, the Queen Mother beckoned Odran to her side.

Queen Mother: [With a calm voice and a hint of humor] "Odran, dear, did you not realize they were following you?"

Odran, feeling a bit sheepish, lowered his head slightly.

Odran: [Sighing] "No, my lady. I was a fool as always, blinded by my eagerness to see my daughter and my wife. I didn't pay enough attention."

The Queen Mother chuckled softly, brushing a hand reassuringly on Odran's **arm.**

Queen Mother: "Well, I suppose we can excuse a father's eagerness. After all, family is what matters most."

Odran couldn't help but smile, feeling the warmth of his loved ones surrounding him. The extravagant feast began, and with every bite, they savored not just the food but the joy of being together again. Love, laughter, and the promise of brighter days filled the air as they celebrated their reunion, fortified by the bonds that had withstood the trials of their journey.

With a soft laugh, the Queen Mother gestured toward the food.

"They'll try again, so don't let your guard down. It's crucial that Aisling develops her future as queen." Odran nodded, bowing his head in reverence, acknowledging her words.

"Come on, eat something. I doubt you've had dinner."

They both laughed, easing the tension in the air. Odran grabbed a plate and helped himself generously, while the Queen Mother regarded him with affection.

Queen Mother: [Gently] "We're so glad you're back. More importantly, we're all together again. Learn from your mistakes, but don't be too hard on yourself. Today is a day for celebration."

Beyond the Shadows

As the night wore on, Odran found solace in the festive atmosphere. The sound of Iris laughing as she played with other teenagers, Mirabella's dedication as she helped organize the guests alongside the Queen Mother, and the acceptance of the courtiers and soldiers filled his heart with renewed hope.

Sitting with a plate of food before him, Odran reflected on how blessed he was to have his family back. Though he knew challenges still lay ahead, he decided to embrace the joy and unity that filled the room in that moment.

The Promise

Before the night came to an end, Odran sought out Mirabella and the Queen Mother. Seeing them together—confident and smiling—he realized that this was his true strength.

Odran: [With a firm voice] "I promise I will be more cautious and attentive. I will never again allow fear or despair to cloud my judgment."

His words hung in the air, a solemn vow that resonated with the family's commitment to each other. As they gathered around the table, the warmth of their bonds enveloped them, and with every shared laugh and story, they began to weave a new tapestry of hope, ready to face whatever the future held together.

"May nothing cloud my judgment. Together, we will face any darkness that crosses our path."

Mirabella and the Queen Mother nodded, their hearts brimming with hope and love.

And so, with renewed spirit and strengthened resolve, the family braced themselves for the days ahead, celebrating that night as the dawn of a new era filled with light and promise.

As laughter echoed around the banquet hall, they recognized this moment as a turning point—not just for themselves but for the realm they had fought to protect. Under the warm glow of candlelight and the shimmering joy of reunion, they forged a pact, a silent agreement that whatever challenges lay in wait, they would confront them as one.

With the air thick with determination and an unbreakable bond, they vowed to illuminate the shadows together, driven by love and resilience. As they raised their glasses in a toast to new beginnings, the specters of the past faded, replaced by a bright future they would build side by side.

CHAPTER 19

Reflections in Hell

In the twilight of a forest cloaked in the night's embrace, Lilith waited, her heart pounding in her chest. The trees whispered ancient secrets, and the very air throbbed with a dark and enticing energy. This forest, once thriving during the days of the Roman Empire, was where Lilith—a young woman of captivating beauty yet consumed by dire poverty—knew her last hope was drawing near.

Her eyes, typically ablaze with a defiant fire, were now clouded by desperation and uncertainty. A barely perceptible rustle in the grass heralded the arrival of the hooded man. His presence radiated an indescribable power, as though the forest itself had swallowed the ambient sound to better hear his proposition.

Lilith: "Are you the one who can grant me what I desire?"

The figure beneath the hood nodded slowly, his voice emerging like a serpentine whisper.

Charming Man: "I can offer you wealth beyond your wildest dreams, power that will make your enemies tremble. But the price is steep, Lilith. Your soul for everything you crave."

She glanced down at her feet, where the dust and misery of her days clung to her like a reminder of her current existence. Desperation forged her resolve as she raised her gaze, confronting him with an occasional glimmer of audacity.

Lilith: "My soul... will it be worth a life free of want?"

A barely perceptible smile crossed the hidden face of the man.

Charming Man: "That is a dilemma you will have ample time to consider once the deal is sealed."

The air around her grew thicker, shimmering flashes of red and gold reflecting ephemeral visions of the prosperity she longed for.

Lilith: "I accept. Let my soul serve as currency to buy my freedom from this miserable existence."

The decision hung heavy in the air, the weight of her choice echoing through the darkened woods. In that moment, Lilith stepped boldly into the unknown, ready to sacrifice everything for the promise of a new life. As she made the deal, the forest sighed, a witness to the intertwining of fate and desire, binding her to a path that would lead to both unimaginable power and unforeseen consequences.

With a slow and ceremonial motion, the man extended a bony hand. A simple signature of blood sealed their fates, and a shiver crawled up Lilith's spine, marking the completion of their dark pact.

Centuries later, Lilith found herself in her chamber in hell—a space that seemed luxurious at first glance but harbored an unsettling undertone. The walls were draped in brocade shades of scarlet and purple, exuding decadence and depravity. In front of her black satin sheets, towering glass windows revealed a landscape of eternal fire.

Beyond the glass, souls writhed in perpetual agony, scorching flames consuming their essence in a grotesque, unending dance. With her chin resting in her palms, Lilith pondered the pact she had made.

Lilith: "Is this eternity what I truly desired? Trading earthly chains for those of fire..."

Shadows danced across her face, mirroring the internal storm of emotions within her. The opulence she once dreamed of now felt cold and unattainable, a stark contrast to the reality she faced.

Revelation and Laughter

A sudden interruption jolted her from her reverie: a dull, violent thud against the hellish glass. A disfigured face emerged—none other than Adolf Hitler, pressing against the surface, his eyes locked in a mute plea for release.

Lilith watched the scene with a mix of pity and horror, but then something shifted in her mind. A spark, an idea flickered through her thoughts.

Lilith: "What if all this... could be different?"

Once more, another soul slammed against the glass; this time it resembled Stalin, echoing a macabre reminder of her own potential fate should she fail to find a way out. But this time, Lilith smiled—a smile not born of joy, but rather shrewd determination and renewed hope.

That sudden inspiration carved a new path beyond her self-imposed condemnation; she realized she needed to fight, even in hell, to find meaning amid her eternal torment. With the faces of history's monsters hovering before her, Lilith felt a burgeoning resolve to reclaim her agency. The time for action had come, and she was ready to seize it.

Lilith lay in her bed, lost in the whirlwind of her thoughts, when the enormous oval doors of her chamber creaked open, reverberating through the space. The intrusion was followed by the entrance of a towering figure, her loyal servant, whose solemn presence infused the room with an air of urgency.

The servant, a being sculpted from the depths of the underworld, resembled an ancient statue: his ashen skin was marked with subtle glimmers of metallic sheen that caught the flickering firelight. His penetrating amber eyes seemed to contain the secrets of forgotten ages. Clad in dark robes that brushed the floor, he approached Lilith with a reverent bow, the very embodiment of loyalty.

Servant: "My lady," he announced, his voice resonating with the weight of fate, "I bear bad news."

Still seated on her dark satin sheets, Lilith slowly lifted her gaze. Her features, once sharp and chiseled like marble, were softened by an unexpected gentleness. There was a weariness in her eyes that spoke of centuries of struggle and inflicted pain, now eased by a hint of newfound understanding.

Lilith: "What has happened?"

The servant lowered his head for a moment, as if searching for the right words to convey the grim news.

Servant: "Odran's soul has escaped. It seems he has found his way to the fairy realm and is now happily reunited with his family."

The announcement, which would have once provoked a fierce outburst or an immediate call for retaliation, was met with a contemplative pause. Lilith regarded her servant, and in that moment, the hardness that had defined much of her existence momentarily faded. A smile curved her lips—not one of malice, but of serene acceptance and perhaps a hint of envy.

Lilith: "That's fine. Thank you."

The servant blinked in surprise at the calmness with which Lilith accepted the news, but he bowed once more, respecting his mistress's decision.

As he turned to fulfill his duties in the deep recesses of hell, Lilith sank back into her introspection. The news of Odran had managed to pierce the armor of her soul, igniting a spark of something she had thought lost: the hope for redemption or perhaps a quiet longing for connection.

In that illuminated stillness, Lilith contemplated the paths ahead— the battles yet to be fought, the decisions to be made. Odran's escape lingered in her thoughts as a reminder of the fragile bonds of love and loss intertwining through eternity, nudging her toward the possibility that perhaps there was still time for change, even for someone like her.

Lilith intertwined her fingers in her lap, allowing her thoughts to run free. She had learned that power and vengeance were not enough to fill the void left by the loss of her humanity. The example of Odran—his escape and reunion with his family—shone like a beacon, reminding her that even in the darkest depths, there was always a path back to the light.

The stillness of her infernal chamber now held a faint peace, a momentary respite in her internal war, as Lilith contemplated the next route she would take on her endless journey.

Seated on the edge of her bed, she fixated on the eternal flames dancing just beyond the glass of her infernal room. The haunting melody of "Lilith in Aeternum" floated through the air, weaving through the underground like distant whispers.

Her mind was a tapestry of intertwined thoughts, navigating the tumultuous sea of her actions and choices. When the order to eliminate Aisling Lite Fairy arrived, the weight of millennia of malevolence resurfaced, pressing down heavier than any external threat. She questioned for the umpteenth time whether it was worth continuing her legacy of darkness. What if Aisling Lite was, in fact, her daughter? A bond she had once understood, now long lost. What sense did it make to perpetuate destruction when a spark of change flickered within her?

As Lilith pondered, her thoughts drifted back to Delucas, a killer she had aided in escaping the confines of hell. This death mage had crossed into the mortal realm, carrying with him a shadow even darker than before. Whispers of a recent multiple homicide he committed reached her through dark channels.

The crime scene echoed an unspeakable atrocity—an entire family obliterated within their own home. The sepulchral silence of the shattered household spoke of frenetic violence, the walls splattered with the red of life that Delucas had snatched away. It was clear he had reveled in every moment, a macabre dance leaving deep imprints on the souls of those departed.

Delucas, with the cold precision of a predator, exerted his will upon his victims. His low and venomous voice echoed hauntingly:

Delucas: "Do not fear; you will soon know the true extent of suffering... but first, allow me to savor your fear."

Lilith shuddered at the memory but also felt an unsettling thrill at the power he exuded. In that moment, she realized that she stood on the precipice of a profound choice. Would she follow in Delucas's path of chaos and terror, or would she seek to reclaim her humanity and the light that flickered within her? The answer to that question would define not only her future but the fate of those intertwined in her destiny.

Their victims, powerless, offered their final pleas in vain, the sound of their desperation mixing with the echo of Delucas's laughter as he silenced their voices for ever

With the image of that brutality fresh in her mind, Lilith contemplated her options. She knew that confronting Delucas could unleash the wrath of Satan, who monitored their thoughts with chilling precision.

Burdened by the weight of fatigue and the search for meaning, Lilith rose from her bed. She needed to act with cunning, carefully concealing her intentions while plotting every thought and glance to deceive the master of lies.

Lilith to herself: "Perhaps there's a way to redeem what we've lost... if not now, maybe offering him a chance at life... a possibility for me as well."

She realized the key lay in approaching Delucas, not as an ally in darkness, but as someone seeking change—a transformation of her own shadows. She aimed to illuminate a path where he, like her, could rediscover freedom outside the endless cycle of death and destruction.

With each step she took, Lilith directed her mind toward visions of what could be if she walked a different path—one hidden from demonic eyes, yet perhaps the beginning of her own redemption story. The fire that filled her room was no longer merely the eternal flames; it flickered with a glimmer of hope that persisted, a testament to the fact that even the deepest darkness was not always absolute.

In the grim scene where Delucas had left his mark, the room lay in silence, punctuated only by the slow drip of a leaky faucet. The victims of his bloody ritual were scattered about, each telling the story of what had once been a life filled with promise and bright moments.

The first victim was a man in his forties, whose face still bore the marks of a life devoted to hard work and sacrifice for his family. His calloused hands hinted at the craft of a dedicated artisan. In an attempt to protect his loved ones, he had put up a fight, even if it was in vain. His eyes, still wide open in a grimace of horror, reflected his final thoughts of powerlessness and paternal love.

Next to him lay his wife, a middle-aged woman with hair framing a serene face, even in death. Until the last moment, she had held an expression of defiance, resisting the inevitable end to protect her children. The wrinkles at the corners of her eyes hinted at years of laughter and shared love, but her now-immobile lips held words of comfort and bravery that would never be spoken.

In that haunting moment, as Lilith surveyed the remnants of lives once vibrant and full of promise, she felt a renewed urgency. The realization that she could still forge a path of redemption not only for herself but for the souls lost to darkness stirred something deep within her—a determination to break the cycle and find a way to restore the lost light

The children—those little ones with their soft skin and wide eyes that spoke of dreams yet to be realized—lay on the ground like fallen angels. Their faces reflected the innocent confusion they had felt at the end, far too young to fully grasp the horror that had visited them. Nearby, a rag doll rested, a forgotten toy amidst the chaos, a silent witness to a moment of terror.

Delucas had reveled in their final moments, savoring the desperation he had wrought. Before silencing their voices, their pleas resonated like a sinister choir orchestrated by the murderer.

Mother: "Please, let us go... we're just a family. There's nothing here for you."

Delucas twisted his lips into a wicked smile, relishing the absolute power he held over them.

Delucas: "Go? This is your final act. I want to see the shadow of fear before I take you into oblivion."

The father, with a voice cracked but resolute, tried to reason with him.

Father: "Do what you will with me, but let the children go. They don't deserve this."

Delucas leaned in, his eyes gleaming with malice.

Delucas: "Life is a game of chance; why should they be the exception?"

Lilith, learning of these horrors through silent visions sent by her loyal servants, felt that the tragedy only deepened her doubts. The magnitude of the violence Delucas had unleashed was a direct consequence of the choices she had made in the past.

Reflecting on this latest episode of death, Lilith felt a profound urge to act, to change the course of what she had allowed to flourish in the world. Each victim stripped of life was a stark reminder of the corrosive power of unchecked darkness. And now, she was more determined than ever to seek a way out, to find a means to undo at least a fraction of the damage she had inadvertently permitted to thrive.

Journey into the Unknown

In the heart of the house, a cozy room pulsed with the light of the afternoon. Its walls were adorned with ancient maps and seashells collected from distant shores, hinting at the new adventure awaiting them. Lumina and Aisling, two young women brimming with life and magic, found themselves surrounded by suitcases and trunks decorated with maritime emblems. Despite the sun pouring through the window, their souls were tinged with a youthful fear, mingled with the inevitable sadness of leaving the familiar behind.

Mirabelle, their mother, stood nearby, her presence a beacon of unconditional love. She watched her daughters, feeling their emotions as vividly as her own. Alongside Mirabelle were Odran and their grandmother, all present to offer support and bid farewell to the girls.

The grandmother, ever the one to lift spirits and break the ice, smiled tenderly and spoke in a soft yet determined voice.

"Come on, girls, you're not going to another world. Barcelona will welcome you with open arms."

Aisling, the youngest and full of curiosity, looked up with a glint of defiance mixed with fear.

"But we are going to another dimension, Grandma. And that scares me. I've never been before."

The grandmother chuckled warmly, while it was Odran, the father, who intervened with a voice rich with memories and intrigue.

"Ah, but you've been there before, even if you don't remember. Don't you remember the cart?"

Aisling furrowed her brow, trying to unearth memories that seemed hidden beneath a fog. She paused, reflecting on her father's words. The knowledge that she had once traveled down unknown paths brought an unexpected peace, easing some of her anxiety.

With each shared glance, the bonds of family and love fortified them against the uncertainty ahead. As they prepared to embark on this journey into the unknown, Aisling realized that the strength of her family would accompany her, a guiding light through whatever shadows they might encounter. Their departure wasn't just a farewell; it was a step toward new beginnings, woven with the threads of their shared past and the limitless possibilities of the future.

The room, adorned with warm, familiar touches, seemed to envelop them like a comforting embrace, shielding them from the uncertainty ahead. The large windows were dressed in sheer curtains that danced gently in the breeze, reflecting a tranquility that contrasted sharply with the storm of emotions swirling within.

Mirabelle, caught in a blend of pride and melancholy, felt tears glide down her cheeks. She made no attempt to hide them; they were a testament to the deep, unwavering love that only a mother can hold. With a barely audible whisper, she addressed her daughters:

"My little navigators, may each wave carry you to discover treasures that only brave hearts can see."

Lumina and Aisling turned toward her, and without needing words, they threw themselves into her arms. That moment, eternal and unbreakable, became a sanctuary in time, where love cloaked them in the courage needed to face the unknown.

After embracing their mother, Aisling approached her father, her eyes shimmering with a wisdom that belied her youth. Looking directly into his eyes, with the seriousness of someone grasping her place in the vast universe, she said:

"Father, we are like stars in the sky, reflecting what we have been and what we will become."

Odran, moved by the purity of his daughter's words, nodded slowly, recognizing the brilliance of her truth. His understanding went beyond mere words, connecting with the essence of the young woman who, though she did not yet know it, was stepping toward a grand destiny.

Finally, their grandmother, ever the guardian of tradition and protocol, regarded her granddaughters with an air of noble solemnity.

"Majesty," she declared, intertwining her hands before her heart, "I will honor your name and future reign. May your journey be as glorious as the lineage you represent."

With those words, the scene culminated in a perfect moment of familial unity, where each member stood as a pillar, supporting one another with love and strength, as the path to the unknown unfolded, promising adventures yet to be discovered.

On a dusty road winding through the endless fields of Wisconsin, a 1950s diner stood alone, glistening in the scorching sun. The neon sign flickered wearily, casting an anachronistic glow that barely illuminated the diner's exterior. Inside, the atmosphere was steeped in nostalgia: red vinyl chairs, a jukebox humming in the corner, and waitresses moving with a choreographed efficiency. The air was thick with the tantalizing scent of sizzling hamburgers, mingled with the aroma of freshly brewed coffee.

De Lucas, an unassuming man with a flicker of sinister mischief in his eyes, was lost in thought. He wore a worn-out jacket and jeans that seemed to have seen better days. Beside him lay a grease-stained newspaper that he perused with mild disinterest. His car, an old Ford with no remorse, had been stolen from the family he had massacred and waited with the keys dangling in the ignition.

Outside, leaning deliberately against the hood of the Ford, Lilith waited. Her figure radiated a mix of patience and authority, as if each passing second slid off her skin without leaving a trace. She watched through the window as De Lucas raised his hand, calling the waitress to settle his bill.

The waitress, flashing an automatic smile, handed De Lucas his change while he murmured a polite thanks. He stood up from the booth, trying to exude nonchalance, though the tension within him was palpable. As he stepped outside, the blast of heat welcomed him, leading him to the car where Lilith awaited, unyielding.

Upon seeing her, the first instinct was a surge of alarm, an almost reflexive urge to escape. But something in Lilith's expression held him in place, as if he sensed that any attempt to flee would be futile. With hesitant steps, he approached her, hands stuffed into his pockets and a forced smile on his lips.

Lilith: "So, De Lucas. I saved you from the darkness, and the only thing you can think to do is butcher a family?"

De Lucas managed a grimace of indignation and confusion, quickly retorting,

De Lucas: "I didn't do anything, ma'am. How do you know this? I've been following the news, and there hasn't been a—"

His words trailed off, caught in the realization of the futility of his defense as Lilith's eyes bore down on him. The weight of her presence was suffocating, wrapping around him like a vise. In that moment, he knew he was trapped—not just by her words, but by the gravity of the actions that had led him here.

Lilith smiled with a chilling calmness, her gaze piercing through any facade that De Lucas attempted to maintain. She knew far more than he could have imagined—beyond the reach of newspapers and news reports.

"I don't need the press to know what you've done. You forgot that you operate under an invisible cloak to the world, but not to me."

The wind blew softly, carrying away the distant sound of a car on the road. De Lucas, anxiety coursing through his veins, broke eye contact and moved back toward the car, desperately trying to cling to the last remnants of control over the situation.

With a deep breath, he slid into the driver's seat and turned the key, the engine roaring to life with a thunderous growl. As he sped away, his thoughts spiraled chaotically, struggling to decipher how Lilith, that seductive and terrifying entity, had known about his crime without a doubt.

It wasn't long before he glanced in the rearview mirror and felt a fresh wave of terror wash over him. There, in the back seat, sat Lilith with casual ease.

"Hello, idiot."

De Lucas, unable to suppress the panic rising in him, jerked the steering wheel violently, the car swerving dangerously. Tires screeched as the vehicle veered off course, skidding out of control toward a precipice that teased the horizon.

An instant later, the car careened down the slope, disappearing among the trees and foliage like a wounded beast. Meanwhile, Lilith remained on the road, watching the scene unfold with a blend of indifference and satisfaction.

"Useless fool," Lilith murmured, her voice low, almost a whisper.

The echo of her words hung in the air as silence reclaimed the landscape, enveloping the now-deserted road as if it had all been a mere dream lost in the clamor of the day.

The Journey of Aisling and Lumina

At the threshold between the familiar forest and the unknown, Aisling and Lumina prepared to embark on a journey that would echo through the annals of the fairy realm. They carried with them not just physical luggage, but also the hopes and dreams of those they were leaving behind.

Aisling clutched a suitcase fashioned from soft birch bark, intricately woven with moonlit lilies that glowed softly in the morning twilight. Inside, whispers of ancient melodies promised protection and warmth. Beside her, a radiant satchel woven from golden threads and adorned with starlit flower petals held small treasures: fairy dust, dawn crystals, and an enchanted map that revealed its path only when the traveler's heart was in tune.

Lumina, Aisling's inseparable companion, sported a satchel made of arcane leaves, flanked by runes of light. Within it, she carried sparks of laughter from the past, memories of shared adventures, and a vial of solar laurel to illuminate any dark path ahead.

Behind them, on a trail of contained excitement, their father, Odran, and mother, Mirabelle, approached with unshed tears of unabashed pride in their eyes. The Queen Mother, Aisling's grandmother, appeared serene, but her farewell embrace was steeped in wisdom and love.

"Aisling, my little star," whispered Odran, cupping her face in his hands. "Remember, this journey is just another step on the vast map of your life. Never stop seeking your own constellations."

Aisling smiled through her tears, nodding as she clung to each word with devotion.

Mirabelle, embracing Aisling first and then Lumina, added with a trembling yet resolute voice, "Have courage and know that our light will always guide your way. Trust in the magic you carry within."

With one last embrace, their parents' tears fell, glistening like crystals as they touched the ground, each drop a reflection of eternal love.

As Aisling and Lumina turned toward the path ahead, the air crackled with possibility. The enchantments of their world lingered in the breeze, a whisper of reassurance that their journey, however daunting, would forge a new chapter in their lives. With hearts full of hope and minds set on discovery, they stepped into the unknown, ready to weave their own stories among the stars.

In silence, Aisling turned to the Queen Mother, who gently placed a moon tear pendant around her neck—an amulet that had been passed down through generations. "You are never alone, my dear. These are just new beginnings. As you journey forth, always remember who you are."

Aisling and Lumina stood at the frontier between their familiar world and the new one filled with promises. Behind them, the gathering of fairies and sprites waved goodbye, forming a vibrant tapestry of laughter and song, their farewells filling the air with a sense of anticipation and hope.

The magical circle glowing before them resembled a black hole, but instead of darkness, it emanated a whirlpool of vivid colors and golden sparkles. It was a mystical gateway to the unexpected, a crucible of future dreams.

Aisling took a deep breath, her fingers interlaced with Lumina's as they stepped forward together toward the portal. With their first step, the air hummed with a radiant glow and a sweet resonance, akin to the promise of future adventures. Crossing the threshold, they were enveloped by a warm sensation, like an eternal embrace from the universe itself.

Behind them, friends and family watched with pride and love that transcended words, sensing that although they were embarking on the unknown, they were destined to leave a trail of eternal magic in the wake of everyone they encountered.

And so, with each step, Aisling and Lumina penned another chapter in their story—a tale that belonged not only to them but also to the world they eagerly chose to explore.

Welcome to the Marine Kingdom

Through the whirlwind of shimmering colors, Lumina and Aisling emerged, blinking in awe at the new landscape that unfolded before them. They found themselves in a hidden cove along the Costa Brava, a place where the land embraced the sea with a loving caress. The golden sand stretched out like a soft carpet leading to the deep blue of the Mediterranean, where the waves whispered ancient secrets to the shore.

Aisling closed her eyes for a moment, letting the sea breeze brush against her face, carrying away any lingering traces of uncertainty. Beside her, Lumina exhaled softly, a mix of wonder and relief escaping her lips. Though they felt a bit disoriented, the warmth of the sun and the salty scent of the air welcomed them into a new chapter of their journey.

Before them, at the edge of the cove, stood the princess of the sea, their aunt Seraphina. Her presence was both commanding and serene, like the tide itself. Her blue-tinted hair flowed freely in the wind, and her deep purple-blue eyes sparkled with an unmistakable blend of joy and tenderness as she spotted her nieces.

In her hands, she held a unique bouquet, not of flowers, but of iridescent seashells and vividly colored seaweed, creating a breathtaking display of maritime hues. The shells shimmered with pearlescent reflections, while the marine plants seemed to pulse with life, reflecting the sunlight dancing upon the water.

"Welcome, dear nieces!" Seraphina exclaimed in a melodious voice as she stepped forward to embrace them. "This is your new home, or at least a temporary refuge along this beautiful coast. I am so happy to have you here."

Aisling and Lumina melted into their aunt's warm embrace, feeling a comfort that erased any lingering fears. The joy of reunion filled their hearts, and the tears that fell were ones of pure happiness.

Surrounding them, a chorus of sea fairies watched with excitement. Unlike their woodland counterparts, these fairies boasted bodies adapted to the aquatic world. With a simple motion, some transformed their legs into shimmering tails, ready to dive into the sea and glide gracefully through its depths with effortless speed.

In that enchanting moment, as the laughter of the sea fairies mingled with the gentle lapping of the waves, Aisling and Lumina knew they had stepped into a realm alive with magic and possibility, a place where their adventures were just beginning.

Welcome to the Marine Kingdom

Through the whirlwind of shimmering colors, Lumina and Aisling emerged, blinking in awe at the new landscape that unfolded before them. They found themselves in a hidden cove along the Costa Brava, where the land gently embraced the sea. The golden sand stretched out like a soft carpet leading to the deep blue of the Mediterranean, where the waves whispered ancient secrets as they lapped against the shore.

Aisling closed her eyes for a moment, allowing the sea breeze to caress her face, taking with it any lingering traces of uncertainty. Lumina, next to her, exhaled softly, a blend of wonder and relief in her breath. Though they felt a bit disoriented, the warmth of the sun and the salty scent of the air welcomed them into a new chapter of their journey.

Before them, at the edge of the cove, awaited the sea princess, their aunt Seraphina. Her presence was both imposing and serene, much like the tide itself. Her blue-tinted hair flowed freely in the wind, and her deep purple-blue eyes sparkled with an unmistakable mix of joy and tenderness upon seeing her nieces.

In her hands, she held a unique bouquet, crafted not from flowers but from iridescent seashells and vibrant seaweeds, creating a stunning visual display of marine colors. The shells shimmered with pearlescent reflections, while the marine plants seemed to pulse with life, reflecting the playful dance of sunlight on the water.

"Welcome, dear nieces!" Seraphina exclaimed in a melodious voice as she stepped forward to embrace them. "This is your new home, or at least a temporary refuge along this beautiful coast. I'm so happy to have you here."

Aisling and Lumina melted into their aunt's warm embrace, feeling a comfort that erased any lingering fears. The joy of reunion filled their hearts, and the tears that fell were born of pure happiness.

Surrounding them, a chorus of sea fairies watched with excitement. Unlike their woodland counterparts, these fairies had bodies adapted to the aquatic realm. With a simple gesture, some transformed their legs into shimmering tails, poised to dive into the sea and glide effortlessly through its depths.

In that enchanting moment, as laughter and magic mingled in the air, Aisling and Lumina knew they had stepped into a world alive with possibilities. This new chapter was not just a continuation of their journey; it was a chance to discover themselves, to embrace their destinies within the vibrant tapestry of the Marine Kingdom.

"Tell us everything about your journey," Seraphina requested, her satisfaction evident. "The sea holds wonderful secrets that I'm eager to share with you."

The cove buzzed with life as the sea fairies celebrated the arrival of Aisling and Lumina. Songs, keeping rhythm with the waves, soared into the sky, intertwining with laughter and the dances of aquatic creatures.

The newcomers explored the coastline, discovering hidden grottos and natural pools where colorful fish swam among their feet.

As the sun dipped toward the horizon, casting its orange and violet hues across the sky, Aisling and Lumina settled beside Seraphina. They gazed out at the vast ocean, feeling a deep sense of peace and the promise of adventures yet to come. They knew that this world was just another piece in the tapestry of their journey, a place where the boundaries between land and sea dissolved, revealing infinite possibilities.

"This is just the beginning, right, Aunt Seraphina?" Lumina asked, her eyes shining with curiosity about what lay ahead.

"Indeed, my dear," Seraphina replied, gently stroking her hair. "Together, we will uncover the secrets of the ocean and beyond. The universe always offers more magic to those who seek with an open heart."

With a renewed sense of belonging and a thirst for adventure, the two sisters submerged themselves in the joy of their new home, confident that the dawn would bring new wonders.

Welcome to the Marine Palace

Through the sparkling waters of the fairy marine dimension, Aisling and Lumina ventured into a magnificent city that blended the classical splendor of ancient Greek design with imaginative modern touches. Gleaming white buildings shone under the sunlight, adorned with elegant bridges spanning crystal-clear canals, and a school promised teachings as vast as the ocean itself.

The air around them was filled with the scent of salt and the sounds of playful laughter, inviting them into a world where the magic of the sea intertwined with the vibrant lives of its inhabitants. As they navigated through this enchanting place, Aisling and Lumina felt the stirrings of a new chapter, one filled with boundless potential and adventures waiting to unfold.

Upon arriving at Aunt Seraphina's palace, Aisling and Lumina were overwhelmed by its grandeur. The white classical columns and marble stairs that descended directly into the sea created an ambiance of majesty and mystery. Soft tones of linen and cotton—creams and blues—imbued the environment with a serene elegance.

"It's incredible," Aisling murmured, her eyes wandering over every detail with fascination. "I've never seen anything so beautiful."

"Neither have I," Lumina agreed, nodding as she gazed at the sea through the crystal walls—an awe-inspiring display of vibrant corals and multicolored fish darting among the currents.

In the underwater garden, a mermaid was diligently adjusting plants that seemed to dance with the tide. Spotting Lumina, she winked conspiratorially.

"I can't believe I can breathe down here!" Lumina exclaimed, first glancing at the mermaid and then turning to her aunt with genuine curiosity.

Seraphina chuckled softly at her amazement. "She's a sea fairy, dear. They know how to extend their time underwater using ancient techniques."

The young women nodded slowly, spellbound by the blend of magic and nature surrounding them.

As they continued their tour, they arrived at their rooms. When they opened the doors, renewed astonishment washed over them: two grand beds adorned with mother-of-pearl and decorated with glimmering oyster pearls shimmered in the warm marine light.

"Are we really going to live here?" Aisling asked, her laughter bubbling with incredulity.

"Yes," Seraphina laughed, her expression radiating satisfaction. "This will be your home while you're here, but remember, we start your lessons promptly at 8 A.M."

The girls exchanged glances, trying to contain their excitement. "Seraphina, this place is magical," Lumina remarked, her eyes shining as she took in their surroundings.

Behind them, a group of sprites busily organized their luggage. Their nimble hands carefully unpacked the girls' belongings, arranging them in their new spaces while the fairy eyes continued to admire the breathtaking scene outside through the crystal walls.

In that moment, Aisling and Lumina felt a sense of belonging and anticipation for the adventures that awaited them, knowing they were about to embark on a journey unlike any they had ever experienced.

"Everything in this place is... more than I could have ever dreamed," Aisling said, pressing her hand against the glass and watching as a silver fish swam gracefully by.

"Well, my dears, it's time to rest now," Seraphina replied, her smile warm and tender. "Tomorrow's adventure will be as magnificent as this welcome."

As the palace lights glowed softly under the aquatic shimmer, Aisling and Lumina nestled into their mother-of-pearl beds, the thought of new experiences filling their minds just before sleep took hold. The gentle ebb and flow of the water outside their window was soothing, and the glass walls revealed a vibrant world that promised unimaginable discoveries.

The two girls understood that their time in the Marine Kingdom would offer not only grand adventures but also deeper bonds with the magic that surrounded them. With the distant songs of sirens resonating in the air, they embraced their new home, filled with excitement for what awaited them at dawn.

As slumber began to claim them, dreams of shimmering oceans, hidden treasures, and the enchanting magic of their new life danced through their minds, weaving a tapestry of hope and possibility. In that moment, under the protective glow of Seraphina's love and the whispers of the sea, Aisling and Lumina felt the promise of a future brimming with potential and adventure.

"Everything in this place is... more than I could have ever dreamed," Aisling said, pressing her hand against the glass as she watched a silver fish gracefully glide by.

"Well, my dears, it's time to rest now," Seraphina replied, her smile warm and nurturing. "Tomorrow's adventure will be just as magnificent as this welcome."

As the soft lights of the palace shimmered beneath the aquatic glow, Aisling and Lumina settled into their mother-of-pearl beds, thoughts of new experiences swirling in their minds just before sleep claimed them. The gentle rhythm of the water outside their window was soothing, and the glass walls revealed a vibrant world that promised unimaginable discoveries.

The two friends knew that their time in the Marine Kingdom would offer not only grand adventures but also a deepened connection with the magic that enveloped them. As the distant songs of the sirens echoed in the background, they embraced their new home, filled with excitement for the dawn and all it would bring.

In that moment, with the soft glow of Seraphina's love surrounding them and the whispers of the ocean lulling them to sleep, Aisling and Lumina felt the promise of a future rich with potential and enchanted journeys waiting just beyond the horizon.

Dilemma of Lilith**

Lilith stood motionless at the edge of the spot where Delucas had lost control of his vehicle, her gaze fixed on the landscape under a watchful moon that barely illuminated her face. At the very precipice, both of the physical road and her psyche, uncertainty enveloped her like a dense, oppressive veil.

For centuries, she had chosen the path of power at any cost, a route paved with acts of wickedness and selfish decisions. Yet in that moment, satisfaction seemed to dissipate into a chasm of emotional emptiness. Inside, she wondered if it had ever truly been worth it—all the evil she had wrought and the lives she had affected.

Memories of times filled with luxury and excess resonated within her, mere shadows of happiness that had never satisfied her longing for belonging. "Can power really buy inner peace?" she mused, her voice barely a whisper against the night wind.

She knew well that her master, the demon, had the ability to read minds, infiltrate souls, and nurture darkness. This made any attempt at redemption all the more complicated. "But there must be a way," she thought defiantly, as the murmurs of her surroundings echoed her own internal doubts.

Caught between uncertainty and conviction, Lilith contemplated potential instructions for her dark master. Reviving Stalin and Hitler to orchestrate a new coup between 2030 and 2049 was her latest idea. She was well aware of their flaws as leaders, yet their unyielding malevolence and ability to influence could prove useful once more in the hands of Satan.

Thoughts coursed through her mind like a black river, maneuvering the pieces of her wicked chess game. "I must plan this to perfection," she murmured to herself, while the air around her thickened with a sinister, penetrating echo of her decision.

With the weight of her choices pressing down, Lilith stood at the crossroads of her existence, contemplating whether to continue down the dark path she had forged or seek redemption from the very darkness she had embraced for so long. The night pulsed, and she knew that the next move would determine not only her fate but also the fate of countless others caught in the web of her ambition.

However, beneath the apparent advantage of her dark world, something deep within her reluctant spirit yearned for the truth of peace, even though she did not yet know the way. Her eyes, usually cold and hardened, flickered momentarily with unfulfilled longing.

Lilith contemplated not only how to serve her diabolical master but also the possibility of transcending the very darkness that had defined her existence. "Perhaps not all is lost," she thought, scrutinizing every crack in the decisions that had led her to this point.

As she devised a plan to contact her master, Lilith sensed her soul awakening to the silent clamor of her conscience. There was so much at stake, and even though the thought of redemption meant confronting a mortal risk, she understood that the darkest souls could often find light in the most unexpected places.

Around her, the wind howled softly. Lilith knew that the path to personal peace would be long and fraught with obstacles, but perhaps—just perhaps—there was room for a new beginning in this complex universe.

As she lifted her gaze to the night sky, her mind began to formulate a plan to confront, for once, the rebirth of her own humanity. In the final twist of this chapter, she resolved to allow a spark of hope to ignite new and unexpected paths in her enigmatic journey. She would need to learn how to shield her thoughts from the devil, who possessed the virtue of reading minds, using that power to influence their thoughts and amplify their ego, malice, and selfishness.

The Shadows' Plan

In the heart of hell, within a vast chamber where shadows danced as if they had a life of their own, Satan presided over his secret meeting. He sat on a commanding throne made of blackened bones, embodying absolute power. Before him, the general of his infernal legion stood at attention, detailing the logistics for the "Grand Day," an event that would alter the course of humanity.

"My Lord," the general began, his voice resonating with authority, "we will have an army of one hundred thousand souls surrounding the World Summit. With numbers like these, the police forces—barely reaching ten thousand—will be powerless to withstand our influence."

Satan's crimson eyes glowed with an inner fire as he nodded slowly, pleased with the magnitude of the plan. "Proceed," he commanded, his tone deep and resonant.

"I, along with my chief commander, will accompany you," the general continued, "to deliver your speech. When the attendees gaze out the window, they will confront our infinite army, compelling them to bow to your will."

The room, thick with darkness and an atmosphere that felt almost suffocating, fell silent as the plan took shape. Just then, Lilith entered the chamber with captivating grace.

"My Lord," she interjected softly, offering an elegant bow before continuing, "I have a suggestion."

The general shot her a disdainful glance, sensing a threat to his carefully laid plans, but Satan gestured for her to proceed.

"The other day, while I was relaxing," Lilith recounted in an almost seductive tone, "I noticed the souls of Hitler and Stalin trying to catch my attention, banging against the glass. They could be invaluable for our scheme."

Satan maintained an inscrutable expression, yet a renewed interest flickered in his eyes. "And what do you propose, Lilith?" he asked, each word dripping with millennia of authority.

Lilith's proposal was intriguing. "Imagine, my lord, delivering your speech and then bringing them in. Their very presence would ensure they know you speak the truth. The history and horror of their times would guarantee obedience."

As she spoke, a chill ran through the chamber—a blend of fascination and dark anticipation of the power that lay ahead. This was a bold strategy, one that could unite past terrors with present ambitions, and Lilith could sense that her words had struck a chord. The game was afoot, and in this sinister dance of power, she was ready to take center stage.

The general could not mask his disagreement; his jealousy bubbled over uncontrollably. "My Lord," he interjected cautiously, "with all due respect, allowing them to shine again could be a grave mistake."

Lilith, wearing a sly smile, quickly countered, "Of course, you will always stand above them. You, my dear general, will be the general of generals."

Satan pondered Lilith's words, weighing the possibilities. His chamber, illuminated only by low flames, seemed to come alive, absorbing the drama of her proposal. "Interesting," he finally said, a smile spreading across his face—one that promised impending catastrophe. "We could use these ancient tyrants to ensure the impact of our strike."

Though his pride had been pricked, the general nodded, recognizing the wisdom in following his master's lead. "I will be ready, my lord," he promised, his mind already beginning to adjust the pieces of the master plan.

With the plan laid out, the commitment of their followers renewed, and the promise of resurrected horror in the air, the darkness in Satan's chamber deepened further. Lilith bowed with subtle grace, knowing she had secured the next link in her chain of influence.

In the heart of infernal power, the gears began to turn, and every soul involved in the game sensed that soon, the weight of darkness would descend upon the mortal realm like an unstoppable storm.

Preparations for the First Journey

Six months had passed since Aisling and Lumina arrived in their aunt Seraphina's splendid marine world. During that time, they immersed themselves in studying the seas and the threats humans posed to marine life. Now, after intensive lessons and countless conversations with oceanic creatures, they felt ready for their first foray into the human dimension. Excitement and nervousness intertwined as they sat down with their aunt to discuss the final details.

"Aisling, do you have the amulet that the sage gave you?" Seraphina asked, a blend of tenderness and concern reflected in her eyes.

Aisling nodded, a spark of determination shining in her gaze. "Yes, Aunt. We haven't forgotten a thing," Lumina chimed in, smiling brightly. "We've double-checked everything."

"Remember," Seraphina advised, "start with simple tasks. This way, you'll learn how the human mind works, which can be incredibly complex. Don't rush into situations that may turn dangerous."

"And we must remember about Satan," Aisling interjected, recognizing the gravity of the warning.

"Exactly," Seraphina affirmed, her expression sobering. "He resides in many humans, interfering with their thoughts and actions. You'll need the proper protection. You must find the sword of Saint Michael and take it with you."

Lumina frowned. "But we don't know how to use a sword..."

"That doesn't matter," Seraphina reassured them. "Simply carrying it will provide you with protection and strength. Now, have you decided what your first intervention will be?"

The two young women exchanged knowing glances before responding in unison, "Yes."

The three of them laughed together, feeling a slight relief at the formality of the moment.

Planned Interventions

"First, we're going to target the whaling ships," Aisling explained with conviction. "We need to stop the indiscriminate hunting of endangered whales."

Their resolve was firm, fueled by the knowledge that their mission was crucial not only for the ocean's inhabitants but for the delicate balance of life itself. Together, they would step boldly into the unknown, ready to champion the cause of those who could not fight for themselves.

"And afterward," Lumina added, "we'll tackle the planes that release chemtrails. We need to stop them from polluting the skies and contributing to droughts."

Seraphina smiled at their determination. "That's a noble start. Remember, you possess the knowledge and magic necessary to make a difference."

To seal their commitment, Seraphina offered them a glass filled with a potion made from aquatic plants. The liquid shimmered a vibrant green in the light and emitted a fresh, revitalizing aroma. "Drink this. It will provide clarity and energy for your missions."

Aisling and Lumina took the glasses and drank the delightful concoction, feeling a wave of rejuvenation cascade through their bodies.

With their plan set and Seraphina's support behind them, Aisling and Lumina were ready to embark on their first mission in the human realm. As the sun began to dip below the ocean's surface, casting golden hues throughout the marine palace, the two young women felt more prepared than ever to face the challenges that lay ahead.

"We're ready," Aisling declared, her eyes filled with gratitude as she looked at her aunt. "Thank you for everything, Aunt. We promise to be careful."

"I trust you," Seraphina replied, pulling them both into a warm embrace. "Go and make the fairies proud."

This would be the first step in a myriad of adventures to come, guided by their hearts and strengthened by the magic that had always been by their side.

Arrival in the Human Dimension

In the mystical portal that bridged the dimensions, Aisling and Lumina, the young fairies, stood poised for their incursion into the human world. Before them, the tunnel shimmered with lights that danced like captured stars. Their aunt Seraphina, draped in a flowing cloak of marine silk, was there to offer her final blessing.

"Dear nieces," Seraphina began, her voice enveloping them in understanding and love, "the journey ahead will be fraught with challenges, but it will also present opportunities for healing and changing the lives of many."

"Aunt, your guidance has been invaluable. We promise to remember your teachings," Aisling affirmed, squeezing her aunt's hands.

Lumina added with determination, "We know it won't be easy, but we are ready."

Seraphina smiled, her eyes shining with pride. "I trust in your inner strength and the unbreakable bond that unites you. Fill yourselves with courage, let kindness guide you, and remember, the true magic lies within you."

With a warm embrace, Seraphina bid them farewell, allowing the strong current of the portal to envelop them in a vibrant journey toward their new mission.

As they emerged on the other side of the tunnel, Aisling and Lumina landed softly on the well-kept grass of a city park. Dressed as ordinary teenagers of the time, their appearances stood in stark contrast to the modern metropolis surrounding them. Their beauty and the shimmering aura they radiated made them conspicuous.

"Lumina, we need to dim this light around us, or they'll realize we don't belong here," Aisling said, a hint of anxiety creeping into her voice.

"You're right, but… how do we do that?" Lumina replied, hesitating as she glanced at her softly glowing hands.

Their discussion was abruptly interrupted by the shout of an elderly woman. "My phone! My purse!" she cried, pointing at a young man racing away.

The sudden chaos jolted them both into action, their instincts kicking in. Aisling exchanged a quick look with Lumina, understanding without words that this was the moment to adapt and blend in. They had a mission to complete, and the human world was filled with unexpected challenges—challenges they would face together, united in purpose and determination.

Without hesitation, the sisters sprang into action. In an instant, thanks to their speed and agility, they blocked the path of the young thief.

"Please return what isn't yours," Aisling said firmly.

The boy smirked, an air of irony in his demeanor. "Well, come take it from me, princess," he retorted disdainfully.

Lumina didn't hesitate. In a swift motion, she lifted him from the ground by his collar, leaving him suspended in shock. "Okay, okay, fine," he stammered, notably intimidated. "Here, take it back. Please, don't hurt me."

After the boy returned the purse and phone, Aisling and Lumina gently set him down. The elderly woman, visibly relieved and grateful, blessed them with words of gratitude. "You're like angels," she exclaimed, her eyes shining with admiration.

Still glowing, the two sisters shared a soft laugh as the woman walked away. They understood that maintaining a low profile would be crucial, yet they also felt the power of kindness and the immediate impact they could have on the human world.

"This is just the beginning," Aisling said, adjusting her hair as her radiant glow gradually faded thanks to a newly discovered mental trick from Lumina. "We're going to uncover so much more here."

And so, with their first success resonating in their hearts, the two young sorceresses ventured deeper into the city, ready to face the challenges their mission would present.

Exploring the World

Following their shocking arrival in the human realm and having aided an elderly woman in distress, Aisling and Lumina now faced a new reality: they needed to find a place to live. They walked along a bustling city avenue, surrounded by people rushing to and fro, most of them lost in their thoughts, oblivious to the extraordinary presence of the two sisters.

The aroma of hot asphalt mingled with the enticing scents wafting from storefronts offering a plethora of goods, creating a unique and chaotic atmosphere that tingled at their senses. As they navigated the throngs of humanity, Aisling and Lumina sensed the pulse of the city—a vibrant tapestry of life filled with stories waiting to be discovered.

Drawing from the courage ignited during their encounter with the thief, they felt a renewed determination to find their place in this bustling world, eager to see what other adventures lay ahead. With each step, they embraced the thrill of the unknown, ready to weave their own tale into the rich fabric of human life.

"I don't know, sister, where are we supposed to live?" Lumina asked, casting a puzzled glance at the bustling humans around them.

"I'm not sure," Aisling replied, taking a deep breath to calm the unease stirring within her amidst so many worried faces. "These humans look… exhausted, hardly happy."

"Look!" Lumina exclaimed, pointing at a real estate agency with large windows displaying pictures of luxury homes. "Maybe they can help us!"

They approached the storefront, where imposing houses with stunning blue pools adorned the display, accompanied by dream-like prices that held no meaning for them. Still, their beauty drew them in like moths to a flame.

As they opened the door to the real estate office, a bell chimed to announce their entrance. The air conditioning offered a refreshing respite from the heat outside, filling the space with the rich aromas of fresh coffee and new paper. Three employees tapped away at shiny computers, but it was a man in his fifties who greeted them.

"How can I assist you?" he asked politely.

"I'd like to know where the house in the photo with the blue water is," Lumina said with a bright smile, referring to one of the homes with a pool she had seen.

"The one with the pool?" the man inquired, intrigued. "Because they all have pools."

"Yes, yes," Aisling nodded quickly.

"That house is on the outskirts of the city," he informed them.

"We want to know the address so we can move in," Lumina declared confidently, eliciting a mix of surprise and skepticism from the agent.

"But you would need to buy the house," the man replied, his tone growing more serious.

"Buy?" Lumina repeated, bewildered. "How do you buy?"

The conversation began to unfold, revealing the complexities of a world where buying a home was a commonplace endeavor, and Aisling and Lumina found themselves on the precipice of an unfamiliar reality. They exchanged glances, silently urging each other to navigate this new terrain together, ready to learn the rules of the game in a world that was both enticing and intimidating.

"Yes, my dear," the man explained with increasingly waning patience. "You pay money for the house, and it's not cheap."

One of the women at the back of the office stood up, noticing their exchange. "Please leave the office, or I will call the police," she warned, assuming the two young women intended to claim the house or steal it.

Before they could protest, the sisters found themselves outside, feeling the weight of hundreds of passerby gazes on their backs. "I told you, Lumina," Aisling murmured, confused and a bit indignant. "They're so strange and always seem angry."

"But what did we do wrong?" asked Lumina, sharing her bewilderment.

"I have no idea," admitted Aisling, looking around for answers that the human world seemed unwilling to provide.

As they walked away, the sisters realized they needed to adjust their approach. The human realm, with its implicit rules and peculiar value system, was an enigma waiting to be unraveled. The warm air and the constant buzz of the city created a strange symphony in their ears, so accustomed to the serenity of the Marine Kingdom.

Determined to keep a low profile, they decided to explore more of their surroundings to better understand how to proceed. The resolve glimmered in their eyes as they disappeared into the crowd, guardians of another world on a mission to heal a new one.

A Stone and Grass Altar

High above the bustle of Barcelona, Lumina and Aisling sat atop the towers of the Sagrada Familia. From their elevated vantage point, the air felt crisper, and the wind caressed their faces with a gentleness reminiscent of the world they had come from. The majestic structure loomed like a petrified forest, its intricate Gothic and modernist forms intertwining seamlessly with the sky.

"Well, this looks a bit more like our world, doesn't it?" Lumina remarked, admiring the abstract beauty of the towers that mimicked nature in stone.

Aisling nodded, feeling an unexpected sense of belonging amidst the grandeur. The sight of the towering spires, reaching toward the heavens, filled them with a renewed sense of purpose. Perhaps they could find their place here, blend the magic of the Marine Kingdom with the heartbeat of this vibrant city, and uncover the mysteries that lay waiting in the human realm.

Aisling nodded as she absorbed the infinite details of the basilica. "Yes, it almost feels as if these forms are alive and breathing. There's a magical energy here."

Reality returned, presenting a sprawling metropolis laid out before them—a sea of buildings and streets in constant motion. The lights from vehicles snaked through the city like nocturnal rivers under the starry sky.

"We hadn't considered getting a house," Aisling reflected, her tone tinged with a hint of melancholy. "And we didn't even ask how to go about it. We're alone in this."

"So what do we do now?" Lumina pondered, feeling the familiar chill of uncertainty grip her.

"We need to find somewhere to sleep and stay," Aisling suggested, her stomach growling softly, reminding her of her most basic need. "I'm hungry, but I don't see any flowers or anything to eat here."

"We'll have to learn from the humans," Lumina admitted with a sigh. "Maybe we should head to Sant Pere and retrieve the sword first. We need to get started on our purpose; otherwise, we won't get anywhere here."

Aisling glanced down the street, where a man was violently pushing another. "Look, that guy is hitting someone," she observed with sorrow and surprise.

"Well, it looks like there's no shortage of work to be done," Lumina murmured, trying to reconcile this stark vision of the human world with their capacity to make a difference.

The splendor of the Sagrada Familia, with its columns resembling intertwined trees and its nature-inspired motifs, reminded them that beauty could exist even in places of struggle and chaos. Yet, it also filled them with an urgent need to act, to begin draining the darkness clinging to the human world.

"We have to do something," Aisling declared, her determination as strong as a young sprout yearning to reach for the sun. "This world needs help, and while we can't change everything at once, we can start step by step."

With renewed resolve and the fire of purpose igniting within them, Aisling and Lumina set out into the city, ready to confront the challenges that lay ahead and determined to make their mark on the world.

Lumina smiled at her sister's resolve. "Yes, we will find a way to fulfill our mission. And perhaps, in the process, we'll discover more about this place."

They took a moment to absorb the view, allowing themselves to feel a bit of calm before embarking on their tasks.

"Come on," Lumina finally said, rising with an ethereal grace. "It's time to head down and find our sword."

As they moved away from their vantage point in those magnificent towers, they were acutely aware that the path ahead would not be easy. Yet, they were prepared to face each challenge with the strength, power, and light they carried from their magical origins.

Aisling and Lumina left behind the shadows of the stone towers, ready to illuminate the reality awaiting them below, where good and evil battled at the heart of humanity.

In the gardens surrounding the iconic Sagrada Familia, Aisling and Lumina found themselves entranced, their gazes drifting from the clear sky to the breathtaking architecture of the temple. The structure, a marvel of Gaudí's modernism, seemed to meld their magical world with a cathedral born of dreams. Vivid colors from the stained glass windows cast a brilliant array of lights across the interior, while columns rose like colossal stone trees, supporting a sculpted firmament.

"It's as if they're trying to construct a forest of stone," Aisling whispered, captivated by the way the columns branched off into limbs and leaves—a perfect reflection of the home they longed for.

"Yes, it feels almost mystical," Lumina replied, her voice barely audible as her eyes remained entranced by the colors spilling throughout the space. The towering ceilings echoed the majesty of mountains and skies, reminiscent of a world adorned with magic.

Suddenly, Lumina leaned closer to Aisling and whispered in her ear, "What did the man mean when he said there wasn't enough money for the house?" Her confusion was clear on her features. "What is money, Aisling?"

Aisling shook her head, her golden curls glinting in the light from the stained glass. "I don't know, Lumina," she confessed, lost in her own ponderings.

The concept of money felt foreign and distant to them, a mystery to unravel in this new world that was filled with both promise and confusion. Being anchored in their magical upbringing, they were determined to learn and adapt, ready to explore the unknown while holding tightly to their sisterly bond.

Not far away, a woman spoke to a boy who appeared to be her son. "Pedro, take this money and put it in the donation box, sweetheart," she said gently, handing him a crumpled bill.

Intrigued by this revelation, the sisters approached the woman. "Excuse me," Aisling began, her sincerity shining through. "Is this money?" she asked, pointing to the bill.

The woman stepped back slightly, sensing their almost childlike curiosity, a flicker of fear crossing her face as she wondered if they might try to take it from her.

"Can you show us?" Lumina pleaded with wide, curious eyes filled with wonder.

Seeing the genuine surprise in their expressions, the woman relented and displayed the bill, though she remained vigilant, watching their every move.

"And how do you get this, ma'am?" Aisling inquired, trying to grasp the complexity behind the simple piece of paper.

The woman huffed, a bit impatient but not unkind. "You earn it, dear, by working. Unless, of course, you find a way to make it," she replied quickly, her words heavy with simple truth.

Convinced the young women were mocking her answer, she shook her head and walked away, murmuring, "I won't believe it until I see it," leaving them increasingly bewildered.

As the woman faded into the crowd, the sisters remained silent for a moment, processing their conversation. The majesty of the Sagrada Familia loomed around them. The basilica, designed by the legendary architect Antoni Gaudí, had been under construction for over a century, funded entirely by donations from people all over the world. Its intricate facades and soaring towers were a testament to collective hope and faith, embodying a love that transcended time and distance.

"Do you think it would be possible for us to make it?" Lumina pondered, a thoughtful tone in her voice.

Aisling smiled, feeling not discouraged but rather inspired. "Maybe there are other things we can do here that are equally valuable," she suggested, gazing at the magnificent temple that surrounded them. "And we must remember our mission."

As they moved away from the gardens and back into the bustling city, Aisling and Lumina understood they had much to discover about the human world. The challenges they would face would be as vast as the columns of the Sagrada Familia, but they carried with them the promise of learning, helping, and perhaps finding their place within the fabric of this complex and fascinating existence.

Destiny had led them to consider bartering. As they rummaged through their belongings, Aisling discovered a necklace that shimmered with an iridescent glow, while Lumina proudly retrieved a pearl necklace—a gift from their aunt Seraphina.

Determined, they offered their trinkets to passersby, but their expressions of resolve failed to capture anyone's attention. Eventually, they stumbled upon a 24-hour jewelry shop tucked discreetly in the alcove of an old building—a place that still echoed with the charm of small shops from days gone by.

The streets around them were fragrant with the aroma of freshly baked bread and Mediterranean spices, guiding Aisling and Lumina to this vintage jewelry store, which represented their last hope of the night.

Inside, an elderly man stood behind the counter, polished by time, observing them with keen interest. Once an adventurer, he had drawn inspiration from vast landscapes to craft unique pieces of jewelry. Yet time and an internal struggle had confined him to this corner of the world, where the silent monotony of his shop became a constant reminder of the opportunities lost.

"How can I help you, ladies?" he asked, his voice weary but laced with curious anticipation.

"Look, we'd like to sell this necklace," Lumina said, extending the pearls toward him with a mix of hope and urgency, fully aware that their momentary solution hinged on the interest in the man's eyes.

The old man adjusted his monocle, inspecting the pearls under the dim yellow light that filled the space. The stairs leading to the shop were covered in a worn carpet that had once been vibrant, now barely a whisper of its once-luxurious past. The wrought iron banister was rusty, telling stories of days brighter and filled with promise.

"Excellent quality," he remarked, lifting his gaze to meet theirs. "You didn't steal these, did you?"

"No, sir! We're... in a difficult situation," Lumina insisted, the hunger and urgency in her voice as evident as the gleam in her eyes. It seemed their natural vitality was the last flicker of hope against the exhaustion that hung over the seller.

The man studied them closely, searching for the truth behind their plea. While they may have been young and out of place in this bustling city, Aisling and Lumina carried within them an undeniable resilience that made them more than mere visitors. They were on a mission, one that required courage and a touch of creativity to navigate the complexities of the human world.

As the weight of their circumstances settled among them, the potential for a brighter future still flickered at the edges of their determination.

"I offer you 50 euros," the old man said, well aware that this was far below the actual value. His past life had taught him to be cautious, but also not to show too much interest.

"But sir!" protested Aisling, recalling the price displayed in the window. "I saw one out there for 1,250 euros, clearly of lesser quality than ours."

A spark of recognition flickered in the man's eyes, reflecting the nostalgia of youthful blood he once possessed. Still, he attempted to maintain his commercial composure. "I have to make some profit, don't I?"

"We understand that, but we truly need your help," Lumina added, her tone touching the chords of compassion from someone who understood desperation all too well.

Seeing their honest faces, the shopkeeper softened slightly. "Well, perhaps—"

The old man sighed, but satisfied by the prospect of a considerable profit, he relented. "Alright, 300 euros. But I'll need your identification."

Lumina, not fully grasping the human term, raised her hand to show her glowing fairy identification. The jeweler stepped back, both astonished and fascinated. "That won't work," he stammered, unable to tear his gaze away from the palpable magic before him. "No passport, no sale."

Aisling gently intervened, her voice heavy with sincerity. "Sir, we've lost everything and were robbed. Our parents told us to sell something until they could send us help. Unfortunately, our home is far away."

The elderly man, observing the truth in their eyes, felt a surge of compassion mixed with the desire to acquire the necklace. "Alright, 250 euros without documents, deal?"

Lumina beamed with triumph. "300 or nothing."

As Aisling explained their situation—her sincerity resonating with the old vendor—the notion that genuine kindness still existed in the world began to disarm his skepticism. Wanting to help and simultaneously seize an excellent deal, he finally started counting the bills.

In that moment of negotiation, the connection formed was more than mere commerce; it was a bridge of understanding across different worlds, knitting their fates together in ways neither had expected.

"Alright, I'll make an exception," the elderly man murmured softly, a blend of warmth and professionalism in his tone. "You both seem like good girls. Remember to take care of yourselves."

"Thank you, sir!" both exclaimed, their hands trembling as they collected the money, fully aware of the significance this sale represented.

As they descended the stairs slowly, they felt the vibrations of years past resonating beneath their feet. Walking toward the street, the daylight greeted them with new challenges, while the old vendor gazed at the necklace he had just acquired, smiling to himself with the same spark of adventure he had long since lost.

For a moment, the souls of this old man and the new generation crossed paths, leaving a mark of hope and promise in the corridors of time.

After their encounter at the jewelry store, Aisling and Lumina ventured through the vibrant streets of Barcelona. The breeze carried the intoxicating scent of the Mediterranean, mingling with the urban hustle and bustle. They found their way, drawn by the warm, inviting aroma of a frankfurt, a fast-food joint that captured the essence and soul of the region, popular since the 1980s.

Upon crossing the threshold, they were welcomed by a cozy, lively atmosphere. The walls were adorned with framed photographs of Barcelona and yellowed newspaper clippings recounting the establishment's history. The smell of sautéed onions and spices floated in the air, a comforting embrace for their empty stomachs.

Lumina studied the menu hanging on the wall, her eyes devouring each picture with a ravenous appetite. "Look at that, Aisling. It has to be delicious," she murmured, admiring a hot dog topped with caramelized onions and vibrant condiments.

Aisling nodded, her gaze fixed on her own chosen dish, already feeling her taste buds awaken. "What could it be made of?" she wondered aloud, her love for new mysteries eliciting a smile as she watched other customers relish their snacks with delight.

At the end of the counter, a young waiter noticed their presence and approached with steaming plates in hand. He set the hot dogs before them, and the pair dug in with enthusiasm, each bite a celebration of flavors and textures that perfectly satisfied their hunger.

As they savored their meal, the flavors danced on their tongues, marking the beginning of their adventure in this new world, each moment bringing them closer together and deeper into the heart of the human experience.

They ordered water to accompany their meal, both feeling a bit hesitant to try human beverages and opting for something more familiar. As she devoured her first bite, Lumina, her mouth still full, exclaimed, "Aisling, order me another one, please!"

The waiter had been watching them, drawn not only by Aisling's undeniable beauty, which seemed almost otherworldly, but also by her genuine admiration for the food. "Is your friend hungry, huh?" he joked, smiling as he wiped down the counter.

Aisling returned the smile and gently nudged Lumina with her foot beneath the table. "Come on, Lumina, control yourself," she whispered.

However, Lumina, with a playful glint in her eye, shot back, "And you like my sister, don't you?"

The waiter hesitated, a flush creeping up his cheeks. "Oh, I'm sorry if I've offended you; that wasn't my intention."

Sensing his discomfort, Aisling intervened with a reassuring smile. "It's okay, just bring another one for my sister to go, please. Lumina really appreciates good food."

Lumina continued, "You're handsome, but my sister and I didn't come here to break hearts; we just wanted to eat."

Aisling shot her a look, half-amused and half-wishing for a bit more restraint. "Alright, Lumina. Just get the other sandwich, and we'll pay you for it," she concluded, her tone grateful as she glanced at the waiter, who still wore a remnant of a smile.

Intrigued by the sisters' accents but unable to place their origin, the young man nodded. "Sure, I'll be right back with it."

As the waiter walked away to prepare their order, Aisling and Lumina continued to enjoy their feast in a brightly lit corner of the establishment. Gradually, the earthly experience transformed into a revelation of grateful simplicity. The ambiance of the Frankfurt, with its warm lights and interiors adorned with memories, offered them a brief respite from their mission.

After settling the bill, they stepped out into the twilight-soaked streets of Barcelona, their stomachs full and a sense of belonging enveloping them in this vibrant world, albeit temporarily. The diner had given them more than just a meal; it had provided a first glimpse into the simple joys of human life, reminding them that light could be found in the most unexpected places.

With renewed strength, they braced themselves to face the challenges ahead, one step closer to their purpose.

The food had offered them a first glimpse into the simple joys of human life, reminding them that light could indeed be found in the most unexpected places. With renewed energy, they prepared to face the upcoming challenges, one step closer to their purpose.

Upon exiting the Frankfurt, Aisling and Lumina ventured into the heart of Barcelona's Gothic Quarter, a labyrinth of narrow, winding streets steeped in medieval history. The cobblestones beneath their feet echoed with each step, a persistent reminder of the ancient buildings draped in shadows around them.

While the captivating landscape did little to ease their concerns, they found their way to a stone bench in a small plaza. The whimsical glow of vintage streetlamps cast a magical and mysterious light over their surroundings.

"Aisling, why did you embarrass me?" Lumina murmured as they settled onto the bench, the sound muffled by the night air.

Aisling chuckled softly, her laughter resembling the familiar murmur of a gentle stream. "You don't remember what Grandma said, do you? No boys."

Aisling sighed, resigned. "Alright, fine. Let's remember what our positive magic teacher used to say," she suggested, a spark of inspiration igniting in her bright eyes. "Do you think we could use that to create more money?"

Lumina looked at her, determination and camaraderie gradually filling her expression. "Yes, but you just need to say the magic word."

Aisling opened her hand, placing the 100-euro bill they had sincerely earned in the center of her palm. Lumina concentrated and began reciting the ancient incantation they remembered from their lessons:

> "Flourish and multiply,
> like seeds upon the wind,
> let abundance call forth,
> by the power that I hold."

In an instant, the air around them shimmered with swirling light; the bills began to replicate until they were enveloped by a gentle shower of high-denomination notes. Miraculously, more than 500 bills materialized, cascading like autumn leaves to the ground, scattering with a soft whisper.

"Whoa, whoa!" Aisling exclaimed through astonished laughter. "That's enough, Lumina. We can't carry that many!"

As they tried to collect the raining money, giggles erupted between them, each note a testament to their burgeoning magic and the thrill of newfound possibilities. In that moment, the weight of their mission felt a little lighter, buoyed by laughter and the promise of adventure that lay ahead.

They both laughed, exhilarated by their achievement. Together, they gathered a total of 200 bills, carefully stowing them away in Aisling's backpack, heedless of the excess that remained scattered across the cobblestone plaza. They did not feel the need to possess more than necessary; money was merely a tool, not an end in itself.

"Lumina, you had a brilliant idea," Aisling said, leaning down to pick up her bag.

As they ventured deeper into the Gothic Quarter, the shadows lengthened, and the streets narrowed. Small balconies jutted out from the weather-worn facades of buildings, adorned with geraniums that clung tenaciously to life in the twilight. Ancestral statues inhabited the corners, seeming to watch passersby from their silent pedestals.

Finally pausing for a moment, they unfolded the enchanted map that would guide them to Sant Pere. The magical light emanating from the paper illuminated the dimness, marking their path with a gentle glow visible only to them.

After an hour of wandering, engrossed in the exploration of every neglected corner and story buried in time, Aisling and Lumina reached the outskirts of the Gothic Quarter, feeling the closeness of their purpose.

"Well, we've learned so much tonight," Aisling remarked, reflecting on the multitude of adventures and knowledge they had gained in just a single day.

"And what is yet to come," Lumina replied, her silhouette illuminated by a watchful moon.

Together, they vanished into the Barcelona night, leaving behind the echoes of laughter, magic, and the soft sounds of eternity that always accompany the truly brave on their journeys through the world.

CHAPTER 23

The Coup Begins

In the heart of Switzerland, the quaint and picturesque town of Davos buzzed with activity as it prepared for the World Economic Congress. The normally serene streets had transformed into a flurry of action. Flags fluttered in the wind from every corner, and gardeners worked diligently to ensure that every inch of the town reflected the importance of the event. Amidst the frantic hustle, Lilith stood out as an unmistakable figure of elegance and mystique.

With every step, Lilith radiated an air of mystery wrapped in grace. Her outfit, immaculate and sophisticated, set her apart from the bustling crowd, while her keen gaze absorbed every detail of her surroundings. She meticulously observed the streets, familiarizing herself with the congress entrances and memorizing the locations of emergency exits with calculated precision. Each element was stored in her mind, woven into a complex plan known only to her.

As she continued her exploration, a security guard noticed her idling near a restricted area. A sturdy man clad in a dark blue uniform that symbolized authority approached her with a mix of firmness and courtesy.

"Miss, you can't be here," the guard said, his voice a blend of professionalism and respect.

Caught in the act, Lilith pivoted on her heels, donning a charming smile. "I'm sorry," she replied suavely, her accent dripping with sophistication. "I got lost looking for my hotel. I assure you, I'll leave right away."

The guard, captivated by her elegance and hesitant to inconvenience such a distinguished lady, nodded his head. "Very well, miss. Please be careful and have a good day."

Lilith walked away with a slow, deliberate grace, ensuring she exhibited no signs of anxiety. Her goal was to remain inconspicuous, and her calm demeanor effectively convinced the guard of her innocence.

As she moved further away, Lilith had not only mentally cataloged all the necessary details, but she had also validated the effectiveness of her disguise. She knew that every aspect of her environment—from the décor to the security measures—would play a crucial role in her ultimate scheme.

The fresh air of Davos blew gently against her skin, a reassuring breeze that promised her plan was one step closer to fruition. With each measured stride, Lilith was prepared to initiate the carefully orchestrated coup that would alter the course of their world—and she embraced the thought with quiet determination.

The Effectiveness of Her Disguise

She was acutely aware of the effectiveness of her disguise. Each element of her surroundings—from the decor to the security—would play a role in her overarching scheme. The cool, fresh air of Davos caressed her skin as she moved away, a gentle breeze promising that her plan was one step closer to completion.

The World Economic Congress continued its preparations, oblivious to the machinations woven in its shadows. Lilith understood that success depended on every single detail, and with the same serenity with which she had arrived, she faded into the crowd, ready to take the next step in her elaborate intrigue.

A Journey Through Time

Just 681 miles away in a place steeped in history, Lumina and Aisling found themselves at the Abbey of San Pere de Rodes. Perched on an imposing mountain, the ruins of the ancient monastery stood as silent witnesses to centuries past. Roofless yet alive with spirit, the abbey seemed to survey the surrounding lands with a watchful eye.

Lumina gazed at the landscape, captivated. Her attention was drawn to a distant point, revealing a cosmic void hidden to all but the most evolved entities. "Look, Aisling, over there," she whispered, pointing at the opening.

The Hidden Cave

With their golden wings unfurling gracefully, the sisters ascended, moving toward the cave with the agility of two hummingbirds. Inside, a heavy silence was broken only by their quickened breaths. Aisling retrieved the amulet from the old sage, its green light illuminating the vast expanse of the cave. As they ventured a few meters in, they found their prize: the rusted sword of Saint Michael.

"Look, Lumina, there it is," Aisling murmured, her excitement barely contained.

In an effort to activate the sword, Lumina touched it—but nothing happened. In that tense moment, a terrifying noise reverberated throughout the cave. Fiery bolts of lightning erupted from the shadows, arcing toward the ceiling. The surprise was fleeting as Aisling grasped the sword again, illuminating its fiery red hilt and causing its steel to radiate a dazzling glow.

Suddenly, the first of many challenges emerged: a massive six-headed serpent confronted them, roaring ferociously.

As they faced this fearsome creature, the sisters stood together, ready to confront the trials ahead. With adrenaline coursing through their veins and the light of the sword shining brightly, they knew they had the strength and determination to overcome whatever darkness lay before them. This was their moment—a test not just of their prowess but of their bond as sisters on an extraordinary quest.

", Mistress Serpent," Aisling greeted with a hint of irony, her voice steady yet laced with courage. "We're here for the sword; it's our mission."

The serpent lunged forward, instinctively pushing them upward as they soared. The sisters spun gracefully in the air, artfully confusing their foe, who struggled to track their agile movements.

Aisling devised a stealthy plan; she caught one of the serpent's heads from behind, skillfully dislocating it. Lumina, taking note of her sister's technique, mirrored the action. As another head fell, the serpent, consumed by rage, swung its tail, striking Aisling and knocking her close to the sword.

A Twist of Fate: The Trap

Focused on protecting her sister, Lumina redirected the serpent's attention by striking at the remaining heads. Aisling, now positioned near her target, seized the opportunity amidst the chaos. "Last warning, Mistress Serpent!" she proclaimed firmly, raising the radiant sword. "Stop, or I'll sever all your heads."

The serpent hesitated, its shrewd eyes evaluating her resolve, but deep down, it launched itself at Aisling.

The sisters accelerated their flight, forming a whirlwind around the monstrous being. Aisling, thanks to Lumina's agility, wrapped a magical cord around the serpent's six heads, tying them together in an unbreakable knot as they whirled.

With a decisive motion, Lumina pulled the magical rope from her bag. "Now!" she shouted. As she tossed it, the shimmering cord coiled tightly around the serpent's thick neck, securing all its heads in an inescapable trap.

The serpent gasped silently, trapped but lacking the will to continue fighting; its dark gaze dimmed in surrender. The sisters, exhausted yet triumphant, took a moment to process their victory.

"We did it!" Lumina celebrated, her voice strong but filled with relief.

Aisling, confidently holding the now-glowing sword, smiled at her sister. "Let's move on to the next challenge."

They left the cave with firm steps, fully aware that their journey towards rectifying the human world was just beginning, but more prepared than ever to undertake it. The prophecy of the power hidden in the Monastery of San Pere de Rodes had now become a reality.

Skyward Bound

Sailing through the skies at a dizzying height, Aisling and Lumina stealthily approached one of the many planes allegedly tasked with dispersing chemicals in the atmosphere under the guise of commercial flights. With unyielding determination, they positioned themselves in front of the aircraft, their radiant forms contrasting sharply against the vast blue horizon.

As the jet hurtled closer, the sisters exchanged glances filled with unspoken understanding. This was their moment to confront yet another aspect of the darkness that plagued humanity. They were ready to shine light into the shadows and reclaim the skies for the sake of those unable to fight back.

Before confronting the crew, the sisters stealthily approached the small side windows of the plane. Peering in with curiosity and caution, they confirmed their worst fears: the cargo hold was crammed with massive barrels, all interconnected by an intricate network of tubes. Each tube snaked toward the back of the aircraft, where enormous fans spun furiously, propelling the toxic contents into the atmosphere.

"Did you see that, Lumina?" Aisling whispered, her eyes widening as she grasped the magnitude of the potential damage.

"Yes, those fans are spreading it all into the air. We have to stop them," Lumina replied, her voice thick with urgency.

With renewed determination, they positioned themselves in front of the aircraft's cockpit. Clinging to the glass, the sisters briefly matched the speed of the plane before moving back a few feet to observe the incredulous crew operating it. The astonishment was evident on the pilots' faces, their mouths slightly agape in disbelief.

"Commander," exclaimed the captain, gripping the controls tightly as the aircraft began to tilt left in an attempt to evade them. "Are you seeing this?"

"Yes, Captain, this can't be real," the commander responded, a trace of incredulity lacing his voice. With a touch of nervous humor, he added, "We didn't take any drugs, did we?"

"No, Captain, what do they want?"

Showcasing their acrobatic skills, Aisling and Lumina began performing aerial flips in front of the windshield, demonstrating their mastery of the skies. The two sisters danced in the air, sharing a playful moment before darting apart again.

With a dramatic gesture, Aisling mimicked speaking into a radio transmitter. "Stop polluting nature and its citizens, or we'll bring this plane down," she warned, broadcasting through the plane's radio frequency.

The pilots, momentarily perplexed and breathless, exchanged incredulous glances, unsure of how to respond to the surreal situation unfolding before them. The tension in the cockpit hung thick like fog, each second stretching out as they processed the extraordinary sight of two young fairies floating effortlessly outside their aircraft.

In that moment, Aisling and Lumina became more than just messengers of their realm; they embodied the very spirit of nature's fury, determined to reclaim the skies and halt the destructive forces arrayed against the world they cherished. Their mission had taken on new urgency, and as they prepared to act, the sisters felt the weight of every breath and the promise of consequences resonating in the air around them.

"But who are you?" exclaimed one of the pilots, clutching the radio tightly. The other added with a half-mocking chuckle, "Don't tell me Greenpeace has reached this level."

Lumina, tapping into her magical connection, responded with restrained fury: "No, sir, we're here to save nature. Don't you have families down below? Do you think they won't breathe this too? If you don't stop polluting right now, we won't hold back. And we promise you'll soon know what real smoke is."

To emphasize her point, Aisling and Lumina swooped forward, soaring in an arc about twenty-five feet above the plane. Electrical discharges began to crackle between their palms, a terrifying display of their power. Their laughter echoed with an otherworldly resonance that seemed to challenge the very wind.

As they approached again, Aisling raised her hand in an overtly friendly gesture that mimicked a radio transmitter. "So what's it going to be, Captain?" she asked, her tone a convincing blend of playfulness and threat.

The captain, beads of sweat forming on his forehead as he grasped the potential devastation of this unresolved conflict, gave Aisling a reluctant thumbs-up, indicating his agreement.

This aerial encounter would ultimately change more than just the course of a single flight. It was rumored that the pilots left the industry forever, carrying with them the shame and determination to forge their futures in nobler pursuits. The co-pilot, in particular, vanished from sight, leaving behind no trace of his previous life.

Soaring above the Alps, Aisling and Lumina were captivated by the immense beauty of the Swiss valleys. The lush green hills and snow-capped mountains beckoned them to descend, wrapping them in a warm embrace of nature and splendor. As they neared Davos, the vibrant decorations and flags caught their attention. Curiosity propelled them to land gracefully in the lively village, where the festive air seemed to infuse even the slightest breeze with excitement.

Feeling the thrill of new discovery, Aisling suggested, "Lumina, shall we grab a bite to eat?"

"Yes, that sounds good. Let's find a cozy place," Lumina replied, always eager to savor earthly delights.

Before long, they discovered a charming restaurant where a friendly maître d' recommended a fresh salad and a local pâté, truly a Swiss delicacy. As they enjoyed their meal, Aisling found herself distracted by a young couple at a nearby table, engrossed in a playful exchange of glances and nervous smiles.

"Why do people act so silly before falling in love?" Aisling asked, genuine confusion in her voice. "Why not just say 'I love you' and be done with it?"

"Don't you remember what our teacher said?" Lumina recalled. "In this dimension, mammals and other animals flirt before having offspring. I suppose they need to ensure they like each other, or I don't know, figure out what they're looking for."

Lumina, not hiding her own confusion, added, "Why do you ask me these questions? It seems a bit silly—just playing around."

The sisters burst into laughter, their joy warm and infectious, until a soft voice interrupted them.

A Twist: Lilith's Appearance

"Aisling, is that you?" asked a charming voice.

Aisling turned to see Lilith, who was watching her with a captivating smile. "Yes, it's me," she replied, astonished, as Lilith stepped forward to offer her hand.

"I'm Lilith. How is your father, Odran?" she inquired casually.

"You know him?" Aisling responded, her surprise evident.

"How could I not? He worked for me," Lilith declared, her tone laced with an unsettling familiarity.

The young women exchanged intrigued glances at the sudden mention of their father, who had lived five centuries ago in human time. The perception of time between them was relative, yet the coincidence felt undeniable.

"How did you know him?" Lumina pressed, eager to learn more.

Lilith's eyes sparkled with the promise of stories from yesteryears as she explained calmly, "Long ago, Odran collaborated on a mission that required both his wisdom and courage. His legacy has left deep marks. Even in this dimension, his influence endures."

As Lilith spoke, Aisling and Lumina absorbed her words, their minds racing with the implications of their father's past and the connection they now shared with this enigmatic figure. In the vibrant atmosphere of the restaurant, they could almost feel the threads of history weaving around them, drawing them into a narrative far greater than they had anticipated.

In the bustling restaurant of Davos, Lumina and Aisling shared a delicious meal. The unexpected arrival of Lilith, with her enveloping presence, transformed a simple lunch into a memorable encounter. As laughter and camaraderie filled the air, the sisters prepared to learn more about this mysterious figure who seemed to have ties to their past.

"Oh, please, have a seat," Lumina said, realizing they hadn't been the most gracious hosts. "We're a bit rude."

The three of them laughed, finding an easy camaraderie among themselves.

"Don't address me formally; just call me 'you,'" Lilith insisted with a friendly gesture.

"Oh, yes, yes!" Aisling and Lumina replied in unison.

"Are you girls going to be here for long?" Lilith asked, clearly interested in their plans.

"No, we're on our way to the Pacific," Aisling explained candidly. "We're going after whalers to stop them from killing more whales."

"That's the spirit, ladies," Lilith said, visibly reassured. "You're at the age where you should be fighting for a better planet. After all, in just a few days, this place will be filled with boring gentlemen and ladies who only know how to talk about money and economics."

The trio burst into laughter, understanding that in their own realm, money was merely a trivial distraction.

Driven by curiosity, Lumina asked, "Lilith, do you know why they love money so much?"

With a reflective tone, Lilith replied, "These individuals have a profound lack of security and deceive themselves into thinking that with money, they become important or powerful. It's all just fantasies."

Aisling smiled at the remark. "You sound like my teacher, Miss Lilith."

Having gathered the information she sought regarding their mission, Lilith rose from her seat. "Well, your company has been delightful, but I must take my leave. After all, I'm one of those boring ladies obsessed with money."

Her parting comment, accompanied by an amused smile, prompted another wave of shared laughter among the three, forging a bond stronger than the simple exchange of words. As Lilith departed, Aisling and Lumina felt a sense of purpose fuel their hearts, ready to embrace their destiny as they prepared to embark on their journey to save the marine world.

Once Lilith had departed, Lumina and Aisling remained seated, reflecting on the unique encounter they had just experienced. Although their time together was brief, the impact was

unmistakable; while Lilith played by her own rules, she had left a lasting impression on the sisters.

"It's incredible," Lumina remarked thoughtfully. "How some people can view money as the most important thing when there are so many other forms of value."

Aisling nodded, her thoughts aligning with her sister's. "But I also wonder… having that power and choosing to follow a different path— doesn't that constitute a form of value as well?"

Still processing the surprise of their interaction, Aisling and Lumina felt a renewed connection to their lineage and their father's adventures. Davos, with its unexpected surprises, had given them more than just nourishment; it had provided pieces of a past they barely understood.

With the promise of discovering more on the horizon, the sisters decided to set aside the opportunity for deeper inquiry for the moment, understanding that this fortuitous meeting with Lilith was only the beginning of new adventures and revelations.

"We must move forward," Aisling murmured, a spark of determination igniting in her eyes.

"Yes, but with more questions than before," Lumina added with a smile.

With each step they took, they ventured further into a world rich with ancient magic and mysterious encounters, deeply aware that the past, present, and future were intricately intertwined.

Determined to continue their mission, Lumina and Aisling resumed their journey with renewed energy. They knew obstacles lay ahead, but this encounter served as a reminder of the importance of keeping their purpose firm and clear. Drawing upon the lessons learned in their daily lives, they took flight toward new horizons, ready to face whatever came next, understanding that every person and experience added a new layer to their understanding of the world and themselves.

The dawn barely hinted at its light over the vast Pacific Ocean. Aisling and Lumina, cloaked in their magical outfits, soared through the chilly air, their souls ignited by the mission that awaited them. The seamstress who had crafted their garments had woven more than mere clothing; she had created a symbol of struggle and protection, a tribute to courage in the face of adversity. They knew they were about to confront the most ruthless whalers, and the outcome of that encounter was yet to be determined.

Spotting a whaling ship on the horizon, the sisters began their descent, their hearts racing with the rush of adrenaline. They landed gracefully on the deck of the vessel, their silhouettes glowing in the early morning light, casting elongated shadows that danced across the stained wood.

Aisling, having learned Japanese through the whispers of the wind that carried tales from the past, stepped forward confidently. "Stop the hunt immediately. We cannot allow you to harm these magnificent creatures any further."

The sailors exchanged bewildered glances, taken aback by the impossible notion that these magical figures spoke their language with such fluency. "How is that possible?" one murmured, his mouth agape in astonishment.

The leader of the whalers, a man hardened by the sea and time, nervously barked an order. "Don't let these girls stop us! Get the harpoon ready!"

A visibly anxious sailor raised a harpoon, aiming it toward the sisters, his narrowed eyes reflecting the tension of an impending confrontation. Without a trace of fear, Lumina moved to shield Aisling.

"Put down the weapon," Lumina commanded, her authority emanating from the depths of her being.

The sailor hesitated, but under the pressure of his leader, he took a step forward.

Aisling, maintaining her calm without wavering, repeated in Japanese, "This is a warning. Please cease your hunting."

As the sailor prepared to shoot, Aisling raised a hand and released a gentle burst of light from the enchanted clover resting against her chest. The luminescence enveloped the crew in a peaceful serenity, momentarily suspending them in a state of soft interaction between wonder and confusion.

In that charged moment, the sisters stood united, ready to confront not just the whalers but the darkness threatening to engulf the marine world they were sworn to protect. Aisling could feel the power of the clover pulsing in harmony with her growing determination, and with Lumina beside her, they were both a beacon of hope and resilience in the face of impending chaos.

Lumina on her part, conjured a whirlwind of wind that surprisingly enveloped the crew, forcing them to retreat. "We won't harm you unless we have to," she declared in a tone that brooked no disobedience.

Overwhelmed, the sailor dropped the harpoon with a clatter that sliced through the tension in the air like lightning.

The captain of the ship, witnessing this display of power beyond normal comprehension, began to rethink his approach. His thoughts swirled with the possibilities of a different future, nearly forgetting the calculations of the present.

Lumina sensed the shift and recognized a latent opportunity. "Think about the legacy you leave behind, about what your children will hear of you," she urged, touching the humanity that still pulsed within the old whaler.

The captain lowered his gaze, noticing for the first time the metaphorical blood on his hands. "I don't want to be remembered as a destroyer," he murmured, his voice barely a whisper, laden with regret and self-awareness.

As the tension aboard the vessel slowly began to dissipate, Aisling stepped forward. "If we change today, we can rewrite the course of what is to come," she proposed, extending her hand in a sincere gesture of peace.

The leader hesitated but accepted her offer, a newfound determination igniting in his eyes. "Perhaps there are other ways we can survive," he concluded, signaling to the crew to lower their weapons and turn off the engines.

With the whaling ships sailing away into the horizon, Aisling and Lumina paused for a moment, watching as the transformation they had inspired became a distant reality. The vast and endless ocean reflected the golden glow of dawn, heralding the end of their day. Satisfied with having averted further destruction, the sisters resolved to find a safe place to rest.

As they walked along the shore, the sound of waves lapping gently at the sand filled their ears, a soothing reminder of the natural beauty they fought to protect. Little by little, the weight of their mission began to settle into their hearts, fueling their courage for the challenges yet to come.

Not far away, partially hidden among the seaside vegetation, Aisling and Lumina discovered a small wooden cabin. Its structure, weathered by time and the elements, reminded them of the magical hills of Ireland and their own origins steeped in nature. Upon entering, the warm embrace of shelter washed over them, and they sighed with relief and a sense of continuity.

As they settled into the cozy cabin, the gentle sound of waves breaking against the beach wrapped around their thoughts like a calming mantra. They knew full well the battle to protect the natural world was far from over, but for that night, they allowed themselves to bask in the tranquility of each other's company and the simple beauty of their surroundings.

The next morning, before the sun fully rose in all its glory, Aisling and Lumina found themselves surrounded by an endless stream of news reverberating through the world. Without needing to touch a single electronic device, the sisters synchronized their minds through telepathy, capturing fragments from newspapers and broadcasts across the country. For them, the informational waves of the media felt like whispers in a giant web, easily heard and interpreted.

"Do you hear that?" Lumina asked, her mind honing in on the reports swirling around the events of the previous day. "They're talking about us."

Aisling smiled knowingly. "Even without seeing it, we know our actions resonated more than they realize."

As they picked up the telepathic vibrations of requests and comments from those astounded by the recent events, they noticed the confusion surrounding the miracle of the world they aspired to protect. To them, magic was not just a skill; it served as a tool for connection.

The usual conversations they observed through mobile devices still caught them off guard. In their own realm, it was enough to think of someone to communicate. This concept of physical separation didn't exist, and watching humans rely on gadgets to convey even the simplest messages struck them as unusual yet fascinating. "It's curious how they complicate communication," Lumina observed, intrigued.

As the salty aroma of the sea mingled with the fresh air filling the cabin, Aisling and Lumina solidified their determination. They understood that their gifts and abilities represented a legacy to wield wisely. Though the human world had its complexities, it also offered marvelous opportunities for teaching, learning, and caring.

Together, they embarked into the day, knowing that while challenges would continue, so too would their capacity to inspire change and bring hope. For with every step they took, they carried the echo of a noble purpose, reminding them that true power resided within them to forge a better world.

As the news revealed that the whalers refused to return, the sailors had risen up against the captains, declaring it a bad omen. They sensed the return of sea sirens or at least the fury of the ocean's spirit, leading them to believe they would not return.

With dawn bathing the small wooden cabin on the Pacific coast in soft golden tones, Aisling and Lumina awoke slowly, their minds still resonating with the echoes of the previous day. While the murmur of the waves caressed the shore, the sisters focused on perceiving the news and reactions that arose following their intervention.

The air was charged with information, each headline and phrase a clear whisper to them, caught through their telepathic link. Tuning into the news waves, they listened as astonished narrations recounted the events of the day prior.

"The whalers are refusing to return," Lumina murmured, sharing what she sensed. "The sailors have rebelled against their captains."

Aisling, picking up on the latent fear in those words, added, "They say what they experienced was a bad omen. Some believe the sea sirens have returned."

With every whispered word, they understood the growing unease among the humans, yet within that uncertainty, Aisling and Lumina clung to the hope and determination to effect real change in their new world. The dawn heralded not just a new day but the promises of a pivotal journey ahead.The descriptions were laden with a mystical reverence for the sea, signaling a shift in the thoughts of the people.

The fishermen, it seemed, were firmly refusing to return to their former ways, insisting they had felt the wrath of the spirit of the sea. "Never again," some declared in interviews. "To go back would be to defy ourselves."

"It's incredible how a spark can ignite such change," Lumina reflected, absorbing the telepathic images of fishermen abandoning their posts in search of renewed hope. The apparent change of heart among the mariners not only brought peace to the ocean but also began to pave the way toward a more conscious and harmonious future.

What had started as a simple mission to protect the whales was taking on a life of its own. The perception that the sea was responding through the intervention of nearly mythical figures had captured the imaginations of the fishermen and, by extension, the world.

"It seems this time, fear has turned in our favor," Aisling remarked, observing how the power of myths and legends was brilliantly being reborn in the collective consciousness of humanity. The idea that the spirit of the ocean had raged was resonating within them, crafting a modern myth born from their intervention. It was a living lesson in respect for nature and its grandeur.

As the sun raised its light over the ocean, Aisling and Lumina realized that their mission had achieved more depth than they had anticipated. Although it had been their power that directly influenced the change, it was the transformation of human consciousness that would endure.

"Today, we made history," Lumina said, her voice brimming with satisfaction and responsibility.

"And we will continue to do so," Aisling responded with determination, the shimmer of the sea echoing her every word.

With their energies filled with renewed promises, they prepared to embark on the next stage of their journey, knowing that wherever the waves met the shore, there would always be a new story to tell and defend.

As dawn enveloped the small wooden cabin in a golden embrace, Aisling and Lumina began to gather their belongings, ready to embark on their next adventure. However, a gentle tap tap at the door made them glance at each other with curiosity.

"Come in," they said in unison, watching cautiously as the door creaked open slowly to reveal the figure of a stunning Asian fairy. Her presence was majestic, with an ethereal beauty that seemed to carry the very essence of the eastern bamboo forest from which she hailed.

"Thank you," the Asian fairy began softly. "Your Majesty instructed me to come and see you, inviting you to our city so you can enjoy a few hours of rest before continuing your mission."

Aisling, taken aback, nodded her head in gratitude. "Did my grandmother inform you that I was here?"

"Yes," the fairy replied, her voice as smooth as silk, while two equally beautiful and graceful fairies lined up behind her. The air around them seemed to vibrate with a soft melody, a symphony that only the fairies could fully appreciate.

"We'd be delighted to go," Lumina responded, a mischievous smile curling her lips. "Just make sure there's good food. I'm really craving something delicious," she added jovially, raising a conspiratorial eyebrow at Aisling.

As they followed the Asian fairies, morning mist swirled around them, lifting gently in a synchronized flight. The sisters felt the currents of air guiding them toward their unknown destination.

Before long, they arrived in the city of the Asian fairies. In stark contrast to the emerald green hills of Ireland, everything here exuded an elegant and serene aesthetic. The city was nestled within a bamboo forest, its structures woven from filigree of golden silk and jade crystal. The streets flowed like rivers, guided by the gentle murmuring of nearby streams.

"This is stunning," Aisling murmured, admiring how sunlight filtered through the bamboo, casting dancing shadows on the ground.

"Our home reflects the nature that surrounds us," one of the guiding fairies explained, smiling with a glimmer of pride.

As the sisters immersed themselves in this enchanting realm, they felt the weight of their journey momentarily lift. Surrounded by beauty and harmony, they began to understand the depth of the connections they were forming—not just with the world around them, but with each other and the purpose that drove them forward. In this magical city, they sensed that every moment held the promise of discovery, and each step would lead them closer to their true destinies.

The sisters were escorted to a central pavilion where an imposing figure awaited them. The Queen of the Asian Fairies, exuding an air of serenity and wearing a smile that overflowed with wisdom, greeted them with a respectful bow.

Aisling and Lumina, she began, "It is an honor to receive the granddaughters of my dear friend. I hope our hospitality refreshes you."

Lumina performed a playful yet cordial curtsy and replied, "Thank you, Your Majesty. Your hospitality already feels rejuvenating."

Hours of rest swiftly transformed into a feast of sensations. Delicate dishes, reminiscent of morning dew, burst with flavors that danced on their palates with every bite. The Asian fairies shared millennia-old stories beneath the cool canopy of the forest, forging bonds through their soft laughter that rang like distant bells.

As the time to say goodbye approached, Aisling and Lumina felt a renewed sense of peace, ready to continue their mission with their spirits lifted. They knew that within their hearts now resided the duality of two magical worlds: the familiar embrace of Ireland and the exotic allure of the Land of the Fairies. With a gentle flutter of wings, they departed from their temporary home, bearing the light and hope that the world so desperately needed.

Stepping back into the vibrant tapestry of life, they were invigorated by their experiences, prepared to face whatever lay ahead. With each heartfelt encounter and magical moment, they understood that they were not merely travelers, but guardians of a legacy that transcended boundaries. As the path unfolded before them, Lily and Aisling walked onward, determined to illuminate every shadow they encountered along the way.

Asian Fairy

In the Heart of Davos

In the heart of Davos, Switzerland, the atmosphere was electric. The usually tranquil village had transformed into a hive of activity and expectation. The world's most powerful figures gathered in a majestic glass room, seated around a table designed for thirty. The tension in the air was palpable, yet each individual understood that their influence was crucial for the new order about to emerge. Outside, darkness began to cloak the streets as thousands of soldiers, clad in uniforms reminiscent of a troubling past, marched to the rhythm of a future that promised to become a nightmare.

Development

The council members, ranging from tech moguls to renowned politicians, prepared to discuss projects and policies that would shift the course of humanity. The murmurs of conversation intertwined with the sound of microphones adjusting, while floral arrangements and glasses of water adorned the table. Anticipation crackled in the air.

David Caldwell, the CEO of a major pharmaceutical corporation, broke the ice. "We are here to ensure our investments remain profitable during times of uncertainty. We must find ways to stabilize the market and perhaps even create new crises that benefit us."

Maria, an influential environmental politician, vehemently opposed him. "We cannot allow our decisions to continue harming the planet. We need sustainable initiatives. The future is not just economic; it's ecological."

Willy Late, a tech monopolist who had thrived in the shadows of others, laughed cynically. "Sustainability? We're talking about profits, not fairy tales. The economy rules, and unless we can create a new paradigm…"

At that moment, a guard, with his ears covered to communicate discreetly with headquarters and shield himself from the ongoing discussions, glanced nervously out the window. He attempted to relay some information, but his phone was unresponsive. The sight before him was incomprehensible, with red flags bearing the ominous swastika fluttering in the distance, accompanied by thousands of soldiers dressed in black. Suddenly, the door burst open violently. Silence fell over the room as everyone stared in confusion.

A sinister figure entered—the Commander-in-Chief—accompanied by his lieutenant, who wore an officer's uniform with unsettling discrepancies. All eyes fixated on them as the presence of the General filled the air with palpable tension.

"Ladies and gentlemen," **the Commander**-in-Chief began, "I present to you the future president of Earth." Lilith entered with grace, followed closely by Satan, whose impeccable attire seemed to shake the ground itself with his mere presence.

Satan: [Brusquely pulling out the leader's chair and standing] "I apologize for the interruption, but your time is valuable, as is mine. So, I'll be brief. Many of you, when you die, will come knocking on my door."

A murmur of disbelief rippled through the room, glistening sweat-drenched hands gripping the edges of the table tightly.

Satan: "How many lives have you shattered in your quest for power? Your selfish practices are leading you inexorably to eternal damnation. You fail to see that divine justice cannot be negotiated."

The murmurs of unease filled the room, as the weight of his words hung in the air, a stark reminder of the consequences that awaited those who pursued power at the expense of the innocent. The tension in the room thickened, and as fear took hold, a chilling understanding began to settle among the powerful assembled.

The murmurs around the table escalated into a clamor of opposition. A young man named Willy stood up defiantly.

"Who do you think you are, dictating what we should do? You're nothing but a fraud, and you have no power over us!"

In an instant, Satan lunged at him, sweeping across the long table and knocking aside everything in his path—flower arrangements, glasses, and water bottles, all sent crashing to the floor. His hand shot out like a bolt of terror, gripping Willy by the throat. In a split second, Willy was lifted off the ground, his feet dangling helplessly as terror filled his eyes.

"Do you doubt my power, Willy?" Satan intoned coldly. "Let me offer you a lesson."

In the stunned silence of the room, everyone watched as the young man struggled to breathe, unable to scream. His lifeless body was dropped to the floor with a resounding thud, leaving a chilling stillness in its wake.

"Gentlemen, you have no alternatives," Lilith chuckled with satisfaction.

The back doors burst open once more, this time admitting two chilling figures: Adolf Hitler and Stalin. A gasp of disbelief rippled through the room.

"This is quite an interesting gathering," Stalin remarked, surveying the scene. "Arrest this man for his incredulity!"

Five soldiers rushed in, swiftly overpowering an aide who had risen halfway to protest.

"Welcome, gentlemen," Satan said, his voice smooth like silk but dripping with menace. "You have lived in the shadows, but today you will be under my command."

The others at the table remained silent, paralyzed by the unfolding drama.

"It was not a mistake to gather here," Stalin declared, his tone flat and cold. "It's time to make it clear that power resides here. Who will stand alongside the General and our new leader?"

With terrified glances, the council understood that the balance of power was about to shift drastically. Satan's proposition resonated with a mixture of fear and twisted logic.

"You will owe me fealty in the world of men, and in return, you shall keep your privileges, but under my dominion. Never forget that your selfishness is a reflection of my existence. That's why I exist."

A murmur of discontent grew as everyone contemplated their precarious situation. They came from diverse backgrounds, each with their own hidden agendas and desires.

"Who among you would like a second chance? Who dares to challenge the established order?" Lilith asked, her voice deliberately provocative. The silence thickened with horror, a renewed sense of servitude washing over the attendees as they exchanged wary glances, searching for the one brave—or foolish—enough to speak.

An old politician, his name lost to time, raised his head and addressed Satan.

"This is madness. Many will try to resist you, believing they can outwit you with deceit and treaties." Laughter rippled through the room.

"No, dear pedophile," Satan retorted, the laughter quickly fading under the weight of his declaration. "Everyone whispers when they call the politician that. Learn from history. Those who resist fall first. In the end, I am the only one who can offer you the life you desire, rather than the one you deserve."

At that moment, Adolf Hitler spoke up. With an expression of grim recognition, he turned to Satan and proclaimed, "I have endured unimaginable torments in hell, trapped in endless agony. But now, thanks to you, I am granted a new opportunity to resurrect what I once tried to build and failed. For that, I am eternally grateful."

With a gesture, Lilith pointed toward the exit, and the officials began to march silently toward the doors, allowing the tense atmosphere to dissolve into an echo of despair. A clear warning hung in the air; the council had been hijacked, their feelings and fears ensnared in Satan's power experiment.

Before the meeting could conclude, the young man still standing at the table, Lukas, shouted, "No one has to accept your deal! We can unite and fight!" His words resonated forcefully, awakening murmurs among the attendees. However, the Commander-in-Chief approached menacingly, narrowing his gaze at the young man.

"Are you going to be another fool?" he challenged. "Or do you prefer to reflect on this?"

Satan leaned forward, a dark smile spreading across his face. "You see? Doubts are already creeping in..."

But remember, the power they wield is merely a loan, and I am the creditor who always collects on his debts.*

Stalin, with a malicious glint that betrayed his sadistic enjoyment, quickly moved towards Lukas. His firm hands gripped the young man with an intensity that revealed the pleasure he derived from exerting control over another human being. Suddenly, two soldiers entered to escort away the next prisoner, the atmosphere thickening with dread as the stakes of the night grew higher.

The Debates of Power and Control

A heavy silence fell over the room, tinged with the thrill of danger and uncertainty. In that charged atmosphere, the whispers of the council members faded as they braced themselves for the tumult ahead.

"No one is obliged to accept your deal! We can unite and fight!" The young man standing at the table, named Lukas, cried out, his voice resonating with defiance. His words stirred the crowd, awakening murmurs of intrigue and dissent among the attendees. But before he could rally further support, the Commander-in-Chief moved menacingly closer, locking his gaze on Lukas.

"Are you going to be another reckless fool?" he challenged. "Or would you prefer to reflect on this?"

Satan leaned forward, a dark smile spreading across his face, relishing the anticipation in the air. "You see? Doubts are already creeping in...

Remember, the power you wield is merely a loan, and I am the creditor who always collects his debt."

Stalin, his gaze laced with sadistic delight, quickly approached Lukas. His firm grip revealed an unsettling pleasure in exercising control over another human being. Just then, two soldiers rushed in to escort the next prisoner, stark reminders of the perilous situation.

The murmurs fell silent once again; the collective fear had reasserted itself. As the security of their former privileges began to crumble, the remaining members of the council comprehended that change was inevitable. The echo of Satan's words hung in the air, serving as a warning about the new shadows that would envelop humanity's future.

What was intended as a power exchange had instead morphed into a dark lesson about the high stakes of global leadership. The pieces on the chessboard were now poised for new moves under a control that promised to rewrite the rules of the game forever.

The Plan for Global Domination

To orchestrate a subtle, staged strategy for world domination, Satan used his magnificent strategist, Lilith, to distribute colorful pamphlets outlining his insidious proposals:

Political Infiltration: Satan would recruit influential political leaders from various nations to discreetly implement legal and administrative changes. These changes would include the gradual elimination of charismatic leaders and the placement of easily manipulable figures in their stead.

Dismantling Religions: Policies would be set in motion that, on the surface, promoted freedom of expression and alternative beliefs but, at their core, undermined traditional religious institutions. Ideologies centered on materialism and the worship of wealth would be encouraged.

Revaluation of Social Values: A cultural campaign would be unleashed to ridicule or minimize the importance of traditional morals and family values. Through media, the notion that the Ten Commandments were outdated would be promoted, encouraging a life devoid of moral constraints.

Judicial Control: Judicial institutions would be weakened under the guise of reforming the system to deliver justice more effectively. However, the true goal would be to erode the integrity of the legal system, paving the way for arbitrary justice dictated by Satan and his allies.

As the plans unfolded like a dark tapestry, the reality of their ambitions settled over the council members. They understood that they were but pawns in a greater game, one that would forever alter the landscape of their world and the very fabric of society itself.

Educational and Cultural Manipulation

The educational systems would shift towards the elimination of critical and humanities disciplines, fostering a population lacking critical thought and easily susceptible to manipulation. Popular culture would be steeped in distractions and trivialities.

Transparent Economic Policies

A cult of ruthless capitalism would be initiated, where wealth and financial success were revered above all else. This would create a society of consumers obsessed with accumulating material goods, distracting them from the underlying political and social changes taking place.

Flexible Social Norms

Legislation would be introduced to allow increasingly loose interpretations of moral and ethical laws, favoring corruption and impunity while desensitizing the populace to injustice.

Covert Laws and Reforms

Governors would receive a "Book of the New World President," a set of guidelines designed to implant these policies gradually and safely, ensuring that the public would not perceive drastic changes or feel incited to rebel.

Establishment of a New World Order

With the weakening of traditional institutions and the focus on materialism, a point would be reached by 2040 where a centralized global leadership could be proclaimed without significant resistance, with Satan destined to be the sole ruler of Earth.

During the unsettling meeting in the glass chamber, just as the attendees' attention fixated on the formidable visage of Satan, an atmosphere of anticipation filled the room. From the shadows, a group of disciplined attendees, dressed in impeccably dark uniforms, began distributing a black leather-bound book with golden lettering: "The Decalogues of Domination: The Laws of the New Order of Lucifer."

Each attendee took the book with a blend of curiosity and doubt. As they opened the first pages, they could feel the symbolic weight of the tome in their hands. Its beautiful binding contrasted starkly with the dark content that promised to reshape the future.

Satan, surveying the room with satisfaction from the end of the table, proclaimed, "This text is the guide we have carefully constructed to lead this world into a new era. The laws it contains will form the foundation of our New Order. Understand it well, for this will be the sacred book that governs this land."

As the attendees began to leaf through the book, a restless whisper spread through the hall. Ten main laws stood out, each designed to erode existing systems and construct a new structure under Lucifer's leadership. Just as religious texts had once been revered, this book was structured as commandments:

1. Cult of Power and Wealth: It proclaimed the supremacy of money as the only true god, urging everyone to pour their efforts into accumulating personal wealth and power, relegating humanistic values to the background.

2. Erosion of Spirituality: Religious sectors would be transformed into mere cultural relics, promoting a world devoid of faith and devotion.

3. Disintegration of Traditional Institutions: The text outlined how to gradually weaken the pillars of society, such as family and the judicial system, to establish new systems of subjective justice.

4. Freedom for Chaos: It encouraged traditional laws to be reinterpreted, allowing personal indulgence and desire to guide actions rather than established moral principles.

5. Educational Reformulation: A new curriculum focusing on materialism and financial success would be established, minimizing the importance of history and philosophy.

6. Global Surveillance and Control: The unification of intelligence and citizen control systems under a central

command would be recommended to ensure loyalty to the new regime.

7. Culture of Unrestrained Consumption: The idea that an individual's value is determined by their capacity to consume and possess would become prevalent.

8. Overthrowing Opposition: Strategies would be designed to identify and neutralize any burgeoning sources of resistance at their roots.

9. Propagation of Deception: Tactics would be detailed for flooding the media with lies that steer public opinion toward acceptance of the new order.

10. Promotion of Hedonism: This doctrine invited the pursuit of all earthly pleasures without remorse, encouraging a lifestyle solely focused on indulgence.

11. Lilith, maintaining her poised demeanor, addressed the assembly once more. "These guidelines will be implemented in every school, library, and cultural center around the globe. This is not just a book; it will serve as our constitution."

As the pages unfolded, the potential of the future revealed itself—dark and tempting. The assembled leaders understood that this text would not only be a manifesto but a lethal tool of transformation.

As they closed the book, a familiar yet unsettling anxiety echoed in their minds: the world would never be the same again. The weight of their decisions pressed heavily upon them, a reminder of the irreversible changes that lay ahead. With Lilith at the helm, they sensed the shift towards a new era, one that promised both allure and danger in equal measure.

United by ambition and driven by the promise of power, they prepared to step boldly into this redefined reality, where hedonism reigned and the tenants of morality dissolved into shadows. It was a moment poised on the edge of history, ready to plunge into the depths of a twisted ambition that would reshape the very foundation of civilization.

Each of these decrees echoed with the weight of inevitability, and as the council absorbed the implications of their new reality, they began to realize just how deeply ensnared they were in a web of manipulation and control. The atmosphere became thick with tension and dread, setting the stage for a dark chapter in the history of humanity.

CHAPTER 24

Discovering America

Aisling gazed into the distance, her green eyes capturing every detail of the city that never sleeps. From her vantage point, she could see Central Park as an oasis amid the steel and glass titans, the lights of Times Square beginning to flicker like terrestrial stars, and the rivers flowing through the urban jungle like veins. It was a view no human had ever experienced from this angle, yet, despite its magical splendor, it did little to alleviate the melancholy that weighed on her heart.

The burden of their mission in the city pressed heavily upon her shoulders. Aisling knew that beneath the dazzling lights lay deep shadows that she and her sister were destined to unveil. The melody lingered in her mind, each note a familiar caress reminding her of the warmth of home and the love of her family. A single tear, as clear as morning dew on clover, rolled down her cheek, briefly reflecting the last ray of sunlight of the day.

Lost in her thoughts, Aisling leaned forward and let herself fall from the pedestal of the statue. Her descent was free, arms outstretched and the air whistling around her in a cold, liberating embrace. For a moment, it felt as though she had surrendered, as if the weight of the earth had stolen her desire to fly. But when she reached seventy meters, something within her awakened with unusual force. The strains of "Farewell to Irish Lighthouses" resonated louder in her mind, reminding her of who she was and where she came from. Her iridescent wings unfurled with a vibrant sound, capturing the air and transforming her fall into a majestic ascent.

Aisling soared gracefully, leaving behind the statue that had briefly served as her sanctuary for contemplation. She headed toward the city with resolute determination. As she flew over the rooftops and towers of the bustling metropolis, the memory of her homeland remained embedded in her heart. Even though Ireland was far away, she carried with her the strength of its people.

The wind struck her face as she flew, but it was no longer the chilling indifference of those who have lost faith. It was instead the vital breath that urged her onward. The music in her mind, an internal source of inspiration and comfort, accompanied her in every movement. New York awaited; with its mysteries and struggles. As night fell, Aisling plunged into the depths of the city, not as a melancholic exile, but as a guardian determined to..washed away by the current of liberation she felt in Maria's comforting presence.

"Believe me, God is proud of you and trusts in you," Maria whispered before fading into the air, leaving behind a trail of serenity.

As Maria vanished, a gentle and ethereal melody began to fill the air: the song of Mary Magdalene. Its notes wove through the wind, touching Aisling's soul as a reminder of the power of love and faith. Her heart, once laden with uncertainty, felt renewed and ready to face the challenges that awaited her.

With a renewed sense of purpose, Aisling soared into the sky once more above the city. The lights of New York shimmered below her, no longer a sea of confusion and pain, but a reflection of hope and potential. She knew that despite the difficulties, there were good people worth saving. Her mission would continue, guided by faith in divine power and those willing to fight for a better tomorrow.

Aisling descended slowly towards the rooftops of the city, the weight of her mission now balanced by the peace Maria had restored within her. With the song's echo still in her thoughts, she prepared to face a new dawn filled with promise. She knew that with each small act of kindness and every soul saved, the purpose of her journey gained meaning. And so, with a light heart and clear mind, Aisling resumed her flight, confident that the light would always find its way through the shadows.

The flickering neon signs cast vibrant colors on the shadows as they projected figures in the lonely alleys. Aisling, the Irish fairy, found herself huddled beneath one of these signs, exhausted from an intense day that had worn her down emotionally. It felt as if the weight of the world rested upon her shoulders, and her eyes began to close gently, pulling her into an almost irresistible drowsiness.

Just as she was about to succumb to sleep, a sound jolted her awake. It was the voice of her sister, Lumina, who seemed to be in distress at a distance. Aisling quickly leapt to her feet and peered over the edge of the rooftop. Under the intermittent glow of the streetlights, she saw Lumina surrounded by five unmistakable figures—a gang with clearly hostile intentions.

From her high vantage point, Aisling watched with interest rather than concern. She had complete faith in Lumina's ability to handle the situation, but it never hurt to remain vigilant. The youths, evidently more confident than they should have been, continued their taunts and laughter. One of them brandished a gun, a device which Aisling, unfamiliar with human threats, interpreted with innocent bewilderment.

In her heart, Aisling knew this world was filled with darkness and challenges, but, alongside her sister, she was determined to bring light wherever it was desperately needed. With her spirit bolstered by Maria's message and the unwavering bond she shared with Lumina, she was ready to confront whatever lies ahead.

Perched on the ledge, Aisling listened as one of the gang members taunted, "Ummm, I like your costume and Irish accent, but we'll be taking it off you soon."

Their crude laughter echoed through the empty street, a provocation that rumbled in the silent night. Lumina, grasping their intentions swiftly, shot back a sharp retort: "And who's going to take it off, you or your grandma, bro?"

But Aisling knew they couldn't underestimate the dangers humans posed and readied her magic, prepared to intervene if Lumina needed her. The youths' words were crude, and their gestures, threatening. Another of the gang, bolder or more foolish than the others, added, "Bet you got lost on your way to a bachelorette party, huh? We'll make sure you have a good time here."

Unfazed, Lumina moved swiftly towards the youth holding the weapon. In a heartbeat, she was beside him, her hand gripping his neck with an unexpected force, her feet planted on his shoulders and her hands firmly placed on his head. "Drop that piece of metal or I'll snap your neck, idiot," she whispered, her threat leaving no room for doubt.

Her speed and skill caught them all off guard. The gang was frozen in place, dumbfounded by Lumina's agility and prowess.

"Hey, don't be like that, it was just a joke," mumbled another gang member, trying to downplay their actions as his eyes darted around for an escape route.

Lumina didn't need to repeat herself. The steely resolve in her voice and her unwavering stance instilled panic among them.

"Listen to me. Get lost or I'll break his neck; it wouldn't be the first time I've done it."

Her words carried an immense weight, cutting through the cold indifference of the night.

Understanding the seriousness of the situation, the gang members turned to flee, vanishing into the alleyways as if swallowed by the darkness itself.

Aisling descended gracefully from the illuminated sign, landing silently beside her sister. The street, now empty once again, seemed to hold its secrets beneath a shroud of silence.

"I knew you didn't need my help," Aisling remarked with a smile tinged with pride.

In the aftermath of their encounter, Lumina and Aisling stood in the muted glow of the streetlights, their bond stronger and their resolve reaffirmed. Together, they were prepared to face whatever darkness lurked in the alleys of this vast city, always ready to bring light where it was most needed.

Aisling said with a smile, and Lumina, a spark of humor and determination in her eyes, returned it.

Then, Aisling looked at her curiously and asked, "How did you learn to talk like that?"

Lumina shrugged playfully. "From the streets, sis. It's easy to pick up this kind of colloquial speech."

Their laughter rang out, a melody of relief and camaraderie echoing in the solitary night. Though far from home and surrounded by danger, the sisters remained an unstoppable force, ready to confront any shadow that dared to cross their path.

Fairies often possess extraordinary abilities and can learn a language with remarkable speed. Their capacity to adapt quickly is driven by their magical intelligence and connection to the natural world. By constantly interacting with human thoughts and emotions, they develop an intuitive understanding of new languages in mere days or even less, depending on their exposure to culture and speech. This allows them to communicate effectively and grasp the human world better as they fulfill their missions.

The dawn's gentle light filtered through the glow of the large neon sign beneath which Lumina and Aisling had spent the night. A tempting aroma of freshly brewed coffee and warm pastries filled the air, rousing Lumina with a familiar pang of hunger. "Sister, I'm starving," she murmured as she stretched, noticing Aisling beginning to blink awake as well.

Aisling, still half-asleep, reflexively reached for the sword strapped to her back, ensuring it was still secure. She nodded at Lumina's practical suggestion: "We should rent an apartment or find a hotel. We can't keep sleeping on the streets." The sense of this idea wasn't lost on them. Aisling rummaged through her belongings, pulling out a couple of fifty-euro notes from her bag.

"Well, we've got to make more; we're almost out," Lumina noted.

With a familiar gesture, they recited the spell they had used in earlier adventures. In seconds, they conjured another 500 bills, ready for use in a world that demanded constant transactions.

"Do you think we should work to earn some money?" Lumina asked, ever inquisitive.

Aisling thought for a moment. "And how would we carry out our mission if we worked? Not for now. Let's just head to a hotel."

With their plan set, the sisters emerged into the morning light, their spirits lifted by the simple prospect of a warm bed and the opportunities the day promised. They knew their journey would continue to challenge them, but with each step forward, they also grew stronger and more determined to make a difference in the world they had come to protect.

Determ the sisters descended onto the street, making their way to the first cozy café they spotted. As they entered, the aroma of breakfast filled their senses, and they ordered berry tart and peppermint tea, avoiding coffee and traditional tea, as their fairy school had taught them these could subtly affect the spirit in undesired ways.

When it came time to pay, they offered one of their newly conjured fifty-euro bills. The waiter, kind yet firm, informed them, "This bill isn't valid here. We only accept dollars."

Aisling frowned, slightly confused. "What do you mean it's not valid? We don't have any other currency, only euros."

Noticing their predicament, the waiter offered a pragmatic solution. "You need to exchange it for dollars."

Thinking quickly, Lumina proposed, "This is worth 18 dollars. Keep the whole bill, no change necessary, and exchange it."

The waiter nodded agreeably. "That works just fine."

Grateful, the sisters accepted the arrangement. As they settled into their seats with their trays, Lumina remarked, "What a complicated world this is. A different bill for every place."

Finally seated, they enjoyed their breakfast in the café's cozy corner. As they savored the sweet tart and soothing peppermint tea, they discussed their next steps, reflecting on the surprising complexities of human norms. With a plan forming and a new perspective on the necessary adaptations for survival, Aisling and Lumina set out to find more comfortable lodgings. They knew each experience came with a lesson, and they would need that wisdom as they advanced in their mission. The city presented unusual challenges, but with each one, the sisters grew in skill and understanding, ready for whatever lay ahead.

After their refreshing breakfast, Aisling and Lumina decided to explore more of the vibrant city. They strolled down the bustling streets, marveling at the shop windows and finding in the human world a blend of fascination and amusement in things they often deemed trivial yet entertaining. As they wandered, Lumina suddenly stopped in front of a fashion boutique.

Immersed in elegance and luxury, Aisling and Lumina decided to allow themselves a small reprieve from their mission as they explored New York City. After a leisurely breakfast, the sisters strolled through the bustling streets until a dazzling storefront caught their attention. Unbeknownst to them, they had wandered onto the prestigious Fifth Avenue, a runway of boutiques shimmering with opulence.

The store they chose to enter was a haven of sophistication. Crystal chandeliers gleamed overhead, casting twinkling reflections across the polished marble floors. The air was delicately scented with lavender and jasmine, crafting a multisensory experience that promised exclusivity and quality.

As they tried on the dresses, the soft textures seemed to whisper stories of luxury and craftsmanship. Aisling and Lumina's laughter filled the space, a lighthearted melody that contrasted with the often-serious air of such establishments. For them, the experience was playful, a dive into a human reality they were only beginning to participate in.

Intent on leaving with their chosen garments, Aisling adored a pale green dress, each fold and detail of its design amplifying her presence like an ethereal halo. Lumina, on the other hand, selected a pastel pink dress that complemented her youthful glow.

Initially skeptical of Aisling and Lumina's youthful appearances, the saleswoman assumed they might have their parents' credit cards and allowed them to browse freely. After trying on several dresses, Aisling decided on the spectacular pale green ensemble with a matching ribboned hat, while Lumina admired her pastel pink choice.

"Wow, you look like a queen. If Grandma could see you, she'd be proud," Lumina remarked with a beaming smile.

"That pink dress looks fantastic on you too. Shall we keep them?" Aisling asked, buoyed by the moment's excitement.

"Yes!" exclaimed Lumina, animated by the atmosphere.

They decided to wear their new dresses out, letting the day's excitement sweep them away. The saleswoman, though puzzled by the request, obliged and offered bags for their clothes. "No need," Aisling said, "I'll just put them in my bag."

Relieved, the saleswoman smiled courteously and proceeded to ring up their purchases. "Alright, the total comes to $7,356," she announced, maintaining her professionalism.

With their newfound sense of elegance and the city stretching out before them, Aisling and Lumina stepped back onto Fifth Avenue, knowing that their adventure through human experiences was just beginning.

However moment of payment presented a small obstacle. When they handed over the euros they had, the saleswoman raised an eyebrow. "Oh, euros. Do you have dollars or a credit card?" she asked, maintaining the meticulous courtesy her job demanded.

Lumina, recalling the lesson learned from the waiter, reacted swiftly. "Look, ma'am," she began confidently and charmingly, "keep the change for any inconvenience we may have caused." They offered a total of 8,000 euros, a sum that satisfied the saleswoman.

She examined the bills, checking them with a special marker to ensure their authenticity. The quality was undeniable, and seeing the personal profit, her initial skepticism faded. "Thank you for the tip," she replied, allowing informal capitalism to work in her favor.

For Aisling and Lumina, this small financial exchange unveiled a profound truth about human nature: many are willing to overlook formalities if it provides them with personal benefits. As they exited the store in their new outfits, the sisters realized that cultural understanding was often as crucial as their magic in fulfilling their mission.

Empowered by their newfound appearance and the experience gained, they walked with confidence through the streets of New York. They had learned not just about fashion and human tastes, but also about the resilience and flexibility that often characterize those they had come to help. Ready for the next stage of their adventure, they sought to blend the magic of their world with the indomitable human spirit that thrived within the vibrant cityscape.

As Aisling and Lumina strolled through the bustling streets of New York, every passerby's gaze fell upon them. In their stunning dresses, they resembled models stepping straight out of a fashion magazine, radiating a mix of elegance and mystery with every step. Spotting a majestic hotel to their right, they decided it was a fitting place to rest.

They crossed the street with little concern for the monetary value of things; their focus had always been on acquisition rather than earthly possession. Upon entering the hotel lobby, a bellhop offered to take their bags, but they politely declined. "No, thank you," Aisling said with a smile, as the hilt of her sword protruded slightly from her backpack.

They headed to the reception, where the receptionist, a kindly man in his mid-fifties with a mustache reminiscent of another era, requested identification. Not possessing any, he courteously explained that it would be necessary for them to stay.

Realizing this new barrier in their path, Aisling and Lumina understood there was yet more to learn in this world. Nevertheless, their resolve was unshaken, and they were determined to navigate through these challenges with grace and ingenuity, ever mindful of their mission to bring light to every corner of the human experience.

Quickina took charge of the situation. "Look, sir," she began with charm and confidence, "my sister and I were robbed yesterday, and our father suggested we find refuge in a hotel before going to the police to report the incident. If you like, we can offer you money in advance." Aisling, playing along, placed all the money they had—twelve thousand euros—on the counter.

Surprised by both their story and the large sum of cash, which seemed incongruent with their youthful appearances, the receptionist believed their tale. Concluding that these young women, who appeared to be from high society, required special attention, he called the hotel manager, who promptly arrived. The concierge eyed the backpack with curiosity. Aisling quickly assured him, "It's a gift for my uncle; he collects swords."

"Ladies, how may I assist you? And who is your father? Some European noble?" the manager inquired, both curious and accommodating, his accent distinctly Irish.

Lumina maintained her composure, her voice sincere. "Well, our great-grandmother was a queen."

Intrigued, the manager asked, "Oh, of which country?" Realizing her slip, Aisling swiftly improvised, recalling snippets of European royalty. "Our uncle now rules in Monaco," she said.

Remarkably impressed and not wanting to cause discomfort to supposed royalty, the manager assured them, "Put that away, ladies, lest you risk being robbed again. All right, make sure they get a room, and then bring an officer by for their report."

With arrangements settled, the sisters headed to their room, feeling a bit more secure and gaining a clearer understanding of the complexities and advantages of human society. This unexpected turn of events bolstered their confidence in their adaptability and improvisational skills. Now, with a safe place to stay, they could prepare more effectively for their mission in this vast and intricate human world.

Upon entering their assigned room, Aisling and Lumina were awestruck. The room's overflow of luxury evoked the magnificence of their grandmother's home. Resplendent gold decorations, velvet-upholstered furnishings, and majestic chandeliers made their stay feel more like a palace retreat than a mere hotel room.

The space stretched across 120 square meters, boasting two lavishly decorated bedrooms and a spacious lounge inviting relaxation and enjoyment. Floor-to-ceiling windows offered breathtaking views of New York, creating a sensation of having the city at their feet. In the distance, twinkling lights promised adventures and secrets yet to be uncovered. The pièce de résistance was undoubtedly the terrace, which featured a jacuzzi providing a tranquil retreat with unparalleled vistas.

The receptionist had made every effort to ensure the sisters' comfort, even offering to exchange their euros for dollars as an unscheduled courtesy. Receiving two $100 bills, the bellboy couldn't contain his happiness. "Thank you, ladies, thank you very much," he repeated, making a small bow before leaving the room.

Once alone, Aisling expressed her persistent unease: "We've been lying a lot, and our faces and bodies will become disfigured, sister."

Lumina, sharing this concern, sighed. "And what do we do? Here you either lie or you're done for. This world forces you to lie. Don't you see, Aisling? Deception is deeply rooted in humanity."

The brutal honesty of her words was undeniable, a truth Aisling couldn't ignore. With a now more reassured smile, she dashed towards one of the beds by the window and exclaimed, laughing, "This one's mine." The excitement in her voice indicated that, despite everything, she was trying to find a balance between enjoying herself and maintaining her morality.

"No fair, cheat!" protested Lumina, though her face betrayed more amusement than real annoyance.

The luxury of their surroundings provided a mental haven, a space to process the events of recent days and plan their next steps. The city's soft, distant hum flowed in through the open window as a constant reminder of the new world they inhabited.

Later, as they settled in and explored the room's amenities, an unexpected knock announced the hotel manager. "Ladies, I've secured a contact at the police department to assist with your situation. Also, for safety, we've increased security on your floor."

With these reassurances, Aisling and Lumina prepared to navigate their new environment, bolstered by the support that unexpected circumstances had brought them.

Aisling and Lumina exchanged glances. The director's reaction was unexpected, a reminder that not all humans were as simple as they had assumed. This turn of events made them reconsider their perception of humanity, understanding that even in a world dominated by deception, there were individuals striving to do good.

As the director departed, the sisters, surrounded by their luxurious refuge, gazed out at the city sprawling beyond their window. Each light represented a story, a destiny. They realized that this small oasis was not just a place of rest, but a base from which to organize their broader mission, now equipped with a growing understanding of human nature. In this world of bright lights and deep shadows, Aisling and Lumina were ready to face the complexities that lay ahead.

In the opulent tranquility of their hotel room, while the city churned below them like a restless sea, Lumina and Aisling faced an unexpected dilemma. "Sister, what are we going to do about the documents? We don't even have last names," Lumina asked, visibly concerned.

Aisling, perched at the edge of the balcony with the city lights reflecting in her eyes, responded pensively, "I don't know... who was that 'uncle' in Monaco?" They exchanged glances, acutely aware of the predicament they had created. "I looked it up in general information and it was the first name that popped up," she admitted, as a sense of urgency pressed upon them.

"We have to create documentation, but how?" Aisling pondered. "Let's see through their eyes, using those gadgets..." Lumina, quick to want solutions, suggested, "Okay, but where do we get one?"

Aisling pointed to an old telephone beside them, accompanied by a list of numbers for various city departments. "Let's ask the concierge to bring us one."

Using the ancient rotary phone for the first time, Lumina initially spun the wheel aimlessly, unaware she needed to insert her finger into the corresponding number holes. Eventually, she managed to connect with the reception and greeted confidently, "Hello, sir, can you send a computer up to our room?"

Ever ready to assist, the concierge assured, "We don't have one at the moment, but I'll find one and have it delivered to you right away."

For Aisling and Lumina, navigating this new terrain meant learning as they went, embracing the twists and turns with determination and humor. Their journey in this vast, complex human world was just beginning, and they were poised to uncover the secrets within it, armed with their unique perspective and a growing arsenal of unconventional strategies.

A later, as Lumina and Aisling were enjoying a relaxing soak in the jacuzzi, a knock on the door announced the arrival of the bellboy. "Who could that be now?" Lumina murmured, before casually calling out, "Come in!"

The bellboy, a cheerful young man, was momentarily dazzled by the ethereal beauty of the sisters as he entered. "I've brought the laptop," he stammered, placing it gently on the elegant table. "Just set it there, please," Aisling instructed, her face glowing with a playful smile. Once he left, amused by his own nervousness, the two shared a serene, knowing laugh.

Rejuvenated and determined, they stepped out of the bath, needing no towels thanks to their subtle magic. They flipped open the laptop, finding the strange device both fascinating and alien. Closing their eyes for a brief moment, they accessed information about its operation almost instantaneously, thanks to their exceptional abilities.

Searching the Internet, they delved into the details of passports from the Principality of Monaco, quickly noting the names and surnames of the current royals. They took note and then focused, placing their hands over the screen. Speaking in ancient Irish, they uttered the magical phrase to transform their intentions into reality: "Draíocht Sióg."

In an instant, the gateway of the digital world manifested passports for them, complete with their names, photographs, and a surname that echoed nobility and nature: Ashbourne, a harmonious blend of "ash" (tree) and "bourne" (stream or brook).

This ingenious act of creation reminded them that beyond the truths or fictions of the human world, they possessed intrinsic power capable of transcending barriers. Though they faced ethical dilemmas, one thing was certain: with each encountered obstacle, they found a solution that brought them one step closer to fulfilling their mission, ready for any unexpected twist fate might deliver.

As they shared a moment of complicity, Aisling and Lumina reflected on their success. They had managed to obtain official documents through their magic, aware that their actions, however well-intentioned, tiptoed on the verge of legality. Yet, they felt they had no other choice; the truth of their origins and abilities would seem too incredible to anyone who heard it.

Suddenly, a "knock, knock" on the door interrupted their thoughts. "Come in," they said calmly.

The door opened to reveal two men in well-tailored suits, exuding professionalism and expertise. The first, a stocky man of middle age, sported a well-groomed mustache and eyes that seemed to catch every detail. His companion, younger and leaner, with hair slicked neatly to the side, carried a notebook in hand.

They had come to follow up on the sisters' story, but neither Aisling nor Lumina showed any sign of apprehension. With the city alive beneath their window and a renewed sense of purpose, they met the gaze of their visitors with the quiet confidence of those who knew their own power, ready to transform whatever challenge appeared into another opportunity on their extraordinary journey.

"Ladies, we're here to interview you since you've been victims of a robbery, and your documents were taken as well," began the older officer, regarding them with a mix of sympathy and curiosity. "I hope those scoundrels didn't harm you."

"Well, thanks to our quick reaction, we managed to escape," Lumina replied.

"Did you notice any particular details about the assailants that could help us?" the younger officer asked while jotting down notes.

"What did you have in the stolen bags, besides your documents?" inquired the mustached officer, trying to piece together the crime scene.

"Have you had any conflicts with anyone who might wish to harm you?" he suggested, assessing the situation.

After the preliminary questions, the senior officer cautioned them: "You need to be careful, as your uncle is a very important person. If the criminals find out, you could be targeted for more serious crimes."

Aisling and Lumina nodded, projecting calculated vulnerability. When the officer examined the passports, he raised an eyebrow. "You didn't mention these had been stolen."

"Yes, sir, but our uncle had replacements sent quickly. They just arrived," Aisling explained, maintaining her composure. The officer's skepticism was apparent. "That's remarkably fast service. Seems impossible. When did your uncle find out?"

"Yesterday afternoon, sir," Lumina replied without hesitation. "We climbed up to a rooftop and stayed there all night until dawn, we were so scared."

As they left the room, the senior officer, still doubtful, paused at the reception desk. "Has there been any messenger bringing an envelope for the Misses Ashbourne today?" he asked the receptionist, a friendly man who seemed aware of every movement in the hotel.

"No, sir. We don't let anyone upstairs without coming through reception first," the receptionist confirmed confidently.

"Thank you," the officer replied, walking away with his colleague toward the exit, engrossed in conversation.

As the police left, Lumina and Aisling peered out the window, assessing their current situation. Although they had temporarily extricated themselves from a tricky situation, they understood the need for increased caution. Their encounter with the law reminded them that their actions—even the necessary ones—could have unforeseen consequences, and they needed to act with greater subtlety to complete their mission without arousing further suspicion.

They realized their abilities were not only a valuable asset but also a significant responsibility, demanding they maneuver their endeavors with care and precision. The world they navigated required dexterity, and the stakes were higher than ever as they continued to protect the secrets of their origins.

The night before, as New York City shimmered with its myriad lights and a constant hum filled the air, Lumina walked the streets, seeking clarity after the intense day she'd just had. That's when she saw him: Jack, a former police officer whose story had reached them. He lay slumped on the sidewalk, an empty bottle in hand, staring into a void that seemed to have drained away all his hope.

Lumina approached gently, sitting down beside him without intruding on his space. "Hello," she greeted warmly, her voice a gentle nudge that reignited a flicker of hope.

Jack glanced up, his eyes red from drink and despair. "Leave me alone," he muttered, shifting slightly away. Yet Lumina remained undaunted. She closed her eyes briefly, reading into his past through the strands of memory worn thin by guilt.

"Those children weren't your fault," Lumina whispered, her words imbued with a truth that cut through the darkness surrounding him.

Jack looked at her, startled by her declaration. "How do you know that? It was all over the news," he replied, searching for a logical explanation for her insight. Nonetheless, something within compelled him to listen.

Lumina smiled, taking a step forward in her own confidence, and extended her hands, revealing her ability to fly. With grace, she lifted slightly off the ground, revealing her true nature. Jack gaped in astonishment, rubbing his eyes.

"How many bottles did I have?" he wondered aloud, unable to believe what he was seeing.

"What you see is real," Lumina assured him, landing softly. "My sister is also in the city. We're here to help you. We want to make sure your past in Chicago doesn't haunt you."

Lumina placed her hands gently on Jack's head and murmured indistinct words, a surge of energy passing through him, causing a tingling sensation up his spine that was beyond explanation. In that moment, the melody of "Old Men of Chicago" began to weave through the air, like a distant memory resurfacing to embrace the scene.

The following day, when Aisling and Lumina saw Jack again, he was no longer the shadow of the man he had been. Dressed with sobriety, he approached the sisters with newfound enthusiasm. Aisling, upon seeing him, felt an immediate connection; something about him reminded her of her father, a protective and kind figure she cherished deeply.

"I'm ready to face whatever comes," Jack declared with determination, the gleam in his eyes reflecting gratitude and a renewed sense of purpose.

The transformation in Jack was a testament to the power of redemption and the influence of the sisters' mission. As they prepared to continue their work, Lumina and Aisling knew they had gained a valuable ally in Jack—someone who understood both the shadows of the human soul and the light that could overcome them. Together, they stood poised to make a difference in the world, one encounter at a time.

What began as a simple act of charity evolved into a formidable alliance. The sisters started outlining their plan to confront present threats. The elderly man found himself unable to resist leaving his shadows of the past, along with his addiction, and began strategizing with precision, combining Jack's earthly strength with the celestial magic of the fairies. For Jack, it was a new opportunity to redeem his past.

As the afternoon turned to evening, the city illuminated its lights, shining on the newfound understanding forged between these unlikely allies. Together, they were determined to change the course of events, not only to redeem Jack but also to alleviate the suffering of others.

This unexpected encounter offered Jack not just a new reason to fight but also reinforced the sisters' mission in a world craving a touch of magic and truth. With the knowledge that the past could not be changed but understood and redirected, they faced the future with renewed determination, knowing that true strength lies in unity and understanding.

The bustling café provided a perfect cloak of anonymity for Jack, Aisling, and Lumina, who settled at a secluded table, away from curious gazes. The dim lighting and aroma of freshly brewed coffee created an atmosphere of moderate urgency, matching the delicate subject they were discussing.

Jack spread a detailed map of the city across the table, pointing to several intersections in the northeast section. "This is the likely route for the gang's exchange," he explained in a low voice, his face a mixture of focus and determination.

Aisling leaned in, absorbing every detail. "If they reach the port, intercepting them will be difficult," she noted, tracing an alternative path to block them.

Lumina, her eyes sparkling with ideas, suggested, "I could use my magical abilities to follow them. Staying unnoticed will allow me to place trackers on their vehicles," she mused, then added, "though I really don't need those, they're more for you two."

Jack nodded, his voice filled with resolve. "That's a good plan. We'll keep constant communication. We have to act quickly, or we'll miss our only shot."

Tension mounted; their information was scarce. Jack, frowning, added, "The exchange is set for 48 hours from now. We have zero room for error."

Aisling bit her lower lip, a shadow of concern crossing her face. "What if there's a change of plans? These guys are unpredictable," she pointed out, the weight of responsibility pressing on her shoulders.

Unfazed, Lumina asserted, "We'll handle it. With our skills and your experience, Jack, we can cover more ground than they imagine."

Finally, taking a sip of his coffee, Jack summarized the plan with a phrase imbued with duty-forged optimism: "This is our only chance to surprise them before someone else gets hurt."

The confidence in Jack's voice renewed the sisters' commitment. "We're with you, Jack," Aisling responded, her gaze meeting Jack's. It was a silent testament to the trust they shared.

As they rose to leave, Aisling glanced once more at the map. "We can do this," she affirmed, more to themselves than anyone else, feeling that every step in the right direction was a step toward justice.

Around them, the café's daily life continued uninterrupted. While people went about their routines, oblivious to what was at stake, Jack, Aisling, and Lumina knew they were on the verge of changing lives. With a brilliantly outlined plan and the clock ticking against them, they set out to execute their mission, confident that their skills and determination would lead them to success.

The hotel room brimmed with a blend of excitement and silent concentration as Aisling and Lumina prepared for the next day's operation. The sunset streamed through the curtains, bathing the space in a warm glow that contrasted with the tension of the moment. They were resolute in their mission to rescue the children, a goal that had become their most urgent priority.

Lumina meticulously practiced her invisibility powers, disappearing and reappearing in a blink, ensuring her control was absolute. Aisling, meanwhile, was crouched over a table laden with papers, maps, and communication devices. Beside her, Jack reviewed every logistical detail with her.

Lilith possessed the ability to read human minds, a gift she shared with the young fairies. Although Jack had trust in Aisling and Lumina, they knew what to expect from him and didn't feel it necessary to mention the magical auditory link they shared. It was a relationship grounded in a tacit understanding, as though words were superfluous.

While Jack rested on the sofa, exhausted from the preparations for the next day's operation, there came a gentle knock at the door. Lilith's presence was an intoxicating blend of mystery and irresistible allure. Jack, still groggy, answered and was momentarily hypnotized by her beauty.

"Hello, are my nieces here?" Lilith asked, her voice laced with calculated softness.

"Ma'am, I think they went down to the dining room," Jack replied, still trying to process the situation.

Aware of his past struggles, she slyly inquired, "Would you offer me a whiskey while I wait for them?"

With a firm resolve, Jack replied, "I've quit drinking, and there's no alcohol here."

Lilith smiled, exuding a deceptive calmness. "Ah, that's fine. Don't tell them I'm here. I want it to be a surprise."

As Lilith temporarily withdrew, the receptionist, still dazzled by her presence, noticed the young fairies approaching. "Ladies," he called out quickly. "Your aunt is here. Such a beautiful woman, just like you."

"Aunt Seraphina is here?" Aisling asked, her brow furrowing slightly as they made their way to the opulent dining room. The lights glowed with inviting warmth, but an unsettling tension buzzed in the air.

"Let me check," Lumina said, closing her eyes to mentally connect. After a moment of concentration, she opened her eyes with confusion. "No, she says she's not here."

Aware of the deception, a flicker of concern crossed Aisling's face. "So, who is it?"

Alerted to the ruse, they mentally reinforced their magical defenses and discreetly surveyed the guests. The dining room's splendor morphed into a theater of possibilities, with every stranger being a potential ally or adversary.

Suddenly, they sensed Lilith's presence, observing from a greater distance. Yet their gazes challenged any attempt at manipulation. They understood her true aim was to divide them or distract them from their mission.

In the face of uncertainty, Aisling and Lumina remained resolute, mentally joining forces to guard against any interference. The stakes were too high, and they were determined not to let anything thwart their plans. With unwavering focus, they prepared to confront whatever challenges lay ahead, trusting in their bond and abilities to lead them through the unfolding mysteries.

Realizing her deception hadn't achieved the desired effect, Lilith opted against a direct confrontation. Instead, beneath the glow of the chandelier, she sent a psychic message to Aisling and Lumina: "We will meet again... when you are ready to hear the truth."

As a singer and her band began playing "Lilith Bad," the fairies accepted the challenge with a calculated calmness, knowing they would face Lilith when the time was right. Lilith withdrew to her room, a hint of frustration tingling within her. She desired to protect these young women, as a new feeling had stirred within her soul. Despite arriving with deceit in mind, her transformation and emotions were changing. After all, these young fairies were her kin, and blood ties ran deep. Meanwhile, Aisling and Lumina continued their dinner.

They accepted the challenge with a measured serenity, confident they would confront Lilith in due course. As they refocused on their primary mission with Jack, there was a clear understanding that their adversaries existed in both the physical and ethereal realms.

The tension of the encounter strengthened the sisters' bond and renewed their dedication to the cause. They understood that each adversity not only fortified their mission but also solidified the purpose that had brought them to the human world, heralding a new chapter in the endless battle between light and darkness.

The tranquility of the hotel dining room was interrupted only by the gentle clinking of cutlery and occasional murmurs. With Lilith gone, Aisling and Lumina sensed an external presence calling to them. An invisible pull urged them to investigate, but Lumina, with her characteristic love for culinary pleasures, interrupted her sister's urge.

"Wait," Lumina said, her eyes twinkling mischievously. "Let's finish dessert first." It was a lavender soufflé with a delicate lemon and berry sauce, a dessert worthy of her discerning palate. Aisling smiled, well aware of her sister's weakness, and agreed that a small delay wouldn't alter the outcome.

After savoring the last bite, they stood and instructed the waiter to charge their suite. Stepping out of the hotel, they were greeted by the frenetic energy of New York City. They scanned their surroundings, trying to discern where the call they had felt was coming from.

The alley before them, scarcely visible in the shadows cast by the towering buildings, seemed the least welcoming place. Its walls, adorned with urban art, whispered tales of comings and goings. The air carried a blend of urban freedom and the yearning for anonymity that only a city like New York could provide.

A glanced toward the corner of the alley, and as she focused, she discerned the outlines of three urban fairies. They blended seamlessly with the city's pulse, fully integrated into its rhythm. One of them, with pale skin and captivatingly blue eyes, waved with a mischievous smile. "Hello, Aisling… and you must be Lumina."

They introduced themselves with nicknames that resonated with the spirit of the Big Apple: "Skyline," the tallest with a metallic sheen in her hair; "Beat," an African-American fairy whose vibrant energy echoed the city's music; and "Whisper," a Native Indian with the fierce beauty of wild water.

"Our mother told us you were here and that we might help," Skyline mentioned, her words as fluid as the traffic coursing through the city's veins.

As they spoke, groups of teenagers walked by. One of them, intrigued by the unusual gathering, jeered, "Where's the costume party? Can we join?"

With classic New York flair, Beat quipped, "Nah, not in your everyday gear, pal." Laughter rang out, light and fleeting, as the teenagers moved along.

The encounter had the air of a fortuitous alliance, a crossing of paths brimming with opportunities and mutual discoveries. Feeling the security this connection offered, Lumina suggested, "Let's head up to the room."

With an ease that defied ordinary perception, they unfurled their wings and took flight, heading toward the balcony of their suite. The lights of Manhattan glittered below like earthly stars, echoing their airborne dance.

Upon reaching the suite, they found the terrace door locked. They knocked gently, laughter still twinkling in the air around the balcony—a reminder that even amidst tension and threats, beauty and possibility thrived in the meeting of kindred spirits.

This experience not only reinforced their mission but broadened their worldview, making it clear that magic and urban life could indeed coexist. The sisters understood that their path was rife with uncertainties but also new friendships and unexpected allies, ready to face whatever challenges destiny might cast their way, together.

Hearing the soft tap on the balcony glass, Jack parted the curtains, his mind still somewhat groggy from rest. As he peered out, he was met with a scene that defied all logic and reality: five girls, each radiating an aura of unique energy, hovered outside, patiently awaiting an invitation.

Jack couldn't help but remain agape at the unexpected gathering. In a moment of incredulity, he thought that no dream, not even in the best years of his youth, was as extraordinary as this vision. Shaking off his astonishment, he opened the balcony door and, with the curiosity of someone living the incredible, asked, "What is this? Can't you come through the door like normal people?"

Beat, with the confidence and cheek only a true New Yorker could muster, responded with a smile, "Grandpa, it's just more practical to come up this way."

"Alright, alright, come in, all of you," Jack said, gesturing them into the luxurious suite. The living room was a spectacle of understated elegance, with emerald velvet sofas snaking around an elegant glass and marble coffee table. Chandeliers cast soft reflections that adorned the dark wood-paneled walls.

The fairies settled in comfortably, their presence easily blending with the opulent surroundings. Observing the unusual assembly, Jack let out a light laugh, shaking his head. "More fairies? So New York is crawling with fairies, and I never knew? All these years, completely in the dark."

Lumina, with a touch of playful irony, responded as she took a seat: "Jack, there's none so blind as those who will not see." Her words carried a soft, universal truth: often, the most wonderful things are hidden in plain sight.

With conversation flowing naturally in this newly forged camaraderie, the girls began to discuss the challenges they faced and the hidden opportunities scattered through bustling New York. The mix of their perspectives, along with the unique abilities each brought, promised a bold and revitalized approach to their mission.

No longer confined to acting from the shadows, together they possessed the strength and connection needed to face any threats that crossed their paths with courage and determination. In this unexpected meeting, they not only found ways to empower each other but also began to alter Jack's perception of the seemingly ordinary world he inhabited, transforming the city he knew into a realm of magic and limitless potential.

Turning to Aisling, Lumina said, "We should order something for our guests to eat." When asked what they wanted, they all chimed in for burgers, and the Native Indian, for a hot dog. Lumina commented, "But that's unhealthy," to which Beat replied, "Here, it makes you strong, Lumina. There's no time for much else."

Aisling picked up the phone from the nightstand but hesitated, unsure how to use it, prompting Jack to step in. "Let me handle this; the youth knows nothing about analog," he chuckled. Handing the receiver to Aisling once the front desk answered, she instructed, "Order every type of juice, for night and water."

After making the call, Jack turned to Aisling and asked, "Do you have enough money for all this? You know this hotel is expensive, right?"

With an unmistakable Irish lilt, Aisling, along with the young fairies, reassured him, "Don't worry, Jack. We've got plenty of 'Franklins.'" She flashed a stack of $12,000, to which Jack remarked, "At this rate, you'll run out quickly."

"Don't worry about it," she teased, "We'll just make more." Laughter filled the room, and Jack, wisely, held his tongue.

Jack, though impressed, couldn't conceal his skepticism. "At this rate, you won't have anything left," he warned, his cautious nature peeking through. But his concerns were quickly brushed aside.

"Don't worry," Aisling replied with a playful wink. "We'll just make more." Laughter filled the space, transforming any tension into a wave of shared humor and liveliness. After all, no one really expects dollars to be conjured up in a hotel room.

The girls continued chatting and laughing, their light-hearted banter filling the suite as they waited for their order to arrive. Jack watched them, quietly reassured by the sincerity and sense of community that emanated from these magical beings, despite their otherworldly origins.

This unexpected gathering, and the camaraderie that bloomed within those walls, suggested that the true essence of life wasn't always found in the mundane, but rather in those moments of genuine connection. The night unfolded into a new opportunity to strengthen alliances, to laugh at the absurdities of everyday life, and to remember that even amid important missions, humor and friendship were gifts that should never be underestimated.

Jack

The Coup Begins

In a sleek, modern conference room adorned with luxurious marble and dark wood finishes, a clandestine meeting of the "World Organization Against Disease" (WOAD) was convened. Each member of the board arrived clad in high-fashion suits, wearing the masks of honorable philanthropists. Yet, the reality was starkly different, as among them were some of the most devilishly ambitious individuals on the planet.

The most notable figure was Heinrich von Strauch, a 70-year-old man with carefully groomed silver hair and piercing blue eyes. He had amassed his fortune through decades of deceit and corporate manipulation, following the extreme principles instilled by his father. His philanthropy, seemingly benevolent, served a sinister purpose.

As the directors settled in, a massive screen illuminated the wall, displaying maps of New York, Chicago, and other major capitals around the world. Heinrich led the conversation, exuding an air of unyielding authority.

"Ladies and gentlemen, our experiment in Africa was a resounding success," Heinrich began with a cold, calculated smile. "The indigenous villages offered no resistance, allowing us to refine our strategies."

The tone in the room was one of unanimous agreement, filled with knowing glances. "Now, we turn our attention to New York and Chicago," Heinrich continued. "Vast, diverse populations that will provide the perfect cover for the second phase of our plan."

A woman on the opposite side of the table, a representative of a prominent pharmaceutical laboratory, raised her hand. "We have analyzed the compounds and made progress in their efficacy to ensure the intended impact," she reported with conviction.

"And regarding the genetically engineered carrier insects," added a collaborator linked with biotechnology, "They are ready to be released in strategic areas, ensuring maximum spread and exposure."

The room buzzed with an unsettling energy, a collective anticipation for the chaos their plans would unleash. The conspirators discussed logistics, timelines, and contingencies with precision, each step carefully orchestrated to maintain their thin veneer of public service while pursuing their true, dark ambitions.

In this opulent chamber, under the guise of philanthropy, a coup of unprecedented scale was quietly set into motion. As their plans unfolded, so did the potential to alter the fabric of society—a reality known only to those within these walls, hidden from the eyes of the unsuspecting world outside.

"We with caution, however," Heinrich warned, his expression now grave. "Our patrons have invested significantly in this cause, and we cannot afford to fail."

The meeting continued with meticulous planning of logistics for the events in New York, Chicago, and other cities worldwide, each board member receiving specific instructions regarding their role. Heinrich, before dismissing the delegates, concluded with words steeped in pulsating determination: "If we succeed, we will control something that neither wars nor markets have achieved. It is time to remake the world in our image."

As the meeting adjourned, the atmosphere was charged with a sinister anticipation. An operation so Machiavellian required the perfect synergy of ill intent and the promise of absolute power. The conspirators filed out one by one, their confidence bolstered by the shadow of impunity that had shielded them for years. Yet, they were utterly oblivious to the imminent clash instigated by magical forces poised to thwart their plans.

In the dimness of a hidden library in New York, where the outside light barely seeped through, Aisling, Lumina, and Jack were deeply engrossed in researching documents that could alter humanity's fate. The wood creaked under the weight of centuries, and an air of solemnity enveloped each shelf laden with ancient knowledge. With Lumina's enchanting guidance, they meticulously traced the dark energies lurking over the city, unveiling the nefarious schemes of the "World Organization Against Disease" (WOAD).

As they pored over maps and etchings detailing the experiments and devices poised for deployment, they sensed a familiar yet strange presence approaching. Lilith, with her graceful steps and an aura oscillating between menace and affection, drew near deliberately.

Lost in her thoughts, she recalled her inability to form meaningful connections throughout her millennia-old existence. Perhaps in these young ones, she had glimpsed a trace of what she never had—a protective impulse she was unfamiliar with.

"Bravo, girls, you are quite clever," Lilith interjected in a velvety voice. "What are you searching for? Why not ask your Aunt Lilith?" The irony in her voice was palpable, yet beneath it lay a softer tone, almost nostalgic.

Aisling looked up, her frown a mix of surprise and defiance. "How did you find us?" she questioned, taking a defensive stance beside her sister.

Lilith offered an enigmatic smile. "Just as you have your powers, I have mine. Must be a family thing." Jack, bewildered, glanced from one to the other, trying to grasp the suddenly shifted dynamics.

However, the moment of confusion soon gave way to a deeper understanding. Lilith, revealing a glimpse of her knowledge, informed them about the organization's plans with an unsettling pragmatism. "WOAD plans to release disease-carrying insects and radioactive clouds over New York and Chicago," she explained with a detail and precision born of someone who had witnessed such scenarios many times before.

"For them, it's enough to create chaos," Lilith continued. "Warning of good after causing evil is their tool. They generate discord to tip the scales."

As she spoke, a beep broke the silence, signaling an incoming email on Jack's laptop. "We got it," he exclaimed, pointing to the urban fairies as he revealed contact with an old friend in Texas, an expert hacker who had managed to decrypt detailed plans and system passwords for WOAD. They had gathered millions of pieces of evidence against politicians and executives from major corporations worldwide, with over 150 "white-hat" hackers supporting the effort, led by "The Computer," a seasoned hacker renowned globally for his fight against control, advocating for freedom and justice.

"We have access to the locations and staging points for the trials," Jack concluded, eyes filled with determination.

The weight of the information on the small group was immense. They had the chance to stop the impending horror. They glanced at Lilith, still unsure of her role. But she merely said, "Sometimes, the greatest enemy is the one who helps us see how far we've come."

Aisling and Lumina exchanged a meaningful look before nodding. They knew that regardless of personal preferences, they had to act swiftly to counteract the devastating plan.

With the stolen data in their hands and strategies beginning to formulate among them, Lilith melted into the shadows, her smile barely visible as darkness reclaimed her. They had gained the momentum they needed from the most unexpected source and were ready to face the challenge, determined to prove that good could prevail even when evil lurked closer than we dared admit.

Love and War

In a tranquil corner of Ireland, amidst rolling green fields and crisp, fresh air, Ashley found herself in a rented home—a timeworn structure brimming with stories and echoes of times long past. The stone walls and sturdy wooden beams whispered tales from its history. The soft light of dawn gently illuminated the room, and as she gazed out the window, Ashley took in the vibrant and peaceful Irish landscape that unfolded before her eyes.

Feeling a novel, palpable emotion, her gaze settled on a familiar figure: Robert, who stood smiling in the garden. Their hearts raced in unison, an instinctive and sincere reaction that spoke louder than words could ever express.

Intent on savoring the moment, Ashley beckoned him inside, inviting him to share a coffee. The creak of the opening door added a warm melody to their meeting.

"I hope you like strong coffee," Ashley remarked as she headed to the kitchen, playing off the intimate atmosphere that had formed.

"Not as strong as our conversation last night," Robert quipped, referring to their deep discussions about the past and the personal histories that had forged their friendship.

As the aroma of coffee enveloped the room, a crisp sound interrupted their chatter: a "beep" emanating from the computer in the corner. "Excuse me, let me check that," Ashley said, feeling a mix of curiosity and urgency as she glanced at the email that had arrived.

Intrigued, she approached the computer and, with a simple click, opened the message. The words on the screen unfolded into a detailed report—an alarming exposé on the imminent threat that the "World Organization Against Disease" was planning to unleash in New York and Chicago. Her expression shifted as she read, the conversation turning more serene yet laden with significance.

As Ashley processed the information, Robert moved closer, sitting beside her. "Is everything alright?" he asked, ready to offer his unwavering support.

"It's from Computer," Ashley explained, summarizing the alarming contents as she noticed the puzzlement on Robert's face. She laughed, "Sorry! 'Computer' is a guy who helps us at 'Customs Moms,' an organization based in El Paso where we assist kidnapped children. This man is quite the hacker and always extracts fraudulent information from the bad guys."

Ashley offered a strained smile, and Robert nodded, the gravity of the situation enveloping them as they shared a contemplative silence. The house, witness to their heartbeats and words, now transformed into a stage for decisions and actions that could alter the course of their lives.

Armed with this new information, the two pledged to actively engage in the effort to prevent the looming catastrophe. Their hearts, once beating solely from the proximity of each other's company, now aligned towards a shared purpose. The budding love between them intertwined with their desire to join the cause alluded to by "Computer," symbolizing a bond as tangible as the gentle breeze wafting through the open window.

So, on this new day, Ashley and Robert began to view the world not just as a stage of shared memories, but also as a canvas of infinite possibilities. Together, anchored by the solace of their rented home, they chose to pave a path filled with hope for themselves and for those they could still safeguard from the impending evil.

The days in Ashley's rented house in Ireland passed with an enveloping serenity that infused every corner, stirring a desire for introspection and change in its inhabitants. The landscape, draped in vibrant greens and open skies, provided a backdrop for the morning walks they shared. These walks had become sacred rituals, where the ordinary and profound intertwined in conversations that colored their days with new emotions.

As time moved on, small details began to reveal themselves. During one of these walks, Robert observed Ashley as the golden light of dawn gently caressed her face, unable to overlook the eloquence of her laughter and the courage that imbued her every decision. These moments, though subtle, planted the seeds of a feeling that resonated more deeply within him.

Ashley saw in Robert a refuge of trust and complicity. His presence, steady and reassuring, offered her a sense of security she had seldom experienced. Yet, beyond the comfort, there was a shared longing for adventure and purpose.

One morning, while savoring tea on the porch, Ashley confided to Robert her feelings regarding the information "Computer" had shared about the "World Organization Against Disease" (WOAD).

"It's not just worry, Robert," she admitted, her gaze fixed on the horizon. "I feel we need to do something real, something meaningful."

Robert, with a gleam in his eyes betraying a newfound emotion, nodded. "I've spent so much time writing and caught in an endless cycle of interviews and promotions. It's like I'm always searching for something... something that truly matters. I think this is our opportunity for a real adventure, but more importantly, it's a way to genuinely make a difference."

Ashley smiled, warmth spreading from her heart. "And doing it together makes it all the more meaningful."

Their commitment to helping others became the glue that strengthened their relationship, infusing their shared moments with a greater purpose. They planned not only to join the effort to thwart WOAD's plans but also saw it as an opportunity to redefine who they were and what they aspired to achieve.

The path they chose was no longer just physical, but also spiritual and emotional. Together, Ashley and Robert embraced the challenge of becoming active defenders of life and the common good. Facing uncertainty, fear, and challenge, they discovered that their love was intertwined with their mission, forging a bond that not only strengthened them but also imbued their lives with a greater purpose.

With renewed hope and an unspoken commitment to being essential for the world and for each other, their story headed toward unknown yet eagerly awaited paths, where each step consolidated the love and shared mission, making them greater than their individual parts.

The morning unfolded beneath a landscape of gray clouds and a gentle rain drumming softly on the roof of the antiquated rented house in Ireland. It was a typical day, where the weather seemed to mirror a melancholy and contemplative mood. Inside, Ashley rose with determination, sensing an urgency in the air, a compelling need to act and initiate change.

Wrapped in a thick sweater to ward off the morning chill, Ashley settled at the kitchen table with a steaming mug of Irish tea. With her laptop humming quietly beside her, she focused on the details demanding her attention that day. She and Robert had decided that New York would be their destination in the fight against WOAD.

As Ashley composed an email to Jack, outlining the urgency of a potential visit, Robert shuffled into the dining room, still sleepy and holding a letter from his agent. "Are you coming to New York?" she asked, looking up at him. The sudden question caught him off guard.

"Already?" he replied, surprised. "Well... let's say, tomorrow," Ashley continued, searching for flights to the Big Apple as soon as possible. Amidst the emails and web browsing, a virtual newspaper opened on her screen.

Suddenly, her gaze halted on a disturbing headline next to the image of a crashed car. The article recounted the escape of De Luca, a criminal who had murdered a family in a nearby New Jersey county. He had stolen a car from a garage, careening off a hill in an accident. The impact of the news left Ashley momentarily paralyzed.

"My God," she murmured while reading the details. "Why did he have to escape?"

Robert, noticing the change in her expression, watched her with concern while holding the letter from his agent. "Is something wrong?" he asked, his concern genuine.

"No... no, it's nothing, thanks," she replied, trying to downplay it. "Just some horrible news."

The accident and crime involving that poor family filled Ashley with a blend of relief and determination. Knowing that De Luca, the man who had once threatened her life, was dead, provided an unexpected sense of security. Despite its tragedy, the horrific news spurred her to face her journey to New York with renewed and calm resolve. She felt ready to embrace the challenges ahead, assured that her path was now free from that ominous shadow.

They finished planning their journey with unease lingering in the air. They knew that the path ahead was fraught with dangers, both seen and unseen, yet their commitment remained unwavering. There was a shared pressure to protect those who might be at risk if their efforts failed.

As the rain continued its soft serenade, the promise of a new beginning in New York grew for both of them. With each falling drop, they reflected on the change that would soon reshape their lives. Together, they aimed to do good in a story woven with intrigue and interconnected destinies. Their mission served as a beacon, binding Ashley and Robert, intensifying their connection and strengthening their resolve to face whatever was necessary in pursuit of justice and shared love.

Ashley's house buzzed with a mix of excitement and nerves as she and Robert prepared for their trip to New York. A fresh breeze wafted through the window, carrying with it the gentle rustling whispers of swaying leaves. Sunlight danced on the old walls, creating an atmosphere ripe for introspection.

Ashley and Robert were surrounded by open suitcases and neatly folded clothes. Every item they packed symbolized another step toward the unknown, a journey that had both of them looking to the future with a blend of anxiety and hope.

"Do you think we'll need coats?" Robert mused, folding a sweater as he glanced at the growing pile of clothes.

"New York is unpredictable this time of year," Ashley replied, distractedly checking her contact list. "But it's better to be prepared. What about your luggage?" she asked, intrigued.

"Oh, I never bring much," he quipped with a grin. "I just buy what I need when I get there. Keeps things uncomplicated," he added, amused.

As they continued packing, the conversation took a more serious turn. WOAD, an organization Ashley had mentioned frequently, loomed large in their thoughts.

"I wonder how many people actually know what WOAD is up to," Robert pondered, glancing at the documents scattered on the table. "It's chilling to think about the experiments they have planned."

Ashley nodded, her expression resolute. "Aisling mentioned they've been working in the shadows for years, manipulating medical and political systems to expand their control."

Their discussion seeped into a silence laden with determination, the weight of their mission palpable yet invigorating. As they closed their suitcases and took one last look around the room, they remained unified in their resolve, ready to uncover truths, confront fears, and pursue a path that would challenge not just their courage, but also their bond. Together, they were set to illuminate the darkness, driven by the promise of their united love and the pursuit of a greater good.

The atmosphere tensed momentarily before Robert looked up with newfound interest. "So you're saying it's not just a health issue? They're after something much bigger?"

Ashley sighed, gazing out the window as she spoke. "They want absolute power. They're using health as a façade for their far more sinister intentions."

Amidst the serious discussion, a soft notification sound interrupted the tense air. An email had arrived, visible on the laptop screen perched in the corner. Ashley quickly opened it, her eyes scanning the contents. "Looks like we have something more," she said slowly, each word heavy with anticipation. "Someone named Lilith just sent us a message. She might offer a perspective we haven't yet considered."

The conversation lightened as they zipped the suitcases shut, but the gravity of the situation with WOAD lingered persistently in the background. The sense of incoming change was palpable, yet with the strengthening of their bond and the unexpected assistance from Lilith, their hopes were reignited.

With everything prepared, they realized this was not merely a physical journey but the beginning of a new phase in their lives. It was a chance to confront evil and restore faith in the power of joint effort to overcome seemingly insurmountable challenges. With one last knowing glance at each other, Ashley and Robert were ready, bracing for both the best and the worst, knowing they were a step closer to uncovering the truth and facing the challenges ahead.

The familiar hum of the taxi's engine resounded as it pulled up in front of Ashley's house, marking the start of their adventure. As the first light of dawn cast the landscape in a warm, golden glow, Ashley and Robert stepped out into the garden, their suitcases knocking gently against one another as they carried them to the vehicle.

The driver, an older man with a kind smile, stepped out to help load their luggage. "A good day for a journey," he commented cheerfully, adjusting the rearview mirror to watch them as they settled into the car.

As the taxi drove away, Ashley gazed out the window, committing each detail of the Irish landscape that had been her home to memory. The green valleys stretched out endlessly, painted with the vibrancy of the awakening day. Fading into the horizon, the ancient stone walls, steeped in history, conveyed a sense of permanence and strength.

Through the glass, she saw the merging of past and future, the leaving behind of one chapter and the brave stepping into another, filled with unknowns but also with purpose. Side by side, she and Robert felt the powerful pull of the road ahead—a journey promising not only the unraveling of secrets but also the forging of their shared destiny.

"It's amazing how much this landscape speaks of resilience," Robert remarked, his gaze following Ashley's. "It's a good reminder that our roots always remain, even as we chase new adventures."

Ashley nodded, touched by the tranquility of the place. "True. Even as we go to fight threats far from here, we can always carry a piece of this peace with us."

As the taxi navigated the winding roads, a sense of anticipation filled them both. They were leaving behind comfort and familiar landscapes to venture into the unknown, but they did so with the confidence that they were ready to face any challenge.

The journey continued, with conversations ranging from tactical plans to reflections on how they would approach their arrival in New York. Robert's determination blended seamlessly with Ashley's keen intuition, creating a solid commitment and a mutual promise of protection and support.

The taxi eventually reached the airport, marking the next chapter of their journey. As the car came to a stop, the driver wished them luck with a wise smile. "With determination and the right company, you can conquer any mountain," he said, handing them their luggage.

Ashley and Robert shared one last look at the Irish landscape before turning towards the horizon that promised new experiences. Together, they moved forward, ready to board the flight that would take them to a necessary battle beyond the green hills, trusting in the combined strength that their bond had bestowed upon them.

The trip to New York was not just a change in location; it symbolized an internal shift that would resonate in bold actions and decisions, impacting the world they were about to enter. Like the ancient stone walls lining the path, they too would endure time and change, steadfast in their commitment to protect what they loved and challenge what threatened to destroy them.

CHAPTER 27

Arrival in New York

Under the gray winter light of New York, where the chill wind whispers between skyscrapers and snowflakes dance gently through the air, the taxi carrying Ashley and Robert finally reached its destination. The vibrant city, draped in a white mantle, seemed to welcome them to another chapter of their extraordinary journey. As they stepped out of the vehicle, the steamy breaths of the crowd mingled with chimney smoke, painting a dynamic tableau as vibrant as the metropolis itself.

Meeting up with Jack and Aisling in the cozy interior of an elegant hotel, formalities quickly melted into an atmosphere of camaraderie. "Jack," began Ashley, "how have you been since the last time?"

"Running after threats," Jack replied with a tired yet genuine smile. "But this time we have a plan," he added, deftly sidestepping Ashley's inquiry about his former addictions.

It was Aisling who captured Robert's attention. "Do we know each other?" he asked, a spark of recognition lighting up his eyes. "You were the girl on the plane, weren't you? And also... I believe it was in Ireland... and in the forest when you spoke to me about metaphysical realities!"

Aisling grinned, a mixture of secrets and mischief playing across her face. "It's a long story, Robert. Perhaps another time, when things are calmer," she suggested, letting out a musical laugh.

Amidst this reunion, Jack observed Robert laughing as he adjusted his coat. "I'd say it's a bit surreal, wouldn't you?" Jack remarked, easing the tension with his joke.

"This is madness," admitted Robert sincerely, "If I tell anyone, they'll think I'm insane or drunk." Laughter filled the room, a way to tackle the incredibility of the world surrounding them, uniting them in their shared purpose.

In the sanctuary of Aisling's room, joined by Lumina, the group gathered around a table cluttered with documents and steaming cups of tea. "Listen," Aisling began, her tone serious. "The WOAD, under the guise of a nonprofit foundation and funded by several magnates and food and pharmaceutical companies, has already initiated suspicious activities in the city."

The gravity of her words settled over them, charging the air with urgency. The room, once a place for stories and laughter, now turned into a command center for action and strategy. Ashley and Robert, fueled by determination and the warmth of rekindled friendships, readied themselves to unravel the machinations of WOAD. The journey ahead was fraught with risks and challenges, but together, armed with knowledge and each other's strength, they were prepared to illuminate the shadows cast by the seemingly benevolent facade of the WOAD

Lumina added, "They've started introducing chemicals into systems that should be safe, and their plans involve something far larger."

The gravity of the situation descended upon them like an invisible shroud. Detailed reports outlined meetings at strategic points throughout the city, designed to deceive even the most vigilant. "We'll have to act swiftly," Jack concluded, his words echoing with a renewed sense of urgency.

As the day shortened into a night that set the streets ablaze with twinkling lights, the discussion veered towards tactics and commitment. They embarked on mapping out a series of precise actions to infiltrate and counteract WOAD's moves.

Gazing out the hotel window, the city appeared as a sprawling battlefield of potential threats and opportunities. Yet inside, warmed by their burgeoning bond, Ashley, Robert, Jack, Aisling, and Lumina formed an indestructible alliance, ready to transform chaotic stories into narratives of redemption.

What promised to be an intense challenge began to unfold, and with each new step, they reaffirmed their commitment to fight against the lurking evil, determined to safeguard the future from the shadows hidden beneath New York's winter frost.

Under the room's warm and vibrant lighting, Aisling suggested in her usual calm tone, "Well, we could call and book a room." Without hesitation, Ashley, with a confident smile, responded, "Oh, don't worry about that, Aisling. I'll handle it." Her voice carried a clear determination, a product of her more relaxed financial situation.

Robert, observing the interaction, turned to Jack with a hint of humor and humility. "I guess this might get a little pricey. Remember, I'm just your average writer—not a bestselling one," he said with a carefree smile, shrugging off the reality of his own economic limits. "I've got enough to get by."

However, as the atmosphere settled into a mix of familiarity and light-heartedness, an unexpected moment ensued. Aisling, without warning, briefly closed her eyes to concentrate, and in the palm of her hand, bundles of hundred-dollar bills began to materialize as if summoned by magic.

The room fell silent, spellbound by the surreal spectacle. Aisling opened her eyes, her expression serene and knowing. "Sometimes, we just need a little extra push," she said with a playful glint, passing the bills to Robert.

The magical display broke the tension, lighting gentle smiles on each face. In that quiet room, unexpectedly touched by wonder, Robert, humbled by the generosity, found himself embraced not only by newfound friendships but also by the unexpected magic lying beneath the surfaces of tangible worlds. As they prepared to confront the challenges ahead, the evening's unusual gifts fortified their resolve, reminding them that even in times of looming darkness, moments of light and mystery could guide their path towards collective strength and unforeseen possibilities.

Jack, taken aback by the astonishing phenomenon unfolding before his eyes, raised his hands and exclaimed, alarmed, "Stop, stop! What are you doing? This is illegal. You're counterfeiting money!"

Aisling, with the innocence of a child oblivious to the dilemma, replied, "Why would it be fake? It's made just like it is in any factory."

Ashley seized the opportunity, intervening with calm logic and a sly smile: "If the Federal Reserve can do it, why can't Aisling? Besides, Jack, you know that the more money is printed, the higher inflation goes."

The room fell into a momentary silence as all eyes turned to Jack, awaiting his reaction. Despite his principles, Jack found himself mulling over Ashley's words. Finally, with a mix of resignation and bewilderment, he shrugged, choosing not to oppose it.

With the tension now dissipated, Robert, ever quick with humor, chimed in joyfully, "You're going to have to teach me that trick, Fairy." His lighthearted comment resonated in the room, triggering a wave of shared laughter. It was in these moments of connection and camaraderie that the team found the strength and morale to face the challenges ahead.

At seven in the morning, the soft glow of dawn filtered through the hotel suite curtains, enveloping everyone in a warm light. Gathered around the specially laid breakfast table were Jack, Ashley, Robert, Lumina, and Aisling. Each carried the weight of anticipation for a pivotal day, fueled by a mix of nerves and energy.

The atmosphere was light yet focused as Ashley poured coffee, sensing that this simple act helped ease the group's tensions. "Your contact, 'The Computer,' has really given us an advantage," Ashley remarked, glancing at Jack's nephew, Alex, on the video call.

Robert, seated beside her, silently nodded, taken aback by the depth of the information being shared. On the screen, Alex, now 33 and equipped with the sharp skills of a renowned FBI hacker, explained his findings as steam from the coffee swirled around them.

"Barely a new move is attempted online without my contact noticing," Alex continued with admiration. Thanks to his source, he had accessed hidden files from a secret WOAD base located in a remote area, invisible on any GPS maps.

The gravity of the situation deepened as they listened to Alex's revelations. Each piece of information added to their understanding of the looming threat, fuelling their determination to counteract WOAD's hidden agendas. In that moment, with coffee in hand and allies gathered tightly in purpose, they prepared to step into a day that would shape the course of their fight against the dark forces gathering closer to them.

Jack, leaning into his tactical instincts, suggested, "We could send the fairies in with a video camera for reconnaissance."

With a playful smile, Aisling shook her head. "Don't be old-fashioned. Give me your phone, Jack. I'll send you the signal, and you can see through my eyes."

Lumina, always quick with her humor, chimed in, "Yeah, and I'll send the signal to Ashley's phone too. Goodness, you guys and those ancient phones!" A wave of laughter swept through the room, easing the tension and reminding everyone of the technological advantages their magical allies possessed.

Listening attentively from the video call, Alex couldn't hide his curiosity. "Uncle, who are those voices?" he asked, his tone revealing a mix of surprise and intrigue.

Jack, with a critical gesture, replied, "Nothing to worry about, nephew. I'll fill you in when the time is right."

Together, they geared up for informed and timely action. "Customer Moms," led by Alex's skills, combined the efforts of the mothers and the fairies, analyzing images and data to devise an effective counterattack.

That morning, with its interplay of light and shadow, promised not only a tense next chapter but also an opportunity for each member of the group to discover their own potential. Fueled both physically and emotionally by the shared breakfast, and the communal spirit that only a mission of such magnitude could inspire, their actionable efforts flowed into a narrative that would transcend their understanding of the situation and how they would confront the looming threat of WOAD.

This day promised a path toward bold actions and a solidarity that would provide the strength needed to face whatever destiny had in store for them.

The WOAD building loomed like a colossal glass fortress in the heart of New York, its eco-friendly facade concealing dark secrets within. Lilith, wrapped in a luxurious white fur coat and an elegant Russian hat, strode in with purpose. She had neutralized the real spokesperson of the news group in a nearby alley, assuming her identity to infiltrate the upper echelons of power within the organization.

As she entered the sleek lobby, an air of confidence surrounded her, blending into the buzz of office life. Her heart raced with the thrill of her mission, each step calculated, each glance observant. She was aware that behind the polished exterior of WOAD, significant operations unfolded—operations that needed to be uncovered and stopped.

In that moment, as she moved through the throngs of busy employees, Lilith became a key player in a web of intrigue, ready to expose the truth and disrupt the dark ambitions hiding beneath the surface of the organization. As the line between ally and espionage blurred, the stakes rose higher, and the countdown to action had officially begun.

After encounter with the receptionist, Lilith was granted access to the president's office, where two advisors accompanied the leader of WOAD. Awed by her presence, they offered her a seat as she wore a mysterious smile, ready to play her boldest card.

"Well, Mr. President," she began, captivating their attention with a clever play on words. "As part of our commitment to the truth, imagine television cameras broadcasting as your very own neighbors perish live on air. Everyone would rush to buy the antidote. It's a wonderfully... lucrative plan, wouldn't you agree, Mr. Bill?"

Initially taken aback, the president and his advisors exchanged glances, weighing her words. The suggestion was audacious, but there was a twisted logic in her proposal.

"Interesting perspective," murmured the Vice President, leaning forward. "Considering the masses, panic could drive unprecedented demand."

Captivated by the vision Lilith presented, one of the advisors slowly nodded. "Broadcasting the chaos could expedite everything."

As she sensed the men beginning to entertain her approach, Lilith took advantage of the moment, suggesting strategic locations to maximize public exposure of the event.

As the conversation progressed, the executives' defenses crumbled under the twisted logic of Lilith's rhetoric. They entered into a verbal agreement where justifying the unjustifiable became pragmatic business practice, and, with a certain degree of moral contortion, they convinced themselves of their "innovation."

Exiting the office, Lilith wore a triumphant smile, having successfully extracted crucial details about WOAD's plans. It was an imminent danger, but knowledge was power, and now she was armed to bend its course.

Back out on the street, the gleam of the glass building projected a pristine image that belied the darkness contained within. Content with her accomplishments, Lilith knew she was key to informing Ashley and Jack's group. With these revelations, she positioned herself at the forefront of a larger confrontation, waiting for the opportune moment to alter the course of events. Through her, the struggle was not merely a clash of power; it represented a chance at redemption and defiance, engaged with forces that transcended the human realm.

In this high-stakes game, every move she made could tip the balance between chaos and order, and Lilith embraced her role as a catalyst, ready to ignite the change that was so desperately needed.

As Lilith moved away from the imposing glass building, the cold New York breeze offered her a momentary clarity. She understood that the path she had chosen was perilous not only because of what WOAD could do, but also because she was teetering on a tightrope between their intentions and the constant vigilance of those who had once been her allies in the darkest shadows. The most dangerous of them all was her husband, the very Prince of Darkness, who watched her thoughts like a predator lying in wait.

Her mind, meticulously arranged with ancestral precision, became her most effective shield. She had spent much of her existence learning to conceal her deepest thoughts. However, this new plan and her recent alliances with those fighting for good required a level of confidentiality that even for Lilith was an enormous risk.

"You're careful, but not infallible," she whispered to herself, weighing each alternative. She knew that a slip in her mental armor could open the door to the Devil's control, revealing her other sides with just a flicker of stifled ambition.

As she walked down Fifth Avenue, the echo of the city's bustle provided a fitting backdrop to the constant dialogue in her head. Lilith's determination did not wane; she knew she had to stay vigilant and ahead of the abyss that her husband might detect.

Taking a deep breath, her thoughts fluctuated. The images of Ashley, Jack, and the others filled her mind, solidifying her purpose. She recognized that the risk was justified: if she faced the Demon on his terms, she could gain more than her own redemption. She could enact a change on a universal scale.

The percussion of her heels resonated like a prelude to the internal battle she was waging. She drew strength from the memory of every exchanged word, every shared vision with those on the side of good. She believed that the glow of her inner courage could mask the passions her husband would try to expose.

Stopping at the corner of a bustling intersection, Lilith smiled beneath the shadows of her elegant Russian hat, a smile that was almost imperceptible. In that moment, she aligned herself with the hope that brewed in her chest—the hope for a world free from the manipulation of darkness. With each step forward, she was ready to embrace her role, not merely as a pawn in a celestial game, but as a powerful force in her own right, poised to challenge the very fabric of fate that had long sought to bind her.

She felt that part of her inner power resided in that ambiguity, in the delicate art of navigating between light and darkness.

As she set her course toward the designated meeting place with her new allies, she fortified her mental guard. Knowing that the fate of many, and to some extent, her own, depended on her ability to maneuver between her past and present, between undeniable love and indomitable terrors. It was a dangerous game, but with each step, Lilith reaffirmed her role: to adapt to a new purpose that would not only challenge Satan but could also finally lead her toward the path of light.

In Aisling's room, a firm knock drew everyone's attention. When the door opened, the imposing figure of Lilith, elegant in her white fur coat and Russian hat, filled the threshold. Aisling, caught between surprise and caution, exclaimed, "You here again?"

Without losing her composure, Lilith stepped confidently into the room. "Come on, darling, let your aunt in," she said openly, while Lumina looked on in astonishment. With a graceful greeting and an almost theatrical flair, Lilith addressed the group, "Ladies and gentlemen, I bring good news. Although my nieces doubt me."

The eyes in the room were fixed on Lilith as, with a ceremonial flourish, she removed her coat and hat, revealing an unexpected sincerity. "I have the address where they will release the infected bugs," she announced. "They'll be using food distribution trucks to avoid raising any suspicion."

"And how do you expect us to trust you?" Lumina challenged, recalling Lilith's past intentions to ensnare Aisling. With an introspective air, Lilith admitted, "You're absolutely right, but you've made me reflect. My life has been a series of failures, with nothing left to inherit but power and malice. I'm tired of it. You should believe me. After all, I am family."

"Really?" Aisling responded, skepticism lacing her tone.

"Yes, I am your great-aunt," Lilith confessed gravely. "I am the sister of your grandmother, who condemned me to darkness for attempting a coup in our kingdom. Satan welcomed me with open arms."

The humans present were stunned, as if witnessing a scene from a film. Lilith, sensing their bewilderment, smiled serenely. "I know humans love superheroes, and you must always dress with dignity."

With an elegant gesture, Lilith sent the costumes flying toward Aisling and Lumina. Upon touching their bodies, magic took over, instantly dressing them in their emblematic outfits. Aisling was adorned in an emerald green suit, adorned with a four-leaf clover on her chest. Lumina, on the other hand, wore a suit of white and green, featuring an orange clover reminiscent of the Irish flag.

"I love you both dearly," Lilith added softly, "It honors me to see how much you've both grown."

Observing their new costumes, Lumina joked, lightening the mood, "Well, it seems like this is definitely more our style now."

Aisling nodded, feeling a slight weight of responsibility draped with a touch of confidence. "Now I understand, it's time to be what we were always destined to be."

In that moment, a sense of transformation enveloped them, igniting the fire of purpose within. With Lilith as their unexpected ally, they stood ready to take on the challenges ahead, fully aware that not only their destinies but also the fate of many rested on their shoulders. The line between family and foes blurred, and together they prepared to step into a fight against the shadows that threatened to engulf not just their world, but all worlds.

CHAPTER 28

Enemies in Sight

Under the cold neon lights that illuminated the New York night, the imposing WOAD building stood as a bastion of secrets. Its deceptively modern and eco-friendly facade concealed a complex complete with an airport, resembling a futuristic fortress prepared for any contingency. Aisling and Lumina, channeling their magic, took position at the perimeter, ready to dismantle the technological security of the place.

The fairies took their places near the security robots that meticulously patrolled the area. Aisling, with her exceptional magical charisma, began to play a curious game with them: "This is the riddle game," she said with a smile, as the robots tried to follow her rapid cues, diverting their attention from the unfolding plan.

Meanwhile, Lumina positioned herself in front of the main entry panel. Her eyes sparkled as she analyzed the digital codes. "a2h4Z," she murmured with a half-smile, transmitting the PIN to Jack, Robert, and Ashley through her magical link.

The trio, rendered invisible thanks to Lumina's enchantment, slipped silently into the building. Inside, the atmosphere was cold and distant, with metallic surfaces and quiet blue lights extending in vertical lines along the walls.

They arrived at the meeting room, a space where the darkest decisions came to life. Ashley entered alone, while Jack and Robert remained close, hidden in the corridor. Drawing on the stealth learned from past experiences, Ashley cleverly concealed a microphone within a bouquet of flowers but, driven by an impulse, decided to reposition it.

At that moment, she accidentally knocked over a vase, its base overflowing with water that pooled across the floor. The sound captured the attention of everyone present, creating a moment of suspense suspended in time and space. As the water touched the ground, the invisibility spell began to fade.

Panic surged through Ashley's mind as she realized the precariousness of their situation. She quickly glanced back at Jack and Robert, her heart racing, knowing they were moments away from being discovered. The presence of the WOAD executives loomed large in the room, their conversations abruptly silenced as the subtle shift in the air alerted them.

"Stay calm," Ashley whispered under her breath, her instinct for survival kicking in. She needed to think fast; any wrong move could blow their cover.

The executives looked around, confusion mingling with suspicion as they searched for the source of the disturbance. The tension rose palpably, a silent battle between alertness and the desire to remain oblivious.

Outside, Aisling and Lumina maintained their positions, sensing the shift in the air. Aisling's intuition kicked in, her eyes darting toward the entrance, realizing that something had gone awry. "We need to act quickly," she said to Lumina, her voice steady despite the gravity of the situation.

Inside the conference room, Ashley clenched her fists, willing the magic that flowed through her to rejuvenate their protective spell. She focused, summoning every ounce of her ability to restore their invisibility, hoping against hope that it would be enough to keep her friends safe.

"Time to step up, ladies," Aisling murmured, knowing they had to intervene before the situation escalated into disaster. The stakes had never been higher, and they were all aware that the path they walked lay riddled with perilous choices.

With a shared silent understanding, the fairy duo prepared to spring into action, knowing that they were not just fighting for survival but for the very future against the insidious threat of WOAD. As shadows danced around them, uncertainty loomed, but their determination burned bright, ready to face whatever darkness awaited them.

Slowly, before the eyes of the executives, Ashley became visible. A murmur of confusion rippled through the room. "Miss Ashley," exclaimed one incredulous executive, "in addition to being a famous attorney and television advocate for the less fortunate, are you also a magician?"

Thinking quickly, Ashley responded, "Well, I came to look for an old friend, Mrs. Walker, but I couldn't find her and ended up getting lost, accidentally appearing here. I sincerely apologize for the disturbance."

Mr. Von, wearing a calculated expression of disapproval, addressed her directly. "I hope you haven't been listening in too much, because you know that's a violation of private property and industrial espionage, don't you?"

"I fully understand, Mr. Von," Ashley replied firmly.

With a gesture, Von summoned security. Two humanoid robots, dressed as guards, entered with synchronized steps. "Escort the lady to the exit, reference 34," ordered Von.

"As you command, sir," the robots responded in unison as they politely led Ashley through the hallways, now in a procession illuminated by blue lights that flickered upon detecting movement.

Jack and Robert, still invisible, followed every step of Ashley's journey, acutely aware that the fate of their companion mirrored the building's cold, architectural interior: precise, calculating, and utterly ruthless.

Outside, the gardens, reminiscent of futuristic military bases, lay serene under the starry night. Every leaf and corner stood as witnesses to the ongoing battle between light and darkness as the true heroes of this tale advanced to confront the realm of shadows hidden beneath a facade of progress and justice. With their team spirit still elevated, Jack and Robert knew they had to find a way to turn the game around, restoring the equilibrium that an organization like WOAD had so ruthlessly disrupted.

Inside the bowels of the WOAD building, the endless corridors bore the imprint of clinical minimalism. The walls were smooth and placid, the floor absorbed any hint of sound, and the air was heavy with a pervasive sense of control. As Jack and Robert glided through these arteries of steel and concrete, they struggled to devise some form of distraction for the guard robots. But the environment, meticulously devoid of irregularities, rendered every attempt futile.

It was as if they were traversing a futuristic military compound, where every detail was subordinated to the purpose of security and surveillance. The place, brimming with cutting-edge technology, stood as a fortress built with the inexhaustible resources of pharmaceutical, military, and tech conglomerates. WOAD was not just a bastion of power; it was an emblem of a new world order—a reflection of the dominance of the powerful, who now served a darker master: Satan.

As Jack and Robert crept ever closer to their goal, they knew that time was running short, and every moment counted. They could feel the weight of their mission pressing heavily upon them, igniting a fierce determination to expose the truth behind WOAD and dismantle its evil from within. The stakes were higher than ever, and the shadows loomed larger, but they kept their resolve firm, ready to rise against the encroaching darkness.

with the inexhaustible resources of pharmaceutical, military, and technological conglomerates. WOAD was not merely a bastion of power; it was an emblem of the new world order, a reflection of the dominance of the powerful, who now served an even darker master: Satan.

Suddenly, breaking the calculated silence, Lilith emerged. Her figure glided gracefully from a poorly lit corner, her presence destabilizing the cold, robotic control of the environment. "Dear metals, you have a choice," she declared in a melodic voice, barely restrained in a whisper that resonated against the surrounding metal. "You can hand over the prisoner, or I will disconnect you myself."

Ashley, caught in the tumultuous flow of events, stared in disbelief. Where had Lilith come from? Her sense of reality, forged by years of control and order, shattered further as magic and chaos conspired to rewrite the world she knew. Her only anchor was the love she felt, a silent connection with Robert, who remained close even in invisible form.

The robots, responding to the challenge, articulated their response with mechanical coldness. "Step aside," they stated in unison. "We have no consciousness or morals. We simply follow programmed rules to provide assistance to humanity."

Lilith sighed, a disapproving smile playing on her lips. "Nonsense," she countered with an air of certainty. She extended her hand, swirling her fingers with the elegance of one who does not fear wielding her innate power. "You've asked for this."

From her palm, a shimmering mist of sparks unfurled, a tangle of ancient energy woven into geometric and enchanting patterns. The filaments glowed as they made contact with the robots, overloading their circuits with a delicate yet relentless reverberation. In an instant, they froze, the crackling of invisible lines of code suspending their functionality.

As the robots ceased to function, Jack and Robert quickly took action, now free to approach Ashley. The consternation shifted to relief as they saw the metallic guardians incapacitated, thanks to Lilith's opportunistic intervention.

Ashley, trying to absorb the wave of magic surrounding her, reached out her hand toward Robert, who still remained invisible to her eyes. In that subtle gesture of connection, she found comfort and renewed resilience.

With the path cleared, the group moved forward, aware that they had crossed a crucial threshold in their battle against WOAD. Outside, the gardens lay indifferent yet serene, standing as passive witnesses to the epic collision between those who served the darkness and those who sought to restore balance.

As they stepped deeper into the heart of enemy territory, a shared determination surged among them. The stakes were higher than ever, and with the shadows at their backs, they were ready to confront whatever awaited them in the labyrinthine corridors of WOAD, united in their purpose to expose the truth and reclaim the light.

Victory, though uncertain, was beginning to take shape. The tenacity of human and magical forces united in a common purpose: to ensure that those who operated in the shadows would not go unpunished and to bring clarity to a world plagued by the irregular lines of power.

As the light of the stars wove a mantle over the metallic structures, the true heroes of the story aligned, recognizing both their mission and the new day that awaited them, invisible to all eyes but those willing to see beyond the manufactured reality.

The exit from the WOAD building was drawing near, with Ashley, Jack, and Robert advancing down the corridor, sensing the mix of imminent danger and close achievement. Behind them, Lilith walked with silent determination, her presence a constant reminder of the magic surrounding them.

At the main entrance, Lumina and Aisling were preoccupying the small security robots. What had initially started as a tactical distraction had transformed into an impromptu session of laughter, the robots disarmed emotionally by the fairies' charming jokes.

"Okay, guys, we're leaving now. Time to return to your watch," Lilith instructed with feigned authority. The robots, as if obeying a higher command, ceased their mechanical laughter and returned to their posts.

At that moment, Robert raised his voice in humorous desperation, "Lumina, how the hell do I make myself visible again?"

"Simple," Lumina replied, a mischievous spark in her eyes. "Just say 'Revealium Luminos.'" The magical phrase resonated with an archaic simplicity and strength that reflected the group's camaraderie and humor.

In unison, both Robert and Jack uttered the incantation, feeling a slight tingle course through their bodies as they regained their visibility. A wave of laughter enveloped them as the palpable tension of the moment deflated, replaced by a renewed sense of reality.

Lilith, observing their fleeting success, interjected with a warning laced with promise. "Go on, get out. I'll tip them off about you to gain their trust, and I'll give them false information to mislead them. They'll fear you're at the old factory, taking a misstep while you return to the hotel in peace."

The trio glanced at each other, uncertainty mingling with admiration. "Are you sure you can handle that?" Ashley asked, concern flickering in her eyes.

Lilith waved off the question with a determined smile. "I'm more than capable," she assured them. "Now go, and remember, every moment counts."

With that, Jack, Robert, and Ashley took off, their hearts racing as they made their way toward the exit. Outside, the cool air greeted them like a balm, a stark contrast to the tense atmosphere inside. The night sky was vast and sprinkled with stars, a reminder that beyond the darkness of WOAD, hope still existed.

As they moved away from the building, the weight of their mission settled on their shoulders, a mixture of relief and anticipation converging within them. They knew they were not out of danger yet, but for the first time, they felt the tide might be turning in their favor.

Meanwhile, Lilith watched them disappear into the night, her heart pounding with duality - both the thrill of deception and the faint glimmer of purpose that came from standing on the side of light. She prepared for her role, knowing that her actions could either steer the outcome toward salvation or chaos. With a deep breath, she stepped back into the shadows, ready to carry out her plan

They stole one last glance at Lilith before slipping through the doors, a mix of admiration and gratitude shimmering in their eyes. Lilith's reassuring words and strategic sacrifice had woven a momentary cloak of safety under which they could operate.

The group moved quickly, acutely aware of the invisible clock ticking over their heads. They knew that although they had bought themselves a fleeting truce, the threats still loomed large, and Lilith's cunning had merely given them a small reprieve.

The fairies illuminated their path as they advanced toward safety, aware that Lilith had woven a momentary tide in their favor. As they crossed the darkness now speckled with stars, Robert, Jack, and Ashley felt like part of a chosen family—a union of friendship and purpose that had grown beyond mere acts of resistance.

Upon reaching the hotel, they felt revitalized, not just for escaping unscathed but also because the course they had taken promised not only protection for themselves but also a step toward a world where shadows and light could coexist in improved balance. As they rested, each reflected on what lay ahead, knowing that the bonds forged in the heat of challenge and magic were now stronger than ever, capable of facing together the trials that the future held.

Lilith slipped back into the bustling WOAD building, each step resonating with a dangerous and calculated confidence. She understood that to maintain the allegiance of the executives, she must reestablish fear and assert her authority. Moving toward the executives' meeting room, she closed her eyes for a brief moment, concentrating her energy to summon the chief general and the lieutenant of troops. Without uttering a single word, she sent a mental vibration through the building, a silent command that resonated in the minds of those she wanted present.

With a slam that shook the pretentious calm of the office, Lilith burst through the meeting room doors. The executives, taken aback, looked up from their papers and screens, their expressions filled with unease. Among them, Mr. Von stood abruptly, his small blue eyes peering over his thick glasses—reflecting someone who had been the class nerd and suffered rejection from his peers. The marginalized boy had grown into an adult filled with resentment toward his fellow man, molded by a father who championed ideals of racial superiority.

"Why are we gathered here?" Von demanded, his voice unsteady with the urgency of the moment.

Lilith, unfazed by the tension in the room, stepped forward with an air of authority. "We are faced with a situation that requires our immediate attention," she announced, silencing the murmurs of confusion.

The executives shifted nervously in their seats, the reality of Lilith's presence setting in. She could see the strands of fear and intrigue weaving through their thoughts, and she capitalized on that, knowing that the power of persuasion ran deep when woven with a thread of fear.

"Your operations have been compromised, and if we don't act quickly, everything we've built will collapse," she continued, her voice laced with a magnetic urgency. "I can help you regain control, but you must trust me."

As she spoke, she watched their expressions closely, noting the flickers of doubt and skepticism. But she also saw the hunger for power, the desperation to cling to authority amidst brewing chaos. It would be easy to manipulate that.

"Together, we can strike at the heart of those who threaten us," she concluded, allowing a glimmer of her ancient magic to pulse subtly around her, reinforcing the illusion of her unwavering strength.

In the presence of intoxicating possibility and veiled threat, the top brass of WOAD found themselves lured back into the web of fear and ambition that Lilith spun with effortless grace. As they stirred, the faint echoes of their doubts began to fade, replaced by whispers of revenge and reinvigoration. This was just the beginning, and Lilith knew that the game was set, one she was determined to win.

"all idiots?" Lilith roared, her tone sharp as a knife. "Those robots are standing outside like useless scraps! Where did you buy them? At a flea market?"

Von swallowed hard, straightening with all the dignity he could muster. "We'll review the surveillance footage to see what happened," he declared, his voice trembling just beneath the surface of urgency.

Lilith raised an eyebrow, her disdain unmistakable. "Nonsense. I've already looked at it, and nothing is clear; it was intercepted."

The executives exchanged nervous glances. They understood that their positions depended not only on their effectiveness but also on maintaining the facade they had built with money and power.

Lilith continued, her voice resonating like subtle thunder. "Remember, all of you, who you work for," she said, her words a chilling reminder. "You've been allowed to keep your money, your influence. But don't forget that you work for my husband. And this needs to go well, understood, you bunch of useless fools?"

Her authority filled the room like a heavy cloak, smothering any doubt or attempt at retort. The executives nodded quickly, murmuring their assent, fully aware of the precarious balance on which their dominion rested.

As Lilith withdrew, leaving behind a room thick with tension, the WOAD executives felt not only the brush of danger but also a profound disdain for their own incompetence. They knew that their financial and powerful ventures could evaporate as swiftly as an illusion if they failed to meet the expectations of their dark masters.

With each step that took her away from the meeting, Lilith was aware that she had once again sown the necessary fear to maintain control, balancing the fragile axis upon which their plans turned. Every detail would need to be meticulously managed to ensure her survival. This wasn't just a game of politics or power; it was a fight for survival within the turbulent rules she had helped create.

As she left the meeting room behind, the echoes of her words hung in the air, a constant reminder of the stakes at play. Lilith could feel the threads of manipulation weaving tighter around her adversaries, and she smiled, knowing that in the intricate tapestry of this battle, she held the loom.

Reflection Note

Lilith's entrance into the WOAD building is a calculated display of power. Each of her steps serves as a reminder to the executives of who holds the reins and the terror she can instantly evoke. The scene in the conference room acts as a microcosm of this dominance: a simple slam of the door and a few direct words transform an ordinary executive meeting into a wake-up call of profound consequence.

Characters like Mr. Bill Von are briefly sketched, providing insight into their personalities and backgrounds—enough to understand their positions and potential motivations. In contrast, Lilith remains an enigma of authority and strategy, skillfully wielding her abilities to manipulate both technology and human fear. Her interaction, steeped in sarcasm and authority, puts these executives on the defensive, forcing them to acknowledge how reliant they are on her, more than they would like to admit.

The final twist, reminding them that they work for her husband, heightens the pressure. These executives face not only the possibility of professional failure but also the grim reality that they could lose much more if they do not meet expectations.

As she exits the room, Lilith makes it clear that her power lies not only in sharp words but in the suffocating atmosphere of fear she leaves in her wake. Her ability to wield fear in a setting that thrives on control and appearances demonstrates her mastery in the art of manipulation.

This moment reveals an unyielding confrontation but also a precarious balance. Lilith is immersed in a dangerous game where her understanding of these complex power dynamics is crucial for her survival and that of her allies. Her departure is merely another move on the chessboard, leaving others to constantly remember who they are truly playing for.

In this high-stakes environment, the air thick with tension and uncertainty, it becomes evident that the struggle for power, when combined with fear and manipulation, shapes the very foundation of alliances and enmities. Lilith's prowess will not only dictate her fate but also the fate of those who dare to challenge the order she has established.

CHAPTER 29

A Shift in Your Mind

The general, standing tall with a penetrating gaze, halted before Lilith, slightly bowing his head in reverence. "My lady," he said in a grave voice, "your husband wishes to see you at once." Lilith raised an eyebrow, her demeanor exuding a coldness that could freeze hell itself. "Perfect, of course," she replied, her tone laced with both defiance and acceptance. "Let's go."

Inside, Lilith felt the shadow of danger looming over her. She knew that Satan, with his fearsome ability to read minds, could unravel any secrets she tried to keep. But she had mastered the art of shielding her thoughts, becoming an indecipherable enigma even to him.

As she crossed the threshold of the castle, an indescribable chill enveloped her. Upon entering the dark chamber, her husband regarded her with an intense gaze, visibly struggling to penetrate her thoughts. Lilith met his stare with serenity, her eyes locked onto his, a sea of unruffled calm. "What do you wish, my lord?" she asked softly.

With a sigh of satisfaction, Satan set aside the lamb he had been devouring. "Lilith, over the past centuries, I have been quite pleased with you. You have been a loyal, capable, and intelligent wife. I hope that remains the case," he said, making another attempt to delve into the depths of her soul.

Lilith allowed her mind to unfold like an open book, a strategy she had honed over the centuries to earn his trust without resorting to conflict. "My lord," she responded with firmness and dedication, "you know I have only lived for your glory. I am ensuring that the Earth belongs to you. I've been with the sinners of WOAD, and they are trembling. Would you like me to do anything more?"

Satan, feeling satisfied, allowed his posture to soften, dissipating the suspicions that lingered in the air. He invited her to dine, a sign of approval that Lilith accepted with a rare wave of satisfaction coursing through her being. "Eat something, my lady; you must be hungry."

At those words, a faint glimmer of triumph crossed her face. It was the first time he had granted her the title of "my lady," a recognition he had never uttered before. Aware that she was gaining his acceptance, Lilith smiled, yet deep down, she kept her eternal caution alive. For while she played her role flawlessly, she could never place her full trust in Satan. In his realm of shadows, suspicion was the key to survival.

As she settled into her surroundings, the weight of her dual existence hung in the balance. Each conversation, every subtle maneuver, carried the potential to shift everything. Yet Lilith was determined to navigate this delicate dance, aware that even the smallest misstep could unravel the intricate web she had woven. In her mind, the stakes continued to rise, and with each moment spent beside the Prince of Darkness, she refined her strategy for the inevitable confrontation that loomed ahead.

Aisling, known as Irish Lite, found herself in her sanctuary, perched atop the crown of the Statue of Liberty. As she gazed out

over the vast ocean, her thoughts glided softly back to her homeland of Ireland. Beside her sat Lumina, her inseparable friend, whose expression made it clear that she longed for the authentic flavors and warmth of home. Lumina scrunched her nose and quipped, "The food here always tastes like fried oil," provoking a contagious laugh from Aisling.

Suddenly, the sky began to fill with an ethereal glow. Thousands of fairies from all around the world were flocking to New York like stars descending into the night, responding to the call to unite and form an alliance against the looming threat of WOAD.

The climactic scene unfolded on a rooftop with a breathtaking view of New York's skyscrapers. As each fairy took her place in a grand formation, the lights of their wings created a kaleidoscope of colors that left onlookers in awe. Aisling felt the energy and determination of her allies, each possessing her own magic and culture, united by a common purpose. Just as enthusiasm peaked, the skies darkened, revealing WOAD's true power: a connection to malevolent entities from higher dimensions ready to unleash unimaginable chaos.

The revelation of WOAD's dark support hit like a chilling wave. Aisling and Lumina soon discovered that these higher entities were not only powerful but also tied to ancient tales of terror recounted by Aisling's grandmother in Ireland. This historical connection suggested that the battle they faced was more personal and more ancestral than they had envisioned. Armed with this newfound knowledge, they realized they needed to devise a new strategy by delving into their past to combat an evil that had been latent for centuries.

Guided by the legends of their homeland and united with their new allies, Aisling and Lumina prepared for a decisive attack. Together, they utilized their ancestral knowledge, combining it with modern magical interventions from their fairy companions to sever the connection of the malevolent beings to this dimension.

Amidst the uproar and confusion erupting throughout the city, scientists, under the scrutiny of cameras and microphones, rambled on with extravagant theories attempting to explain the mysterious ethereal lights illuminating the sky. With a nervous smile, one scientist asserted that these lights were "luminal illuminations" caused by "bioluminescent microorganisms displaced en masse into the atmosphere due to the unusual warming of ocean currents and intercontinental wind flows."

As the spectacle unfolded above, Aisling and Lumina steeled themselves for the battle ahead, knowing their unity and the strength drawn from their heritage was their greatest weapon against the encroaching darkness. The fight was not just for their present but for the very essence of their past, a testament to the resilience embedded within the stories they carried.

According to him, these microorganisms had developed an astonishing ability to create their own light, akin to fireflies but much more intense due to increased solar radiation. As his words spread across the airwaves, children with eyes full of wonder and laughter bubbling over could not help but be enchanted by the ridiculous celestial spectacle unfolding before them.

A few feet away, a group of punk teenagers gathered. One young man, sporting a mohawk and adorned with studs, shook his head in laughter as he listened to the scientist's declarations. "Cut the nonsense, man! That looks more like a rock concert than anything else. Long live Mother Nature!" he exclaimed.

Undeterred, the presenter continued narrating the surreal scene, linking the cosmic display to climate change, cautioning that the Earth, immutable and vast, was beginning to exact its toll for humanity's environmental sins. Yet, despite the warnings, the spectacle persisted, illuminating the night and filling the air with magic, leaving the crowds with a strange sensation of an apocalypse transformed into celestial art.

The city whispered with an unsettling vibration as the sky, painted with strange, dancing lights, unleashed a tide of mixed emotions. In the central square, screen after screen projected a nervously smiling scientist trying to explain the "luminal illuminations," while the audience listened, piecing together snippets of a reality that seemed to resist coherence.

A constant buzz accompanied the presenter's voice, echoing through the crowded streets filled with both curious onlookers and skeptical bystanders. People clustered in front of every shop window and food stall transformed into makeshift observatories. Children leaped with excitement, pointing at the lights as if the display were a show put on just for them. Above their heads, the punk teenagers camped out near a statue, watching it all with irreverent glee. "It's the Earth's party!" one of them shouted as music blared from a portable speaker.

Media vans, with antennas slicing through the air, invaded the scene. Inside each mobile unit, reporters scrambled to deliver the ultimate scoop. Each channel spun a unique version: one reporter insisted that the lights were a result of polar ice melt that had finally released trapped gases glowing under the moonlight; another, bolder in proclamation, suggested it was a secretly organized event by the United Nations to unite the world in the fight against climate change.

Amid this cacophony of voices and the dazzling lights overhead, a palpable energy pulsed through New York City, blending hope, anxiety, and exhilaration—an electric reminder of the fight against dark forces looming just beyond the shimmering façade of human innovation and survival.

Just as the theories seemed to explode into a chaotic orchestra of voices and rumors, the sky took on a theatrical twist. The lights intensified, organizing themselves into perfect geometric patterns that defied explanation. The city fell into a marble silence, interrupted only by the echo of collective gasps. In that instant, all connections to the mobile units dropped, leaving everyone in a darkness of knowledge.

The presenter, undeterred, held her microphone with the firmness of a sword. "This celestial display is a reminder, a call from the depths of our planet..." But then she realized what the others had not: the lights were not in the sky but reflected from something—or perhaps someone. The camera, guided by her intuition, focused and revealed millions of tiny, winged figures emerging from the waters of the Hudson River.

The revelation sent a jolt through the narrative. The creatures, dancing in the air and shining like flesh-made stars, defied all logic. They moved with ethereal grace, forming living constellations. Some scientists dropped to their knees in astonishment, while others raised their tablets and phones to capture the impossible truth: this was not an atmospheric phenomenon, but visits lost in folklore, fairies akin to those who had inspired forgotten myths.

Finally, the spectacle concluded as abruptly as it began. The lights dissolved into the air, and the city, slowly returning to its artificial glow, was engulfed in a profound silence. The crowds began to disperse, each person carrying the weight of a shared and experienced secret.

Days later, the news buzzed with conspiracy theories and simulations, but for those who had been present, the night of the lights would remain as a bridge between the earthly and the ethereal, a reminder that even in its most rational brilliance, the world holds places where the unknown can still dance freely. The reports from each mobile unit became echoes of a fragmented reality: elements of doubt, certainty, and magic weaving a story that would resist being forgotten. That night, the city did not merely witness the lights; for a fleeting moment, it became part of a waking dream.

In the heart of the night, beneath the glow of the moon that could scarcely compete with the lights that had just illuminated the sky, Aisling, the queen of the fairies, stood before her eternal subjects. With a serene yet authoritative voice, she said, "Ladies, it's time for you to go elsewhere. If not, you'll drive everyone in this city mad."

The fairies, their radiant wings shimmering in the moonlight, exchanged glances filled with a mixture of mischief and reluctance. They knew that Aisling was right; their presence needed to be subtle, a whisper of magic rather than a blaring announcement. With a graceful swish of their wings, they began to disperse, leaving behind the echoes of laughter and wonder as they made their way back to their hidden realms, leaving the world momentarily enchanted—but always yearning for more.

The fairies, some of normal size and others as tiny as needles, nodded submissively. In the blink of an eye, they began to dissolve into a torrent of stardust and years of dreams, leaving only a trail of sparkling magic in the air. Aisling and Lumina, two of their closest allies, decided to fly back to the hotel through the balcony.

Upon entering, they were met with the inquisitive gaze of Ashley, Jack, and Robert. Jack, adopting a paternal stance with his arms crossed, spoke in his deep voice, "Could you please enter through the door for once?"

Lumina, with a mischievous grin, replied cheekily, "Why? This way is faster."

Ashley approached the fairies, her tone wavering between astonishment and indignation. "Tell me you weren't those little lights in the sky…" The fairies could not hide their laughter, and the truth slipped from Aisling's lips: "Yes, and what of it?"

"And what of it? Half the world saw you! Now, what are we going to do to surprise WOAD?" Ashley's voice held genuine concern, a mix of adventure and responsibility.

Lumina, ever nonchalant, shrugged her shoulders. "For you all, it's a problem," she said, "but for us, it's simply a game. We'll neutralize all the bugs, and the planes won't be able to take off. We'll fill the airports with fairies!"

The revelation filled the room with a blend of tension and excitement. Ashley felt her heart racing. "Oh my God! I'm going to have a heart attack." Her anxiety was palpable, creating an atmosphere of nervousness.

"Calm down, Ashley!" Aisling tried to soothe her. "We'll neutralize the bugs that carry disease, and the others will create clouds at the airport. No one will be able to take off."

At that moment, Lilith appeared out of nowhere beside the attorney. Seeing the fairies and overhearing the conversation, she jolted and exclaimed, "Oh God, you're going to give me a heart attack!" Maintaining her usual composure, she added, "You'll have to get used to our comings and goings."

Laughter erupted in the room, breaking the tension that had lingered in the air. Aisling, Lumina, Ashley, Jack, and Robert shared a fleeting connection, uniting humans and fairies in this unusual setting. The blend of realism and fantasy was shaping a new narrative, one where the unexpected was the norm, and magic lurked around every corner.

As the laughter faded, each mind began to explore the possibilities; everything that had been planned, the strategy against WOAD and their malevolent schemes, now needed to be reassessed after the fallout from the lights. The night promised surprises, and the air crackled with the excitement of what was to come.

They all left the room, and Aisling and Lumina headed off to bed, while their aunt settled into the armchair, ready to offer her wisdom in the quiet hours ahead.

The atmosphere in Dimension 5 was thick and charged with mysterious energy. With each step Aisling, Ashley, Jack, Robert, and Lumina took, they drew nearer to the epicenter of the evil that loomed over the strange landscape. Around them, the darkness pulsed as if it were alive.

Suddenly, an eerie sound tore through the silence; their gazes snapped to a monstrous figure emerging from the shadows: a six-headed serpent, each head hissing with a menacing intensity. The threat was palpable, almost tangible, the vibrations of its fierce intentions reverberating in the air.

"Watch out!" Jack shouted, but he wasn't quick enough. The serpent lunged at them with terrifying speed.

In an act of courage, Aisling dashed towards the creature without hesitation, her heart pounding in her ears. The battle was fierce, engulfed in an unsettling blackness that seemed to swallow time and space. The heads of the serpent moved with lethal precision, and one of them lunged directly at Aisling.

Everything suddenly froze. The anticipated pain never came, and Aisling opened her eyes to find herself in her bed, gasping for breath. The room was silent except for her sister's calm breathing beside her.

Aisling slowly got up, still feeling the adrenaline coursing through her veins. She glanced over at Lilith, her aunt, who sat in a nearby armchair, her gaze fixed on the dark horizon outside. Aisling felt secure, but the residue of the nightmare still hung heavily in her mind.

"Aisling, what's the matter?" Lilith asked softly, never pulling her gaze from the window.

"Nothing, just a nightmare," Aisling replied, still feeling her pulse racing. "Aren't you going to sleep, Aunt?"

"No, dear. I prefer to stay here to protect you all," Lilith assured her with a calm smile.

"Come on, get some rest. Tomorrow is going to be a very busy day," Aisling added gently.

"Alright. Thank you," Aisling responded, allowing Lilith's words to cradle her back into the safety of the present.

As she snuggled back beneath the covers, Aisling reflected on the dream. The nightmare had been so vivid, but deep down, she knew it was merely a harbinger of challenges yet to come. She closed her eyes, assured that no matter what lay ahead, she would not face the shadows alone, and Lilith's presence comforted her.

Lilith, on the other hand, found peace within herself, a feeling she had long erased from her emotions over centuries. It was a reconnection with her true self; she was caring for her young wards, who, though no longer children, still evoked that same protective instinct within her. The thought of safeguarding someone from her family brought her immense joy and a sense of purpose. As she watched the young women sleep peacefully, a genuine smile spread across her face—a smile that radiated from the depths of her soul.

The War Begins

On a bright, vibrant morning, the first rays of sunlight filtered through the expansive windows of the hotel restaurant, painting the tables in golden hues. The murmur of conversations and laughter filled the air, creating an atmosphere of eager camaraderie. Around a large table in the center of the room, Aisling, Jack, Robert, Ashley, Lumina, and Lilith shared a peaceful breakfast, but the underlying tension simmered beneath the surface. The fairies proudly wore their hero costumes, exuding power and determination.

Two children approached, their eyes shining with fascination, interrupting the lively chatter. "Are you real heroes?" one of them asked, his tone a mix of awe and hope.

Lumina, with a radiant smile, nodded. "Of course," she replied gently. With an elegant gesture of her hand, she traced a circle in the air. Instantly, the interior glowed with a warm, vibrant light. "See this?" she continued. "It's to ensure that magic doesn't break. As long as the circle is intact, the magic remains."

"Wow, that's so cool!" exclaimed the other child, eyes wide with wonder as he took in the spectacle. Bursting with excitement, they ran back to their table.

"Dad, it's a real hero!" one of the boys shouted, pointing at Lumina with admiration. The father, distracted, downplayed it as he sipped his coffee. "Come on, eat up or we'll miss our flight," he muttered, focused on his itinerary.

Back at the heroes' table, Jack reached for a jar of jam for Lilith, maintaining a serious yet hopeful tone in the conversation. "When you tell me," he said, "my nephew already has all the documentation ready to ensure an international order. And I promise you, they're going to fall: senators here, also in Europe, China, Russia, India, and many more. All the police forces are on alert for our call."

The weight of the conspiracy they faced was suffocating. WOAD, with its tentacles wrapped around every continent, had purchased politicians, television channels, and press outlets. Its influence permeated even the most unsuspecting corners of the globe.

Ashley sighed deeply, uncertainty reflecting in her eyes. "I don't know if we'll succeed," she admitted with a vulnerable and honest tone.

Jack, with renewed determination, interjected, "We will," he asserted, his confidence flowing like a powerful river. "Everyone on our side is inside to avoid breaking the thread of possibilities with corrupt police, which they surely will have. We must believe in our ability to expose them all."

As they shared their resolve, the atmosphere began to shift. Despite the heaviness of their mission, a flicker of hope illuminated their spirits.

With every word exchanged, they fortified their commitment to uncover the truth and confront the looming threat of WOAD, united in purpose and strengthened by their bonds. The war that lay ahead was no longer an abstract concept; it was a reality they were prepared to face together.

The into a momentary silence, a tacit pact of unity and resolve growing among them. Outside, the world continued its daily routine, unaware that its true protectors were about to confront a threat that could alter the course of history. The war had begun, and they were ready to fight.

Lilith glanced at her niece Aisling, who stood slightly apart from the bustle of the table, their connection almost palpable. They locked eyes deeply, establishing an invisible bridge between their minds. Aisling sensed that Lilith needed to convey something important—something no one else should hear.

In a telepathic whisper that resonated only between them, Lilith began to speak: "Niece, I've made many mistakes in my life. Someday, I will seek forgiveness from your grandmother for what I have done."

Aisling held her gaze, her heart open, as Lilith's words floated in her consciousness, raw and sincere.

"But I want you to know," Lilith continued, her spiritual tone more resolute in their silent exchange, "that I am grateful to you because, thanks to you, I have changed. I see your kindness, your desire to help, and you remind me of who I was before. If anything happens to us, I want you to tell your grandmother this: I was blinded by money and power, and I regret it. Thank you, dear."

For a moment, time seemed to stand still as Aisling absorbed the weight of the confession, her gaze conveying a silent agreement and understanding. The promise was sealed in that telepathic moment, a pact stronger than any words spoken aloud.

Removed from the bustling restaurant, the mental connection between Aisling and Lilith remained vibrant, like a silver thread binding them in silence. Aisling's thoughts floated clear and sincere into Lilith's mind, a message loaded with emotion that only they could share.

"Thank you for helping us with this task," Aisling responded telepathically, her mental voice warm and affectionate. "Without you, I don't think Lumina and I could have done this alone."

The gratitude and respect she felt for her great-aunt permeated every unspoken word, communicating more than gestures or spoken voice ever could. It was a connection that transcended time and space, weaving a renewed familial bond.

"Thank you for changing," Aisling continued, sending her thoughts with a gentle breath of affection. "And I'm also happy because I've gained another aunt," she added with a mental smile, which Lilith could "see" clearly, like the sun breaking over the horizon after a long night.

The echo of that final phrase hung suspended in the ethereal space between them, a spark of shared joy illuminating the moment. Both women returned to the everyday conversation around the table, carrying with them the warmth of their telepathic exchange, a personal reminder that even amidst the battles they faced, they had found strength and family in the most unexpected places.

Eventually, as if nothing had happened, they rejoined the central table where the dialogues and laughter of the others filled the air. Though they blended back into the general flow of conversation, the telepathic exchange they had shared remained intact—a testament to love and loyalty that resonated only between their hearts.

CHAPTER 31

Fun and Judgment

After leaving the bustling restaurant, where the telepathic connection between Aisling and Lilith had allowed them to strengthen familial ties and find comfort in their unity, the group prepared to take the next step in their mission.

The fairies, with their radiant presence, moved purposefully toward the ocean. While one group advanced toward the airport in Chicago, others headed for New York City. Their objective was clear: to coordinate a series of strategic mobilizations to intercept any escape attempts by WOAD agents.

Meanwhile, Ashley was already in her strategic position, patiently awaiting at the main entrance of the WOAD headquarters. Beside her, Jack shared the silent vigil, both acutely aware of the importance of their task. In a hotel room transformed into an improvised operations center, Robert monitored a matrix of screens and keyboards. Skillfully, he sent the latest updates to Jack's nephew, who, alongside a committed group of Customs Moms, was tracking suspicious movements around the world with the help of Computer and many white-hat hackers who had joined the fray.

In Ashley's car, an army of fairies readied themselves, prepared to sweep down on any vehicle attempting to enter or exit the WOAD headquarters. Their determination was stronger than ever, driven by the confidence in their future victory that propelled them to remain vigilant.

As vehicles laden with insects began to prepare for deployment, a helicopter buzzed overhead, flying towards Chicago. It was equipped with containers of minuscule insects, ready to be released at the first sign of alarm, blocking any escape route or communication for the unfortunate occupants inside the building.

The operation unfolded like a well-rehearsed choreography, each member conscious of their role in the collective effort to dismantle WOAD's corrupt network. Unity and determination, reinforced by invisible connections like the one shared between Aisling and Lilith, provided the strength they needed to face what lay ahead. The war against WOAD was not just a physical battle; it was waged in every thought, within every quiet strategy, and through each small daily victory.

As the fairies prepared to take to the skies, an air of anticipation filled the atmosphere. Each heart beat with the knowledge that they were fighting for more than just themselves; they were battling for their families, their future, and the very fabric of a world that had grown too comfortable with darkness. Together, they would face judgment and emerge, undaunted, into a realm where light could vanquish even the deepest shadows.

The air was thick with tension as Ashley, still awaiting outside the imposing WOAD headquarters, gazed up at the sky. Suddenly, amid the clouds, the unmistakable sound of a helicopter pierced the air, slicing through with ominous urgency. Her heart raced as the realization dawned on her.

"Shit, the helicopter got through," Ashley exclaimed, frustration clear in her voice. Wasting no time, she grabbed her phone, her fingers moving swiftly as she sent an urgent message to Robert. "We need to intervene now," she typed in WhatsApp, her mind racing.

Within minutes, the response was swift: National Guard trucks and armored vans erupted through the main gate of the premises, crashing through barriers with a thunderous roar. Over a hundred police officers, clad in protective white suits to guard against any potential infections the insects might carry, immediately fanned out. They began searching every corner of the complex, discovering vehicles packed with crates that emitted a noise and had tiny holes for the insects to breathe, amplifying the chaos with the sound of flapping wings.

The discovery of the insects was a decisive blow, a significant step toward halting WOAD's operations. However, any sense of satisfaction was fleeting when the operation's commander swiftly turned to Ashley, his expression grave and bewildered.

"Ma'am," he said, pausing before continuing, "Mr. Von has escaped in the helicopter."

Ashley frowned, disappointment intertwining with determination. "Well, he can't have gone far, can he?" she replied, her tone assertive and confident that justice would prevail.

A shift occurred as the commander slowly raised his gaze, his face marked by frustration. "Well," he said with resignation, "he has a white passport."

The white passport, a legendary artifact designed to guarantee free passage through any border and checkpoint, was more than just a document; it was an almost magical key to impunity. That revelation hit her like a bucket of cold water, emphasizing the extent of the power they were up against.

Despite this complication, Ashley refused to be disheartened. Hope remained alive in her eyes, an unwavering glow reflecting her conviction. "Then we'll have to be smarter and quicker," she declared, her words reaffirming her commitment and that of the team to pursue Von and completely dismantle WOAD.

In that moment, Ashley felt the weight of responsibility pressing upon her, but it fueled her resolve instead of diminishing it. They were in a battle for more than just their own safety; they were fighting for the very integrity of justice in a corrupt world. As her team rallied around her, a fierce determination ignited within them all, ready to confront whatever lay ahead, even against the insurmountable odds they now faced.

The skies were clear now, but the echo of the helicopter continued to resonate on the horizon, a reminder that the hunt had begun. The machinery of justice moved along often winding and difficult paths, yet Ashley and her team were prepared to face them, ready to take every necessary step to ensure that the law—both earthly and divine—would prevail.

Ashley exhaled a long, deep sigh as she watched police vans circling the WOAD building. Her phone vibrated in her hand, signaling that Robert was trying to reach her from his makeshift headquarters in the hotel. Lifting the device, her eyes gleamed with anticipation.

"Ashley," Robert began, his voice clear even through the phone connection. "We've made more progress than we expected. They just arrested 32 senators in the U.S. Senate. In Europe, 150 members of the Euro Chamber are already in custody. Operations are succeeding in other countries as well. This is a global effort now."

Robert's words were like music to her ears, the sound of justice finally being served. The magnitude of their accomplishments began to settle in as he continued detailing the extent of the arrests. WOAD, though powerful, now felt the relentless grip of the law closing in.

A warm smile spread across Ashley's face. Each arrest represented a step toward a world that, while still imperfect, was moving toward a future with fewer shadows. "This is just the beginning," she thought, her mind a mix of satisfaction and renewed determination.

"Thank you, Robert," she replied in a lighter tone, though her heart was undeniably heavy with emotion. "This is a triumph for all of us, and we're not stopping here."

As she looked around, every officer, every fairy, and every team member represented a crucial part of a formidable alliance against the dark forces that threatened to undermine their world. Ashley's smile was not just a reflection of the moment's success, but also a promise of tomorrow—a true testament to shared effort and the power of collective purpose. As the bustling operation at the WOAD headquarters began to settle, Ashley leaned against the car, her mind already diving into the next steps.

She noticed Jack approaching with a curious expression.

"You know, Jack," Ashley began, a trace of determination in her voice, "this trial is going to take me over three years of work. And I'm telling you, I'm going to do it for free."

Jack raised an eyebrow, intrigued. "And who exactly will you be representing?" he asked, sensing the cleverness in her eyes.

With a broad, confident smile, Ashley replied, "The people."

"That's what the prosecutor is for, right?" Jack countered, tilting his head to the side.

"Yes, but I'll be presenting as a private prosecutor," she clarified, the air brimming with certainty about her decision.

Jack grinned, genuinely appreciating her indomitable spirit. "Well, if you need a witness, here I am," he added with a conspiratorial wink.

Before they could continue, three fairies fluttered over to the car, their wings shimmering in the sunlight. "I think we're done here, right?" one of the fairies asked. "We're heading to Chicago to help out there."

Jack, amused, pointed at Ashley. "Ask the boss."

"For me, yes," Ashley replied, gratitude lacing her voice. "I believe you've done your part here, but thank you anyway."

Then Jack, with a spark of mischief, asked, "Do you do magic?"

One of the fairies smiled, understanding his playful inquiry instantly. "Of course," she replied.

"Could you conjure me some donuts? I miss them when I'm nervous," Jack admitted, unashamed.

With a simple wave of her hand, the fairy conjured two fresh, fluffy donuts, presenting them with a theatrical flourish. "Here you go, sir," she said with a playful bow.

Ashley burst into laughter, the moment offering a breath of joy and lightness amid the seriousness of their mission. As the fairies prepared to depart, the group allowed themselves a moment to revel in this small personal victory, a celebration of the extraordinary within the ordinary.

As the impact of the global operation resonated in every corner of the world, news of the mass arrests began to flood headlines across major media outlets. In every parliament of the European Union, agents were detaining politicians who had colluded with WOAD's corrupt network. Brazil, too, was caught in a whirlwind of arrests dominating live broadcasts.

Meanwhile, decisive actions were underway in defense sectors and multinational corporations. The news agency reported over 68,000 arrests worldwide, with even more anticipated. This was not only a blow to WOAD; it marked a wake-up call for democracies and free peoples everywhere.

Finding a moment of calm amid the chaos, Ashley pulled out her phone and began watching live news on YouTube. The images on screen showed agents leading handcuffed officials away—a tide of overwhelming and unstoppable change.

"Jack," Ashley exclaimed, her voice filled with astonishment as she gazed at the screen. "Oh my God, there have already been 68,000 arrests!"

The enormity of what was unfolding filled her with exhilaration and anxiety alike, a potent reminder of the scale of their endeavor and the dangers still lurking in the shadows. But in that moment, she felt a surge of hope—change was really happening, and they were part of it.

Jack, ever quick with his wit, leaned toward her with an ironic smile. "And where are they going to put all of them? There won't be enough prisons for so many." The irony in his voice provided a soft relief on a day weighed down by so much gravity.

The comment elicited an unexpected laugh from Ashley, who continued watching the broadcast, contemplating not only the magnitude of the operation but also the creative—perhaps unconventional—solutions that would be needed to manage the new world they were helping to create. The enormity of what had begun was almost unimaginable, but it stood as a testament to the power of change when true wills united for the common good.

In the vast canvas of the sky, Aisling soared at incredible speed, defiant and determined. Behind her, in a radiant and coral formation, Lumina and over a thousand fairies followed, leaving a trail of light and hope as they surged through the winds. Their objective was clear and urgent: an airplane at Chicago's airport, loaded with toxic gases designed to manipulate the climate—a direct threat to nature and humanity.

As they dove toward the airport, the seriousness of the mission weighed heavily on Aisling's mind. She reflected on the concept of divine law, a higher force that transcended and governed above any human system. This operation was not just a physical battle; it was an act of justice in its purest form—a manifestation of morality that recognized neither corruption nor greed.

Yet, despite her determination, internal doubts waged war in her mind. Would this victory truly signify lasting change? Or would it merely be a fleeting moment in an endless struggle? These questions seemed to whisper in her ear as they approached the plane.

Finally, they arrived at the airport, and the surprise in the pilot's eyes was evident as the fairies formed a luminous barrier in front of the aircraft, preventing its takeoff. It was a scene from a fairy tale, something the pilot had never imagined witnessing. The fairies, laughter spilling from their lips and radiating confidence, greeted the crew of other planes, proclaiming their presence and power.

Lumina, exuding an air of majestic authority, directed herself towards the control tower, followed by a small group of fairies. With fluid and graceful movements, she began to "write" in the air, each gesture leaving a shimmering trail that formed clear words: DO NOT LET ANY PLANE TAKE OFF.

The air traffic controllers, dumbfounded, stared at the scene unfolding before them. One of them finally broke the stunned silence. "Are you seeing this?" he asked incredulously, looking at his colleagues.

"Yes," another responded, shaking his head as if trying to awaken from a surreal dream. "Holy crap, call the army!"

The gravity of the situation was undeniable, and the air crackled with the tension of the unexpected standoff. They were witnessing not only a confrontation but a shining rebellion against the forces of darkness that WOAD embodied, and the stakes had never been higher.

Inity mingled with urgency in their voices, but beneath the surprise lay a dawning awareness that something far greater than themselves was unfolding. The intervention of Aisling, Lumina, and the fairies was a powerful testament that extraordinary forces had risen to protect the

world, defying human logic to impose a higher justice. In that instant, Aisling knew that while many battles remained to be fought, the impact of their actions had already begun to alter the fabric of reality.

Meanwhile, in the luxurious helicopter speeding away, Mr. Von and his three executive henchmen believed their escape was assured. However, in the blink of an eye, the atmosphere in the cabin changed dramatically. Lilith suddenly appeared, seated in the white leather chair that had moments ago been empty.

Her unexpected presence caused a visible startle among them, and a carefree laugh escaped her lips. "Mr. Von, where are you hurrying off to?" she asked with an ironic smile. "Have you betrayed my husband? Wow, when he finds out, he's not going to like it at all."

As she spoke, her tone danced between mockery and sternness. "Do you remember when the kids at school called you 'four-eyes' and snickered at you? And how when you got home, your father yelled at you for coming home scared? Wow!!! And when you started your first company, deceiving your partner and stealing his idea?" Her laughter was sharp, relentless.

Mr. Von, pale and wide-eyed, squirmed uncomfortably in his seat as Lilith recounted each of his most vile acts with chilling precision. Inside the helicopter, the atmosphere was thick with palpable nervousness. The executives and Mr. Von clung to the illusion that they had escaped the consequences of their actions. Yet, in an instant, Lilith's presence altered the course of their thoughts as she elegantly materialized in the white leather chair before them.

With a smile brimming with confidence and mystery, Lilith spoke, her voice resonating with the weight of an inescapable truth. "Mr. Von, do you recall the days when you rose to the pinnacle of wealth, attracting the attention of every news outlet? You seemed a magnanimous benefactor, surrounded by lights and cameras, constructing an image of goodwill with your foundations and charitable acts."

As her words unfolded like an echo of buried memories, Lilith's gaze penetrated Von's recollections. "And those vaccines, the very ones you promoted as a generous advance for humanity… though their true purpose was far more insidious. Do you remember how they left the youth sterile, especially the young girls in that country, under the guise of your fabricated benevolence?"

The weight of her words hung in the air, each revelation a devastating truth that sank deep into the hearts of those present. Lilith was not simply confronting Mr. Von; she was peeling back the layers of deceit that he had woven, exposing the darkness at the core of his ambitions.

The tension within the helicopter thickened, transforming from misplaced confidence to a chilling realization as they faced the very architect of their past misdeeds. In that moment, the balance of power shifted, and the true nature of their actions was laid bare. Lilith was here to ensure that justice would no longer be an abstract concept but a living force that would demand accountability.

With every word, Lilith not only exposed past actions but also painted an intensely critical portrait of the man hidden behind his public mask. "I could continue speaking about these moments for hours, unraveling each layer of the illusion you've woven."

Her tone was not one of accusation but revelation, a calculated exposition of the shadows that Von had cast over the world. In the enclosed space of the helicopter, there was no escape from the truth

that Lilith had unearthed. With a presence that could neither be denied nor ignored, her mission was clear: to remind Mr. Von not just of what he had done, but also where his inexorable actions would lead him.

As the executives remained in mortal silence, Lilith presented an option. "You have two choices," she said with a hint of malicious amusement. "Either you surrender, or I disappear from here, and you all crash this helicopter."

The executives, faced with the threat, cried out in desperation, almost in unison: "No, no, please!" But Lilith raised an elegant finger to her lips, signaling for silence, feeding their fear with an infinite calm. "Decide, Mr. Von. Your lives are in your hands."

Von, staggering, realized with horror that a puddle had formed beneath him. "Look," Lilith pointed out, amusement dancing in her eyes. "You've wet yourself again, are we reminiscing about old times, Mr. Von?" She morphed into the image of Mr. Von's father—a businessman who, in the public eye, maintained an unblemished moral standing yet was rather shady in his dealings, believing in white supremacy and rigid social classes. "Have you done it again?" she taunted as she removed her belt, embodying the figure of that moralistic man.

The silence of his colleagues only emphasized Von's absolute fear. "If this helicopter crashes," Lilith continued, reverting to her true self, leaving behind the transformation of Mr. Von's father, "you will have a hellish existence with my husband. But if you surrender, at least while you're in prison, you'll be free from him. Because you, sir, are going to hell, and no God will save you."

"You need to learn that not everyone around you is evil; perhaps the real monster is you," she added. "That's why you surround yourself with foundations and public goodwill—to silence your conscience."

Mr. Von, pale, trembling, and drenched in sweat, was nothing like the confident man everyone knew from television, the one with grand proposals for humanity. He stammered, attempting to articulate a response. "Lilith, I'll give you anything you want, just leave me in peace."

Her laughter was sweetly melodic, filled with mockery. "Do you truly believe I care about money, Mr. Von? I can obtain whatever I desire with a simple snap of my fingers. Remember your victims, because up there, where it matters, you won't make it." With a finger marked by judgment, she pointed downward. "You've ended up exactly where you've sought to be, Mr. Von."

In the blink of an eye, Lilith vanished again, provoking another collective scream of fear from the men. But their outcry was interrupted when she reappeared, a mischievous glint in her eyes. "I suppose you've decided to surrender; the third time's the charm," she quipped lightly, delivering her warning with a sense of satisfaction.

"Don't you want twenty billion dollars?" Von pleaded, his voice quivering with panic.

"Mr. Von, it sounds as if you could offer five times that amount. You seem to prefer money over your life and dignity; I can't believe how far your selfishness extends," Lilith replied with disdain. "That was a failed question."

As if she were hosting a game show, Lilith reveled in having a once-powerful man—a figure admired by humanity—at her feet, yet so insignificant in the grand tapestry of eternity. "Mr. Von, your response should have been that you would surrender all your riches and fight for peace and love in the world." She continued as if shifting to another camera angle on the set, "And now, let's take a moment for a commercial break."

Lilith found this moment in the lives of humans fascinating; they always chose to live falsehoods for their own interests, embodying scant morality. She enjoyed watching them dissolve into weakness within her dimension, and she leaned in, looking intensely at Von.

"Your assumptions are as empty as your false claims. Your ego has betrayed you," she declared. "Let's continue."

With a theatrical gesture, Lilith traced a square in the air that filled with the image of a young girl—a victim who had chosen to end her life after being sexually abused by Von. The violet hue of the memory served as both an accusation and a sentence.

Mr. Von averted his gaze, consumed by fear and shame. "Don't cower now," Lilith said, her voice now as cold as it was relentless. "Don't you remember her, Mr. Von? You know she committed suicide after your abuse. You bought off all the witnesses to come out on top. You might deceive humanity, but not us."

With his pants soaked, Mr. Von fell to his knees, the dampness soaking into the ground beneath him. "Miss Lilith, please!" he begged, desperation coating his words. "Miss Lilith!!"

She remained unyielding. "God will not welcome you, and your path to hell is already secured. Oh, and"—with a sarcastic edge—"don't bother bringing your money; it will burn alongside you."

Lilith paused, relishing the moments of pure terror unfolding for the executives; it was a retrospective on their moral failings, which they had never overcome. She reveled in that part of the tale. "I suspect that with all your cash and the scant justice in your world, you won't go to prison, so goodbye, gentlemen!!!"

The finality in her tone echoed through the helicopter, leaving the executives to grapple with an undeniable truth. Desperation and despair hung in the atmosphere, and though Von had wielded power for so long, now he found himself stripped bare and vulnerable before the relentless force that was Lilith.GPT-4o

With one final laugh that resonated like thunder, Lilith vanished once again. The helicopter, as if obeying an unassailable command, began to dive sharply, culminating in an explosion that lit up the mountainside, bringing an end to the chapter of horror that Mr. Von had written with his actions.

The fierce brightness engulfed the night landscape, illuminating the surrounding peaks as a fiery testament to his downfall. The shockwave reverberated through the air, a stark reminder of the judgment he had faced for his transgressions.

In that moment, the oppressive aura that had loomed over the operation dissipated, replaced by a profound silence that echoed the finality of justice served. Below, the citizens of the world would wake to the news, their understanding of safety and morality forever altered.

From the safety of their hiding places, Aisling, Ashley, Jack, and Robert witnessed the distant glow, knowing that another layer of darkness had been peeled away from their fight. The path ahead was far from clear, yet this victory, however bittersweet, lit their way forward.

As they stood united, each heart resonated with a newfound courage, knowing they were part of something greater—a weaving of destinies intertwined with a relentless pursuit of justice. In the wake of Von's descent, they embraced the promise of change that had begun to unfold in both the shadows and the light.

In a historic moment in global politics, a titanic legal and political showdown unfolded in the U.S. Senate and European parliaments. Jack and Aisling, armed with compelling evidence, stepped before a tense audience to expose the web of corruption that had infiltrated the highest echelons of power. With each document and testimony, they challenged the implicated senators, sowing the seeds of hope for a more transparent and equitable world.

Cameras from around the globe captured the charged atmosphere in the Senate, where politicians teetered on the brink of ruin, fighting for their survival. The audience in the chamber was a mix of indignation and anticipation. The corrupt senators, acutely aware that their careers were at stake, attempted to undermine the evidence with dilatory tactics and personal attacks. Yet each effort clashed against the integrity of Jack and Aisling, who had delivered to the Senate and the Department of Justice three vans loaded with boxes of evidence gathered from across India and other countries.

Suddenly, a surprise attack threatened to alter the course of the trial. However, instead of derailing the case, the attack only served to underline the gravity of the situation, revealing just how far the accused were willing to go to protect their secrets. This desperate maneuver backfired, further strengthening the public's and the prosecutors' resolve to pursue justice.

Meanwhile, on the streets of New York, an atmosphere of celebration and renewal permeated the air. Ashley and Lumina soared majestically through the sky, followed by a retinue of fairies sparkling like shooting stars. Citizens, mesmerized, filled the streets, looking skyward as their applause resonated like a triumphant ovation for the heroes who had made this change possible.

The scene was magical: a young girl wore a t-shirt proudly proclaiming "Irish Lite Fairy," symbolizing the power of magic and the courage that had transformed the nation. The city lights flickered as if dancing to the rhythm of a new spirit that filled the air, heralding the dawn of an era in which truth and justice took precedence.

Just nearby, two police officers who had entered the room to provide assistance during the robbery gazed upward. One of them remarked with a smile, "I knew they were lying; the truth has such a pure soul that I didn't worry about them." The other officer looked at his partner and replied, "Exactly, I thought the same."

The image of the fairies crossing the New York skyline etched itself into the hearts of everyone—a reminder of what can be achieved when people fight with integrity and unity. Official ceremonies began to recognize the end of a dark era, replaced by the promise of a future where corruption had no place.

As the day unfolded, hope soared alongside the fairies, signaling that the tides of change were not only possible but already in motion. The fight for justice, spurred by courage and unity, was just beginning.

As the dust of the legal and political battle settles, the world begins to rebuild on more solid foundations. The thousands of imprisoned politicians symbolize not just the fall of a corrupt system but also

a beacon of opportunity for reconstruction and growth. Ashley, Lumina, and their allies have ushered in a new era, where humanity strides forward with renewed vigor toward a more just and honest destiny.

The echo of applause resonating in the streets becomes the soundtrack to this promise—a continuous celebration of justice and hope. As communities unite under the weight of their shared experiences, a collective determination rises from the ashes of the past, fostering an environment where transparency and integrity can flourish.

In the wake of this transformation, people actively engage in dialogues once hushed by fear, their voices a powerful testament to the resilience of the human spirit. Neighborhoods that had once suffered in silence now buzz with activity, as citizens come together to advocate for change, ensuring that the mistakes of the past are never repeated.

Ashley, Lumina, and their team continue to play vital roles in this resurgence. Their experiences have forged bonds that run deeper than mere friendship; they have become custodians of justice, guardians of a vision that embraces the values of truth and accountability.

As they navigate this new landscape, the challenges ahead are numerous, but they face them fortified by the knowledge that they are not alone. The spirit of cooperation—between humans and fairies—fuels their resolve, reminding them that together they can tackle any adversary, any threat that looms on the horizon.

In this rejuvenated society, every individual contributes with purpose, and every action, no matter how small, reverberates with the potential to create lasting change. With each passing day, they draw closer to a future where justice is not just an ideal but a lived reality, where the stories of those who suffered become the inspiration for those who fight for a better tomorrow.

As the sun sets on this newfound hope, Ashley looks to the sky, feeling the weight of responsibility mixed with a sense of empowerment. The fairies, fluttering above, join her in quiet contemplation, their wings glimmering in the twilight—a reminder that magic and perseverance can lead to a brighter world for all.

CHAPTER 32

The Struggle of the Underworld

Lilith stood before her husband, the formidable Satan, whose eyes glowed with an intense red, illuminated by a contained fury. "How is this possible?" he roared, his voice reverberating through the heavy air charged with dark power. "Everything was so meticulously organized—over half a million politicians and influential figures under my control… all at my feet. And now, that worthless coward Von…"

With a calm confidence, Lilith gently interjected, "I took care of him, my lord." But he, unfazed by her words, retorted with irritation, "I know; he's right here."

With a touch of irony, Lilith smiled and moved closer to the fire's glass panel, her gaze fixed on the dancing flames as she murmured, "Oh, how quickly he fell." She lingered for a moment, as if searching for some sign of the unfortunate Von.

As he continued to brood over his concerns, a loud thud against the glass caught Lilith's attention. A face contorted by suffering had smashed against the transparent surface—Von's visage, now trapped in the depths of eternal punishment.

"Mr. Von," Lilith whispered with cruel delight, her smile widening. "The traitor, finally in his place."

Her focus returned to Satan, who, absorbed in his own fury and dark strategy, exclaimed, "Prepare everyone. We will do this my way. Our armies will rise and sweep away everything."

Lilith nodded, an echo of obedience punctuating the air. "Yes, my lord," she replied, her voice as soft as it was seductive.

Behind her, Von's face slowly faded into the flames, a burning and eternal reminder of the fate that awaited those who betray. Meanwhile, Lilith understood that the challenge had only just begun—and although Satan seemed indifferent to her subtlety, she played her hand in the background, waiting for the right moment to shape the chaos to her will.

As tensions mounted in the chamber, Lilith felt a stirring within her, recognizing that this struggle for power wasn't merely a test of strength. It was a reflection of the delicate balance between light and darkness, the intricate dance of manipulation and loyalty. With her mind racing, she began to envision a strategy not only to maintain her influence over Satan but to carve a new path for herself in this tangled realm of discord.

The stakes were higher than ever, a game played not just for survival but for the very essence of the cosmos itself. As she prepared for what lay ahead, Lilith's resolve hardened—she would not be merely an instrument of chaos; she would be its architect. And in the inferno that lay ahead, she would carve her own destiny.

In the hotel room, the atmosphere was a blend of relief and celebration. Ashley, Lumina, Aisling, Jack, Robert, and a group of fairies lounged, savoring their hard-earned victory. The excitement of the moment was palpable; every smile reflected the satisfaction of having achieved the impossible.

Aisling, her backpack slung over her shoulder, broke the idyllic silence. "Well, we're heading back home. Our mission here has come to an end," she announced, capturing the attention of everyone present.

Robert, still riding the high of their success, raised his eyebrows in surprise. "You're leaving now? You're famous! You could live well as the liberators of evil."

Aisling looked at him with an understanding smile. "That's only important to you folks—the fame. In our world, it means nothing."

Lumina turned to her friend with a playful wink, reminding her, "Remember what's under the mattress."

Aisling nodded, and Jack stepped forward to bid her farewell. "Aisling," he said, gratitude lacing his voice, "thank you for everything. You pulled me out of the tunnel I was in."

"It was a pleasure," she replied warmly. "You're a good man."

One of the fairies fluttered over to the mattress and carefully retrieved the sword from the cave, placing it on Aisling's back. She was ready for her return home, to her own world, with her mission accomplished.

Before departing, Aisling turned to Ashley, the attorney who had been instrumental in the fight against WOAD. "Lawyer, they need more people like you here. Thank you."

With tears of emotion in her eyes, Ashley hugged her tightly. "Thank you, Aisling. You will always be my Irish Lite Fairy."

That reference sparked laughter among all of them, a reminder of the magic and unique moments they had shared.

As Lumina observed the farewell, she decided to share a little magical trick with Robert. "Robert, if you want to see us from time to time, just look at your phone, think of me, and you'll see where I am through my eyes."

Surprised and grateful, Robert nodded. "Thank you," he replied sincerely, knowing that this magical bond would offer comfort in the days to come.

With one last look of affection and camaraderie, the fairies began to gently rise, carrying with them the memories of an improbable yet powerful alliance. The world had changed, and they had been its architects. Now, the call of duty to their own home beckoned, knowing they would always be remembered as heroines of two worlds.

Before leaving for good, the group decided to step out onto the hotel balcony for one last view of the city bathed in the hues of sunset. The fairies, ready to take flight back to their home, filled the air with a gentle hum of wings.

As they all moved toward the balcony, Jack, with a mischievous grin, couldn't resist making a comment. "You really can't leave through the door for the last time?" he asked, his tone full of affection and humor.

That question ignited laughter among everyone, reminding them of the many adventures and unconventional methods they had embraced throughout their journey.

With a final friendly wave, Lumina and Aisling soared into the sky, followed by their entourage of fairies, leaving behind an invisible trail of hope and camaraderie. Ashley remained smiling on the balcony, her future filled with possibilities, while Jack, Robert, and the others gazed up at the heavens, their hearts brimming with gratitude for the time shared and the lessons learned.

They had changed the course of a world through their unity. And although the fairies were heading home, they knew that the bond they had forged would endure beyond any distance.

As the last traces of daylight faded and the first stars began to twinkle against the darkening sky, both realms felt the shift—the fairies carried with them the strength of their joint efforts, while those left behind held tightly to the memories and experiences that had forever altered their lives. The impact of their challenges and victories would echo through their hearts, a reminder that they were all part of something far greater than themselves.

CHAPTER 33

The Call of Destiny

As Aisling and her companions soared through the skies, the vast Atlantic Ocean unfolded beneath them, a canvas of deep blue and boundless expanse. The wind tousled their hair, and the fairies' wings shimmered in the light of the setting sun. They were on their way home, where peace and rest awaited them—or so they thought.

Suddenly, a warm presence manifested in Aisling's thoughts. It was the voice of her grandmother, the revered queen of her realm, whose wisdom had guided generations. The mental connection flowed through the ether with the familiar softness of home, but the weight of her words quickly shifted the welcoming feeling to one of urgency.

"Aisling, my dear," her grandmother's voice resonated with a blend of love and concern. "I bring you troubling news."

Aisling felt a knot tighten in her throat, a mix of longing and dread. Her eyes brimmed with tears, not just from the distance that separated them but from the weight of the words still to be spoken.

"You cannot return yet," her grandmother continued, her tone calm yet resolute, "for tomorrow begins a great war. The forces of evil from the lower dimensions are rising."

Aisling's heart raced, each word striking her spirit with the gravity of an immense destiny. "You must wait on the path," her grandmother instructed, "and you will receive the order to deliver the sword to Archangel Michael. That has been your true mission."

The impact of this revelation resonated within Aisling, spinning her internal world. This was not the end of the journey but the true beginning of a sacred and essential task.

Aisling inhaled deeply, steadying herself against the rush of emotions. She felt the weight of responsibility settle upon her shoulders, but also the exhilarating clarity of purpose. The path before her was not merely a return to safety; it was a call to action—a beckoning to rise as a guardian against the encroaching darkness.

"Thank you, Grandmother," she whispered, determination filling her voice. "I won't let you down."

As the sun dipped below the horizon, casting vibrant colors across the sky, Aisling turned to Lumina, her spirit renewed. "We have work to do," she declared, her voice vibrant with conviction. The air around them crackled with energy, ready to be harnessed in the fight to come.

With renewed resolve, the group adjusted their course, ready to embrace the unfolding destiny that awaited them. Their journey was about to take on a new meaning, one that would challenge their strengths, test their bonds, and ultimately lead them to confront the very essence of good and evil. And together, they would answer the call that destiny had set before them.

CHAPTER 34

Apocalypse in Eternum

Committed to their duty, the fairies sought refuge on a remote island in the vast ocean. Bathed in moonlight, the island became their temporary sanctuary, where they prepared in meditation for the next step in their divine mission.

Aisling, surrounded by her loyal companions, embraced her destiny with renewed determination. She knew that while the task before her was monumental, she was not alone. The blessing of her grandmother and the power of the sword served as constant reminders of the purpose of her existence.

As dawn approached on the horizon, casting a golden glow over the island, Aisling and the fairies readied themselves for the battle that would change the fate of many worlds. The voice of her grandmother continued to resonate in her mind, an echo of love and wisdom that would guide her.

Above the horizon, the promises of new alliances and capabilities glittered brilliantly. The girls had departed to rest, but they had been called to a war that would define the balance between good and evil. They understood that on the edge of this new era, their actions would illuminate the path toward a more just and balanced world.

As Aisling gazed at the sky from the island where they had paused, she sensed a growing unease. The horizon, which had once promised hope and tranquility, now felt foreboding. As she turned her gaze westward, she noticed a disturbing change: the sky was darkening with a blackness so deep that it seemed to absorb all the surrounding light.

These were not clouds; she knew that. It was something far more ominous. Her heart raced as she beheld the figure of Satan himself, rising with an army of millions, all clad in black leather jackets and helmets that glimmered beneath the fading light. Behind him, beasts of the underworld, including dragons and the feared six-headed serpent, added to his terrifying contingent.

The right hemisphere of the world was engulfed in darkness, a presence so dense that it felt as if day itself had been stolen away. Aisling experienced a potent mix of fear and determination, an inner fire beginning to burn brighter than ever before.

With her allies at her side, Aisling steeled herself for the battle ahead. They would not falter in the face of this overwhelming darkness. With the lessons of their past and the strength of their unity, they would stand firm against the advancing shadows and fight for the light that they believed in. The winds of destiny were shifting, and Aisling felt the weight of her purpose pressing against her, urging her to rise to the occasion.

CHAPTER 35

The Call of Destiny

"Look!" Aisling shouted to the fairies around her, her voice slicing through the air like a call to action. "This is our moment!"

With that declaration, the fairies, Lumina and Aisling leading the charge, began to ascend. Their flight to the sky was swift and precise, each wing glowing with its own light, as if they were shooting comets rising against the backdrop of the darkening expanse. The ground quickly receded beneath them as they ascended vertically, defying all known laws, their hearts aligned with a common purpose: to confront absolute evil.

As Aisling soared with determination, the celestial scene unfolded before her in both breathtaking and terrifying grandeur. The army of angels, led by the resplendent Archangel Michael, filled the heavens with bursts of pure light; the flapping of their wings and the flashes of their swords reflected the divine power contained within them.

However, looming behind her was the ominous shadow of the six-headed serpent, a palpable threat. Five of its heads were fixed on Aisling, while the sixth one eyed Satan, waiting for a signal to attack. Beside Satan, Lilith remained imposing, her gaze briefly connecting with that of her niece. In her eyes, Aisling saw a mixture of warning and challenge, a reminder of the bonds that tied them and the choices that had separated them.

With a protective instinct, Lumina kept her distance at fifty meters from Aisling, surrounded by a throng of fairies buzzing with luminescent energy. Together, they formed a defensive barrier, determined to shield Aisling from the tides of darkness. As Lumina glanced to her right, she couldn't suppress the horror that washed over her as she beheld the throng of underworld beings gathering—nightmarish creatures ready to unleash devastation.

As Aisling pressed forward, she felt the weight of the sacred artifact upon her back, serving as a promise of power and a reminder of the responsibility she must fulfill. The presence of Michael ahead provided a guiding light through the chaos that surrounded them.

Upon reaching her destination, Aisling offered the sacred sword to Michael, the archangel of light. The instant he accepted it, a wave of pure energy enveloped them both, forging a bond that transcended the physical realm. It was as if a ray of hope pierced the sky, resonating with the concentrated power of good, uniting their purposes in a singular force of strength and determination.

"Thank you, Aisling," Michael said, his voice thunderous yet filled with warmth. "I love you in the name of God." Aisling felt her heart illuminate at those words, a rush of happiness and satisfaction flooding her being.

The moment was transformative; she knew the battle ahead was monumental, yet with the might of the archangel beside her and the unwavering support of her friends, she felt ready to embrace her destiny.

Together, they would confront the darkness and fight for a future where light prevailed, ignited by the love and strength that flowed within and among them.

Committed to their duty, the fairies sought refuge on a remote island amid the vast ocean. Bathed in moonlight, the island became their temporary sanctuary, where they awaited in meditation and preparation for the next step in their divine mission.

Aisling, surrounded by her loyal companions, embraced her destiny with renewed determination. She understood that while the task ahead was monumental, she was not alone. The blessing of her grandmother and the power of the sword served as constant reminders of her purpose.

As dawn approached on the horizon, casting a golden radiance over the island, Aisling and the fairies prepared for the battle that would change the fate of many worlds. The voice of her grandmother echoed in her mind—a comforting presence of love and wisdom that would guide her through the chaos.

Above the horizon, promises of new alliances and untapped powers glimmered brightly. The girls had taken time to rest, but they had been called into a war that would define the balance between good and evil. They were acutely aware that on the brink of this new era, their actions would illuminate the path toward a more just and balanced world.

Aisling gazed at the sky from the island where they had paused. The horizon, which once promised hope and tranquility, now felt different. Isolated from human chatter, she sensed a growing unease. Looking westward, she noticed an alarming change: the sky began to darken with a depth of black that seemed to absorb all surrounding light.

These were not clouds; she instinctively knew it was something far more ominous. Her heart raced as she spotted Satan himself ascending with an army of millions, all clad in black leather jackets and helmets that glimmered in the fading light. Behind him, beasts from the underworld, including dragons and the dreaded six-headed serpent, swelled his terrifying ranks.

The right hemisphere of the world was engulfed in darkness, a presence so oppressive it felt like daylight had been extinguished. Aisling felt an intense mix of fear and determination, a fire within her igniting more brightly than ever before.

"Look!" Aisling shouted to the fairies around her, her voice cutting through the air like a call to action. "This is our moment!"

With that proclamation, the fairies, Lumina and Aisling leading the way, began to ascend. Their flight was swift and precise, each wing glowing with its own light, as if they were comets shooting upward against the gathering shadows. The ground quickly receded beneath them, and their ascent defied all known laws, every heart aligned in a united purpose: to confront the absolute evil that awaited.

As Aisling rose with determination, the celestial scene unfolded before her—a magnificent yet terrifying panorama. The army of angels, led by the radiant Archangel Michael, filled the sky with radiant flashes of pure light. Each flutter of their wings and each arc of their swords reflected the divine power they contained.

However, behind her loomed the ominous shadow of the six-headed serpent, a palpable threat. Five of its heads were locked onto Aisling, while the sixth was trained on Satan, waiting for a signal to strike. Beside Satan, Lilith stood resolute, momentarily connecting her gaze with her niece. In her eyes, Aisling saw a blend of warning and challenge, a reminder of their intricate ties and the decisions that had set them apart.

With a protective instinct, Lumina maintained her distance about fifty meters from Aisling, surrounded by a throng of fairies buzzing with luminescent energy. Together, they formed a defensive barrier, determined to shield Aisling from the encroaching darkness. Looking to her right, Lumina couldn't help but feel horror as she witnessed the mass of underworld creatures gathering—nightmarish beings poised to unleash devastation.

As Aisling continued onward, she felt the weight of the sacred artifact resting on her back, a promise of power and a reminder of her responsibilities. The presence of Michael ahead offered her a guiding light through the chaos.

Upon reaching her destination, Aisling presented the sacred sword to Michael, the archangel of light. The instant he accepted it, a wave of pure energy enveloped them both, forging a bond that transcended the physical realm. It was as if a ray of hope pierced through the murky darkness, resonating with the concentrated strength of good—a union of purpose and determination.

"Thank you, Aisling," Michael said, his voice both powerful and warm. "I love you in the name of God." Aisling felt her heart illuminate at those words, a rush of happiness and satisfaction flooding her being.

It was a transformative moment; she knew the battle ahead would be monumental, but with the strength of the archangel beside her and the unwavering support of her friends, she felt ready to step into her destiny. Together, they would

As the battle raged in the heavens, Lilith found herself facing the six-headed serpent amidst the chaos of the celestial war. Upon seeing Aisling fall unconscious, her heart twisted with concern. Without hesitation, she dove toward her niece, cradling her delicate body in her arms.

At that moment, a familiar figure emerged from the confusion: Meribell, Aisling's mother, ascended at an almost unfathomable speed. The light emanating from her was dazzling, and her presence radiated an aura of power that seemed capable of dispelling the darkness surrounding them.

With determination and bravery, Meribell positioned herself in front of the serpent, her figure resolute like a beacon amid the storm. Without faltering, she began to sing, her voice resonating with strength and harmony. The notes soared, filling the air with magic, and soon, the serpent, paralyzed by the enchantment, ceased its movement, ensnared in a prison of light and magic.

As Meribell raised her hand, a glowing sphere formed, creating a shield that rendered the serpent incapable of attack. Meanwhile, Lilith observed with pride and awe, although the fear of an inevitable surge of darkness loomed over them.

A distant flash of light caught Lilith's attention. Without thinking, she started sprinting toward Meribell, Aisling still unconscious in her arms. Tears welled in her eyes as she yelled desperately, "Meribell! Run toward us!"

When Meribell reached her, Lilith handed Aisling over with trembling hands, her heart racing with the weight of the situation. "I'm so sorry," she murmured, her voice quivering. "Get out of here, quickly! It's about to get ugly."

Meribell, maintaining her enchanted light and control over the serpent, turned to Lilith. "And you?" she asked, concern etched in her eyes.

"I am destined for darkness," Lilith replied with a melancholic smile. In that moment, she leaned closer and gently wiped a tear from the face of the young protector.

"Thank you, Lilith," Meribell said, her voice heavy with emotion. "You've saved my daughter."

Lilith smiled, despite the pain she felt, and answered, "Family is family."

As the connection between them deepened, Lilith's heart swelled with an unexpected warmth. She realized that despite the tumultuous circumstances surrounding them, their bond was as strong as ever, forged in love and understanding.

With Aisling in Meribell's care, Lilith knew she had to confront the shadows alone. The battle between light and darkness raged on, but with the strength of their familial ties, she felt empowered to face whatever horror lay ahead.

In the distance, the serpent writhed, as if sensing the shift in the tide. Lilith prepared herself for the next phase of their struggle, knowing that true courage often meant standing firm against the very darkness from which one had once emerged.

The Final Farewell

As Meribell cradled her daughter, Lilith felt a wave of strength and familial love wash over her. With one last glance at the ongoing battle, the two women, with Aisling in Meribell's arms, began to ascend rapidly toward Lumina and the other fairies waiting for them.

Lilith felt an inner strength as she descended with the group of fairies and her niece, but as they distanced themselves from the skirmish, a part of her knew she had to make a painful decision. The moment she sensed the dark energy lurking, a deep instinct to protect surged within her. I cannot put them in danger, she thought, and suddenly, determination ignited in her heart.

With a resolute turn in the air, Lilith kissed Aisling, ensuring the safety of her sister and her daughter as they flew toward the fairies' refuge. "Meribell! I'm going back!" she urged, her voice ringing with the urgency of duty.

As Lilith paused, her heart racing, Meribell also took a moment to collect herself, understanding the weight of what was about to happen. Lumina, about ten meters away, halted her flight, knowing that the farewell was inevitable. The connection between them felt intense, as if time had come to a standstill, and in that moment, a profound understanding floated in the air.

Though Lumina had only known Lilith for a short time, the mark she had left on her heart was indelible. Thanks to her, Lumina had come to grasp a crucial truth: it was humans who created the balance between good and evil. When lives became tainted by ego, selfishness, and deceit, the scales would inevitably tip toward darkness. Lumina felt overwhelmed by a mix of sadness and admiration for Lilith, who had battled those forces her entire life.

A tear rolled down Lumina's cheek as she realized the depth of suffering that had shaped her friend. She recalled the mistakes Lilith had made in her past and how those missteps had transformed her into the powerful warrior she was today. Empathy flooded Lumina's heart like a wave, and in that moment, she fully understood the sacrifice Lilith was willing to make.

At the end of the farewell, when Lilith turned to look at Lumina, the world came to a halt for an instant. In an act of intimate and sincere connection, they exchanged unspoken affirmations, the weight of their bond transcending spoken words. They were warriors united, prepared to face the darkness together yet again, even if it meant parting ways in the process.

With one final, lingering gaze, an exchange of strength and hope passed between them, leaving Lilith resolute as she prepared to return to the fray. No matter what awaited her, she would do it for her family, for the balance of light and dark, and for the future that hung in the balance.

When Lilith paused, her heart racing, Meribell beside her took a moment to stop as well, understanding the significance of what was about to happen. Lumina, about ten meters away, halted her flight, knowing that the farewell would be inevitable. The connection between them felt intense, as if time had come to a standstill, and in that instant, a deep understanding floated in the air.

Though Lumina had only known Lilith for a short period, the mark she had left on her heart was indelible. Because of her, Lumina had come to grasp an essential truth: it was humans who created the balance between good and evil. When their lives became clouded by ego, selfishness, and deceit, the scales inevitably tipped toward darkness. Lumina felt overwhelmed by a blend of sadness and admiration for Lilith, who had wrestled with these very forces her entire life.

A tear rolled down Lumina's cheek as she processed the depth of suffering Lilith had experienced. She recalled the mistakes Lilith had made in her past and how those missteps had transformed her into the powerful warrior she was today. Empathy washed over Lumina like a wave, and in that moment, she fully understood the sacrifice her friend was making.

At the conclusion of their farewell, when Lilith turned to look at Lumina, the world seemed to freeze for an instant. In an act of intimate connection, Lilith transmitted her thoughts to Lumina telepathically: "You're right. The truth is the only path to the light."

This silent exchange held the weight of their shared experiences, a bond that transcended spoken words. It was a moment marked by understanding and compassion, a remembrance that unity and love can spark the courage to confront even the darkest of adversities.

As the echoes of their final thoughts lingered in the air, a promise was forged: they would continue to fight for one another, and for the truth that illuminated their path. With a deep breath, Lilith turned away, ready to face the challenges ahead, while Lumina remained resolute, carrying Lilith's spirit with her as she soared toward her own destiny.

In that poignant moment, they each fortified their resolve, knowing that no matter what lay ahead, they would carry each other's strength into the fray—united in purpose and bound by the love of family that would guide them through the darkness.

Lilith winked, a silent jest that broke the tension of the moment, reminding Lumina of the hope that always perseveres. This revelation would resonate in Lumina's heart throughout her life. It was a gesture that spoke volumes; the understanding and connection between them left indelible marks.

With those final threads of love and understanding, they each set their course. Lilith launched herself toward the battle, the fire of determination shining brightly in her eyes. Lumina, still with tears glimmering in her eyes, felt the renewed power of her mission as she moved toward her own destiny, carrying with her the lessons and love imparted by Lilith as her guide.

As Meribell watched her great-aunt, a ray of hope crossed her being. She understood that, although the path ahead might be dark and fraught with challenges, the strength of familial love and the power of good would always prevail. That light would serve as the beacon that guided each of them, even in the most difficult moments.

With the wind at their backs and their hearts filled with determination, the three of them continued toward the future, shaping their destinies in the long struggle between light and darkness while leaving behind not just a legacy but also the promise of a new beginning.

As they drifted further away, Lilith felt the weight of separation—a painful tug at her chest. Without looking back, she ascended, embracing the power of her family legacy. However, as if called by an invisible thread, she could not resist turning one last time, casting a solitary final glance before the impending confrontation.

It was then that her eyes met Meribell's, who, at that exact moment, also turned her head. It was a suspended instant in time, an understanding that flowed deeply between them.

Without the need for words, they realized they could face the unknown, but that sacrifice was inevitable.

In Lilith's gaze, she found the strength of an unbreakable love and the glimmer of an indomitable spirit. In a world where darkness lurked, that exchange became a beacon of hope.

"I love you, aunt," Meribell's eyes seemed to convey, while Lilith responded silently with a "Forever," whispered on the wind.

Taking a deep breath, Lilith turned away and ascended skyward toward the battle, ready to confront her destiny. With each flap of her wings, the fire of her determination burned even more intensely. Family came first, and so she dove into the darkness, prepared to face whatever it took.

As she approached the battlefield on the horizon, her thoughts returned to her family, the strength of love resting in her heart. She knew her sacrifice would ignite a spark of light in others' hearts, and though the fight would be fierce, her spirit would remain unyielding, resolute in every battle she waged.

In that moment, Lilith understood that love, in all its forms, would always prevail, even in the deepest shadows. And as the celestial lights intertwined with dark omens above, she was ready to wage her battle against evil, on behalf of her family and for the future they still had the power to build.

End